OLD BONES

Also by Douglas Preston and Lincoln Child

Agent Pendergast Novels

Relic*
Reliquary*
The Cabinet of Curiosities
Still Life with Crows
Brimstone**
Dance of Death**
The Book of the Dead**
The Wheel of Darkness
Cemetery Dance
Fever Dream†
Cold Vengeance†
Two Graves†
White Fire
Blue Labyrinth
Crimson Shore
The Obsidian Chamber
City of Endless Night
Verses for the Dead

Nora Kelly Novels

Old Bones

Gideon Crew Novels

Gideon's Sword
Gideon's Corpse
The Lost Island
Beyond the Ice Limit

Other Novels

Mount Dragon
Riptide
Thunderhead
The Ice Limit

*Relic and Reliquary are
ideally read in sequence
**The Diogenes Trilogy
†The Helen Trilogy

By Douglas Preston

The Lost City of the Monkey God
The Kraken Project Impact
The Monster of Florence
(with Mario Spezi)
Blasphemy
Tyrannosaur Canyon
The Codex
Ribbons of Time
The Royal Road
Talking to the Ground
Jennie
Cities of Gold
Dinosaurs in the Attic

By Lincoln Child

Full Wolf Moon
The Forgotten Room
The Third Gate
Terminal Freeze
Deep Storm
Death Match
Lethal Velocity (formerly *Utopia*)
Tales of the Dark 1–3
Dark Banquet
Dark Company

PRESTON & CHILD

OLD BONES

HEAD
of ZEUS

First published in the USA in 2019 by Grand Central Publishing,
a division of Hachette Book Group, Inc.

First published in the UK in 2019 by Head of Zeus, Ltd

9 7 5 3 1 2 4 6 8

A catalogue record for this book is available from
the British Library.

Cover design by Flag. Cover photos of mountains by Getty/Et,
skulls by Getty/Digital Vision, woman by Shutterstock. Cover
copyright © 2019 by Hachette Book Group, Inc.

ISBN (HB): 9781838931056
ISBN (XTPB): 9781838931063
ISBN (E): 9781838931087

Printed and bound in Great Britain by
CPI Group (UK) Ltd, Croydon CR0 4YY

Head of Zeus Ltd
First Floor East
5–8 Hardwick Street
London EC1R 4RG

WWW.HEADOFZEUS.COM

To Michael Pietsch

OLD BONES

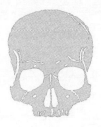

I

October 13

NIGHT HAD COME early to the City of Lights, and by 1:00 AM, with the moon obscured by thick clouds, Paris no longer lived up to its name. Even here, down by the river, it was dark and empty: too late on a weeknight for residents, too cold for tourists and the romantically inclined. Except for a pedestrian hurrying past, coat collar pulled up against the chill, and a long glass-sided boat sliding silently along the river—ghostlike and empty, dinner cruise over, headed to port—the man had the waterfront promenade to himself.

Promenade was perhaps too grand a word for the walkway, paved with ancient stones, that ran along the Seine barely above water level. Still, even late at night this section of it offered a re-markable vista: the Île de la Cité directly across the water, with the dark bulk of the Louvre and the towers of Notre Dame—partly obscured by the Pont au Double—reaching toward a threatening sky.

The man was seated on a narrow bench beside some wooden scaffolding erected to accommodate repairs on the an-cient bridge. Behind him, a stone wall rose some twenty feet to street level, where vehicles on the Quai de Montebello could occasionally be heard as they passed along the artery south of the Seine. Every quarter mile or so, a worn stone staircase led down from this avenue to the riverfront promenade. Occasional lights, fixed high up along the retaining wall, cast narrow pools of yellow over the wet cobblestones. The light closest to the seated man had been removed due to the construction on the Pont au Double.

A gendarme appeared in the distance, dressed in an oilskin coat, whistling a Joe Dassin tune as he approached. He smiled and nodded at the man, and the man nodded back as he lit a Gauloise and casually watched the policeman continue on beneath the bridge, the echoing notes of "Et si tu n'existais pas" receding.

The man took a deep drag on the cigarette, then held it out and examined the burning tip. His movements were slow and fatigued. He was in his late thirties, dressed in a well-tailored wool suit. Between his stylish Italian shoes sat a fat leather Gladstone bag, scuffed, of the sort that might be used by a busy lawyer or a private Harley Street doctor. A shiny new kick scooter leaned against the bench next to him. Nothing would have differentiated the man from countless other affluent Parisian businessmen save for his features—vague in the present darkness—which had an exotic touch difficult to place: perhaps Asiatic, perhaps Kazakh or Turkish.

Now the low hum of the city was disturbed by the whir of an approaching bicycle. The man looked up as a figure appeared at the top of the nearest staircase. He was dressed in black nylon shorts and a dark cyclist's jersey and was wearing a backpack with reflective stripes that gleamed in the headlights of a passing car. Pulling his bike up to the railing, he padlocked it, then came down the staircase and approached the man in the suit.

"*Ça va?*" he said as he sat down on the bench. Despite the chill of the night, his riding outfit was damp with sweat.

The man in the suit shrugged. "*Ça ne fait rien,*" he replied, taking another drag on the cigarette.

"What's with the scooter?" the biker continued in French, shrugging off his mud-splattered backpack.

"It's for my kid."

"I didn't know you were married."

"Who says I am?"

"Serves me right for asking," the biker said, laughing.

The man in the suit flicked his cigarette into the river. "How did it go?"

"A lot worse than your guy made it sound. I figured it would be some remote, empty park. *Putain de merde*, it was wedged right between Gare Montparnasse and the Catacombes!"

The man in the suit shrugged again. "You know Paris."

"Yeah, but it's not exactly the kind of thing you usually see."

They stopped talking and gazed out over the river while a couple strolled by arm in arm, paying them no attention. Then the man in the suit spoke again.

"But it was deserted. Right?"

"Yes. I got lucky with the actual site—right up against the Rue Froidevaux wall. Any farther in, and I would have been visible from the apartment building across the street."

"Was it hard work?"

"Not really, except for having to keep quiet the whole time. *And* yesterday's goddamned rain. Look!" He pointed to his running shoes, which were even more soiled than the backpack.

"*Quel dommage.*"

"Thanks a lot."

The man in the suit glanced up and down the walkway. Nobody but the two lovebirds, now dwindling into the distance. "Let's have a look."

The other grabbed his backpack and unzipped it, revealing additional mud and something covered in layers of plastic tarp, bubble wrap, and soft chamois cloth. A nasty smell arose. The suited man took out a penlight and carefully examined what lay within. Then he gave a grunt of approval.

"Well done," he said. "How long did it take you to bike over here?"

"About ten minutes, using back streets."

"Well, we'd better not hang around longer than necessary." The man leaned over and unsnapped the leather bag between his knees. The top sagged open, and something inside gleamed briefly in the indirect light.

"What's that?" the biker asked, peering. "I don't take plastic or precious metals."

"Nothing. Your money's here." He patted the breast of his suit jacket.

The cyclist waited as his companion reached into his suit pocket. Then the man, hand still in his pocket, glanced up sharply.

"Hold it a minute!" he said in a whisper, leaning in close. "Someone's coming."

Instinctively, the cyclist leaned in, too. His companion put a hand on the man's shoulder, signaling intimacy while also helping conceal their faces from the passing pedestrian. Except there was no pedestrian; the walkway was empty. His other hand came out of the suit jacket holding a Spyderco Matriarch 2: a tactical knife whose thin, reverse-S edge was designed for one purpose only. The Emerson wave feature built into its spine meant the blade was already locked open by the time the knife was out of the jacket.

The weapon was little more than a black blur as the blade slid between the second and third ribs, its edge going deeper as it traveled, severing the major arteries above the heart before it slipped back out again. The suited man quickly wiped the blade on the biker's trunks and returned it to his pocket in a smooth gesture. It all took no more than two seconds.

The biker remained motionless in a combination of surprise and shock. Although his thoracic cavity was already filling with blood, the wound itself was so small that very little was dribbling from the rent in his jersey. Meanwhile, the other reached into his Gladstone bag and removed a heavy length of steel chain and a padlock. The rest of the bag was empty, save for a padded rubber-and-latex liner. Standing and making sure no one had come into view, he grabbed the steel scooter, folded it, pressed it against the biker's chest, then wrapped the biker's unprotesting arms around it and fixed them in place with the chain. He pulled the ends of the wrapped chain tight and padlocked them together. After one more glance along the walkway and across the river, he pulled the cyclist up and dragged him into the darkness beneath the bridge, to the edge of the water. Heaving the man's legs over the curb, he released his grip and let the body slide gently into the river.

Another ten seconds had passed.

Breathing a little heavily, the man watched as the body sank out of sight, weighed down by the chain and scooter. Then he walked back to the bench, carefully transferred the wrapped object from the backpack to his Gladstone bag, and closed them both. He paused to straighten his tie and smooth down his suit jacket. Then he started briskly down the walkway, up the stone staircase, and past the bicycle, dropping the backpack in a nearby trash bin as he went.

He lit another Gauloise and readjusted his grip on the bag before flagging down a cab at the Place Saint-Michel.

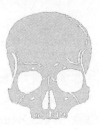

2

One hour later

CLIVE BENTON SLOWED his vintage Ford Falcon to the side of Wild Irish Road, pulled into a turnoff, and eased the car along a dusty track until it was no longer visible from the thoroughfare. He got out of the Falcon, put up the top, and hoisted a small day pack onto his shoulders. Taking out his phone, he loaded a hiking app and located his position, found a bearing, and set off through the forest. The tall fir trees and lodgepole pines were widely spaced, providing an open forest floor that made walking easy. Despite the season, there wasn't even a nip of cold: the air was still deceptively heavy with a drowsy kind of warmth. Looking eastward from between the trees, Benton could see the foothills rising to the distant peaks of the Sierra Nevada, gray teeth against blue. They would soon be covered in snow.

Benton was a historian, and he knew as much about the history of this area as any man alive. It had been the heart of California '49er territory—placer gold country. He could see where hydraulic mining had once scarred the hills with cuts and hollows, the terrain blasted away by gigantic jets of water, which ran the gravel through enormous sluice boxes to capture flakes of gold. But those days were long gone, and these foothills at the western edge of the Sierras, some forty-five miles outside of Sacramento, were mostly depopulated. The scattering of old mining towns—with names like Dutch Flat, Gold Run, Monte Vista, You Bet, and Red Dog—had fallen on hard times. Some had vanished completely, while in a few others, intrepid folk had restored the mining shacks and battenboard hotels as tourist attractions or summer cottages. And the area was in fact beginning to draw a stream of tourists, hikers, and those seeking vacation homes. A development boom had been predicted for years, and now, finally, it seemed to be coming to pass.

Those Gold Rush mansions of the lucky few to have struck it rich could still be found here and there, tucked away in valleys and flats, shuttered and decaying. Benton paused, checking his direction. He was approaching one of those ruined mansions—one that held special meaning for him. The GPS told him it lay a thousand yards to the east of his position, over a low ridge. It was called the Donner House, as it had once belonged to the daughter of Jacob Donner—of the infamous Donner Party.

Benton proceeded carefully, silently, keeping to the shadowy parts of the forest. As he climbed the ridge, he slowed. Through the trees he saw bits of orange and yellow, along with a flash of metal, which he knew were two big bulldozers lined up on an old mining road, ready to descend upon the Donner House and turn it into a heap of brick, stucco, and splintered wood beams, making way for a new golf course and condo development along the Bear River.

As he approached, the outlines of the dozers and the truck that had transported them began to materialize. The truck was idling, and he could smell diesel fumes from its engine, mingled with the scent of cigarette smoke and the murmur of workmen. He made a wide detour around them, hurrying across the road at a point where he couldn't be seen. Moving down the ridge, he could now make out the old house: an early example of the Spanish Colonial Revival style. He came to a low wall at the edge of the forest, which marked the property's boundary. Crouching behind it, he inspected the house carefully. It had once been striking, with a long, low whitewashed portal along one side, above which stood a Moorish dome and belfry. But the red-tiled roofs had caved in; the windows were gone, leaving gaping dark holes; and the extensive gardens and arboretum had grown into a wild and almost impassable jungle of weeds, dead bushes, and specimen trees suffocated by creepers. The building itself was choked in ivy growing up its walls and erupting from holes in its roof. It was a tangible example, Benton thought, of the ephemeral nature of the world: *sic transit gloria mundi.* What a crime that by this time tomorrow it would all be gone, bulldozed into a smoking pile of bricks and plaster. Preservationists had tried mightily to save the old wreck, but the numerous descendants who had been arguing over the property for fifty years could find only one solution—its demolition and sale—and the developer's dollars trumped the preservationists' pleas.

He glanced back up at the ridge. The workmen had finished unloading the dozers and the truck was revving up, belching a cloud of black diesel, starting to pull out. The workmen—four that he could make out—and their personal vehicles were parked down the road, but they were making no move to leave. In fact, it looked like they might be getting ready to make a final recon of the house.

Damn, he'd better get moving. What he was doing was

technically breaking and entering, but he assured himself it was in service to a higher ideal. And could you really break and enter into a house that was about to be torn down, anyway?

Benton leaped the wall and scurried through the overgrown garden, taking refuge on the ruined porch. When all looked clear, he ducked through an open doorway, finding himself in a spare, cool reception hall smelling of dust and old wood. The place had been cleared of valuables, but some worthless broken-down furniture remained. He did a quick search of the downstairs—the salon, kitchen, courtyard, dining room, servants' quarters, pantries, and closets—and found nothing. He was not concerned by that; he did not expect what he was searching for would be there.

He quickly mounted the decaying stone staircase to the second floor. He paused to look out the window and was dismayed to see the four workmen bulling their way down through the shrubbery to the house. He should have come earlier. It was five o'clock, and he'd assumed they would have gone home for the day by now.

A search of the second floor revealed nothing of interest, either. The old chests that remained fell apart in his hands, the closets were empty, and a few rotting bureaus held nothing more than blankets and clothes chewed up into rats' nests. A few chromolithographs adorned the walls or lay broken on the floor, stained and foxed.

He knew an attic sat under the Moorish dome, but he couldn't seem to find the stairs up to it. As he moved about, he suddenly heard voices echoing downstairs, accompanied by coarse laughter.

Would the workmen come upstairs? Of course they would. They would have been told to make a final sweep of the house, looking for anything of value and making sure no squatters were living inside. Which meant they'd look everywhere.

He moved into the center corridor of the second floor, walking slowly, examining the walls. These old haciendas often had hidden doorways. And there it was: a recessed bookcase, holding just a handful of wormy books. Its empty state made the seam along its outer edge all the more obvious. He gave a heave on the side of the case with his shoulder, and as he hoped, it pivoted out, exposing a staircase leading upward. He slipped through and carefully turned the bookcase back into place, hoping— expecting—that the workmen would not notice it. Surely they wouldn't realize the dome held an attic room... would they?

He mounted the steep circular stairs, sending a surprised mouse scurrying away with a squeak. The staircase brought him to a plank ceiling with a trapdoor, which he forced open. The rusty hinges made a loud creaking noise and he paused to listen. The tromping of the men continued downstairs, their laughter suggesting they had heard nothing.

The attic space was small and, surprisingly, still packed with furniture, boxes, armoires, broken mirrors, steamer trunks, an eight-sided poker table, and other bric-a-brac. As Benton pulled himself up and began to move around, a roost of pigeons, living in the belfry atop the dome, flew off with a great beating of wings. There were pieces here with at least some value; this area must have been missed by the movers. Unfortunately, all this stuff meant he could have a longer search. And with the creaky wooden floor, a search might make noise. He'd better wait for the men to leave.

He listened as the voices came up to the second floor. More tromping about and the creeping smell of cigarette smoke. They surely would not find the door.

But they did. He sat up, straining to hear. One of them was exclaiming loudly, and he could hear them heaving on the bookcase and the sliding sound as it pivoted.

His heart suddenly pounding, Benton looked around for a hiding place. There was a large armoire he could hide in—but no, it would likely be opened. He pulled open the lid of a trunk, but it was full of junk. He realized there was no good place to hide. He was trapped.

Now the voices were booming up the stairs. They had not started climbing, apparently egging each other on to see who was going to be first.

There were four of them and one of him. He spied a heavy chest next to the trapdoor. *Yes. That's it.* He seized the corner of the chest and shouldered it across the door, making a loud scraping noise.

There was sudden silence from below.

It might not be heavy enough. He pushed another chest over, and piled several heavy pieces of furniture on top. The silence below told him the men could hear everything he was doing. When Benton had piled as much weight as he could on the trapdoor, he sat back and waited.

"Hey!" one of the men called up. "Who's up there?"

Benton tried not to breathe.

"Who the hell is it?" the man called again. "Come down!"

Silence.

"We're waiting for ya!"

He held his breath.

"Hey, asshole, if you don't come right down, we're going to come up and drag your ass out!"

He heard a muffled thump, then another, as they tried to push open the trapdoor. But with at least two hundred pounds of junk sitting on top, it wasn't going to move. He listened, his apprehension turning to amusement as he heard the men trying to shoulder the door open. They resorted to more pounding. "Okay, pal, we're calling the cops!"

You do that, thought Benton. It would take at least half an hour for the police to arrive, maybe more. He might as well use the time to complete his search.

With no more need for quiet, he began tearing open chests, rummaging through old clothes and blankets, pulling out ancient toys and 1940s-era comic books, crumbling board games and old schoolbooks. He pawed through a wormy set of *National Geographics*, old copies of *Life* and *Stag* and *Saturday Evening Post* and *Boy's Own* magazines, along with bundles of newspapers going back almost to Gold Rush days. As he worked, the pounding and threats continued from below, and then the voices went back down the stairs. He saw, from the belfry window, the men coming out into the yard, one apparently trying to get reception for his cell phone.

Benton continued his search, moving rapidly but methodically from one corner of the small attic to the other. It was discouraging, just a lot of rotting junk without even a hint of what he was looking for. Maybe it wasn't here after all.

And then, at the bottom of a seaman's chest, under a pile of quilts, he found a metal box. Even before he opened it, he knew this must be it. The box was locked, but a rusted metal rod, slipped through the lock's loop, leveraged it off. He opened the lid, hands trembling with anticipation. Within lay a bundle of letters tightly bound with string, and tucked next to it was an old journal covered in dark green canvas, much soiled. He slipped out the journal and, holding it with the utmost care, eased it open.

There, on the front page, written in a precise feminine hand, was a brief legend.

He could hardly breathe. This treasure, so sought after, a holy grail of pioneer American history, actually *existed*. As his limbs trembled with mingled surprise and jubilation, he realized that he hadn't dared hope it might be true, or that he would be lucky enough to find it. Even as he searched, he'd never really believed it was there. And yet here he was, and he was holding it in his hands.

By pure force of will he overcame his impulse to read on. There would be time for that later, but now he had to get the hell out.

He put the diary back in the box and slipped it into his backpack. He went again to the window. Three of the workmen were still outside, and one, now standing on a broken plinth that had formerly held a statue, was talking vociferously into his phone. The jackass really was calling the cops.

Benton quickly moved the chests off the trapdoor and listened. Where was the fourth? Waiting for him? But he heard nothing and finally yanked up the trapdoor. Nobody. The staircase was empty. He descended the stairs as quietly as possible toward the bookcase door, which was standing open. Creeping past it, he looked one way, then the other. The corridor was empty.

He headed down the hall. Suddenly, the fourth workman burst around a corner, ambushing him.

"There you are, you bastard!" the man roared, swinging his fist into his gut.

Benton, taken by surprise, was knocked to the floor, writhing in pain, trying to suck in air and get his breath back.

"He's here!" the man yelled triumphantly. "I got him!"

He turned to face Benton, who was struggling to rise, and gave him a hard kick in the ribs. The violence—and the man's unnecessary gleefulness in employing it—enraged Benton. His backpack had come off when he hit the floor and now he seized it, surging up and swinging it around, the iron box inside whacking the worker upside the head. The man staggered backward, then fell heavily to the floor.

"I'll kill you!" the man screamed, scrabbling up to his feet. But Benton was already running like hell, backpack in hand. He flew down the stairs, ran toward the back of the mansion, vaulted through an open window, and headed for the overgrowth in the direction of Bear River. The workman was right behind, with the other three also pursuing, but the wiry Benton had spent much of his life hiking in the Sierras and they fell back. He tore through the trees, slid down the embankment, and splashed across the sandbars and channels of the river. At the main channel he held up the backpack and plunged into the water, swimming hard until his feet touched sand on the far side. He climbed out and turned to see the workmen standing on the opposite embankment, shouting threats.

He gave them the finger and then jogged into the woods and made a long loop, crossing the river again way upstream. From there he navigated back to his car with his cell phone GPS, relieved to find his gleaming convertible still hidden. He locked the backpack in the trunk and eased out onto Wild Irish Road. Eight miles down, turning onto the highway, he passed two cop cars, lights flashing, and couldn't help but laugh out loud.

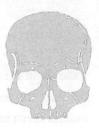

3

Nora Kelly stood up and stretched, muscles cramped from hours of kneeling in the dirt with trowels, picks, and paintbrushes, excavating the fourth and final room of a prehistoric Pueblo ruin.

"Quitting time," she said to her field assistant, Jason Salazar.

The man rose from the square meter he was picking away at and slapped the dust from his jeans. Then he took off his cowboy hat, mopped his brow with a handkerchief, and fitted the hat back on: despite the lateness of the season, the temperature still hovered in the upper fifties.

Nora tipped up the canvas water bag hung on the mirror of the Institute's field truck and took a long swig. The site itself wasn't much to see, but the views were spectacular. The ancient Pueblo people, she thought, always built with a view in mind. The tiny ruin sat on top of a rise of land at the base of Cerro Pedernal, the flat-topped mountain made famous in the paintings of Georgia O'Keeffe. It rose majestically behind her, riven by deep canyons, the higher reaches covered in trees. In front of her, the land swept down to a vast plain the Spanish called the

Valle de la Piedra Lumbre, the Valley of Shining Stone. On the far side, the red, orange, and yellow buttes of Ghost Ranch did indeed seem to shine in the golden afternoon sunlight.

As she walked over to their worktable, she saw a distant corkscrew of dust approaching on the old uranium-mine road that led to the site.

Salazar came up beside her. "Wonder who that is?"

"No idea."

They began packing up their tools and putting them in the prefab storage shed set up next to the site. After a while the vehicle itself appeared, creeping slowly over a rise. They both paused and watched it approach, driven cautiously over the rough dirt road. It was some kind of classic car, Nora could see. It eased up next to the Institute's field truck and waited a few moments for the cloud of dust to roll over it and settle. Then the door opened and a tall, lanky man appeared. A shock of black hair hung down across a bony but fine-looking face, intense blue eyes squinting around. He was dressed in the ugliest paisley shirt Nora had ever seen, all swirls of purple and orange. He appeared to be in his late thirties, a few years older than she.

"Lost?" Nora asked.

His gaze settled on her. "Not if you're Dr. Nora Kelly."

"I am."

"Sorry to arrive unannounced. My name is Clive Benton." He pulled a backpack from the car, came forward, then extended his hand, giving hers a quick shake. "Really, I should have called, but…" He seemed to hesitate. "Well, the Institute said you were out here, and it seems there's no cell reception, and then I was worried I couldn't describe the whole thing properly on the phone anyway—"

Nora gently interrupted the nervous rush of words. "Come

sit down and have a cup of cocoa." She led him to the worktable under the shade, where a thermos sat with some plastic cups.

Benton perched on the edge of a chair.

"What kind of car is that?" Nora asked, trying to put the fellow at ease.

"It's a '64 Ford Futura," he said, brightening. "I restored it myself."

"Not a great car for that road."

"No," he said. "But what I have to tell you can't wait."

Nora took a seat across the table from him. "What's on your mind?"

Benton glanced at Jason Salazar. "Um, what I'm about to say is confidential."

"Jason's a curatorial assistant at the Institute, and I can vouch for his discretion," Nora said. "A lot of what we do as archaeologists is confidential, so you needn't be concerned."

Benton nodded, his black hair ruffling in the breeze. He remained a bit flustered, as if not knowing where to start. Finally he reached down, opened the backpack, and pulled out a plastic Ziploc bag. He opened it and removed an old, tissue-wrapped volume, which he laid reverently on the table between them, unfolding the tissue with delicate fingers.

"The original journal," he said, "of Tamzene Donner."

Nora stared at the book blankly. The name meant nothing to her. "Who?"

"Tamzene Donner." He looked sideways at her and Salazar. "You know, the wife of George Donner, who led the Donner Party? The emigrants who got trapped in winter snows in the Sierras and were forced to resort to cannibalism?"

"Oh. *Those* Donners," Nora said. "So I take it this journal is of historical significance?" She wondered where this was going.

"Incalculable significance."

This pronouncement was followed by a brief silence.

"Maybe I'd better give you some background," Benton said. "I'm an independent historian specializing in nineteenth-century westward expansion. I also happen to be a distant descendant of some of the Donner Party survivors: a family named Breen. But that's not important. I've been researching the tragedy for years. Anyway, one of the few things the Donner survivors agreed on was that Tamzene Donner kept a journal, in which she recorded every detail of the journey. Historians have long speculated one of the survivors must have preserved and carried out her journal, but it's never been found—until now." He made a rather dramatic gesture at the stained and frayed book on the table. "Go ahead—open it up."

With the utmost delicacy, Nora reached forward and opened it to the title page.

"You see what she wrote? *Tamzene Donner, My Journal, October 12, 1846 to...* Note that there's no end date, because she died of starvation and then—" he paused and cleared his throat— "was eaten by a man named Keseberg."

"Wasn't Keseberg also accused of murdering her in order to eat her?" Salazar interjected.

Benton turned in mild surprise. "Yes, that's right. You seem familiar with the story."

Salazar shrugged. "They taught the Donner tale in history class at Goleta High. I found it intriguing." He gave a quick smile. "Who wouldn't?"

Nora agreed. "But where do I come in?"

"Well, I'm here to ask you something."

"All right. Go ahead."

Instead of answering, Benton paused. "First of all, you've

directed several archaeological digs in the Sierra Nevada. You know those mountains."

"To a certain extent."

"You're a top field archaeologist who also has experience with sites where cannibalism occurred, including Quivira—a cliff dwelling you found in Utah."

"True."

"And you have the legitimacy and backing of the Institute."

Nora leaned back. "I'm starting to have the feeling I'm being interviewed for a job."

"You've already got the job—if you want it. You're the ideal person for what I have in mind."

"Which is?" All this dancing around was starting to get on Nora's nerves.

"I have to ask for your word of honor that—for the present at least—nothing I say will go beyond us."

"Isn't that a bit dramatic?"

"I'm sorry," Benton said hastily, nervousness returning. "I know how this must sound, but once you hear what I have to tell, you'll understand why I want to keep it under wraps. It's a long story... and, I warn you, a disturbing one."

Nora checked her watch. It was not yet four thirty. They still had half an hour of sunlight left and it was pleasant out there in the desert. With a faint smile she crossed her arms. Despite herself, she was intrigued by the man's earnestness. "All right. Let's hear it."

Clive Benton took a deep breath, placed his hands on his knees, and began to speak slowly, in measured tones. It was clearly a story he knew by heart.

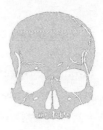

4

"I FIRST HEARD the story of the Donner Party as a young boy growing up outside San Francisco," Benton began. "I mentioned to you that my family—my mother's family—are collateral descendants of the Breen family, who were part of the Donner group. My mother told me the story as a child and I was hooked. It led me into historical studies and eventually a PhD from Stanford.

"The Donner catastrophe was one of the greatest calamities of the westward migration. Here was a group of emigrants who set out to civilize an untamed land—California—but in the process ended up reduced to unspeakable barbarity. It was the American Dream turned inside out.

"The two main characters in the drama were George Donner and his wife, Tamzene. George was a big man with a hunger for land. All his life, he wanted more of it—for farming. His wife was a schoolmarm. She was small and slender, with the manners and education of a lady. But underneath was a woman with an ironbound sense of right and wrong. The two had three daughters together, and George had two other daughters from a previous marriage.

"In 1846, California was still part of Mexico. But war was brewing, and everyone expected the U.S. would soon grab the territory. Donner saw an opportunity to get in on the ground floor, so to speak, and get his hands on some of that rich new land. He was a good talker and he drew his brother, Jacob, and Jacob's family into his vision.

"George, Tamzene, and their five young daughters left Independence, Missouri, in the spring of 1846, with a large group of other emigrants. These were not ragtag settlers: they had money. This was a caravan of well-heeled, even wealthy, pioneers stocked with the best of everything. Tamzene planned to start a ladies' school and had brought books, school supplies, slates and chalk, religious pamphlets and Bibles, even oil and watercolor paints. George had loaded a wagon with bolts of velvet, silks, and satins to sell at high profit to the Californios. Some people carried sums of money with them. A man named Jacob Wolfinger, for example, carried a lockbox containing gold with which he intended to buy land, build a house, and start a business.

"The fact is, aside from their wealth, this was pretty much a normal emigrant wagon train heading west. It would have been forgotten to history except for one thing: a fateful decision they made along the trail. In Wyoming, Donner and the others decided to take a shortcut. It was called the Hastings Cutoff, which was being talked up at the time by a promoter named Lansford Hastings. Donner and about ninety souls voted to take the cutoff. The rest of the emigrant train voted to continue on the regular route.

"So they split up. The Donner Party went southwest into Utah, following the cutoff. The new trail took them through the rugged Wasatch Mountains. Donner and the rest began to realize something was wrong when the mountains turned out to be far worse than Hastings had described. But it was too late to turn around. Once out of the mountains, they were forced to cross the Great Salt Lake Desert. As they struggled on, they began to suffer terribly from lack of water. Some of the children were given flattened bullets to suck on, to relieve their desperate thirst. They ran low on food. Things started to fall apart. Arguments flared up. Indians stole some oxen and shot others full of arrows. Several travelers were also hit—potshots taken from behind rocks and trees—resulting in wounds. Another man, who became unable to walk, was put out of his wagon and left to die by the trail. And all this time, Tamzene Donner kept a careful record of events in her journal.

"As they were crossing the Nevada desert, Wolfinger's wagon became mired. The rest of the train continued on while he stayed behind to dig it out. Soon afterward, two men named Reinhardt and Spitzer volunteered to go back and help Wolfinger. They were gone a few days. When they later caught up with the wagon train, they explained that they'd been attacked by Indians and that Wolfinger had been killed.

"By the time the emigrants reached the foothills of the Sierras in late October, they were badly behind schedule and already starving. But the mountains were still free of snow, and they hoped to hurry across before winter arrived in earnest.

"They almost made it. Less than a day's travel from the top of the pass, a sudden blizzard buried them. At the time, the pack train was strung out along the mountain trail. The blizzard literally froze everyone in their tracks—and there they would remain. Fifty-nine people in the vanguard were caught near Truckee Lake and forced to hunker down. Another twenty-two, including George and Tamzene and their five little daughters, were stuck six miles back in a meadow by Alder Creek. These two camps have been found and excavated by archaeologists.

"But the historical record mentions a third camp—usually referred to now as the 'Lost Camp.' It was a small group in the rear, consisting in part of Reinhardt and Spitzer, a family named Carville, and one Albert Parkin, who deserted his family to seek a new life in California. Nobody is sure what happened but it's likely that, in the confusion of the snowstorm, this group lost the trail and went up a dead-end canyon beyond the mouth of the Little Truckee River. They ended up snowbound deep in the mountains, miles from the main party. Some said the Lost Camp was located in a dark valley, cut off from the sun, encircled by rocky cliffs. So many legends have grown up about the camp that it's hard to tease out the truth.

"At any rate, all the stranded travelers remained snowbound for months, as storm after storm dumped twenty-five to thirty feet of snow on them. It buried the rough lean-tos and crude shelters they had managed to cobble together. In these filthy hovels, they huddled and starved and began to die, one by one. They ate the last of their supplies. Then they ate their oxen and horses. Then they ate their dogs. And then they started digging up the frozen bodies of their companions.

"They peeled off the flesh and cooked it. They went for the organs, eating the livers and hearts, intestines and lungs. They cracked the bones for marrow and split open the skulls for the brains. When all that ran out, they boiled the bones for grease."

Benton took a moment to shift in his chair and glance at the distant horizon. Nora and Salazar were silent.

"I should add that not everyone partook. Many refused to eat human flesh. Even today, historians debate just how many of the party became cannibals. As more died of starvation, it meant more food became available for those left alive. It's almost impossible to imagine what it must have been like, day after day, week after week, stuck in those dreadful camps, overcrowded with men, women, and children in stuffy dens, where the air was so foul from fecal waste and rotting human flesh that it could hardly be breathed. In desperation, a group of fifteen men finally set off to cross the mountains into California to summon help. Seven made it—and then only by eating their companions who had died along the way.

"In February, the first relief expedition arrived. They saw scenes of horror that almost defy comprehension. One rescuer later described coming across some children sitting on a log, their faces smeared with blood as they ate the half-roasted liver and heart of their own father, body parts scattered around them.

"That first rescue expedition could only save a few: they themselves almost starved to death crossing the Sierras to reach the stranded travelers. Tamzene and George Donner were still alive when the first relief party arrived, but Tamzene refused to leave her husband, who was dying of a hand infection. A second rescue expedition brought additional people out of the mountains, and a third, but Tamzene refused to leave George, even while her own children were carried out.

"At some point during all this, a man named Asher Boardman showed up at Donner camp by Alder Creek. It was at the end of February. He had fled the Lost Camp, and alluded to how the place had descended into a kind of cannibalistic madness. Boardman was an itinerant preacher and said he'd run away when his own wife, Edith, tried to kill and eat him. Boardman ended up dying of starvation and exhaustion a few days later, about the time the third rescue expedition arrived.

"All this and much more Tamzene recorded in her journal.

"Finally, in April, the fourth and final relief effort arrived. But in the aftermath of the third rescue expedition, many more had died and the cannibalism had actually accelerated. What those last rescuers found was even more shocking than what had come before. In the Alder Creek camp, they found no one alive. George Donner was dead, his body lying in the melting snow, butchered and partially dismembered, his head split open and brains removed. There was, however, no sign of Tamzene. The rescuers went on to a rude campsite nearby, where they found a single living man named Keseberg. Next to him was a frying pan with a human liver and lungs in it. Under pointed questioning, he admitted they were the remains of Tamzene. He had been eating her body for weeks, he said, and the liver and lungs were all that was left.

"At any rate, that final relief expedition brought out the last of the survivors. The story of the Donner Party became a tale for the ages, retold, reprinted, and sensationalized until it was almost unrecognizable. It has never ceased to fascinate.

"Which brings me to why I'm here. As I mentioned, two primary campsites were identified—the camp near Truckee Lake and the one along Alder Creek. But the Lost Camp has never been found. It was visited by only one member of the third search party. We don't know many details of what he found there, but we do know that after witnessing it he refused to go back. Bad as the two main camps were, what happened in the Lost Camp was apparently worse—much worse. The rescuer found only one survivor in that camp, and brought him out, but he died raving not long afterward.

"The elusive stories about the Lost Camp haunted me. For half a dozen years I searched, following one dead end, one false lead after another...until I dedicated myself to finding Tamzene's diary. Of course, there were plenty of sensational newspaper stories, letters, secondhand accounts of dubious accuracy—but this crucial primary source had been lost for almost two centuries. Everyone believed it must have been left behind, just so much mulch rotting into the forest floor. Thinking it was lost, nobody undertook a systematic search for it. I'll spare you the details, but my patience was finally rewarded in not one but two ways. First, I managed to find the journal—just in the nick of time. And second: it includes not only a list of everyone who was stranded at the Lost Camp, but directions to it as well. Asher Boardman, the man who escaped the Lost Camp, shared information about it with Tamzene before he died. Beyond that, her journal contains notes with landmarks, and a hand-drawn map showing the locations of all three camps. The Lost Camp may have a particularly infamous reputation—and the horrors that occurred there may never be fully known—but we now have a road map to it."

Benton paused again, leaning forward. "And that's the job I'm offering you: to lead an expedition to find the Lost Camp."

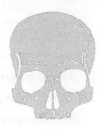

5

November 29

THE ASSISTANT OPENED the door and Nora stepped into the office of Jill Fugit, PhD, president of the Santa Fe Archaeological Institute. Clive Benton followed behind. The office itself, though not large, was warm and cozy and, Nora thought, had a friendly feeling—with an old Spanish tiled floor, adobe walls, and a small fireplace. The windows along the far wall overlooked a garden, now blanketed in white from the previous night's snowfall. A 1920s Two Grey Hills rug adorned another wall, while a shelf displayed a row of Zuni ollas from the late 1800s.

Dr. Fugit raised her head from a stack of papers and rose, shaking both their hands. Her smartly tailored suit, long blond hair, and habitual sense of style were hardly the standard image of a fussy, unimaginative academic—something Nora silently applauded. Fugit had been a controversial choice for president when the post became vacant a few years earlier, but her credentials were impeccable, while her keen and at times acerbic intellect was a pleasant change from the usual mumbling fossils who'd inhabited the office. The Institute was already showing the tangible benefits of her business and fund-raising acumen.

"Nora, nice to see you," she said briskly. "And you must be Dr. Benton. So good to meet you. Please sit down."

She indicated seats for them on either side of the fireplace. Dr. Fugit resumed her seat at the desk and looked at them both with a pleasant but searching expression.

"Can I offer anyone coffee or tea?"

One of the perks of working in the Old Building at the Institute was the coffee service. Fugit picked up the phone and put in their requests. She then pulled a manila folder off the top of the stack, slid it in front of her, and opened it. "So, Dr. Benton. I see you're a Stanford graduate."

"For my PhD, yes. I did my undergraduate work back east."

"My alma mater as well. But let's get down to it. I've read through the report you and Dr. Kelly prepared." She paused. "I knew about the Donner tragedy, of course, and I'm somewhat familiar with earlier archaeological work on the two main camps. But the details you've outlined are remarkably vivid—particularly of this Lost Camp, apparently a scene of exceptional deprivation and despair." She closed the folder. "I couldn't help but notice your spelling of Mrs. Donner's first name. She was perhaps the central figure of the tragedy, and one of the most studied by historians, but I recall her name always being spelled as 'Tamsen.'"

"That's correct. Her mother's name was 'Tamesin' and that was the name she was given at birth. However, she chose to spell her own name as 'Tamzene'—and I've tried to respect her wishes."

"Of course." There was a brief pause. "So—Dr. Benton, you want the Institute to sponsor a search for this camp and excavate it."

"Exactly. I'm a historian, not an archaeologist. The Lost

Camp is almost certainly in the Tahoe National Forest, on federal land, so we'd need to get state and federal permits to excavate. The prestigious reputation of the Institute would be extremely helpful." He paused. "And I'm convinced Dr. Kelly is the perfect person to lead this expedition."

Fugit's penetrating gaze did not waver. As usual, Nora found herself unable to read the president's expression with any accuracy.

"Well, as I said, the proposal is admirably thorough. I've given it much thought. But I don't think it's right for us at this time."

This flat-out surprised Nora. "Why not?" she asked, a little more forcefully than she intended.

"For one thing, high-quality excavations have already been undertaken at the other two camps. Frankly, what more is there to learn?"

Nora took a deep breath. "Dr. Fugit, the last excavation was over twenty years ago. We have new techniques—especially in DNA extraction."

"I'm aware of the new techniques."

"Of course. Sorry." Nora was used to dealing with bureaucrats out of date with technology. "As you can understand, then, with a fresh dig site to work with, we might be able to finally identify some human remains by name. We can figure out who died when, and who..." She paused, trying to make it sound least objectionable. "Who, ah, consumed whom."

At this point the coffee service arrived: a rickety cart pushed by a fifty-year employee of the Institute named Jones, with an urn, cups, cream and sugar, and stale ladyfingers. The discussion paused while they were served.

"At this point, is there tangible scientific value in knowing who consumed whom?" Fugit asked. "Besides, although Dr.

Benton's evidence is persuasive, you're assuming you'll be able to find the Lost Camp. But most fundamental is the question of *cost*."

Nora knew this was coming. Ten years ago, the Institute had fallen into financial difficulties. Now, with Fugit in charge, they were no longer pinching pennies. But one reason for that was because the president was very careful with their budget.

"It's true that, until now, the Lost Camp was, in fact, totally lost," Nora said. "But Dr. Benton's discovery changes all that. By all accounts, the eleven people trapped in this camp underwent some highly unusual sociological and psychological changes. This is an incredible opportunity for the Institute, a high-profile excavation that's sure to get a lot of press."

Fugit turned to Benton. "Dr. Benton, do you have any grant monies to bring to the table? I don't see any mention of support in the proposal."

"No, frankly, I don't."

"Do you intend to apply for grant monies?"

"No."

"Just a moment," Nora interrupted. "Of course we're going to apply for grant monies, but we need the Institute's stamp of approval first."

Fugit continued to look at Benton. "Surely you weren't assuming the Institute would fund it?"

"I was, in fact, assuming that."

Nora frowned. Benton was suddenly on the brink of screwing everything up. But as she opened her mouth to put things back on track, he continued.

"There is one aspect to the story that I didn't put in our proposal," he said.

Fugit put down her saucer. "Which is?"

"It's a part of the story that needs to be kept under wraps—for reasons you'll soon understand."

Fugit waited, hands folded.

"You'll recall from the proposal that a man named Wolfinger was carrying a chest of gold."

"I do recall that."

"Then you'll recall that when Wolfinger's wagon became stuck while crossing the Great Salt Lake Desert, two men—Reinhardt and Spitzer—volunteered to go back and help dig it out. Those two men returned, claiming Indians had killed Wolfinger."

"Yes, yes," Dr. Fugit said, concealing a growing impatience.

"Well, that was a lie. Even at the time the members of the party were suspicious that something untoward had happened to Wolfinger. Reinhardt and Spitzer were viewed with a great deal of suspicion, and the two men afterwards kept to themselves and were somewhat ostracized by the rest. When Reinhardt was dying of starvation in the Lost Camp, he made a deathbed confession: Wolfinger had not been killed by Indians. Reinhardt and Spitzer had gone back, murdered Wolfinger, and taken his gold." He paused. "This information has been known to historians for over a century, but nobody, incredibly enough, thought to ask the next question: what happened to the gold?"

"Please continue."

"Naturally, they must have carried the strongbox back to their own wagon and hid it. And they transported that gold as far as the mountains, where they were snowbound. Because the two of them were basically ostracized, they were forced to make their own shelter some distance from the others. There they died of starvation. Nobody mentioned finding gold or taking it out. Which brings us to the question: where is it?"

A long silence filled the room.

"Are you saying the gold is still hidden somewhere in the vicinity of the Lost Camp?" Fugit asked.

"Precisely. And in fact, probably close to that crude shelter they built from their wagon boards."

Nora stared at Benton, surprised and annoyed. "Why didn't you mention this to me before?"

"I'm sorry. I had to be super careful. Think what would happen if this got out. During their snowbound months, they must have hidden the box. With all that snow they wouldn't have been able to hike very far to hide it. Which is why I think they hid it near their shelter."

Fugit looked searchingly at Benton. "How did you come by this information?"

"Nobody else had thought to do the research. I searched through old bank records from where Wolfinger worked and lived. And in the basement of the historical society, in an old ledger book from the First Depository Bank of Springfield, Illinois, I found a page—dated six days before the expedition's departure—showing a large withdrawal of ten-dollar 'Liberty Head' gold eagles: all dated 1846 and uncirculated, fresh from the Philadelphia mint."

"How many?"

"One thousand."

"And the record specified that the withdrawal was made by Jacob Wolfinger?" Nora asked. She was still smarting from having been kept out of the loop.

"No—I couldn't get the name of the withdrawer. That particular ledger page had been damaged by silverfish. But I have corroborating evidence." He reached into the pocket of his jacket and took out an old piece of paper, sandwiched within archival plastic. "In an adjoining file cabinet, I came across a letter from the First Depository Bank to Wolfinger, dated the following day, hoping he'd found the withdrawal transaction had been to his satisfaction and thanking him for his business."

He passed the letter to Fugit, who looked it over carefully and then passed it to Nora.

"Very intriguing," she said, returning it to Benton. "But how can you be sure it was Wolfinger who withdrew the thousand gold eagles? He could have just withdrawn a few hundred dollars."

"Anything is possible," Clive said. "But consider: This was a small bank. A withdrawal like that would have been exceedingly unusual—and it would have taken time to arrange. They might have had to send to Chicago or even Philadelphia for it. Wolfinger was a wealthy man; he had liquidated a very prosperous farm and business, and he was moving to California. Remember, this was before the days of Wells Fargo. Wolfinger couldn't just wire the money to Sacramento—he'd have to carry it on his person. Ten-dollar gold pieces were the lingua franca of the day, like one-hundred-dollar bills for drug dealers today." Clive leaned forward. "We know a withdrawal of one thousand gold pieces was made right before the expedition set forth. We know Wolfinger made a withdrawal from that same bank. We know he had gold in a strongbox that he was taking to California." He spread his hands. "The evidence is irrefutable."

He sat back, a smile of triumph on his face.

"Ten thousand dollars," Fugit murmured. "That was a great deal of money in 1846."

"Yes. But what's it worth today? We're not just talking about the melt value here—we're talking about the *numismatic* value. A single gold eagle in uncirculated MS-60 or better condition with a date in the mid-1840s is currently valued between fifteen and twenty thousand dollars. In other words, somewhere in or around that camp is a strongbox containing up to twenty million dollars' worth of gold coins."

Benton stopped and the silence in the office was impressive. Finally the president spoke.

"This is all well and good, but if the Institute excavates the site and finds the gold...who owns it?"

"Any artifacts uncovered in a permitted excavation by a qualified 501(c)(3) nonprofit organization are normally owned by the organization."

"So the gold would be ours?"

"Debatable. California will claim the treasure as its historical patrimony. The Federal government will also want it, since it will have been found on federal land. Wolfinger had no descendants that I can find, so there's little concern in that direction."

"I've seen situations like this before. Descendants or no, it could very easily get ugly."

"Yes. But Dr. Fugit—" Benton leaned forward— "here's where the Institute and its stellar reputation come in. As part of the archaeological permitting process, the Institute will negotiate *ahead of time* how any treasure will be divided, should it be found. That arrangement will be written into the permits themselves. The Institute's reputation would ensure no one objected to you getting a goodly share—to increase your endowment. Fund important research. Raise salaries. If the Institute offered a third to California, a third to Uncle Sam, and kept a third, who could argue with that?" He lowered his voice. "In other words, you don't *need* grant money to fund this expedition."

"It would still be a rather expensive gamble."

"If the Institute felt it was too risky, I'd understand. Our joint alma mater, Stanford, has a world-class archaeology program, as does Berkeley."

A line of displeasure creased Fugit's brow. Nora knew the director wouldn't respond well to threats, and she was startled by Benton's directness.

"I'm sure we can find the funds," the president said sharply. "But in this division you propose, where would you come in?"

Benton laughed. "You mean, how much gold for me? None. My interest is purely in history. If I wanted the gold, I could have gone up there myself and searched it out—and nobody would be the wiser."

"Commendable," Fugit said drily. "But how do you know someone else didn't find it years ago?"

"If somebody had, there would be an unusual number of uncirculated 1846 gold eagles floating around. Nobody had any idea where the Lost Camp was located—except us, now, thanks to Tamzene Donner and her journal."

There was a brief silence. Then Fugit closed the folder on her desk. "The Institute will accept your proposal and bear the cost of the expedition. Nora, you will be the archaeological director if you so choose, and Clive—may I call you Clive?—will be chief historian. My office will take care of the permits. We have the winter months, which isn't much time to put together a major expedition."

She stood and shook both their hands. "Dr. Benton, I wonder if you'd give me a moment with Nora?"

"Of course." He smiled at them both, turned, and stepped out of the office.

Fugit watched him close the door. They resumed their seats and she turned back to Nora. "This is a very intriguing proposal." The president's expression remained formal, but her face betrayed a hint of enthusiasm.

"Thank you. I'm glad you think so."

"Where do we stand on that Pueblo ruin out by Pedernal Peak?"

"The final room has been fully excavated and documented. It's just a question of cataloging the potsherds and artifacts. Lab work."

"And that outlier settlement you were working at Bandelier?"

"Our job is complete; I've handed it off to the Antiquities Department to handle the legal issues."

The president looked at her searchingly for a moment. "You know, I've been here almost two and a half years. And in all that time, I can't remember you once taking a vacation, or even just getting your head out of a test trench."

"It's simple: I love my work."

"Is that all there is to it?"

"Yes," Nora said, a little more abruptly than she intended to.

"I'm not trying to pry. But I'm aware of your history. I'm glad you love your work—I just don't want to see you bury yourself in it."

Nora said nothing.

"This expedition may not exactly be a walk in the park. The high Sierras are rugged, dangerous mountains. You know that Ted Curtin is just champing at the bit for a dig like this. Fact is, he needs to get one under his belt. If you want to hand off the fieldwork to him, you could take some time off, and then direct the work from back here and pick up when—"

"Dr. Fugit," Nora interrupted, "I thank you for your concern—truly I do. And I want to see Ted Curtin get his fellowship. But the fact is, Clive Benton sought me out personally.

I don't know how he'd feel about handing the dig off to some-body else. And in all honesty, I'm not burying myself in my work—that work *is* my life. I can't imagine anything more excit-ing than finding the Lost Camp of the Donner Party. There will be downtime over the winter as we prepare—it isn't like I'll be going without sleep or anything."

Fugit remained quiet, listening.

"I know you're aware of my history. Honestly, it's not rele-vant. And ... well, to use your own words, I really do appreciate your sensitivity in not prying."

Fugit's eyes widened almost imperceptibly at this. Silence fell over the office for a moment. And then the president nodded.

"Very well," she said briskly. "Best of luck with your prepa-rations, Dr. Kelly."

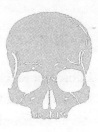

6

AGENT SWANSON?"

The long, echoing room—once apparently a grand chamber of some sort, now broken up into a warren of office cubicles—remained silent save for the low beep of electronic equipment and the clack of fingers on keys.

"Agent *Swanson!*"

Corinne Swanson looked up abruptly, dropping the papers she was leafing through onto her desk.

"Yes?" she said.

The voice belonged to Robert Wantaugh. His head was sticking up from a cubicle at the far end of what she'd come to call their cellblock. He had short blond hair, and it was combed back in a ducktail that would have made an extra from *The Untouchables* proud.

"You're alive. Good. I thought maybe something had happened, and you were as dead as those case files you're studying."

"Not yet." Wantaugh had been on the job only six months longer than she, but since he'd made GS-11 he'd adopted an air of breezy, reckless experience. At least when more senior agents weren't around.

"Just wanted to let you know the pizzas are here. Conference Room B."

"Thanks. You all go ahead, I'll catch up." Not only was Wantaugh a wise-ass, but Swanson thought he might be trying to put the moves on her as well.

She picked up the papers again—eyewitness reports from victims of a bank robber who'd cut a wide swath up and down I-25 three years ago—and tried to get her mind back into focus. Then she turned toward her keyboard and began typing her summary report. Not that there was much to summarize—she knew everything by heart already, and there was nothing new of value to add. Five banks robbed in a space of two months. Two tellers shot, neither fatally. The perp was conscious of security cameras and had walked into the banks wearing a variety of cowboy hats, under which was concealed a balaclava he'd roll down immediately upon entering. Total take, $694,000. Last seen at the Third National Bank in Alamogordo, just off the Mescalero reservation. No ID, no license plates, no nothing; the eyewitnesses could agree only that the guy appeared Caucasian and under forty. Word from a CI was that he'd skipped across the border. And even that word was already two years old.

Swanson let her hands drop from the keyboard, stacked the papers neatly on her desk, and slid them into the official case folder, sighing. It was ironic: the reason she hadn't heard Wantaugh calling her was because she still hadn't gotten used to being called *agent*.

Special Agent Swanson. To think how long she'd dreamed of being addressed like that. It was a dream that had taken her from Medicine Creek, Kansas, all the way to the John Jay

College of Criminal Justice in New York City; followed by the requisite work experience, in her case a year as an assistant probation officer in the lower Hudson Valley; and then, finally, on to the FBI Academy at Quantico for twenty weeks of new agent training. Twenty weeks of endless case exercises and "practicals"; of humping her way over the obstacle course again and again as winter rains turned the dirt to icy mud; of refining her firearms skills and combat tactics in the Hollywood-like set of Hogan's Alley; of executing coordinated spinouts and PIT maneuvers until she felt more like a stunt driver than a law enforcement trainee. And she had loved it—every filthy, exhausting, stressful minute. Because every minute brought her that much closer to being a special agent.

And then at last it came: graduation and the swearing-in, receiving her badge and credentials. It had been the proudest moment of her life. As well as one nobody could have predicted: Corrie Swanson, the foulmouthed, purple-haired goth who'd grown up a latter-day rebel without a cause in a shithole prairie town. Her mother hadn't bothered to come to graduation—drunk, probably—and it had stung that the prime mover behind her budding career, Special Agent Aloysius Pendergast, had been unable to attend...but her father, Jack, had been there, beaming with pride despite his obvious discomfort at being surrounded by so many people with the power of arrest.

And then it was over. She was issued her duty weapon—a Glock 19M with four fifteen-round magazines equipped with orange followers, along with several boxes of Winchester PDX1 +P 124-grain hollow points—and she was off to her new life.

Little did she know at the time that her "new life" would consist of reporting every morning at eight thirty to 4200 Luecking Park Avenue NE—the Albuquerque, New Mexico, field office—

for administrative duties. She'd met Supervisory Special Agent Hale Morwood, the advisor who would manage the first part of Swanson's two-year probationary period. He was the mentor who would "ghost" her, show her the ropes, rate her... and, it seemed, rein in her expectations.

Now she'd spent three months reviewing cold cases and working with the PIO on public relations outreach to the community. Occasionally, for a change of pace, she'd get to accompany Tech Ops... as they put up new pole cams.

This was not what she'd expected. Surely not all new Quantico graduates spent their probationary periods like this. She couldn't imagine getting a worse detail—until Morwood took her to visit the resident agency at Farmington, up by the Colorado border. If Albuquerque was the ugly, dusty ass end of nowhere, then Farmington was the inflamed boil on that ass. If she ever ended up in a satellite office like that, she just might rob a few banks herself.

She could hear a low hubbub of conversation from Conference Room B, where her young confrères were chatting over lunch. But Swanson wasn't hungry. She was eyeing Morwood's office. The door was closed, and the wall of glass beside it was, as usual, obscured by beige vinyl blinds, lowered to floor level. Morwood was on a conference call: the weekly status meeting for Operations. She glanced at her watch: it should be over anytime now. She took a deep breath. And then, as anticipated, the door opened and Morwood emerged, shrugging into the jacket of his dark blue suit. She watched out of the corner of her eye as he disappeared into the maze of cubicles. He was short, in his late forties, a little overweight with a thinning crown of red hair. When she'd first seen him, Swanson had thought he looked more like a train conductor than an FBI supervisor. But that was before she'd had the chance to observe him over a couple of months: the way he kept his own counsel, the sly intelligence that glittered in the sleepy brown eyes.

Now Morwood had re-emerged from the cube farm and was coming back, fresh cup of coffee in one hand. Still sticking to schedule. That meant he wouldn't get called into another meeting for fifteen minutes. Taking another deep breath and composing herself, Swanson picked up the folder, rose from her desk, and exited her cubicle.

Morwood was seating himself back at his desk, stirring Splenda into his coffee. Seeing Swanson approach, he nodded. "Good afternoon, Swanson."

"Afternoon, sir. Do you have a minute?"

Morwood nodded toward one of two identical chairs placed against the glass wall. "Please."

Swanson sat, file on her lap. Something about the detached way Morwood observed her always made her slightly uncomfortable, as if her hair was askew or she'd put her blouse on inside out and the label was showing. Too many years of torn jeans and nearly identical black T-shirts, no doubt. She resisted the impulse to smooth her skirt.

"I've finished reviewing the I-25 robberies, sir," she said.

Morwood took a sip of coffee. "Anything to report?"

Swanson hesitated. She didn't want to appear ineffectual, but on the other hand she didn't want to go on having cold cases dumped on her. "No significant developments. I re-interviewed the tellers and bank employees to make sure nothing had changed in their recollections. I went over the surveillance footage. Even running it through our latest recognition software produced no useful results. Using image enhancement I was able to identify the brand of one of the perp's cowboy hats. It was a manufacturer common to Texas, New Mexico, and Arizona that recently went out of business. Their records proved useless."

"Any new robberies that fit the MO?"

"No, sir. I checked into that carefully, both north and south of the border. Plenty of bank robberies, but none with more than a single-point match."

"I see. Well, good job, Swanson. You'll send me your report?"

"Just completing it now."

Morwood nodded, began to speak, then reached into his pocket and snatched out a handkerchief in time to cover a series of sharp, wheezing coughs. Swanson waited politely for the fit to pass. Morwood was a bit of a mystery. She'd heard her share of rumors. Apparently back in the day he'd been a hotshot Chicago agent with enough commendations to fill a desk drawer. Some said his slow, lethargic movements and heavy-lidded stare were just put on. Others said he'd been in a terrible accident chasing a suspect through an industrial dye plant in Gary that ruined both his lungs and his promising career. Whatever the case, here he was: a man of obvious intelligence and long experience, finishing out his twenty as the FTO for groups of new agents.

Morwood tucked the handkerchief back into his jacket pocket. "Was there something else, Agent Swanson?"

This was it. Swanson took another deep breath. "This is the fifth case I've re-evaluated, sir."

Morwood nodded. "And I've seen a steady improvement in both your approach and your efficiency."

"Thank you." God, getting complimented made this even harder. "Sir, while I appreciate the opportunity to gain experience by reviewing these cases, I was hoping...I feel that..."

She stopped, wishing Morwood would get her drift, finish the sentence for her. He didn't. "That I'd like a new challenge, sir."

"A new challenge. You mean, as in an active investigation?"

"Yes, sir."

"You feel you've learned all you can from these open but inactive cases, and are ready to go out and play cowboys and Indians for real?"

Growing up, Swanson had had a legendary temper, but the years spent at John Jay and, especially, the discipline instilled at Quantico—along with her own gradual maturity—had helped her rein it in. She glanced at Morwood. There was no hint of sarcasm or condescension in his sleepy eyes.

"I'm sure there's always something more those cases can teach me. But I've made no real headway, no actionable breakthroughs, in the three months I've been examining them. I have extensive training in forensic anthropology. I think..."

This time, Morwood helped her. "You think that you've already covered case studies like these at Quantico."

"Yes, sir."

"That after three months spent doing cleanup detail at the fort, you've put in your time and now you're ready for something more useful. More interesting."

Morwood was fond of Western metaphors. Or perhaps, transferred here from Chicago, he was just cynical—Swanson couldn't read him well enough to tell which. "You could put it that way, yes."

Morwood sat forward in his chair. "Swanson, I could answer that one of two ways. I could say that, as a rookie just out of the Academy, what you *hope* and what you *feel* are of no consequence—to me or anyone else in this office. That, in fact, would be the official, the expected, response."

As he spoke, an undercurrent of steel crept into his quiet voice. Swanson felt herself stiffen.

"Or I could say that I understand completely." Morwood put his elbows on his desk, tented his fingers. His voice softened a trifle. "I felt the same way, once upon a time. It's usually worst about now—three months in. I shouldn't tell you this, but the staff psychologists at Quantico even have a term for it."

Swanson sat, still stiff in her chair, uncertain where this was heading.

"Being an FBI agent isn't like being a doctor. Or even like being a cop. There's no single path to getting the right kind of experience under your belt. There are plenty of agents—lawyers, programmers—who don't even wear a weapon and spend their entire careers at their desks. Location makes a difference, too. You happened to catch Albuquerque. A lot of the action around here is drug-related, so the DEA tends to take point." He leaned forward a little. "But I'll tell you two more things, Swanson. First—I'm your FTO. That means I'm your judge as well as your guardian angel. While you're evaluating those cold cases, I'm evaluating *you*: where your skills lie, where you'll do the most good—what weak points need the most work."

Swanson tried not to show her surprise. She'd never considered—certainly never noticed—that Morwood might be watching and evaluating her with any particular attention.

"Second—and you have to believe me on this—your time will come. And it'll probably come when you least expect it. It might not even be an official assignment. Something might happen while you're out installing those damn pole cams. Or driving home at night. It might turn out to be the investigation you were born to solve. Or it might be the most boring, most frustrating catch of your career. Either way, I can promise you this: those cold cases you're reviewing now will come in handy."

He took a sip of his coffee. After a few moments of silence, Swanson realized the conversation was over and that she was being dismissed.

She stood up. "Thanks for your time, sir."

"Don't mention it." Morwood picked up the phone and began to dial.

Swanson made her way thoughtfully back to her desk. As she reached it, she frowned. There was something on it that hadn't been there before—a package, sealed in an oversize buff envelope. Picking it up, she tore it open. Inside lay a fat, well-thumbed folder full of photographs and reports.

Cold case number six.

With a sigh, she sat down, pulled out the folder, and—blinking a little blearily—put it to one side while she finished typing up the summary on the I-25 robber, still at large and sought by the Federal Bureau of Investigation.

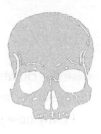

7

THE MAN KNOWN as Bricktop had done a lot of weird shit for money in his life, but this job had to take the cake. Grave robbing was supposed to have gone out of fashion two hundred years ago, but here he was, in a cemetery, digging up a body under the full moon. But for five grand, what the hell—it was better than dealing Oxy, quicker, and a lot less risky.

Although he had driven through New Mexico before, he'd never been in this part of the state, and it was a lot greener than he expected. And mountainous, looking more like Colorado. The cemetery was a good twenty miles east of Santa Fe, on a forested hill, with a wrought iron gate and fence. There was a plaque of some sort at the entrance, which he didn't bother to read. There sure as hell weren't any tourists coming up at this time of night, and there wasn't anything else to do around here except chop down trees. The lights of Glorieta twinkled in the valley below, and a ribbon of I-25 could be seen among the hills, the slow-moving lights of cars crawling along. It was chilly at night up here, but Bricktop was glad of it, as he was working up a sweat digging. They were predicting rain later, but for now the clouds were just patchy and the full moon was all the illumination he needed.

Funny how jobs like this came together. He knew a guy who knew a guy, and all of a sudden he was getting precise directions to the spot. Like the rest of the place, there was no tombstone for the grave, just a small stone monument with some kind of old, official-looking metal medallion—almost like a Rotary Club seal—stuck into the ground beside it.

Bricktop paused for a moment and checked his watch: eleven fifty. He had been working for about an hour and was already halfway done. He took a breather, resisted the urge to light up, and then resumed, sinking his shovel into the loose, dry soil, tossing it out onto the tarp, and repeating, all in an easy, rhythmic motion. It wasn't all that different, he told himself, from working out at his local gym in Kirtland. The song "Brick House" was stuck in his head and the beat provided a rhythm to his work.

Bricktop had not, of course, met the men who actually hired him. All he got was a phone call, in which he was instructed to go to a parking garage and retrieve an envelope with two grand in it and the instructions. Another three grand was promised when he was finished. The instructions not only told him the night and time he was to do the job, with a detailed map, but also included a list of equipment he'd need: a plastic tarp to pile the dirt on, shovel, pick, gloves, a short ladder, and special hooking bars for opening the lid of the casket. He wasn't actually to rob the grave: instead, he was just to expose the casket and open the lid, so the deceased could be examined "to determine identity." The two men who were to make this determination would be arriving at one thirty in the morning, and after they'd had their look the casket would be shut, he'd get the other $3,000, and they'd go away while he refilled the hole. Guys who obviously didn't like to get their pretty hands dirty. Bricktop figured it must be some inheritance business or identity theft, but he wasn't about to ask questions or show curiosity: the note had contained a warning that if he tried to make off with the two grand, he'd receive a visit after which he'd be left with a very, very high voice.

It was not easy digging up a grave, but at least the ground was soft and sandy, free of rocks and roots. Now and then he stopped to listen, but there was never anything except the night noises of the surrounding forest. Down he dug, neatly squaring off the hole as he went, digging first on one side and then the other, still humming "Brick House." Sooner than expected, he heard the blade of his shovel hit something. But it didn't sound like wood. Bending down, he brushed off the dirt and saw to his great astonishment that the old casket under his feet was made of iron, ancient and pitted. It looked more like a frigging treasure chest than a coffin. Shaking his head, he cleared away the rest of the dirt from the top. The casket had a double lid—at least that was something expected. Digging around the sides, he freed up some space to get the hooking bars in place, then lifted the top half of the lid. It was heavy as a bitch. An unpleasant smell arose from the dark recesses. Keeping his penlight below ground level, he flicked it on to examine the man's corpse.

Another surprise: it wasn't a man at all, but a woman. At least, he assumed it was a woman, because it was clothed in a disintegrating brown dress. It was hard to tell from the disgusting face: fuzzy with mold, all shriveled up, more skeleton than visage, mummified lips pulled back in a manic grin. Thank God the identification wasn't his problem. He obviously didn't need to pry open the bottom part of the coffin, if identity was what they were after. He'd done the first part of his job and now he just had to wait for the men to come. He checked his watch: one twenty. He was right on time; ten minutes early, in fact.

He climbed out of the hole, perched himself on a nearby grave marker, and lit a cigarette, taking a deep drag. He was trying to quit and had limited himself to two cigarettes a day. Seeing as how it was past midnight, this would count as his first.

Sure enough, at one thirty sharp he saw a glow of headlights on the winding road that came up the hill past the cemetery, and as the car reached the top the lights went off and the car swung into the dirt lane and pulled up next to his. Both doors opened and two men got out. They walked over to him. One of them held a duffel.

"You're Bricktop?" the man with the duffel asked.

"That's me. Your guy—I mean, what you want—is down there."

He showed the men to the grave. They stood on either side, looking down at the open coffin. Clouds had drifted over the moon, and he couldn't really see their faces. He waited.

Now both guys snapped on latex gloves and put on N95 face masks. One got into the grave and stood on the lower lid of the iron coffin, bent down, and briefly shone a light on the dead woman's face. Then the other guy pulled a long, serrated bone saw out of the duffel he was carrying and passed it down to the guy in the hole, along with a couple of oversize dry bags. The metal saw gleamed faintly in the moonlight. The man bent over the corpse's midriff and Bricktop heard a horrible crackling, sawing sound. It was pretty obvious what the guy was doing—and it wasn't just determining identity. But Bricktop held his tongue. Never ask questions, never show curiosity: that was his mantra.

The man put something heavy into one of the dry bags, sawed some more, put something else in the other bag. Then, sealing them, he handed them carefully to the man standing above. Then he stripped off his gloves and mask and slipped them into a pocket.

"Are we good?" Bricktop asked.

"We're good." The man reached into his coat and withdrew a manila envelope. "Remember: this never happened."

Bricktop nodded, opened the envelope that was handed to him, and saw it contained fresh banded hundreds. Three bands, each labeled $1,000. He riffled through and then slipped the envelope inside his jacket.

"Okay," said the man. "Close the lid and refill the hole."

Bricktop was only too eager to finish the job and get the hell out of there. He bent down, grasping the heavy lid. It was just as he thought—the crazy fuckers had sawed the corpse in half and taken it from the waist up. None of his business. Pulling out the hooking bars, he heaved it closed with a muffled thump.

He felt a sharp tickle against the back of his skull—and that was it.

* * *

The man in the grave bent over the figure sprawled on the coffin, then dispassionately squeezed off a second round from the silenced Maxim 9 pistol, taking off the top of the gravedigger's head. Pulling the latex gloves on again, he gingerly reached inside the man's jacket and took out the envelope with the money, along with wallet, car keys, and the instruction document. He climbed back out and the two men, in silence, dragged the tarp and some of the dirt it held into the freshly dug hole, loosely covering the corpse and his tools. The dry bags and saw went back into the duffel. Dark clouds now began to blot out the moon, the arrival of the predicted front, bringing thunderstorms and heavy rain. The man with the pistol got into the dead man's car, and the man with the duffel got into the other. Bricktop's car went off one way, and a few minutes later the other drove off in the opposite direction.

Hefty drops of rain began spattering into the graveyard, first a few and then many, while lightning split the sky and thunder rolled among the hills.

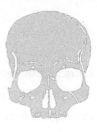

8

April 23

THE PHONE ON Swanson's desk rang. Two short bursts: an internal call.

She picked it up. "Yes?"

"Swanson?" It was Morwood.

"Yes?"

"Would you mind stepping into my office for a moment?"

"I'll be right there, sir."

Swanson pushed aside the files she'd been examining—cold case number seven—and stood up. It wasn't like Morwood to call her into his office like this; not at this hour of the morning. He was quite punctual about their weekly debriefs and review sessions, every Thursday afternoon at two. From long habit, the first feeling she had was of guilt and anxiety. Shit, had she done something wrong?

Over the last couple of weeks, in addition to the ongoing desk work, Morwood had let Swanson ride shotgun with two DEA teams on meth lab raids in northeast Albuquerque. They were low-level busts, and she'd been no more than an observer in body armor—she suspected that Morwood had specifically chosen the ops for their minimal danger potential—but in the process she'd gotten some firsthand experience with interagency rivalry.

She'd already heard the FBI's opinion of the DEA: knuckle-dragging Neanderthals whose main talent was for cracking skulls. But on these ride-alongs, she'd learned the DEA's own impression of the FBI. The assault teams had let her know, in no uncertain terms, that she'd joined the wrong agency, and that the FBI was a sorry collection of pencil-necked, limp-dicked, nerdy accountants who rarely if ever broke leather their entire careers. At first, Swanson had endured the ribbing good-naturedly. But by the end of the second ride-along, just yester-day, one crew-cut-sporting agent in particular just wouldn't let the joke go, and as they'd returned to headquarters—suspects in cuffs, the crank in evidence lockers, and Clandestine Lab En-forcement securing the site—Swanson's anger had gotten the better of her, and she'd let her tormentor know, in graphic detail, precisely where he could shove the meth they'd just confiscated.

It was only later in the evening that she'd learned Breitman, the agent with the crew cut, had been squad leader.

As she approached the open door of Morwood's office, her anxiety spiked. Shit, it had to be that. Almost four months now, and she hadn't blown her top once. Figures she'd do it just at the worst time, and at the worst guy possible. She knew that, as her FTO, Morwood had the power to fire her. While that was al-most unheard of, he could certainly put a note in her jacket that would be an anchor on her career for a long time.

On top of everything else, the Rolling Stones' "19th Nervous Breakdown" had wormed its way into her head and refused to leave. *Here it comes...*

Mouth dry, she knocked on the doorframe. Morwood, who was holding a stapled sheaf of papers in one hand, glanced up. As usual, she could tell nothing from his expression. "Swanson," he said, looking back at the papers. "Come in."

Usually he asked her to sit. Not this time.

She waited while he turned over one page, then another. Then he cleared his throat and—without looking up—asked: "Are you familiar with what happened at Glorieta Pass?"

Glorieta Pass? That road was unfamiliar to Swanson. She racked her brains, recalling the names of the streets in the Alta Monte neighborhood where their raid had gone down— Candelaria, Comanche—but she couldn't recall any Glorieta.

"I'm not sure, sir," she said, bracing herself.

Morwood let the sheaf of papers drop on his desk and finally looked back up at her. "Frankly, Agent Swanson, I'm surprised at you."

"Sir?" *Here it comes, here it comes...*

"A student with your depth of scholarship, and you're going to tell me you don't know about the Battle of Glorieta Pass?"

Now Swanson was thoroughly confused. With a stab of annoyance she thrust Mick Jagger's nasal voice out of her mind. "I'm not sure what you mean. There was no battle; the cooks surrendered without a fight. If you're referring to the incident with Breitman, I want you to know, sir, that I'm sorry if there were any hard feelings—"

"Swanson, are we even on the same planet? I've read your John Jay transcript. It says you took a course on the American Civil War your sophomore year. Or maybe you slept through it?"

Swanson swallowed. "I'm sorry, sir. Are we talking about history?"

"Of course. What did you think we were talking about—that

DEA dustup yesterday? Sure, Breitman called me. I told him to untwist his underwear and forget about it. No, I'm talking about Glorieta Pass—the westernmost major battle of the Civil War. The Confederacy invaded New Mexico Territory in an attempt to cut the West off from the Union, and got their asses royally kicked. At *Glorieta Pass*."

Swanson felt surprise, relief, and then embarrassment. Now that her anxiety was receding, the name did have a familiar ring. But her professor for that class had been boring as hell, and there'd been so many battlefields to remember...

"Yes," she said. "Yes, a class of mine covered it. Sorry, sir."

He frowned at her in what she hoped was mock disappointment. "I'm relieved to hear it. Not exactly Gettysburg, of course, but over sixty men, Yanks and Confederates both, lost their lives in that battle. Several of them are buried up there, at a place called Pigeon's Ranch."

Swanson was silent, listening. As relieved as she was to learn this had nothing to do with the reaming-out she'd given Breitman the day before, she was mystified as to what Morwood was getting at.

"About an hour ago, a body was discovered in the Pigeon's Ranch cemetery. Well, two bodies, perhaps—although that remains to be seen. A man was found shot, lying atop a coffin in a freshly dug-up grave."

Swanson nodded. She wondered if she should be taking notes, decided against it.

"Feel free to chime in anytime, Swanson. Now: Glorieta Pass was a Civil War battle. Part of the battlefield is a national historic park, and that grave was in a small cemetery there."

At this, Swanson did chime in. "That would make the site federal land."

"Yes. You may now keep your diploma. Go on."

"Any crime committed there would be our responsibility to investigate."

"Correction: *your* responsibility." And with that, Morwood picked the sheaf of papers off his desk and handed it to her.

Swanson took the papers gingerly. "Sir?"

"It's quite simple. As I recall, three weeks ago you came to me asking for a new challenge. An active investigation, perhaps." Morwood coughed behind one palm, then waved at the sheaf of papers. "I herewith give you a dead body in a vandalized grave in the cemetery at Glorieta Pass."

When Swanson remained silent, Morwood said: "Isn't this what you wanted? A case of your own?"

Swanson recovered her voice. "Yes, sir, I want that very much. But what do I . . . ?" She fell silent again, seized with panic.

"You don't know exactly what to do? Of course not. It's your first case. But here's the chance to see how that Quantico training and these four months of casework pay off. I'm eager to hear what your budding forensic expertise makes of it all. So: you'll be the initial federal investigator. Liaise with local law enforcement, make sure the site has been secured, examine the body, supervise the collection of evidence, prepare a preliminary report. On your own."

Swanson didn't reply. She was aware of several emotions: excitement, even elation, but at the same time concern, as the ramifications of what Morwood was saying hit home. "What about you?" And, as an afterthought: "Sir?"

"What about me? I'll be in this office, eager to hear your findings."

Swanson swallowed. This was the opportunity she'd been waiting for. But Morwood was FTO for her probationary period. He was supposed to ghost her, mentor her, through just this kind of process. Was this his version of teaching her to swim by throwing her into the deep end of the pool?

"What about, ah, calling in an Evidence Response Team Unit?"

Morwood shook his head. "As the lead investigator, you'll be in charge. That's up to you." He gave her a wry smile. "But keep in mind you'll have local law enforcement and their CSU on hand, with the coroner's office and other support staff. Certainly, if you feel it's necessary to call in the ERTU, do so, but consider the optics first." He picked up his phone. "Take a look at that brief. Meanwhile, I'll get Operations to set you up with a pool car, a radio, and the rest of it."

When she remained motionless, Morwood put the phone down again. "Well? Remove thyself, Agent Swanson. Get thee to Glorieta. It's only an hour away. And it's even a rather attractive drive."

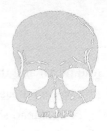

9

As she drove the duty vehicle down the winding, dusty road, Morwood's sheaf of papers—now carefully read, reread, and tucked into a folder—lying on the seat next to her, Agent Swanson found herself beset by unexpected emotions. This was a day she'd dreamed of for a long time: Special Agent Corinne Swanson, lead FBI investigator, on a homicide case. And yet, instead of focusing like a laser on the case, she felt awash in anxiety. Only the most banal thoughts seemed to come, unbidden, into her brain—trivial details of the weather, the color of the road, a broken piñon tree.

She took in a deep breath, then let it out slowly, slowly. She flexed her fingers, adjusted her grip on the steering wheel. Remotely, she was relieved to see her hands weren't trembling.

Get a grip, take it one step at a time, and play it by the book.

She exited at a sign marked GLORIETA PASS BATTLEFIELD NA-TIONAL PARK onto a rutted road that took her higher into the foothills of the Sangre de Cristo Mountains, then leveled off onto a mesa top. Ahead she could see the land dividing, ulti-mately leading to a twin set of ridges that slowly sank away to the north and the south. She wondered, a little idly, if that was the so-called pass, and who Glorieta was.

Now ahead she could see a grouping of RVs and Airstreams parked on the shoulder, their doors open and the occupants standing around in the sun, looking pissed. Another quarter mile, and she found out why: the entrance to PIGEON'S RANCH CEMETERY—GLORIETA PASS was blocked by a sheriff's cruiser, light bar flashing. She stopped and a deputy got out of the cruiser. Swanson had her ID on a lanyard around her neck and held it up for his inspection. The young deputy looked at her, at the ID, and then back again before finally nodding and returning to his vehicle. He revved the engine and moved it so Swanson could pass. Ahead, beyond a gate, a cluster of signs, and a parking turnout, she could see several official vehicles, parked haphazardly.

She took another deep breath.

Pulling in beside the vehicles, she got out and began to walk, first across a paved surface, and then up a gravel path. Weathered graves, each with a number and some sporting small explanatory labels, began to appear on her left and right. She could make out perhaps a dozen people in the distance, in a corner of the cemetery—uniformed officers, national park rangers, a few figures in monkey suits, medical personnel, a woman with a camera, one or two others whose purpose was not immediately identifiable—all standing around as if waiting. As she approached, the heads all swiveled in her direction and she realized it was her they'd been waiting for.

The last of the random thoughts abandoned her and her heart began pumping a mile a minute.

Be cool, she told herself. *You've got this.* As she continued walking, she forced herself to mentally review the case file Morwood had given her, to go over the crime scene training that had been drilled into her at the Academy. With relief she realized that, despite her nerves, she felt a good grounding of confidence beneath her feet. Whatever else happened, she wasn't going to panic.

The group broke up a bit as she drew closer, then one person stepped forward—a middle-aged man, muscular and deeply tanned, with a bottlebrush mustache. He wore the hat and uniform of the sheriff's department.

"Gus Turpenseed," he said, sticking out his hand. "Sheriff, San Miguel County."

Swanson shook it, fingers stiffening as she felt the crushing, intimidating grip. "Agent Swanson, Federal Bureau of Investigation."

"Good to meet you, Agent Swanson," the sheriff said, glancing back at another man wearing the star of a deputy sheriff, who grinned and nodded faintly.

Everyone seemed to be staring at the ID and shield on her lanyard.

"Agent Morwood mentioned you," Turpenseed said, "but I didn't expect—"

"A woman?"

"Someone so young."

"I see." Swanson was surprised to find herself not rising to the bait. It was the FBI shield, she realized; she had it, he didn't, and though he might not like it, he couldn't do shit about it. This realization gave her a tickling sensation of power. Growing up, power was the one thing she'd never had. And so she'd built up a carapace of sarcastic belligerence and resentment toward authority. Ironic how she was the authority now.

She looked around, taking in the other faces, the scene itself—an open grave, surrounded by crime tape, a confusion of dirt, plastic tarp, tools, and a partially covered body at the grave bottom—familiarizing herself with the situation as she let a silence build. Then she turned back to Turpenseed. "You're right, I'm young—and I'm not getting younger standing here. So let's get on with it. Who was first on the scene?"

A blond woman in a ranger's uniform separated herself from the group. "I was."

"Your name?"

"Grant."

"Want to tell me what happened?"

The ranger nodded. "I got here at seven thirty to open the cemetery and prepare it for visitors. One of my duties is to walk the perimeter. As I was doing so, I noticed this mound of earth." She nodded over her shoulder. "Coming closer, I saw the hole in the ground. At first I thought it might be grave robbers, come for Regis. But then I saw that man in the hole, partly covered by dirt. And blood. So I turned and called for Alec."

"Alec?"

"Alec Quinn. He's the other ranger on duty with me today. His car was just pulling in."

"Go on."

Another ranger, apparently Quinn, stepped forward and took over the story. "I thought there was a chance the man was still alive. So I jumped into the hole and began brushing the dirt from him. And then when I saw that—" He swallowed. "That he was dead, I got out and made some calls. There were no ISB agents in the area, so I notified the sheriff."

Swanson nodded. She knew that the ISB, or Investigative Services Branch, comprised the special agents of the National Park Service. She also knew there were a total of about three dozen agents to cover the entire country.

She looked around. "Who's heading the local CSU team?"

A short man of about sixty approached. "Larssen. Santa Fe Crime Scene Unit."

"You've been waiting for the feds?"

"That we have," the man said.

"Sorry to keep you. Please get started, and I'll be with you shortly." Now Swanson turned back to Quinn. "And when did you decide to call the FBI?" she asked.

Quinn reddened. "It's not as cut-and-dried as you might think," he said. "Glorieta Pass has only been ranked a Class A battlefield for the last twenty-five years. And most of it is on private land. Only about twenty percent, the Pigeon's Ranch unit, is technically under National Park Service jurisdiction."

"I called the FBI while we were verifying the authorization," Grant said.

Swanson nodded. "Did you see anything or anybody else?" she asked.

The woman shook her head. "It was like this when we arrived. Once we understood the victim was dead, we backed off and left it alone."

"Nothing out of place? Suspicious in any way?"

Another shake of the head.

"What are the park hours?"

"Eight to six."

"And there's nobody here at night?"

"No."

"You aren't worried about vandals? Souvenir hunters?"

"That's never been a problem before," Quinn told her. "Folks around here respect the dead. We're pretty remote, too, and besides, funding is tight. The trust does what it can, but most of the money is put toward upkeep and restoration.

Glorieta Pass is considered an endangered battlefield. It's got a Priority I rating—one of only a dozen such battlefields to have one."

Swanson had already learned there was a different mind-set in this part of the country. It wasn't all that unlike rural Kansas, really, where she grew up—too much empty land to police effectively, and not enough bodies or money to police it.

The CSU team had now surrounded the hole and were lowering a ladder, preparing to start work. Swanson turned to the sheriff. "Have you secured the scene?" she asked.

"We did, ma'am, as soon as we ascertained the nature of the situation."

The *ma'am* bit temporarily threw her, but she made no sign. It was the equivalent of *sir* and she'd better get used to it.

The sheriff took off his hat and wiped his forehead with the back of one arm. Swanson noticed his head was shaved, the brim of his hat soaked with sweat.

"Sheriff, could you please take your people and look to establish ingress and egress? Note any evidence such as tire tracks for the Crime Scene Unit." She nodded. "That photographer one of yours?"

"Yes."

"Good. Put her to work."

The sheriff hesitated just a moment. Then he turned toward his deputy and spoke in low tones. A minute or two later, about half of the crowd that was standing around began to disperse, a little reluctantly, around the cemetery.

Swanson decided not to call in the FBI's ERTU to supplement the Santa Fe people. It probably would piss a bunch of people off, and Larssen seemed like a competent guy.

She turned back to watch the CSU work. Larssen and another

technician had climbed down the ladder and were standing on the iron coffin, on either side of the body, carefully sweeping the dirt from it, marking up evidence. For now, Swanson was content to observe, let the team do its work. Off to one side, she heard somebody call for a coroner's van, then change their mind and request two vans.

Photographs were taken; the tarp was removed from the hole, followed by the tools, followed by the dirt, in large yellow evidence bags. Almost coyly, the corpse revealed more and more of itself until it lay completely exposed atop the well-preserved iron coffin. Now Swanson descended the ladder to take a closer look of her own. The deceased was dressed in a plaid work shirt, jeans, and steel-toed Dr. Martens. He appeared to be about fifty, but with his clothes on it was hard to be sure: he was lying facedown, the front of his skull blown away. Two shots. The first had dropped him, and the second, point blank to the back of the head, had ricocheted off the iron coffin. No firearm had been discovered. She watched for a few minutes more, then knelt by Larssen.

"What do you figure?" she asked, careful to keep her tone neutral and respectful. "Double tap, execution style?"

"That'd be my guess," Larssen said. "See that?" He nodded at the dent in the coffin.

"Looks like the first bullet entered just above the base of the skull," Corrie said, "causing extreme fragmentation of the occipital bone. The second bullet would have entered a little higher, as he was lying facedown. That's probably what took off his face."

Larssen grunted. "Overkill. That first bullet clearly took care of business."

He was undoubtedly right, but Swanson had been taught that

professional killers didn't improvise. The second bullet was a cheap enough form of insurance. "Based on the limited mush-rooming and the size of that dent, I'd guess solid point, maybe nine-millimeter. I hope your team can recover the rounds."

Larssen nodded.

"No ID," called out the second CSU technician, who had been going through the corpse's pockets.

"Print him, please," Swanson said. Maybe they'd get a hit from IAFIS.

As the corpse's left hand was lifted for fingerprinting, his sleeve slid back, revealing a tattoo of what looked like a half-built wall of red bricks. Swanson pointed to it. "Mean anything to you?"

"Nope," Larssen said.

Swanson glanced at the other. "Prison or biker gang? Military?"

The second CSU man shook his head. "Doesn't ring a bell. Hands are pretty chafed, though—he's almost certainly the one who dug this hole."

"Let's see what the prints on the shovel have to say." Swanson examined the body for another minute or two. Then she stood up. Most of the forensic analysis would be done in the lab.

"Once you've bagged him, let's open the coffin," she said.

Ten minutes later, the unidentified corpse had been carefully placed in a body bag, removed from the hole, and set on a morgue stretcher for transport to the coroner's office. What evidence had been located around the body had been tagged and removed as well. Swanson remained in the hole, feet balanced along one edge, looking at the coffin. It had a double lid and was still in good condition. The top half of the lid, she noticed, looked a little scarified, freshly disturbed by metal tools.

Someone had recently opened—or been about to open—the coffin.

She called for Grant, who quickly came over and looked down into the open grave.

"You said something earlier," Swanson told her. "About grave robbers maybe having 'come for Regis.' The body buried in this coffin was named Regis?"

Grant nodded down at her. "Florence P. Regis."

"A woman? Buried in a Civil War cemetery?"

Grant smiled for the first time since Swanson had met her. "She's the closest thing we have to a celebrity around here. Florence was about as die-hard a Confederate as they come. Her father, Edward Parkin, was a big slaveholder in Georgia. He taught her to shoot at an early age. And her husband, Colonel Regis, led a Confederate battalion until he was killed by a Yankee sniper right after First Manassas. Following his death, Florence pulled up stakes and moved to El Paso. When she heard General Sibley was sending half a dozen companies up the Rio Grande in preparation for an attack on Fort Union, she was determined to avenge her husband's death. She donned a Confederate uniform and joined the ranks, pretending to be a man. After the truth came out following her death in battle, the general ordered her buried with full military honors."

No doubt this was the story the ranger disgorged to tourists on a daily basis. Swanson looked down at the coffin with fresh interest. Despite the grisly scene, she felt the investigation was going well, and she hadn't made any major screw-ups. Every now and then she felt the nervousness spike, but each time she pushed it away—if she was going to have a meltdown, she'd do her best to stave it off until she was back in her apartment that evening, where a bottle of Cuervo Gold was handy.

She nodded at Larssen, who—having secured the dead body—had clambered back down into the hole. "Mr. Larssen? Time to open the coffin."

"Very good."

Larssen bent over and, with a grunt, opened the top half of the coffin lid.

Swanson looked down in surprise. Except for a few scattered chunks and slivers of dried bone and tatters of clothing, the upper coffin was empty, its rotting velvet lining drooping into dust.

"Hoo boy," said Larssen.

This was bizarre. It seemed the victim had been shot after the body was stolen.

She tried to sort the sequence of events into some kind of rational order. Under what circumstances would somebody unearth a body, remove it, then get shot and left on the coffin? The man with the brick tattoo was, it seemed, hired help. Dispensable hired help. This killing was looking more and more professional.

Turning to Larssen, she said: "Let's take a look at the bottom half of the coffin."

They climbed out of the hole, and then Larssen had his men lower a hook and snag the lower lid. With some effort, they raised the hook. The lower half of the body came into view, badly decomposed—the desiccated bones and tattered remains of flesh were clearly visible through holes in the ancient dress Florence Regis had been buried in. The corpse had been crudely sawed in half.

Quinn, the young ranger, crossed himself.

"That's no way to treat a lady," came a familiar voice at her elbow. Swanson turned to see Morwood, hands behind his back, looking down into the hole and shaking his head. She'd been so engrossed that she hadn't heard him approach.

"Hello, sir," she said quickly. Behind him, she could see several others in various uniforms advancing—FBI support staff to complete the CSU work.

"Solved the case yet?" Morwood asked.

"Sir, I—"

"Never mind. It looks like you have things well in hand here—why don't you brief me back at HQ." He nodded at Larssen, who waved familiarly back.

Now the sheriff, Turpenseed, approached. He did not look happy. His cowboy boots were dusty from the search for evidence.

"Special Agent Morwood," he said, removing his hat again and wiping his bald pate. "Glad to see a...more senior agent taking charge of the case."

Swanson bit her lip.

"Looks to me like Agent Swanson has been doing quite a creditable job, sheriff," Morwood said in an even tone.

"Oh, no doubt." He grinned. "I just wasn't aware the FBI was hiring out of high school these days." He gave a guffaw and winked at her.

It came out before she could stop herself. "And *I* wasn't aware mental deficiency was a requirement of being a New Mexico sheriff. These days."

Morwood shot her a warning glance. Then he nodded to the sheriff and began making his way back down to the parking area. Swanson followed.

"The time-out stool for you tonight, Agent Swanson," he said as they arrived at their vehicles.

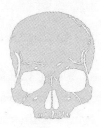

10

May 1

Y OU'RE GOING TO want to take these," Skip said, picking up Nora's binoculars from her desk and brandishing them. "You know a comet's supposed to appear in ten days or so. You'll get a great view up there in the high Sierras."

"Good idea." Nora took the binoculars from her brother and laid them out on the living room floor with the rest of the equipment. Her golden retriever, Mitty, was roving around, and she could tell he was worried. He knew something was up—humans didn't normally wake for the day at 5 AM—and had been following her around the house, constantly underfoot and whining anxiously.

She paused in her packing to give him a reassuring scratch. "Skip's going to look after you," she said, smoothing his fur. "Don't you worry."

"That's right." Skip was walking around in his bare feet, holding a clipboard with a list of all her personal equipment, checking off each item as she put it in the duffel bag.

"There's no muffler," he said, frowning at the list. "It's going to be cold up there at night, you know, even in May."

"I've got a winter hat and scarf; that's enough."

"Nothing is as warm as a muffler, but okay, if you're sure. And what about long underwear?"

"Right over there."

Skip had been a fountain of freely offered advice during the packing process. If it were up to him, she'd be taking five trunks full of everything from umbrellas to an espresso machine. He had been extra solicitous of her the last several years, ever since she'd lost her husband in New York City under tragic circumstances. She had returned to Santa Fe, where she'd grown up, and been rehired by the Institute, where Skip worked as a collections manager. The Institute had assigned him to be a "liaison" with the expedition, which essentially meant he would be responsible for monitoring the Institute's satellite phone. The phone would be the expedition's only reliable link to the outside world while in the mountains.

"Long underwear, check," said Skip, marking it on the list. "Woolen socks, check. Glove liners, check. French ticklers—"

"Knock it off." Nora surveyed the gear littering the floor. It seemed a bit much—after all, they weren't bound for the Himalayas, or even the remote canyons of southern Utah. The presumed location of the Lost Camp was only about a dozen miles from Interstate 80, which followed the route of the original California Trail. The Institute was supplying the expedition with the best of tents and outdoor gear. Fugit had also arranged for them to have access to the latest archaeological technology, including a resistivity meter, a portable magnetometer, and a handheld XRF analyzer.

Knowing a good PR opportunity when she saw one, Fugit had invited a local reporter from the Santa Fe *Express* to interview Nora about the expedition at her Institute office. Nora hadn't been especially happy about this—she considered it bad luck to talk about an expedition until after its successful conclusion—but it was good for the Institute, so she'd consented, remaining vague and being careful to avoid any and all specifics that might attract the curious to their intended worksite. And of course, any mention of gold was absolutely forbidden.

"Anybody I should say goodbye to for you?" Skip asked with a knowing leer. "That guy Morris, for example?"

"The brainiac pencil pusher from Los Alamos? I haven't talked to him in months."

"Pencil pusher? Huh. He's a nuclear engineer." Skip played idly with the dog. "What about that professional climber, then? The one who led the expedition up K2 last year?"

"Parker Frampton? His biceps measurement was greater than his IQ."

"Okay. So the nuclear engineer is too smart, and the mountain climber is too dumb."

"Skip, don't start."

"Start what? I'm just saying."

"I know what you're just saying. And we have work to do."

"You're young—well, relatively speaking. You're attractive as hell. But as your brother, I've got to say: if you keep looking hard enough, you'll *always* find a reason why some poor guy isn't going to measure up."

Instead of replying, Nora began collecting the gear from the floor.

"Look. I know you still grieve. I do, too. But it's been half a dozen years. You have to move on. That's not a betrayal, and it doesn't mean you love him any less. He'd *want* you to be happy! There's more to life than your job, these four walls, and doting on Mitty. If Bill were here he'd say the same thing."

Nora felt her face flush. "Well, he's not. And mind your own business. Seems to me you've got your own hands full with that blond bartender over at the Cowgirl Tavern. Talk about a hot mess."

"You're always throwing shade at Georgetta! Anyway, we're just friends."

"Try telling her boyfriend that."

This observation produced a storm of protest and self-justification. Thank God, Nora thought, that her brother was an easy person to redirect.

* * *

Soon everything was checked, packed in the duffel, and ready to go. Mitty was looking more anxious than ever, whining and trying to nuzzle Nora with his cold wet nose at every opportunity.

"Remember," she told Skip. "One cup of food in the morning, one in the evening, always mixed with a raw egg, plus raw hamburger twice a week. And give him a real beef marrow bone from time to time, never one of those fake chewy things…"

"He eats better than I do."

"That's how it should be. But no beer for him."

Skip threw up his hands in mock dismay. "How could you even think—?"

She glanced at her watch. "We'd better get going. The rendezvous at the Institute's in half an hour."

Skip helped her load the duffel and day pack into her car and got into the driver's seat.

"Wait. One more goodbye to Mitty."

"You love that stupid dog more than me."

Nora went back to the house and gave the dog a hug, told

him to be a good boy, and assured him she'd be back. She eased out the door and saw him appear moments later at the window, propped up on his front paws, watching her leave with sad eyes and drooping tail.

"He's going to be fine with me," said Skip as she got back in the car, "and so's your house. I promise. Mitty will get a hike every day." He patted his belly. "And I'm going to lose five pounds in the process."

"In that case, you'd better lay off the beer. *And* Georgetta, while you're at it."

"Jesus, what a taskmistress. How long did you say this expedition's going to last—four weeks? Sure you can't make it eight?"

They wound through the narrow predawn streets of Santa Fe to the outskirts of town, where the Institute had its twenty-acre campus, an attractive spread of adobe buildings tucked among gardens and piñon trees. Skip turned in through the gate. In the main parking lot, the Institute's field archaeology truck was idling, already packed. Skip pulled up nearby and heaved out Nora's bag, which two assistants took and loaded in the back of the truck. Jason Salazar was there, spiffed up in Indiana Jones khaki and canvas, with one side of his Australian-style cowboy hat's brim snapped up. Nearby was Clive Benton, dressed in jeans and yet another ugly shirt, this one with tiny Day-Glo paisleys scattered about a field of green. His black hair escaped from under an Orioles baseball cap. He was talking on his cell phone and looking both nervous and excited. He'd been hanging around the Institute for the last ten days, driving Nora crazy with his eagerness to get started.

Standing off to one side a bit awkwardly was skinny, towheaded Bruce Adelsky, Nora's graduate student from the University of New Mexico. He had a vape in his hand and he took a drag on it. She had been a little worried about his ability to get along in the wilderness, but he was one of the most promising students she'd ever had, and he badly needed the field experience for his degree.

"You can't take something like that on an expedition," Clive said as he ended his call, pointing at Adelsky's vape. "This calls for stouthearted men of iron—not weenies."

"Is that right?" Adelsky said, taking another quick drag and then tucking the vape into his pocket.

"Damn straight it is. Once we get to the site, I'll give you one of my cigars."

"Ugh," said Adelsky. "They're as dated as that shirt of yours."

"Okay," Nora broke in, looking around. "Let's get in the truck and go."

And now, coming out of the Old Building was Jill Fugit herself, brisk and well coiffed as always. She was not one for ceremony and glad-handing, but Nora could see that not even the Institute's president could hide a look of pride and anticipation.

"It wouldn't look right if I weren't here to send you off," she said, smiling.

The sun was just rising toward the adobe rooflines of the main building as she shook everyone's hand, murmuring words of encouragement. Nora got into the driver's seat, Clive swung in shotgun, and Jason and Bruce climbed in behind. Nora had driven the F350 with its panel-truck body many times before, and as she started the vehicle up it felt like an old friend. She waved goodbye to Skip and the others as she exited the gate and headed out of town, merging onto the westward interstate.

"Just like the pioneers of old," Clive said, pointing at his cell phone and then slipping it into his pocket with a grin.

11

THE DRIVE HAD taken two days, with an overnight in a nasty
motel outside Las Vegas. As they entered the mountains, the
heat and dust of Nevada changed to the forests and snowcapped peaks of the Sierras. As the interstate gained altitude,
Nora began to see patches of snow not just on the mountain-
tops, but in the shady areas under trees on either side of the
highway.

They reached Truckee, California, around noon. As they exited the freeway, Nora was disappointed to find the town a
rather shabby resort of cheap battenboard buildings and houses
tucked among fir and spruce trees. The parking lot next to the
Pioneer Monument was full of idling tourist buses disgorging
people clutching cell phones and selfie sticks, diesel fumes hanging in the air.

"Somehow I expected this place to be a little more…
dignified," she said as they drove past the monument entrance.

"The Donner tragedy's become an industry," said Clive. "A
couple of hundred thousand people visit each year. Doesn't help

that the interstate passes so close to the location. Hard to believe something so horrific happened in a place so ordinary."

They continued on through town. Soon Donner Lake appeared on the left, a sheet of blue shimmering in the sunlight. Taking a turnoff, they drove through a ranch gate hung with an elk skull and into a dirt parking area. This, Nora thought, was a lot more like what she'd expected: an old-time lodge made out of chinked logs, with bunkhouses, barns, corrals, and horses—all tucked in among tall firs.

They pulled up in front of the lodge and got out. It was a cool day, the air smelling of resin. The lodge door opened and a lanky man with a handlebar mustache strode across the porch, boots thudding. A giant mug of coffee was held in one hand. He took off his cowboy hat as he came down the porch stairs.

"Welcome to Red Mountain Ranch," he said. "I'm Ford Burleson, but everyone calls me Burl. You must be the archaeologists."

They shook hands. Nora observed him curiously. He was almost freakishly tall, around six foot seven, and like many people of unusual height he was permanently bowed from having to look down on the rest of the human species. He was every inch the cowboy, but Nora knew from a background check that he had once been a Harvard-educated divorce lawyer and had abruptly given up a highly lucrative legal career to buy a horse ranch not far from where he'd grown up. He had a deep, gravelly voice that Nora thought must have been unusually effective in the courtroom. There were three outfitters in the area, and Nora had looked closely into all of them before choosing Red Mountain Ranch.

They introduced themselves and shook hands. "You must've had a long drive," Burleson said, fitting the hat back on his head. "Come on in."

Nora entered the main house, followed by Benton, Salazar, and Adelsky. It was an impressive room, dominated by a stone fireplace, leather furniture, and rustic wooden tables and chairs. A mounted elk head and an expensive-looking rifle hung above the fireplace.

"Please, sit down." Coffee, tea, and cocoa had already been laid out on the large coffee table in front of the sofa.

"That's quite a rack," said Clive, nodding at the elk as he helped himself to coffee.

"Four hundred and two on the Boone and Crockett scale," said Burleson proudly. "A local record." He took a sip of coffee. "They say you're a Donner Party descendant."

"My great-great-great-grandfather was a Breen."

"Can't imagine how it must feel, coming up here."

"It's hard to describe. They did what they had to do—that's how I see it."

"And that's how I see it, too." Burleson turned to Nora. "The Lost Camp has always been the subject of tall tales and myths around here."

"I can imagine," said Nora. She wondered just what those tall tales might be.

"It's not a myth," Clive added. "The camp's a documented historical fact. It's the location that's never been ascertained."

"Well, that's always the problem, isn't it?" Burleson pulled a manila folder out of a battered leather bag, laid it on the table, and flipped it open. "I got your list of supplies, added my own. It's all purchased, sorted, and ready to pack. We leave tomorrow—if that's still your wish."

"It is."

"I'll want you to unload your own gear on the porch so we can have a look at it—size- and weight-wise—and figure out how many horses we're going to need to pack it all in. We'll leave at dawn." He turned to a young man who'd been hovering around. "Call in the team."

A moment later three people entered. Nora had the impression they'd been waiting just outside.

"Jack Peel, our new wrangler, just arrived from Nevada, where he worked on a dude ranch outside of Reno." Burleson pointed to a compact African American man.

Peel went around, shaking hands silently, face grave. He was wearing a white cowboy hat stained with dirt, sweat, and dust, which he did not remove. As he walked, the spurs on his boots jingled faintly. His eyes were gray.

"Maggie Buck, our cook."

Maggie's personality seemed the polar opposite of the laconic Peel: she came thrusting forward with a grin on her face, almost bowling Bruce Adelsky over in her eagerness. "Pleased to meet you!" she said. She looked, Nora thought, a bit like a fortysomething Charlie Brown in curls.

"Maggie's a wizard with a Dutch oven. Wait till you try her biscuits."

"I hope y'all like home-style cooking. We got any dietary restrictions here?" She looked around with a disapproving expression on her face. Nobody responded. "Good! I can cook tolerable vegetarian, but I draw the line at gluten-free."

"And this is Drew Wiggett, assistant wrangler," Burleson said. "He's a vet student from Berkeley, looking to spend some time with horses in the mountains."

If it was possible, Wiggett looked even younger and lankier than Adelsky. Flipping his long hair out of his face, Wiggett offered his hand around, nodding and smiling.

"Our turn," said Nora. "Clive Benton, historian and Donner

Party expert. Jason Salazar, field assistant with the Institute. And Bruce Adelsky, graduate student in the Anthro Department at UNM, working toward a dissertation in Southwestern archaeology."

A slightly awkward silence fell over the group.

"Well," said Burleson, "we'll get to know each other soon enough in the mountains. Maybe too well!" He laughed and turned to Nora. "Like you asked, we're all sworn to secrecy. Right, Maggie?"

"What're you looking at me for?" she said. "He thinks I talk too much." She looked at Nora, winking.

"Before we go any farther, I'd like to say a few words. About the risks." Burleson's tone turned serious. "Where we're going is pretty much trackless wilderness. Don't let the proximity of so-called civilization fool you. A dozen miles into rough country can be like a thousand: look at the Donners. Things can go wrong fast. Even in May a blizzard can blow up out of nowhere. Speaking of snow, we had a big winter and the mountain ridges still have cornices."

"Cornices?" asked Adelsky.

"That's a pileup of snow, blown by the wind along one side of a ridge. Those cornices build up and can be a hundred feet deep. While May avalanches are rare, they can happen. The important thing is not to tramp through snow fields, especially atop a ridge, because you might dislodge a cornice. Always stay on solid rock."

He poured himself another mug of coffee. "As for animals, there are only two to worry about: bears and mountain lions. Bears can be dangerous, especially mamas with cubs. We'll be hanging our food in trees. Don't keep any food in your tents. If you encounter a bear, back off slowly. Look as harmless and unafraid as possible. Let it retreat. With mountain lions, do the opposite. Act belligerent, make yourself big, open your coat up and flap it, spread your arms and make a lot of noise."

"What about snakes?" Adelsky asked.

"What about them?" Burleson replied.

"He's got a phobia of snakes and spiders," Nora said, glancing at the graduate student.

"We'll probably see a few rattlers, despite the altitude. As for spiders, just shake out your boots in the morning before putting them on." Burleson slapped his hands on his knees and stood up. "Now let's see that map of yours," he said to Nora. "I've only got a general idea of where we're going."

"Sure thing."

Adelsky, who was holding the tube, handed it to Nora, who slid the map out of it and spread it over a nearby table. It was a USGS topo map on which she and Clive had worked out their planned search area. Burleson weighted down the corners with coffee mugs. He bent over and examined it, muttering under his breath.

"So this is where you want to go?" he said, pointing to the markings.

"The Lost Camp is somewhere up one of those canyons," Clive told him.

Burleson frowned.

"You familiar with that country?" Clive asked.

"No, and I daresay few are. That's true high-country wilderness. Rough, remote as hell. Not like Winnebago Central down here."

Clive pointed at the map. "The probable location of the Lost Camp is along one of these creeks—Sugarpine, Poker, or Dollar Fork. Tamzene's map only shows one creek, but she drew it from a description given by a dying man and she never saw the camp herself. She mentions a couple of landmarks, but the crucial one is this: from the Lost Camp, you could see the profile of an old woman on a rocky cliff to the north. Tamzene noted it was like New Hampshire's Old Man of the Mountain, except an old woman with a hooked nose."

Burleson nodded. "That must be pretty unique. I've never seen anything like that up here."

"The plan is to make our first camp up in here somewhere—" Clive pointed to an area of less dense topographical lines— "and use it as a base camp. We'll conduct the search from there, concentrating on the three streams that flow into Hackberry Creek. The Lost Camp must be in one of those canyons."

"Hellacious country. Why did they go up that way? There's no way out."

"The simple answer," said Nora, "is they got lost."

"Here's what apparently happened," said Clive. "The emigrant train was spread out as they entered the mountains. A group fell behind—eleven individuals. As the snow began falling, they missed the trail over the pass and drifted northward into that maze of ravines. Then they went up one of these side canyons, where they became snowbound. A few months later, a single person managed to reach the Donner camp at Alder Creek, only to die of starvation not long after. But it was from him Tamzene got the information about the Lost Camp, including its location."

"Was anybody rescued from the Lost Camp?"

"One person. A single rescuer got up there and found everyone dead save a man named Peter Chears, who was babbling and died raving mad shortly thereafter. What that rescuer saw at the site was pretty awful. He gave a short description to someone who committed it to memory, but the rescuer never spoke of it again."

"What do you expect to find?" asked Burleson.

"Human and animal remains, personal effects, abandoned supplies and equipment from the original wagons. Crude shelters. The most important thing is to extract DNA from the human remains, so we can identify them by name. It will help us reconstruct exactly what happened in that camp."

Nora said nothing about the stash of coins; her own two assistants had been told of it in strict confidence, but she and Clive had agreed that it would only complicate things if Burleson's party knew a fortune in gold might well be hidden somewhere in the vicinity of the Lost Camp.

Maggie Buck put down her coffee cup. "What about the legends? You know, the Donner Party ghosts? The ones who went mad before they died—or, maybe, *after*?"

There was a brief silence. Then a sprinkling of uncomfortable laughter went around the room.

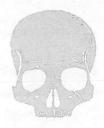

12

As the laughter at Red Mountain Ranch was dying away, Agent Corrine Swanson was entering the front hall of a three-bedroom condo in the well-groomed suburb of Scottsdale, Arizona. She flashed her shield at the cop standing at the door, unsmiling and wearing the kind of blue-mirrored sunglasses currently popular with thirtysomething males below a certain income bracket.

"Is Lieutenant Porter on the scene?" she asked.

The cop nodded. "In the kitchen."

From the front hall she could see the kitchen situated at the far end of a carpeted hallway. She moved toward it, noting the blond wood walls, the recessed lighting. A deep, thumping bass made the air tremble slightly around her. The entrance to the living room was to her left, and she could see even in her peripheral vision that it was expensively furnished. To her right, a yellow strip of crime scene tape had been strung, almost as an afterthought.

Lieutenant Porter was a tall, youngish man in a tan suit,

leaning against a kitchen counter and drinking coffee. He shook her hand. "Agent Swanson."

"Lieutenant Porter. Thank you so much for this opportunity." This was not mere politeness: Swanson was, in fact, grateful to the lieutenant for providing her access to a scene where the feds had no clear jurisdiction. Just as she was grateful to Morwood for letting her chase this lead of hers, despite his being highly skeptical and giving her only one day to run it to earth.

So far, despite her best efforts, she'd been unable to develop any solid case out of the Glorieta battlefield killing. They'd identified the dead gravedigger as Frank Serban, a small-time thief, drug dealer, and grifter whose red hair had given him the nickname of "Bricktop" and in turn explained the tattoo. And the body in the iron coffin—the bottom half of it, anyway—was indeed Florence P. Regis, unlikely casualty of the Battle of Glorieta Pass. Thanks to the rain that night, they'd been able to determine that two vehicles left the cemetery around the time of Serban's death. One—Serban's—had been found abandoned a few miles away. She hadn't been able to trace the other vehicle. Larsson, to his credit, had recovered two 9mm slugs after a meticulous search. Rifling marks indicated they had been fired from a noise-suppressed gun, most likely an exotic, integrated model like a Maxim. Beyond that, they had collected a lot of incidental forensic material that she feared would yield nothing.

Just as troubling as the lack of crime scene evidence was the question of motive. Other than the fact that she'd been a woman combatant in a historic battle, Florence Regis was unremarkable. Was it possible some crazy collector wanted her remains as a trophy? But then why kill Serban, whose role had been just to do the manual labor? It would have been much easier to take

Regis's body, refill the grave, and leave the site looking undisturbed: nobody would have been the wiser. No, Serban had to
die so no witnesses would be left, and that implied the stakes
must be high.

*I'm eager to hear what your budding forensic expertise makes of it
all,* Morwood had said. So far, "it all" was damn little to go on.

Until—maybe—today.

The one item of interest Swanson had learned in the course
of her widening digital searches had to do with Florence Regis's
maiden name: Parkin. Almost seven months ago, in Paris, a
grave in the Cimetière du Montparnasse had been violated and
a corpse—part of a corpse, at least—stolen. The missing remains belonged to one Thomas Parkin, an American expatriate
painter who had died in 1943 during the Nazi occupation. And
then, this February, another Parkin corpse had gone missing—
Alexander Parkin, a schoolteacher from the tiny town of Nelson, New Hampshire, who died of old age in 1911 and was
buried in the town plot. He had rested in peace for over a century until somebody yanked his long-cured carcass out of the
ground and, no doubt, gave the hamlet of Nelson something to
talk about for the next century.

Three Parkins, their deaths spanning eighty years, but all dug
up within six months of each other. And now, this…

She glanced at her watch: quarter to one. Even though she'd
started out at dawn, Phoenix was a good six-hour drive from
Albuquerque. She'd be lucky to get home before midnight.

"Sorry I've made you keep the crime scene open," she said.

Porter shook his head. "Team's just wrapping up. Want to
talk to them?"

Even with her inexperience, Swanson understood how the hi-
erarchy worked. "That's not necessary, thanks. Why don't you

give me the details, if you can spare the time, and then maybe I can take a look?"

"Sure. Given the amount of blood, our coroner tells us whoever it came from would be mighty incapacitated and quite possibly dead." He cleared his throat, consulted a tablet. "Rosalie M. Parkin, twenty-seven, unmarried, newly minted lawyer from U of A Law School, now an associate at the Pritchie and Wilkins firm over on McDonald Drive. Both parents dead—that Airbus A380 that went down over the Pacific a few years back, some malfunction, no survivors, maybe you remember it?"

Swanson said she did.

"Well, they were on it. Returning from a vacation in Singapore. The father was a banker, left enough for Ms. Parkin and her brother to live comfortably. For a while, anyway."

"Brother?" Swanson asked.

Porter nodded. "The little punk's in there," and he nodded across the kitchen, past a hallway with a guest bathroom, to a closed door. It was this room, she noticed, that was the source of the thumping bass. Another uniformed cop stood outside that door.

Swanson was still adjusting, not only to being an active FBI agent—walking around with a firearm hidden under her blazer—but to the ballet among different law enforcement agencies. She decided to keep her questions brief, neutral, and to the point, and to betray no opinion or judgment of her own. After all, these people, whatever their jurisdiction, had a lot more time on the job than she did.

"Would you mind giving me the background?" she asked.

Porter nodded again, pleased to be given free rein. "Ms. Parkin was due in court yesterday at ten AM. She never showed up. By lunchtime, the firm got worried, had a paralegal call her cell. No answer. So around six, one of the partners came over. When nobody answered, he let himself in."

"How?"

"He had a key."

"And who was this?"

"Ken Damon."

He had a key. "Did he and Ms. Parkin have, um, anything going on?"

"Ken Damon's forty-one, married, with two kids." The expression on Porter's face told Swanson, *Yeah, they had something going on.*

"Then what happened?"

"When Damon found no sign of Ms. Parkin, he called us."

"Okay. Thank you. I'd like to see the scene now, if you don't mind."

"Sure." Porter led the way back out of the kitchen, made a left, and stopped at an open door marked with the crime scene tape she'd seen earlier. Beyond lay a large bedroom with expensive new furniture, the kind that a young woman with money and a promising career might favor. Everything was in its place and spotlessly clean. A walk-in closet and a private bathroom lay beyond. The bathroom looked equally clean, nothing out of place except a bath towel that appeared to have been tossed to one side, ready for the hamper.

Porter lifted the tape for Swanson and she stepped inside. The room was unoccupied except for one member of the CSU team, obviously finishing up. There were pins and flags in various places, along with a couple of chalk scrawls. But the thing that immediately caught her attention was the huge pool of blood in the middle of the room. It had been soaked up by the plush carpeting, but even so, she guessed from the deep color and the glistening sheen that at least a liter of blood, maybe two, had been spilled here.

Near the stain was a Turkish rug of embroidered black and red, one end flipped back.

"And this bloodstain is the only physical evidence so far?" she asked.

Porter nodded. "No blood spatter anywhere, no signs of a struggle, no droplet trail from a body being dragged or carried. Nothing broken or missing that we can determine. Of course, we only have the one person familiar with the place, so it's a little hard to be sure."

"You mean the brother?"

"No. Mr. Damon. The brother refuses to talk to us."

She looked at the room again, taking it in now with a more critical eye. It was as the lieutenant had said. Nothing seemed to have been disturbed. If the rug hadn't been lifted to expose the stain, nobody would have been the wiser. The way Porter referred to the brother, and given the cop on guard outside his door, it seemed he might be their number-one suspect.

She pointed to the carpet. "Who pulled it back like that? Mr. Damon?"

"No. But he knew that carpet was usually located in the hall. That's why he called us."

Smart, Swanson thought. Not only was he boning his young associate, but he knew the apartment well enough to see when a rug was out of place—and not to touch it. "Any idea when this happened?"

"Based on the blood chemistry, they're saying around thirty-six hours ago. The blood type is hers. We'll be confirming that with DNA."

Thirty-six hours. That would have been one, maybe two o'clock on the morning of May 2. "Fingerprints?"

"Her fingerprints everywhere, of course. And Damon's, in the kitchen, the bathroom, the living room, the bedroom."

"And the brother?"

A pause. "We haven't printed him yet. But there don't appear to be any prints from a third party in the bedroom, and no sign of wiping down."

"Got it. Any idea who was last in contact with her?"

"According to her phone records, she called a few friends on the night of May first. She called Mr. Damon around twelve thirty on the morning of May second."

"Twelve thirty?"

A flicker passed across Porter's face. "Damon confirms it. He says the call was in regard to their court appearance at ten AM yesterday morning."

"And I suppose Damon has an alibi for the rest of the night."

A brief pause. "He was in bed with his wife, and she confirms."

Half a dozen snarky observations came to mind, and Swanson bit them all back. "Anything else of interest? Controversial cases she was involved in? Drug problems? Past history? Enemies?"

"Nothing we know of. And there's no body—which adds investigative and legal complications. There's no indication of forced entry or exit from either the apartment or the building. Unlike her shitbag brother, she wasn't under suspicion for anything, so it's doubtful she fled—no items of clothing are missing that we know of, no sign of packing. Nothing's been stolen, again as far as we can tell. Her car is parked in its assigned spot downstairs. No eyewitnesses. There hasn't been any activity on

her credit cards. As for enemies, you might want to ask him."
And he nodded in the direction of the brother's room.

"Why's that?"

"Because more than once neighbors have complained of dis-
turbances. The two argued frequently. The brother also showed
signs of physical aggression. One morning, he ran after her as
she was driving away from the building and hit the trunk of her
car with a hammer. She refused to press charges."

As Porter spoke, Swanson was taking one more look around
the room. But she could already tell there was nothing to see
here—not, at least, without a microscopic investigation. She
tried to empty her mind of outside influences, such as her opinion of Ms. Parkin's taste in furniture or her curiosity about
the expensive-looking porcelain figures in the glass cabinet on
the far side of the room. *Let the room speak to you*, one of her
instructors had said.

Three other people with the same last name had been dug
up, their bodies stolen over the last six months. Now, a
fourth—a living Parkin, this time—had gone missing. No indication of forced entry or a struggle; nothing stolen or missing. Except the woman herself. Nothing strange—besides, of
course, the massive quantity of blood, hidden casually beneath
a Turkish rug.

Swanson's mind went back to the Glorieta Pass cemetery, and
the hole in which Frank Serban died. That was a professional
job. And this one was looking professional as well. Nothing disturbed, nobody seen, nothing heard. In her mind, she visualized
two figures in black entering the bedroom. One grabbed Rosalie Parkin and hauled her from the bed, hand over her mouth.
He dragged her to the middle of the room. The other one took
careful aim and stabbed her with a blade, cutting a major vein—

maybe the subclavian or the vena cava. That would spill a lot of blood, but at a low pressure, like 20 mmHg, so it would flood rather than spurt and not splatter the perps. As Parkin's ability to resist dropped, they bound her hands and taped her mouth, and maybe bundled her into a waterproof bag that would contain additional bleeding. Then they pulled over the rug to cover the stain, to buy a little more time.

She glanced at the nearest window, which looked down onto a back alley. If they parked there, they could be in and out without anybody noticing. Even the brother.

The brother.

Shaking away this scenario, she turned toward the lieutenant. "What's the brother's name?"

"Ernest," Porter said, handing her the tablet. "Feel free to talk to him; he's been Mirandized. I hope you can get more than we did."

Swanson made her way through the apartment in the direction of the thumping. The cop outside the brother's door stepped aside and nodded as she approached. She tried the knob, was surprised to find that it turned, then realized the mechanism was broken—perhaps by the cops. She opened it and was almost physically pushed backward by the wall of heavy metal music.

She quickly stepped in and closed the door behind her. As her eyes adjusted to the darkness, she began to make out details: black plastic over the windows to keep out the light; a battered desk with a large Buck knife jammed into its top; an Ibanez flying-V guitar lying in a pile of stomp boxes next to a Fender amp. Posters on the wall displayed thrash bands like Slayer and Metallica, along with cult films such as *Audition* and *The Relic*. A smell of weed and unwashed socks lingered in the air.

A twin bed sat to the right of the door, its covers twisted up in a ball at the foot. A figure sat on the bed: a man, or rather a boy, wearing torn black jeans, black low-top sneakers, and a jean jacket with metal studs in it. His hair was long and spiky, and it flopped over his face, concealing the features. His knees were drawn up and he was hugging them to his chest with two tattooed arms. His eyes flickered up toward her a moment before drifting back down to stare again at nothing.

The volume of the music had been too high for her to process it before, but now she recognized it: "The Wanton Song," by Led Zeppelin. Judging by the bass riff that had been shaking the apartment since her arrival, the kid had been playing it over and over. And now she noticed, on the scuffed table, a decent-looking sound system, with an amp and speakers and—to her surprise—a turntable with a stack of vinyl records next to it.

She turned to the youth on the bed. "Hey!" she shouted. "Would you mind if we turn it down for just a minute—"

In response, Parkin picked up a set of headphones and slid them over his ears.

Swanson took a seat beside the desk and began rotating it slowly back and forth, looking around. She knew that to Parkin, she must look like just another government drone, with her slacks and blue blazer, making negative assumptions about him. What the kid didn't know was that she could easily have been him six years ago, right down to the ripped jeans and the little network of red lines on the inside of his arm where he'd practiced cutting himself. He couldn't guess that his costume had been her costume, too, and that the blazer she was now wearing happened to be one of only two she could afford, a blue and a black, and that she was carefully rotating them until the next good sale. And he couldn't guess that, as a result of all this, she might have a clue to what he was feeling—and how he was reacting—right now.

Parkin wasn't in a gang—the tattoos weren't right, and they were too professionally done. The record player, in place of some streaming Bluetooth device, indicated he cared enough to search out and curate a collection of music. Despite the smell of weed,. he didn't look like a big-time user, and according to Porter's rap sheet the crimes this "shitbag of a brother" was suspected of were two accusations of shoplifting from big-box stores, the charges dropped in both cases. He'd been a decent student, too—until three years ago, when the plane with his parents disappeared into the ocean.

She reached over to the old Marantz receiver and slowly turned down the volume knob until the music was background noise.

The kid pushed the headphones down around his neck and glowered at her. "Hey, what the fuck? Turn that back on. I already told the others I don't know anything. So leave me alone."

Instead of answering, she reached over to the turntable, removed the record, and returned it carefully to its torn white sleeve. "I like your rig," she said, putting the sleeve back in the record jacket. "Interesting taste in music, too. I mean, the way you're rocking it old school. You know what? I've tried to get into hip-hop—I really have. But I've more or less given up. To me it sounds like a bunch of bragging and ranting and bitch-slapping, chanted over the beat of a dime-store drum machine. And then when they do condescend to sing a little— like, during the hook, maybe—the voices all sound so clinical and similar, Auto-Tuned up the ass." She shrugged and nodded toward the door. "Of course, those characters out there don't even know Merle Haggard's dead. Don't tell them—you'll ruin their day."

Parkin didn't say anything during this monologue. But he didn't curse at her again, either; just looked at her with curiosity. Now she took a moment to replace the album atop the stack. "I was more into dark ambient, but I always did like Zep," she said. "They took even older material and respected it, made it relevant. Made it their own. That's how the best music endures. By the way, my name's Corinne—Corrie to my friends." She paused and then, because she had to go by the book, added, "FBI." She touched the lanyard on which her ID was strung.

But this didn't seem to faze the kid.

"I know you're Ernest. Do you mind if I—?"

The kid watched as she began to look through his records. Swanson had already gotten what she'd come to Scottsdale for—it wasn't much, but it was all she could hope for—and now she was just confirming her instincts. "In ninth grade," she said, "I used to carry around a Les Paul—a knockoff, anyway—totally broken, no pickups or anything, but I didn't care. I wore it low slung, practically down to my knees, like Page."

Her fingers stopped on another album, with a cover showing nude figures creeping up a slope—presumably toward a sacrificial altar. "This is it!" she said. "*Houses of the Holy*. There's a song on here—'The Ocean'—that totally changed my musical perspective. That opening guitar riff…I mean, it comes out of nowhere, breaks all the rules of rhythm, seems to start over again even before the end of the second bar. Here, I'll play it." She took off her jacket and let it drop on the dirty chair—pretending to be unaware her shoulder holster was in plain view—pulled out the record, flipped it to side B, set it on the platter, moved the needle to the last track, and cranked the volume back to where it had been before.

They listened for all four and a half minutes of the song. Then a second time, and then a third. And then Swanson put the tone-arm back on its stand. There was a moment of silence, broken only by a faint hum from the speakers.

"What do you want?" Parkin finally asked.

Swanson didn't answer immediately. She was winging it and had been ever since she stepped into the kid's bedroom. There was nothing like this in the book, and Morwood would probably shit a brick if he saw her. This wasn't her case—but she understood this frightened and lonely youth better than any of the cops outside did.

"I want you to know I'm not here because of you," she said. "Your sister's only been gone for—"

"Don't bullshit me, you know she's dead!" Parkin said, suddenly sitting up straight on the bed, face flushing, tendons showing in his neck. "*Dead!* And those motherfuckers out there, hanging around, doing nothing to find her...they might as well be jacking off. They obviously think it was me—*hope* it was me. That would make their lives easier, wouldn't it? Fuckers."

"Is that why you won't talk to them?" she asked.

Parkin's answer was to lean back again and turn his face to the wall.

Exactly what she would have done in the same situation. Not if her mother vanished—that would be cause for a Kansas state holiday—but if her father had. He *had* left, truth be told...but not suddenly, like this. Not with apparent violence. She could just imagine it: cops crawling all over their double-wide, Sheriff Hazen concluding right away that it was her—hell yes, she'd have reacted just like Parkin. Except he had it worse. It was obvious that things had fallen apart for him after the death of their parents. His sister, several years older, had weathered it a lot better than he had. She'd gone on with her life, found a job, found someone to date—even if he was married. Meanwhile Ernest had just drifted.

And now, this.

"Why do you say she's dead?" she asked as casually as possible.

Parkin answered without turning away from the wall. "All that blood in there—didn't you see it? Her car in the garage. Her purse, her cell phone, still here. And she wouldn't just go away without telling me. Not even with that asshole."

"You mean Damon? The one who came in, found the blood-stain?"

Parkin may have nodded; in the dark, it was hard to tell.

"Ernest, I have just one more question. Why weren't you the one who discovered she was missing? Why did it take until six PM the next day for someone to come looking for her?"

"I came home late," he muttered, "like usual. I was quiet—she hated me waking her up. Her door was closed, as always. She doesn't want me touching her stuff. So I went to bed. And I slept in. She goes to work long before I get up. I didn't hear anything."

Suddenly, he shifted on the bed and began pounding the wall violently with his fist. "Fuck!" he yelled. "Fuck, *fuck!*"

She jumped out of her chair just as the cop outside opened the door. She gestured for him to leave and he withdrew.

"Ernest," she said in a low voice. "Hey. Don't hurt yourself. You don't know for a fact she's dead. You need to hope for the best."

He started to weep.

★ ★ ★

She found Lieutenant Porter still in the kitchen.

"Get anything out of him?" he asked.

"He says he came home late, slept late. Didn't hear anything. It's not surprising he didn't notice she was gone or see the blood. If you ask around, you can probably find out where he was and secure him an alibi."

"If you say so." Porter made another notation on his tablet.

She turned to face him. "Lieutenant, I sincerely want to thank you for your time and courtesy. I wouldn't presume to tell you your business. But if this woman turns up dead, I'd bet you my car that kid had nothing to do with it."

"Yeah? What kind of car?"

"Um, a 2002 Camry LE."

The lieutenant merely shook his head and laughed.

★ ★ ★

On her way back, she got stuck behind a jackknifed tractor-trailer on I-40 and didn't get home until long after midnight.

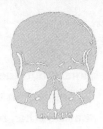

13

THE MORNING HAD dawned in crystalline perfection, an ideal send-off for their expedition, Nora thought as she loosely held the reins of her horse. They were following a mountain stream that burbled among smooth rocks, the banks lined with alders and willows. Birds chirped in the thickets and a golden eagle soared overhead, making a whistling noise. Burleson had been right: they were less than a mile from the ranch, but it already felt like they'd entered another world. Ahead, above the trees, she could see mountains upon mountains rising in the distance, their peaks patched with snow.

Burleson led the group, riding a seventeen-hand gelding named Blackie. Nora followed, riding a brown-and-white paint called Stormy, although his docile demeanor didn't seem to live up to his name. Clive rode behind her, and Nora couldn't help but notice the easy way he handled his horse, his back straight as a preacher's. She would have to ask him where he'd gotten his riding experience.

Maggie brought up the rear of the train with Jason Salazar and Bruce Adelsky. Salazar seemed comfortable enough with horses, but Adelsky was another matter. He had actually put the wrong foot in the stirrup and started to get on the horse backward, to the great hilarity of Maggie. Behind the train, Wiggett and Jack Peel led the five pack horses carrying their supplies and equipment in plastic panniers and buckled-on top packs. Among the supplies was a padlocked strongbox carried on a mule, to hold any jewelry or other valuables that would be discovered during the dig, but also to store the legendary gold—if it existed…and if they found it.

Nora could hear Maggie telling Salazar and Adelsky a story, punctuated by gusts of laughter, about a disastrous expedition she'd been on the year before. Nora could only catch parts, but it seemed to involve drunken idiots falling off horses, a man shooting himself in the foot, a helicopter rescue, and a bill for twenty thousand dollars.

The trail started out well used, but about five miles in it began to peter out. At a certain point Burleson stopped. He and Clive consulted a map.

"This is where they got off the trail," said Clive. "They should have gone left, but for some reason—probably confusion caused by the snow—they went right."

The fateful right turn started up a broad canyon between gray cliffs. The going was easy at first, but then the canyon walls began to narrow and loom higher above them until they were riding in shadow. The air was increasingly chilly. In a few places—passing through deep woods, or in shady spots at the bottom of rocky cliffs—Nora could still see patches of snow. Amazing how quickly they'd left civilization behind and entered a primeval landscape.

They stopped for lunch near a pile of fallen rocks. The pack train had fallen behind, but Burleson was in contact with Peel over walkie-talkie. Nora checked her cell phone and found that, as expected, they had gone out of cell range. For the next month they'd be relying on the sat phone Nora carried in her saddlebag—with Skip hopefully manning the other end.

Nora munched on a roast beef sandwich while Burleson finished his conversation with Peel over the walkie-talkie. He pulled out his own sandwich and took a deep breath, looking around. "I love these mountains," he said. "Every time I come up here, I feel renewed."

"So you just gave up a lucrative career as a lawyer, quit the rat race to come out here?"

"A *divorce* lawyer. Not a fun line of work, representing some bloodsucking young woman intent on breaking a prenup and prying money out of some rich old bastard of a husband. Or vice versa. You rarely meet good people in a business like that, either as clients or opponents. The decision to get out wasn't entirely mine; I became crosswise with the California Bar Association and was given a nice, unfriendly push out. Every time I'm up in these mountains, I send them my silent thanks."

"Crosswise?"

Burleson laughed. "I'm not a good rule follower. Perhaps I represented my clients a little too well, you might say."

Nora was pleasantly surprised by his candor. She had done some basic searching on Burleson before hiring him, but none of this had turned up. It was probably one of those things that didn't reach the level of news, she thought.

They mounted up after lunch and rode past yet another scree slope of gray rocks, spilling down a steep ravine and into a dark forest of towering fir trees, with more snow in the shadows. As evening came on, the trees gave way to a meadow surrounded by cliffs.

"Those Donners were really lost," said Maggie, looking around.

"Here we are, at our first campsite," Burleson said, dismounting.

Nora halted her horse. It wasn't a particularly welcoming place—a bedraggled field cut by the stream—but she reminded herself they would be here only a couple of days. When they found the Lost Camp, they would move closer to that location.

The others dismounted. Burleson and Drew Wiggett went around, helping here and there, unsaddling horses and hobbling them in the meadow. As they returned, Peel arrived with the pack train. He parked it at the far end of the field, and he and Wiggett began unpacking, lining up the boxes in rows.

"Fire's going here," said Maggie, indicating a raised spot on the verge of the meadow. She pointed at Nora and Clive. "You all gather up some wood. Birch, alder, and oak—none of that fir or spruce! Jason and I are going to build a fire pit. Jason, let's put some muscle on those arms of yours! You, too, Bruce."

"Sorry, not in my job description," said Adelsky with a grin as he settled down on a fallen tree, fumbled in his pocket, removed his vape, and fired it up. He leaned back and issued a stream of smoke. "I'll watch you work."

"Bum," Maggie said. "By the way, Arizona recluse spiders just love to lay their eggs in dead trees like the one you're squatting on."

Adelsky leapt to his feet and brushed frantically at his jeans, vape falling to the ground, while Maggie's belly laugh echoed across the field.

Nora and Clive headed into the trees at the edge of the meadow and started collecting wood.

"So far, so good," Clive said. "Burleson seems to know his business. Interesting, though, that he gave up a lucrative practice to start this outfit. It makes you wonder if there isn't more to his backstory than we've been told."

"It's quite an eccentric crew he's put together," Nora said. "Maggie, who talks a mile a minute; Peel, as silent as the grave; and Wiggett. He's hard to pin down but he looks, well, *hungry*."

"What do you mean?"

"You know, the kind of person who's never satisfied, always looking for greener grass."

"Nothing wrong with ambition. And you seem to be a striver, too, right?"

"I hope it's not too obvious."

"Why not be obvious?" He paused and gave her a big smile. "Isn't that why we're here, as partners? Ambition, thirst for knowledge, wanting to make our mark."

Nora knew he was right but felt odd hearing it put so baldly. "There is one thing I've been meaning to ask you. I've been wondering why, when you first told me your story—out there at my dig—you never mentioned the gold. I have to admit...that kind of bothers me."

Clive chuckled. "I knew you were going to ask me that. First, Jason was there and I didn't want him to hear it. But more than that—I wanted to see what kind of interest you had in the project before you heard about the gold."

"So you waited until that meeting with Fugit to spring it on me."

"Look at my position. It could screw up everything if word got out there was twenty million in gold lying around, just waiting to be found. Also...well, I wanted to make sure you had the—forgive the expression—stones for the job."

Nora frowned in surprise. "What are you talking about? You know my credentials. You searched me out. This isn't my first brush with controversy. I've even dealt with cannibalism before."

"I know," Clive said, picking up a piece of wood. "But this goes beyond even cannibalism."

Nora straightened. "How so?"

"I've tried to deflect idle talk about some of the more salacious stories about the Lost Camp, as you might have noticed—but the fact is something truly strange and awful happened there."

"What could be worse than cannibalism?"

Clive paused a moment, looking out over the meadow. "I mentioned that one person managed to escape and make it back to the Donner camp at Alder Creek—an itinerant preacher named Asher Boardman. He ran off, he said, because madness overwhelmed the Lost Camp. He later died of starvation—but not before Tamzene wrote down his story. When the lone rescuer, a man named Best, finally reached the camp, he found only one person still alive—Peter Chears. He was singing songs and playing with a pile of human bones, gore stuck to his cheeks and matted into his hair. Best hauled the man out with the last of Tamzene's camp. Chears survived the trip back to civilization, but died soon after, hopelessly insane."

"Jesus," Nora said. "And how do you know these details?"

"The historical record. A lot of it is suspect—exaggerated newspaper articles, chapbooks written by people who weren't directly involved—but the primary documents can't be ignored. In addition to the details included in Tamzene's journal, there's the diary—admittedly sensationalized—of a survivor, Mrs. Horne, who described Boardman's staggering into their camp. And then there's the account of the rescuer, Best. Best himself didn't write it down, but he spoke of it to a few people back in Tamzene's camp. Best was a tough customer, but what he saw at that Lost Camp must have shaken him to the core. What remains of those horrific secondary accounts are viewed by historians as examples of 'generation loss' and the unreliability of oral tradition. The farther you are from the primary source, the harder it gets to be certain the details are one hundred percent accurate."

"One hundred percent or not," Nora murmured as these details sank in, "that's a hell of a lot more than you told me that first day. No wonder Maggie's so full of tall tales."

"Some are less tall than others. I wanted to be certain of your gumption. As the excavations uncover the details of what happened, it might get...a little disturbing."

"And?"

"I'm reassured."

Nora shook her head. "I wish I'd known these details earlier. I don't appreciate being blindsided."

"Sorry. You're right. I apologize."

"Accepted," said Nora. "But now that we're actually searching for the camp—no more secrets between us. Agreed?"

"Wholeheartedly. But remember, that goes both ways."

"Of course." Nora wondered what exactly he meant by that.

They dragged a number of dead branches back, piling them up near the fire. The camp was in the last stages of coming together. Their wall tents were up, the fire was blazing, and Maggie was fussing with a wooden pantry box, unloading two Dutch ovens and organizing the pots, pans, dishes, and silverware in various compartments.

"Oak!" she said approvingly. "Good work! Jason, grab that ax and let's chop this up."

Wielding an ax herself, Maggie expertly chopped the oak

branches into manageable lengths while Jason started hacking away.

"Hellaboy, you're going to cut your legs off doing it that way." Maggie came up behind and, wrapping her ample arms around him and holding his elbows in place, demonstrated how to aim and swing an ax. She glanced over at Adelsky. "See what you're missing?" she asked with a salacious laugh.

"My loss." Adelsky waved his vape.

Folding chairs had been stacked against a tree, ready to be placed in a circle around the fire. Jason Salazar pulled one over, opened it, and flopped down on the seat, his face red and covered with sweat. "That woman's a slave driver," he said.

"I heard that!" Maggie said while forking steaks onto the grill with a searing noise.

"I meant you to hear it."

"I'm just putting some meat on those bones of yours. You've had your nose in books too long."

The others came back from their tasks and gathered around the fire as the evening descended.

"Some wine?" Burleson asked, fetching a bottle out of the basket and drawing the cork. He poured it into tin cups and offered them around. "Good Napa Valley cab. Might as well take advantage of the bounty of our great state. No roughing it in my camp."

The dinner was everything Nora could have asked for, and more: the steaks perfectly grilled, the potatoes crisp, the salad just right—and key lime pie for dessert. Unexpectedly, Jack Peel led them all in a blessing before dinner, which seemed oddly appropriate in the vast wilderness setting. When the dishes were done, Maggie pulled a guitar from among the gear and sang "Tumbling Tumbleweeds" and "Lovesick Blues" by the crackling fire, her surprisingly pure contralto rising into a vast black sky filled with stars. She finished up the mini-performance with an atmospheric rendition of "Ghost Riders in the Sky."

"Plenty of ghost riders in the sky around here," she said, lowering her guitar. "I grew up in Truckee, and I could tell you some stories."

"You implied as much back at the ranch," Adelsky said eagerly, leaning toward the fire. "So what are you waiting for? Put your money where your mouth is."

"You pint-sized little varmint," Maggie said amiably. "Okay, you asked for it. Ever heard the story of the ghost of Samantha Carville?"

Peel rose abruptly and disappeared in the darkness, heading for his tent.

"What's with him?" asked Maggie, turning to Burleson.

The man shrugged. "Damn good wrangler, but he's not much for conversation."

"Go on," said Clive. "What's a campfire without a ghost story?"

"Well," said Maggie, her voice growing hushed, "in my hometown, the old-timers still tell stories of what *really* went on out here. Like Samantha Carville. She died of starvation up at the Lost Camp, aged only six."

Clive nodded. "There was a family by that name in the party."

"They buried her body in the snow. And there Samantha stayed. For a while, anyway. As the starvation time began, two men snuck out one night, dug up her body, chopped off part of her leg, and ate it."

"There's nothing about this in the historical record," Clive said. "It's hard to believe they would have started with a child."

"You hush!" Maggie scolded him. "You'll ruin a good story." She turned back to Adelsky. "Those two men were bad 'uns, but after starting in on her leg, even they couldn't finish. They threw away the bone and covered Samantha's body back up again."

She paused, her voice deepening.

"And so they say, even today, that on a moonless night, deep in the forest, you can still hear her wandering around, looking for her leg bone. You can't mistake the sound—a kind of shuffling, knocking, like a one-legged person hobbling on a stick." And in a sudden, chilling display of mimicry, Maggie put her hands to her mouth as if preparing to yodel, and made a peculiar hollow sound: *Ssshhhhhh-KNOCK. Ssshhhhhh-KNOCK.*

Nora felt her skin crawl.

Maggie's voice trailed off, and there was a moment of silence as everyone seemed to be listening in the dark. Then Adelsky began to laugh.

"Wow! Now, that's a ghost story! We'll all be lying awake tonight, listening for little Samantha knocking about the trees, searching for her leg." Huffing and blowing, Adelsky tried to imitate the sound but failed. Then he laughed again, only this time without quite the same gusto as before.

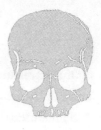

14

THE FOLLOWING NOON, resting in the shade on a flat rock by
Hackberry Creek, Nora pulled from her pack the lunch Maggie
had made for her. Clive sat down beside her with his own lunch
packet. They had made good progress that morning scouting up
the creek, and were almost ready to begin a search for the actual
Lost Camp.

"There's something I've been worrying about," Nora said.

"Let me guess. The gold again." Clive unwrapped the tinfoil
to find a BLT sandwich.

"When we find it, it's going to be really awkward explaining
that we were looking for it all along."

"Just like it was awkward for me, deciding when to explain it
to you."

"Maybe we should tell them now. They might be upset at
being kept in the dark."

"We don't know anything about Burleson's gang. I mean,
look at Peel—the guy is so silent. Practically the only thing I've
heard him say was that prayer last night. Even a normal person
might do something really stupid for twenty million dollars."

"I'm sure Peel's okay. There's nothing wrong with having faith."

"Agreed. But if they learn about the gold before we actually find it, we might have a mutiny on our hands. And what if word leaks beyond the group? This whole area will be crawling with yahoos carrying metal detectors."

Nora shook her head. "I don't like keeping secrets."

"So you've said. But we *have* to keep this secret. When the time comes to explain—with the gold locked safely in the strongbox—then we'll do so."

They ate in silence for a while, and then Nora asked: "Weren't you ever tempted to find the gold and keep it for yourself?"

Clive laughed. "Honestly? Yes. You can't help but think how that kind of money would change your life. But then I considered all the complications. How do you turn that much gold into cash? How would you pay taxes on it? If you try to sell the coins, you'd flood the market and dealers would know immediately some treasure trove had been found. Even if you were able to sell them, you'd still be faced with the crazy task of laundering twenty million dollars." He shook his head.

"I can see you really *did* think about it."

He laughed again. "It's only human nature."

They finished their sandwiches. Clive took a Trimble GPS out of his day pack and checked it against a photocopy of Tamzene's map. "Here are the clues," he said. "It seems Tamzene drew one creek on the right when there are actually three. But the camp was definitely down one of those smaller creeks. She also mentioned a couple of landmarks. Not far up from the creek's mouth was a place where the canyon seems to have narrowed. She wrote: *the Carville party's wagon scraped the wall of a rocky defile and lost a running board.* Beyond that lay the meadow where the third group camped. After Boardman later staggered into Tamzene's camp, she wrote: *Mr. Boardman stated in his fever that the only true marker to that dreadful place was the rocky profile of an old woman, visible high on a bluff, as distinct as the famous Old Man of the Mountain in New Hampshire."*

"That's the key clue," said Nora. "Let's go find the old woman."

They finished lunch and hiked up Hackberry Creek. They passed a couple of canyons to the left of the stream, which they ignored: their destination was to the right. At last, Clive nodded toward a gap in the rocks, almost hidden by trees. "According to my GPS, that's the mouth of the first creek— Sugarpine."

"Shall we check it out?"

"What if we go up it two miles, looking for the 'rocky defile,' and then if we don't find it move on to Poker Creek and, if necessary, Dollar Fork?"

"Sounds like a plan."

They gathered up the remains of their lunch and shrugged into their backpacks. With Clive and his GPS leading the way, Nora followed. They waded across the creek and soon came to the junction where Sugarpine flowed in. They followed it upstream. Instead of a single defile, it seemed to Nora the entire creek was lined with rocky cliffs that a wagon would have to squeeze past. As it was, they had to cross the stream multiple times, and her boots ended up getting soaked. They found no meadow and no old woman's profile, and finally reached a bottleneck beyond which no wagon could have gone.

They returned to Hackberry Creek and hiked up to the next checkpoint on their list—Poker Creek. This one looked much more promising. It went up a mile and then squeezed past a rocky defile like the one described in the journal, with a cliff on one side and the creek on the other.

"I'm getting a good feeling here," Clive said, quickening his pace.

Nora felt a similar flush of excitement. The stream took a turn and they tramped across it and passed through a screen of dead trees to where the canyon opened up into a long, broad meadow. Steep ravines covered with scree and cliffs of gray basalt surrounded them, framed against a darkening sky.

"This seems a likely place!" said Clive enthusiastically, turning slowly around with his hands raised.

It was a damp meadow of about ten acres, mostly flat, surrounded by tall firs and slopes of broken scree. Both sides of the valley were lined with dark cliffs riddled with holes and cracks. Looming above were masses of dark clouds. Poker Creek gurgled its way through the middle, a deep, narrow gully almost hidden in grass. It was a bleak place.

Clive came over. "Now to find the old woman on one of these cliffs."

Nora nodded toward the mountains. "Looks like weather coming."

"Yeah. You'd better take the right side and I'll take the left."

Letting her pack slide from her shoulders, Nora walked slowly, scrutinizing the cliffs on her right, squinting, looking at every rock formation from multiple angles. Once in a while she saw something that looked more or less like a face but on further scrutiny just didn't seem striking enough to qualify as an old woman. At the far end of the valley, where the stream came out from a stand of trees, she met up with Benton.

He shook his head. "Let's switch sides and go back."

When they met again at the base of the meadow, they still had seen nothing.

Nora frowned. "Do you think it might have fallen off, like the one in New Hampshire?"

"Anything's possible. After all, it's been a hundred and seventy-five years." The disappointment in his face was plain.

The wind was picking up, flattening the grass.

"I think it's more likely this isn't the place," he continued. "We'd better move on to Dollar Fork."

She felt a drop of moisture, and then another. Up the canyon, dark shafts of rain rapidly approached.

"Looks like we're in for it," said Nora, pulling a waterproof shell out of her pack and putting it on. Clive did likewise.

The storm hit with a blast of cold wind and a torrent of rain that swept over the meadow in sheets and obscured the peaks around them.

"It's three thirty," said Nora. "We can do Dollar Fork tomorrow."

"Sure you don't want to check it out now?" Clive's question was almost drowned out by a sudden rumble of thunder.

"I don't know. Do you?"

"Um...I guess not. I've seen what lightning can do up here. Like that big spruce down the trail, trunk split right to the ground." He tugged the waterproof plastic tighter. "Me for a steaming cup of Maggie's coffee."

Another peal of thunder sounded before Nora could reply. Instead, she just nodded her agreement.

By the time they got back to camp, the rain was turning into sleet and the temperature had dropped into the low forties. Nora and Clive took refuge in the dining area, sheltered under tarps strung between trees. They stripped off their dripping rain gear and hung it on branches.

"Come and get some grub before it's all gone," said Maggie, hovering over a simmering kettle of stew. "Better warm your butts by the fire. You look like drowned rats." A Dutch oven smelling of freshly baked bread stood to one side. Salazar, Peel, Wiggett, Adelsky, and Burleson were sitting around the fire circle, sipping coffee.

"Sorry we didn't wait," Salazar said.

"I'm not," said Adelsky. "When Maggie rings the dinner bell, I know to come running."

Nora and Clive helped themselves to dinner and took their places by the fire.

"Did you find it?" Burleson asked.

Clive shook his head. "Tomorrow. For sure, tomorrow."

Maggie joined them. "Your young man here pestered me for another story. I was just about to tell them about the legend of the two prospectors. Happened back in 1872. Maybe 1873. Maybe you know it: one of them was blind in one eye, and the other had a hook for a hand."

She proceeded to tell a hair-raising story about a pair of life-long friends who found a vein of gold in the mountains, got greedy, and one stormy night—a night like this one—they laid traps for each other, managing to both die in the process. With relish, Maggie added lots of graphic details, especially about the man with the hook. It was amusing to watch Adelsky's reaction: he was the one who'd asked for a ghost story, but by the time it was over he appeared a little green about the gills.

Later, Nora crawled into her tent, cold and wet, but she had trouble falling asleep. Thoughts of Clive—his stubborn yet appealing ways, his boyish enthusiasm—came unbidden to her mind. She realized she was noticing him more than perhaps she should, and she resolved to keep things strictly professional. In a small, isolated group like this, any sort of relationship could destroy the team's equilibrium, and with this thought she drifted off to sleep.

She was awakened in the middle of the night—suddenly—by a strange rumbling, like the scurrying of countless giant rats down a mountain slope. She opened the entrance to her tent and glanced around, but it was pitch-black and the sound was already dying away. Nobody else seemed to take any notice.

The sleet pounded down the rest of the night.

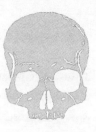

15

May 6

W HEN NORA ROSE at dawn, she could see her breath inside the tent. A light sleet was still tap-tapping on the waterproofed nylon.

She dragged herself out into the icy air and put on her clothes. At the fire, Maggie was cooking a breakfast of bacon and eggs and corn bread, her usually cheerful face a damp mask of annoyance. Burleson was sitting on a log, nursing a cup of coffee, speaking in low tones to Jack Peel about the horses. Clive had emerged from his tent in a brand-new paisley shirt, this one purple, orange, and pink.

"Help yourself to coffee," said Maggie, gesturing toward a pot standing on a rock beside the fire. "You look like you could use it."

"I heard something strange late last night. A low rumbling, like a herd of tiny elephants coming our way."

"That was just a rockfall. Tumbling boulders. It's not uncommon in the spring. Nothing to worry about—unless one lands on your tent, of course."

Nora poured herself a cup and warmed her hands with it

as Jason Salazar emerged from his tent, hair askew. He walked over, trying to flatten it with one hand and finally, giving up, putting on his hat. Adelsky and Wiggett were nowhere to be seen.

"You and Clive going out again today?" Salazar asked.

"Sure are."

"If you need a third person, I'd like to come."

Nora glanced at the sky. Salazar, of course, already knew about Wolfinger's gold, as did Adelsky. "You sure? Going to be a nasty day."

"Better than playing solitaire in my tent."

Maggie plucked strips of sizzling bacon out of the pan and laid them on a paper-towel-lined plate to drain. She poured most of the grease into the fire, which flared up, and then started making scrambled eggs. She stirred the eggs, still frowning.

"Rotten weather," said Nora.

"Don't mind the rain. It's the snow I don't like."

"Snow?" Salazar asked.

"You can bet it's snowing like hell in the high country." Maggie shook her head.

"Is that a problem?" Nora asked.

"Maybe." Maggie gave the eggs another stir.

"How so?"

"Avalanches—remember those boulders you heard last night? Or if it melts too fast, the creeks will flood." She picked up a cowbell and gave it a few whacks with a stick. "Breakfast!"

* * *

Nora, Clive, and Salazar set out after breakfast, hiking in the rain. Hackberry Creek was running high, rippling over boulders. Once again, they had to cross multiple times, the icy water filling their boots, the rocks slippery.

They hiked up Hackberry past Sugarpine and Poker Creeks, both of which were pouring into the main stream. The canyon broadened and big meadows appeared to their right, sweeping up to a ridge cloaked with mist. They crossed rushing water once again, holding hands for support as they scrambled over the rocks and turned up Dollar Fork, a stream smaller than the others.

"Wonder why they call it Dollar Fork," Nora said.

"Back then, silverware was expensive up here," said Salazar, to a chorus of groans.

As they ascended, Nora noted that the valley was wide enough to accommodate a wagon. A mile up, the canyon narrowed—just as Tamzene's journal had described—and then it opened up again into a vast meadow. The sleet stopped and the low clouds started to lift, mists rising from the flattened grass.

"Looks like another good candidate," said Clive, stopping and looking around. "Great campsite. Plenty of rock walls for displaying an old lady."

They split up and again walked slowly through the meadow, scrutinizing all the rock formations for the image of an old woman.

"Bingo!" Clive called out. "Here she is!"

Nora and Salazar hustled across the creek and joined Clive.

"It's a face?" said Salazar. "Maybe. Sort of."

"Come on, it's an old woman's face!"

Nora shook her head. "We're looking for a *dramatic* face—otherwise they wouldn't have made special note of it. That thing is more like a Rorschach blot."

Clive turned to her. "Rorschach blot? Anyone can see the hooked nose, the pointy chin!"

"Anyone but me, I guess."

"Or me," said Salazar.

"Come on, you two! Are you sure you're looking at the same thing I am?"

After some additional squinting and fruitless arguing, they decided to continue searching the valley walls in case a better face turned up. But there was nothing more. They gathered once again at the spot.

"I'm sure this is it," said Clive. "I can feel it in my bones. If so, we must be near the campsite. In fact, it should be right around where we're standing."

"I don't buy it," Salazar told him. "The ground slopes here."

Benton turned to him. "So what?"

"When you're lying down, you can feel even the slightest incline."

"There was *snow* on the ground, for Christ's sake!"

Nora listened to this exchange and Clive's raised voice. One thing was clear: despite the historian's normally chipper veneer, finding the Lost Camp meant a great deal to him. And the fact was, he might well be right: the camp could be just beneath their feet.

There was a moment of silence, during which Clive pulled a long cigar with a Dunhill wrapper out of his coat pocket and used a lighter to fire it up.

"How about this?" she said. "We do a test pit or two."

The look of annoyance on Clive's face cleared. "Okay," he said through a cloud of blue smoke. "That's a good idea."

"Jason will dig where you think the camp was most likely, while I go back down to Poker Creek."

"But there was no old woman there."

"Maybe she fell off."

Clive nodded as he puffed on the cigar. "If that's what you think best. Jason, let's you and I get to work. Nora, we'll plan to meet you back in camp."

Nora was silent a moment, looking at the two of them. Then she shouldered her day pack, turned, and walked back through the meadow, toward the rocky trail down the mountain.

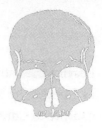

16

SPECIAL AGENT CORRIE Swanson stood before a mirror in the ladies' room on the second floor of the Albuquerque FBI building, examining herself with a critical eye. Her hair was combed more carefully than usual, and she'd put on her best business attire before coming to work. She had even refrained from eating her usual lunch salad, to ensure no stray piece of green got stuck between her teeth. She wore no makeup except a light application of lipstick, but even that got the once-over, the dab of a Kleenex here and there.

She was aware of a combination of excitement and nervousness. As part of her probationary training, she was required to take part in what was known around the field office as the Firing Squad—the weekly meeting in which new agents debriefed their FTO and colleagues on the status of whatever case they were investigating. Normally, Corrie had found this to be a pretty straightforward exercise—this cold case examined and shelved; that cold case examined and shelved.

But not today. Today she was going out on a limb.

She glanced at her watch: five minutes to two. Game time.

Leaving the bathroom, she returned to the office and—stopping by her desk to pick up a stack of files—navigated through the cubicles to Conference Room B, with its lingering odor of pizza that never seemed to go completely away. It was a large room, with a table that held at least a dozen people. There were computers for digital slide shows and videos, and a seventy-five-inch smart touchboard for interactive demonstrations, but they were rarely used for meetings such as this. Only Bob Wantaugh, the GS-11 douchebag, had employed the interactive whiteboard, in a spectacularly unedifying update the week before on his pet case: something involving extortion, money laundering, and perhaps human trafficking along what he was calling an "underground railroad" between Albuquerque and Ciudad Juárez, just over the Mexican border. His evidence was colorful but highly circumstantial, and after last week's presentation even the normally patient Agent Morwood suggested Wantaugh might want to cut down on his diet of Robert Ludlum novels.

Corrie entered the conference room and took a seat. She waited as the handful of other new agents—Supervisory Special Agent Morwood's flock—arranged themselves around the room. To her consternation, she saw that a couple of senior agents had parked themselves at the far end of the table. Higher-ups sitting in on a Firing Squad was a common enough occurrence; she just wished these two had picked some other week for their evaluation.

Last in was Morwood, carrying the usual cup of coffee. He shut the door with his free hand, then took a seat at the head of the table. He had no notebook, tablet, or other writing instrument with him.

"Hear ye, hear ye," he said. "This tribunal is now in session, the Honorable Hale Morwood presiding. All would-be crime

fighters and upholders of the American way present and accounted for, I see? Good." His perpetually sleepy eyes surveyed
the room. "Swanson. Why don't you start?"

Corrie almost jumped in her seat. Morwood never picked her
first—her litany of cold cases usually came last. She'd expected
more time to mentally prepare herself.

"Me?" she asked, realizing as she said it how stupid it sounded.

"You. Please: enlighten us with your forensic expertise."

He would say that. Corrie cleared her throat, shuffled through
her papers. There was a cough from across the table: Bob Wantaugh, his blond ducktail shaking faintly with displeasure. He'd
become used to going first.

"Patience, Agent Wantaugh. We'll get to the latest, ah, chapter in your saga soon enough." Morwood looked back at Corrie.
"Go ahead."

Corrie cleared her throat again. Only she and Morwood
knew the specific details about the case she'd been investigating.
Even Morwood didn't know all of it. She fervently wished he
didn't have to hear it for the first time in front of all these others.

"As I mentioned in last week's meeting," she said, "I investigated a crime scene at a cemetery in the Sangre de Cristo Mountains, about eighty miles northeast of here. The cemetery—
Pigeon's Ranch—is a national historic site commemorating a
Civil War battlefield, which is why this is a federal case. Upon arrival I found an unearthed grave, containing the iron coffin of a
Florence Parkin Regis, who had died in 1862. Her remains were
partially disinterred. Lying on top of the coffin was the body of
Frank Serban, age fifty-four, of Denver. He had no identification
and was later ID'd from prints. He'd been shot twice in the back
of the head, execution style, the night before. No evidence of
this shooting was found at the scene save for the bullets, which

evidently had been fired from a silenced weapon. Serban had a long history of petty crimes."

As she heard herself talk, Corrie realized she'd been over this ground the week before. When she was nervous she tended to overexplain. She made a conscious effort to pick up the pace.

"Forensic work by myself and the Crime Scene Unit ascertained that Serban had probably unearthed the coffin himself. The top portion of Regis's remains was removed, the coffin closed, and Serban was shot and left on the coffin lid. Presumably this was a job for hire and he was eliminated as a potential witness."

So far, so good. Here, Corrie knew, was where it got a little dicey.

"Not all the forensic evidence gathered at the site has been analyzed, but little of value has yet turned up, and it probably will not, beyond the two 9mm rounds. This appears to have been a clean and professional operation. However, when I started widening the parameters of my search, I came across something suggestive. In an effort to link this crime with others of a similar MO, I discovered that in two other cases, graves had been robbed with only the top portion of a corpse removed. One of those was a recently deceased mobster in Joliet, Illinois, named Carmine Scarabone. His grave had been desecrated, the coffin partially removed and his headstone vandalized. The other corpse belonged to Alexander Parkin, who had died in Nelson, New Hampshire, in 1911."

She glanced at her papers. "In pursuing this MO, I widened the scope of my search. I found that six months ago in Paris, the grave of Thomas Parkin, an American who died in France during the Second World War, had also been disturbed. In that case only the skull was taken. But when I looked more closely,

I realized there was an unexpected connection among all three cases."

Here she paused and looked around. She was both gratified and made anxious to see she had the room's undivided attention.

"Florence Regis, née Parkin; Alexander Parkin; and Thomas Parkin obviously shared a common surname. I checked census records and a genealogical database, and discovered that, in fact, all three shared a common ancestor as well."

"What genealogical database might that be?" Morwood asked. "Is this some FBI asset I'm not aware of?"

Corrie paused. She hadn't mentioned this part to Morwood before. "Uh, no. It's Ancestry.com, sir."

The two senior agents in the back exchanged glances. Morwood looked at her in disbelief. "You consulted *Ancestry.com?*"

Wantaugh tittered.

"I took advantage of it as a tool, a stepping-stone. I know it wouldn't be admissible as evidence in court, sir."

She glanced around again. The faces looking back at her were now waiting for the punch line.

"Three days ago, I learned that one Rosalie Parkin, twenty-seven and unmarried, a lawyer in Scottsdale, Arizona, had gone missing. With Agent Morwood's approval, I went to Scottsdale, liaised with the local police, and examined her apartment. While there was no sign of a struggle, there was a very large amount of blood on the premises. The type matched Rosalie Parkin's."

"Any eyewitnesses?" somebody asked.

Corrie's thoughts flitted briefly to Rosalie's brother. "No. But the police are now treating it as a criminal missing persons case."

She paused.

"Go ahead," Morwood said. "Tell them the rest."

"I checked, and the missing woman is related to the other three Parkins."

"Checked on Ancestry.com?" Wantaugh asked.

Corrie decided to ignore this. "They are all descendants from a single line."

"What about the incident in Joliet?" another junior asked. "The mobster?"

"Unrelated. The individual was not a Parkin relation, and the vandalism was most likely the result of the individual having been a CI."

"What is your operating hypothesis?" Morwood asked.

"That there is a party or parties out there with a special interest in this particular family line."

"What kind of interest?" Morwood prompted. This was his modus operandi—pushing and prodding, looking for holes in theories or gaps in investigative method.

"Maybe it's a descendant," Wantaugh offered. "With a peculiar collecting hobby." There was faint laughter in response to this equally faint witticism.

One of the two senior agents shifted in his chair. "If this woman was abducted because of her relation to the disinterred," he said, "why the sudden change in MO?"

This was the question Corrie had been asking herself, and the one she dreaded. "I don't have an answer to that yet."

"Kidnapping is dangerous and risky," the senior agent continued. "And far more serious than grave robbing."

"I agree," Corrie said. "So is homicide—as in the execution of Serban."

"Beyond the Parkin connection," Morwood asked, "what other evidence do you have to connect these cases?"

"None yet, sir."

"And no doubt you've contacted other Parkins, living and directly related, to see if they know anything about this—with negative results?"

That had proven time consuming. "Correct as well."

"And you've checked to see how many other Parkins still lie in their graves, undisturbed?"

That had proven even more time consuming. "Yes. There aren't many—the family line is thin."

"Do you have any leads beyond the Parkin connection?"

"Not beyond, sir."

Morwood took a sip of coffee, a sure sign he was preparing to pass the floor to another agent.

"There is one thing." Here it was—the other part Morwood didn't know about.

The supervisory special agent raised his eyebrows inquiringly.

"I spread my net pretty wide. And in the course of doing so, I flagged some information that—well, seemed to me of interest."

Morwood put down his coffee. "Agent Swanson, surprise me."

"Any archaeological excavations on federal land require extensive paperwork. Several months ago, the Santa Fe Archaeological Institute in New Mexico submitted paperwork proposing an excavation of a campsite of the Donner Party."

She looked around the table, to be greeted by blank faces.

"The Donner Party. They were the pioneers whose wagon train got snowbound for an entire winter in the Sierra Nevada, in 1847. Many of the survivors resorted to cannibalism to stay alive."

Now some of the faces registered recognition.

She continued more quickly. "One of the party who died that

winter was Albert Parkin. It turns out this Albert Parkin is the direct common ancestor of all four Parkins in our case. The Santa Fe Archaeological Institute is currently searching for that campsite and intends to excavate it."

Morwood was, indeed, now looking surprised—and not in a good way. "And?"

"I spoke to the president of the Institute, a Dr. Fugit. This is a legitimate organization and the excavation is approved by both the feds and the state of California."

"I ask again: and?"

"Well, sir, this means that, if they're successful, yet another set of Parkin remains might be excavated—legally this time. It seems like a strange coincidence that should be investigated."

"I see," said Morwood. "And let me guess. You want to go out to the Sierra Nevada, track down this archaeological expedition, and in one way or another make their lives miserable."

"That—" Corrie began, but decided not to finish.

There was a brief silence around the table. Out of the corner of her eye, Corrie could see Wantaugh smirking.

Morwood sighed. "Let me remind you, Agent Swanson, what you were tasked with: discovering who killed that gravedigger at Pigeon's Ranch."

"And that's what I'm doing, sir," Corrie replied. She felt herself growing hot under the collar.

"You have already taken a trip to Arizona in pursuit of this theory. *And* accessed unapproved civilian databases to further your investigation. What you are suggesting would take several days, at the least. On what can only be called the thinnest of leads."

"With respect, sir, Albert Parkin is the common link. The

ancestor of them all. Doesn't it seem strange to you that, out of nowhere, Parkins are being dug up all over the world?"

"Please don't take this the wrong way, Swanson—but I believe you've fallen into a rookie trap."

"Which is?"

"You've let the case lead you, rather than leading the case. It's a common problem among first- and second-year agents, nothing to be ashamed of."

Corrie, tense in her seat, balled her fists below the table. Nothing made her angrier than being patronized. Well, except some jackass sexually harassing her—which had been a problem at the Academy.

Morwood's voice was quiet, even gentle, but the words cut her like a knife. "This is a good object lesson, and one that everybody in this room either has learned or will learn soon enough. Focus on the case at hand, and don't chase after every circumstantial lead." He looked pointedly at her. "Ask yourself: what could this Albert Parkin, who died in 1847 in the mountains of California, possibly have to do with the homicide of Frank Serban in a Civil War cemetery almost two centuries later? Albert Parkin's remains haven't even been found yet. And you yourself said this excavation is being conducted by a highly accredited organization with all the required permits—nothing like nighttime grave robbing."

He took a deep breath. Corrie could see he was about to draw the lesson for everyone in the room.

"There's an insidious danger we all face in our job today: computers are too good at giving us information. We at the FBI are faced with an overwhelming deluge of data. It becomes difficult to determine which leads are valuable and which are just coincidence... or wishful thinking."

He paused to let this sink in.

"And so what I'd suggest for your next action steps, Agent Swanson, is to continue the good work you've been doing. Continue the investigation into the Serban homicide. And while you're doing that, keep an eye—a distant eye—on this Parkin family connection. Watch for any other incidents involving the family line. Wait and see if that expedition in California ever finds the remains of Albert Parkin."

He gave Corrie a smile of encouragement along with an approving nod, but she could see the *no* in his eyes as well.

Morwood then took a hearty gulp of coffee and turned to Wantaugh. "All right, Agent," he said. "We're now ready for the next chapter in this thriller of yours."

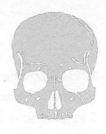

17

Nora hiked back down Dollar Fork to Hackberry Creek, taking particular care—being on her own—not to slip on a rock or twist an ankle. She had to cross multiple times going downstream before she reached Poker Creek. By then her feet were freezing and making a squelching sound with every step. The clouds were lifting, revealing a fresh snow line laid down by the storm. The line looked a lot closer than it had on the first day they packed in.

She started up Poker Creek and in forty minutes had reached the defile, then the wall of dead trees. Instead of looking for the profile of an old woman, she walked along the base of the cliffs searching for freshly fallen rock that might indicate where the profile had once been. The job wasn't difficult: rock had been falling for tens of thousands of years, leaving long scree slopes and boulders, but most of it was covered with lichen and buried in soil. The rock faces were riddled with cracks and holes. As she worked her way along, a pair of ravens flew overhead, cawing their displeasure. The air smelled of fir trees. A strange, icy feeling took hold as the mists once again descended, obscuring the peaks and turning the valley into a lake of ghostly mist.

She reached the end of the valley and started back down the other side, almost immediately coming upon a fresher rockfall—recent enough that the trees it had knocked down could still be seen rotting among the broken rocks. She backed away and looked up. Along the edge of the bluff, below the line of melting snow, she spied an area of lighter, newly exposed rock where the canyon made a turn.

This seemed an ideal vantage point for a stone face to be visible—*if* what was now rockfall had once resembled a face.

She backed up further, sizing up the hollow with a practiced eye. The ground fell away from the valley edges, leveling out into a smoother area—smooth enough for a campsite. It was three, maybe four acres: much larger than the archaeological site itself, which would probably occupy no more than a quarter of an acre.

So where, exactly, might they have pulled up the wagons? She tried to put herself in their heads. At the time, there was about a foot of snow on the ground and it was falling fast—the leading edge of a blizzard that was about to alter their lives forever. The remote landscape had changed little, if at all, since 1846, and Nora knew that—except for the lack of snow—she was seeing much of what they would have seen.

If she were leading the group, where would she have made camp?

She moved about, walking a transverse first to the right, then to the left. Closer to the creek the ground sloped down again. They would have stopped somewhere in the middle of the flat area. From which vantage point would the now fallen face have been seen best, the sharp granite corner most visible? It was hard to be sure, but after a bit of squinting up at the still snowy cliff she settled on a spot that somehow felt right. The hollow was larger than it looked from a distance. The grass was wet from the rain here, thick and healthy. Unusually thick and healthy. And there were flowers.

There were no flowers anywhere else in the damp meadow. As an archaeologist, she was trained to watch for areas of soil that were unexpectedly rich, or where there was a sudden change in vegetation.

She knelt and pressed her hand into the icy grass. Should she?

She was qualified, and they had all the proper permits. There was no reason not to.

Kneeling, she took off her pack and removed an archaeological trowel, gloves, and a face mask from it. After measuring and cutting a fifty-centimeter square in the thick grass cover, she edged the trowel underneath, working the roots loose, and lifted free the plate of grass to expose the muddy soil below. Slowly, with exquisite care, she began scraping back the layers of dirt, bit by bit. A 175-year-old site would not be far below the surface, especially at this high altitude, in a meadow where soil would have accumulated slowly.

At three inches, the trowel tapped something. Changing to a light brush, she exposed the object.

It was a tooth.

* * *

When she returned to camp, the weather had fully cleared, the fleeting clouds tinged a blood red from the setting sun. The freshly whitened peaks were afire with alpenglow. Jason and Clive were still out, and Nora said nothing while Maggie cooked dinner and the wranglers fed the horses their evening oats. Finally, just as she was beginning to grow concerned, Jason appeared in camp. Clive followed, his face a mask of discouragement.

"What a bust," he said, dumping his pack. He picked the ever-ready coffeepot off the fire and poured himself a cup, sitting down on the log.

"No go, eh?"

Clive shook his head.

"Nothing at all? Really?"

"Not so much as a button."

Jason poured himself a cup as well.

"Jason, what do you think?" Nora asked.

He shrugged. "If there's a camp, it's not up Dollar Fork."

Night was falling quickly and Nora heard the hoot of an owl. She turned back to Clive. "Kind of selfish, don't you think?"

He looked at her in incomprehension. "What? Who is?"

"You. All this whining about what you didn't find. Why haven't you asked me what *I* found?"

Both men turned. "You found something?" Clive asked.

She nodded.

"What?"

"A human molar."

Clive leapt to his feet. "No shit! Really?"

Everyone started talking at once, asking questions.

"It was just over a mile up Poker Canyon, in that hollow we first explored."

"Nora, my God, that's *fantastic*," said Clive, giving her a hug before recollecting himself, stepping back, and shaking her hand vigorously. She was gratified, and a little surprised, by

Clive's lack of envy that it was she, not he, who'd made the discovery. On top of that, she realized the hug had left her with a faint tingle.

"Amazing. Phenomenal." He sat down again, still laughing with joy, his blue eyes flashing. "Tell us how you did it."

She briefly told the story, while Burleson broke out a bottle of wine and poured glasses all around.

"A toast," he said, holding up his tin cup.

That bottle was followed by another, as Maggie served dinner. Afterward they sat by the fire, and the conversation—consisting mostly of excited speculation—eventually fell off into silence. The only sounds were the crackling of the fire, the hooting of an owl, and the faint sigh of wind in the trees.

"We'll move camp tomorrow," said Nora. "There's a flat area along Poker Creek only about half a mile down from the site."

Burleson nodded. "I'll get Jack and Drew on it at first light."

Again they lapsed into silence. And then Jason sat up. "Did anyone hear that?"

A long silence. Nora heard a knocking sound, very distant and faint.

"There it is again," said Jason.

"Woodpecker," said Clive.

"They don't peck at night," said Maggie.

"Sure they do. Don't they?"

Another distant knocking sound, this time a little nearer. The wind sighed in the trees.

"Anybody missing from the campfire?" Maggie asked. "Off answering nature's call?"

"Nobody'd go that far," said Peel.

They did a quick head count anyway. Everyone was accounted for.

"Okay," said Maggie loudly into the darkness as she rose to her feet. "We know you're trying to scare us. Well, it worked. So show yourself, now that you've had your fun."

They waited and, as if on cue, there was another knock, followed by a low thump.

Nora stood up and flicked on her headlamp.

"Where you going?" Maggie asked.

"Out there to see what it is."

Nora walked quickly across the verge of the meadow, ignoring the various voiced warnings from the campfire. She reached the tall trees and walked into the forest, the trunks like giant pillars in a cathedral, disappearing into the darkness above her. She paused and looked back. The glow of the fire was visible through the trunks. She walked farther, then paused to listen. Nothing but barely audible voices from the campfire, no doubt calling her back.

Then the thumping sounded again—closer. It could be the wind, Nora thought, knocking two trees together. Or perhaps an elk moving about in the dark, rubbing its rack on tree trunks.

The sound came again and this time she zeroed in on the direction, walking fast through the trees, keeping to a straight line. After a few minutes she stopped to listen once more. This, she judged, should be the approximate location of the sound. She waited, and waited some more. But no sound came.

Taking a few more steps, she passed through a particularly dense stand of trees and suddenly emerged into a roughly circular clearing. Odd: there was no reason for a break like this in such thick forest. She shone her light around, but there was nothing: just a soft bed of green moss, undisturbed by tracks, and a few scattered boulders.

She waited five minutes, but the sound did not return. She turned and began retracing her steps. Despite being an experienced woodsman, she hadn't marked her back trail, and in the dark every trunk began to look the same as every other. Just as she was starting to panic, thinking she'd lost her way, she saw a faint gleam through the trees and headed for the welcoming fire.

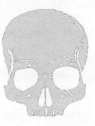

18

May 8

Two mornings later, Nora stood near the base of the cliff and looked around. What had been an empty meadow the night before last was now a full-fledged archaeological excavation. And, she had to admit, a damn fine one.

The prep had gone like clockwork. Salazar and Adelsky had gridded out the central site, driving pegs into the ground at one-meter intervals and tying Day-Glo orange string to create a six-by-ten-meter grid—each of the sixty grid spaces representing a square meter, from which every speck of soil would be removed and screened. The proton magnetometer—a device that looked like a high-tech lawnmower—had already been run over the entire area, giving them a rough idea where buried artifacts might be located, especially ferrous objects such as nails, bolts, and tools. Since this was a pristine area, free of human settlement, Nora assumed any ferrous object located in the ground must have been left by the Donner Party. And there were a lot—all concentrated in the middle of the hollow. That was probably where the hearth and the remains of the shelter would be found.

Clive had pitched in with gusto, asking questions about how this worked, or that, showing a keen interest in how archaeology was done and an eager desire to help. He was like an enthusiastic boy, really, thrilled to be on his first dig.

Meanwhile, Maggie and the wranglers were busy shifting their base camp from Hackberry Creek up Poker Canyon, just over half a mile from the site. Peel was leading the pack train to and from the ranch into the mountains on a daily basis. He would pack in equipment, overnight the animals in the campsite, and then lead them out again for another journey. Their living quarters had already been set up along the banks of the creek, and the move should be complete and everything in place by the following night.

At the Lost Camp itself, a large wall tent—cheekily labeled HQ by Adelsky—had been set up adjacent to the archaeological site. It contained worktables and storage containers for sorting, photographing, and conserving the artifacts, along with a computer and Wi-Fi transmitter, attached to solar panels and a small backup generator. The Wi-Fi couldn't connect them to the outside world, but it would be effective in communicating and transferring files among themselves. The strongbox went into a corner, and on the opposite side was an area for storing the proton magnetometer and other archaeological equipment. Adelsky and Salazar were at the far end of the meadow, finishing up the magnetometer survey. In the aftermath of the storm, the weather had been sublime: warm during the day and above freezing at night.

As she watched, Clive emerged from the work tent and came over to where she was standing. "Beautiful morning," he said. "I'm really curious to see how this is going to progress. I've never worked on a dig before. We historians spend most of our time shut up inside libraries and archives, accumulating dust and withering away."

Nora smiled. "Nice shirt," she said, nodding at yet another paisley horror show. "How many of those did you bring? It's going to get awfully dirty, you realize. That is, if you're really serious about helping."

Clive grinned, tugging on the collar. "I know, I know. I can't help it: I just like paisley. But I am serious. Really. We're partners and I want to be useful, not just some bump on a log."

"Okay. I think that can be arranged." Nora thought back on how solitary her life had been since her husband's death, how used she had become to working alone. Well, perhaps it was time to engage with life a bit more.

"That's great," said Clive. He gestured at the snowcapped mountains. "Sierra Nevada. Snowy Mountains. They sure live up to their name—it's mid-May and they're still covered with snow. I can't believe how thrilling it is to be out here, working on this." He looked around. "You think we should give this meadow a name?"

The same thought had occurred to Nora. She'd considered "Tamzene's Meadow," but decided that wasn't suitable: even in the early morning sunlight, the damp hollow held little charm. And it was not only because of what had happened here. The rocky walls seemed to loom over them almost menacingly. Where they narrowed at the far end, the cliffs were still topped by heavy scallops of snow. In particular, one vast lip of snow the size of an apartment building hung over the edge of a steep col high above them. It seemed to defy gravity, and she wondered what kept it in place.

"I guess that's one of the cornices Burleson warned us about," she said, nodding toward it.

"Good thing the dig site's nowhere near it. I wouldn't want to be under that baby when it gives."

Nora continued her visual survey. The trees that formed the edge of the vale were dark and forbidding, cloaked in almost constant shadow, and many were partially or completely dead. At a low point near the end of the valley, the creek temporarily widened into a black, ice-skimmed tarn before continuing on its sinuous way. All in all, it was—not to put too fine a word on it—spooky.

"Let's call it Lost Meadow," Clive suggested.

Nora considered this a moment. It seemed both simple and appropriate. "Good idea."

At that moment, they heard the distant voice of Maggie, calling them down to breakfast.

* * *

Nora finished her bacon and eggs and gulped the last of Maggie's strong black coffee. Seated nearby, Salazar and Adelsky were both wolfing down their food. Now that the site was prepared, they knew what the day had in store: serious work.

She rose and put her plate in the dish tub. "What do you say, Jason?" she asked the field assistant. "Ready to get dirty?"

"Damn straight!" He was on his feet in an instant.

"Count me in," said Clive.

Moments later the four of them—Nora, Salazar, Adelsky, and Clive—were headed back to the gridded-out dig site, Maggie wishing them good hunting at the top of her lungs.

At the work tent, Nora picked up one of the iPads that ran the Institute's cutting-edge excavation app. As she fired it up, Clive came and looked over her shoulder. "How does it work?"

She swiped open the app. "It's pretty amazing. You input all the levels, soil types, and every artifact and its position. All you have to do is photograph the artifact and the app maps it in situ using the picture. It stitches all the pictures together to create a complete dig site image, layer by layer."

"Amazing. Can you teach me...?"

"To use it? Sure. I'll show you the details. But you'll also need to know the rudiments of basic dirt archaeology. I'll show you as we go along. You can observe and follow what we do today, and maybe tomorrow I'll give you some actual work to do."

"Thank you, this is very exciting for me. History is always one step removed from the real thing—but right here, to be able to see and feel...It's so much more immediate, so real. It's like touching the past."

"You put your finger on exactly why I love archaeology," Nora said. She realized she would have to rein in his eagerness until she was sure she could trust his competence in field technique, but she was more than a little pleased at his lively interest.

Nora motioned to Salazar and Adelsky. "Grab your trowels and equipment and let's go. And don't forget gloves, hair nets, and face masks." Nora had worked out an exacting protocol for the excavation work, so as not to contaminate human remains with their own DNA.

They connected their iPads to the local network and calibrated them. She assigned Salazar and Adelsky to one-meter squares, then she herself took the grid in which she'd found the tooth, B3. Salazar's and Adelsky's squares were not adjacent to hers—she wanted to open the site in different places, get a feel for the broader outlines, develop a sense of where things were.

As she put on her kneepads and knelt in the grass, Clive standing behind her, she felt butterflies in her stomach. This wasn't a typical site—it was where an unspeakable tragedy had occurred. The place was owed a certain reverence. And dealing with historic human remains, where there might be living descendants—there *were* living descendants, like the man whose shadow was half covering her as he looked over her shoulder—made it an entirely different story.

Working carefully but efficiently, she removed the tarp from the sod layer she'd cut out two days before—labeled with a meter number—and examined the area of black earth where she'd found the tooth. She'd already discovered that the 1846 soil "horizon" was only ten inches down—an incredibly shallow excavation.

As she proceeded, she patiently explained each step to Clive. Taking the edge of her trowel, she gently removed soil a millimeter at a time, placing it in a bucket next to her, to be later dried and screened or put through flotation in search of carbonized organics and human hair.

She could hear the two others starting on their squares: scrape, dump; scrape, dump. A moment later, her trowel touched something else. Once again switching to a brush, she began to clean the surrounding area carefully.

"It's the top of a human cranium," she announced after a moment.

Clive dropped to his knees and looked at it closely, his head almost touching hers. "This gives me a really...strange feeling," he murmured. "Seeing these human remains."

"Me, too."

Salazar and Adelsky immediately came over. "That didn't take long."

Nora brushed it off, exposing it to the edges. It was a piece about the size of two silver dollars, discolored brown edging to a crumbling whitish powder, crazed with fractures.

She worked ever so slowly, uncovering more of the skull. Her work revealed the forehead, eye sockets, and nasal opening, along with the mandible that had held her initial discovery—the tooth.

"Probably male, from the brow ridges," she murmured.

They all watched in focused silence as she continued.

"That's the coronal suture," she said, pointing with the tip of her brush at a squiggly line running through the bone. "I'm no physical anthropologist, but I'd guess from its state of fusing this skull belonged to an adult."

There was a silence. "The Lost Camp, according to my census, had seven male adults," said Clive, his voice low. "A seventeen-year-old, three in their twenties, two in their thirties, and one who was forty. But Boardman, who was in his late twenties, escaped to the Donner camp, and the forty-year-old, Chears, was eventually rescued. So it couldn't be either of them."

"I'd guess this was one of the thirty-year-olds."

Clive squatted closer. "Can you tell anything else from looking at it?"

Nora took a deep breath. "See these marks here and here?" She fished out a loupe and allowed him to examine them closely. "Those look like 'anvil strike' markings. They're one of the six classic signs of cannibalism: the kind of scratches caused by a skull being placed on a rock and bashed open with another rock."

Clive shook his head in faint horror.

She pointed at another spot. "And here we have a second classic sign: the crumbling edge on this bone could only have been the result of heating and cooking." She sat back. "This person was decapitated, his head put in a fire and cooked, and the brain pan was bashed open to get at the, ah, cooked brain."

This was greeted by a brief silence.

"Glad I kept my hands off that bacon at breakfast," said Salazar.

"Brings it home pretty strong, doesn't it?" said Clive. "So what are the other four signs of cannibalism?"

"Scraping marks inside the bone to get out the marrow; butcher marks made by stone or metal tools; the mashing of spongy bone to extract the nourishment—and pot polish."

"Pot polish?"

"That's where broken bones are boiled in a ceramic or iron pot to extract the grease. As they turn in the boiling water, the sharp ends become microscopically polished by the sides of the pot." She paused. "Back in the lab, a physical anthropologist will examine these bones under a stereo zoom." She stood up. "There's probably a lot more of it—I mean him—to be found in this immediate area." She hesitated. "Let me excavate just a little more before deciding on our next move."

She knelt and began to work again, with Clive, Adelsky, and Salazar watching. Almost immediately she uncovered two more pieces of cranium and the burnt rim of the orbit. There were no vertebrae connected to the skull, but next to be exposed was a femur and what appeared to be a humerus.

"I'm no archaeologist, but the density of stuff is surprising," Clive said. "I thought it would be more spread out. But it looks like a jumble, those skulls and long bones..." He shook his head.

"Well, I hate to put it this way," Nora said, "but the area we're working in appears to be a midden heap—where food trash was tossed."

"As in, a lot of cannibalized bodies?"

"Yes." She stood up again. "Jason, Bruce, under the circumstances I think you should leave your assigned quads for now and concentrate on the quads adjacent to this one, starting with B4 and A3. If this is a midden heap, it's where the biggest cache will be."

The men nodded and moved off to collect their equipment. Nora stepped back from the immediate worksite and Clive followed her.

"Ever worked on a site like this before?" Clive asked.

"In a way, yes. I worked on a site years ago that held the remains of young people murdered back in the nineteenth century by a serial killer. And I helped excavate a major prehistoric Pueblo cannibal site in Utah. That's where I met my husband."

"I didn't know you were married."

"My husband, Bill...well, he died."

"I'm so sorry. I had no idea." He took her hand spontaneously. She thought of withdrawing it, but didn't. There was nothing more in the gesture than friendly concern, she told herself.

"I'm working on getting over it." She didn't want to tell him it had been more than seven years. In the past months, she thought she'd finally gotten over the worst of Bill's death, but his memory and the hurt always seemed to resurface when she least expected it.

"I lost a girlfriend," Clive said. "Fiancée, actually. Pancreatic cancer. Caught too late, as it so often is. In two months she was gone."

"How terrible. I'm so sorry."

"You grow up thinking everything's fine and bad things

happen to other people, and then, out of the blue, life drops a piano on you. I couldn't believe the pain. And the surprise."

She nodded. He had been through it, too. And yet he seemed to be getting over it. "When did that happen?"

"Two years ago. It feels like yesterday. But we move forward, right? We do what we have to do to continue our lives."

Again she nodded. He was still holding her hand. After a long period of quiet, he gave it a friendly squeeze and released it. "Nora," he said. "I'm ready. I'd love to have my own grid to work on."

She hadn't expected the conversation to take this sudden turn. "Clive, I'm not sure—"

"You taught me a lot last night, and I've learned more just from watching you today."

"A couple hours of observation might not be enough—"

"I promise I'll be slow. And super careful. And if I find anything, I'll immediately let you know."

Nora mulled this over.

"Look. My own ancestors, the Breens, were on this mountain. Patrick and Peggy Breen had seven children, ages one to fourteen. They overcame their scruples for their children's sake and fed them human flesh. They were the only family that didn't have a death, and forever after they were marked: *Those are the kids who lived on human flesh.* It seems horrible, I know, but if their son Edward hadn't resorted to cannibalism, I wouldn't be here. He was my great-great-great grandfather." He took a deep breath. "Now that we've found these remains, I...well, I find I just want to delve in, be part of this, get my paisley shirt really, really dirty."

Nora couldn't help smiling. She knew exactly how he felt. Even so, she wasn't going to take too big a chance. She consulted her iPad. Perhaps she could assign him a square in the most distant quadrant of the meadow, closest to the woods, where he was least likely to find anything of significance—or, for that matter, do any damage. E10 would be a good place for him to start—the proton magnetometer had registered something in this area, but it was faint and far from the main scene of action.

"Okay," she said. "If you promise to take it slow. No deeper than ten inches, please. And stop to notify me the moment you find anything. Even so much as a pebble."

"I promise."

"You can take grid E10." Nora put her iPad aside. "Come on—get a mask and gloves, and I'll show you where it is."

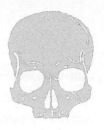

19

THE DISCOVERIES WERE so exciting, and coming so thick and fast, that nobody wanted to stop for lunch, so Nora just let them keep going while the afternoon lengthened. At first, she checked on Clive every half hour, but when it was clear he was doing a slow and painstakingly methodical job, she decided he could be left to his own devices. Thanks to the joint efforts of Salazar and Adelsky, the midden heap was yielding up more and more artifacts: not only a third skull and numerous other human bones, but scraps of clothes, buttons, lockets, and jewelry. Everything was carefully tagged and logged and situated using the suite of powerful archaeological software on their tablets. Salazar pointed out that here and there the midden heap showed signs of animal disturbance, but it looked old—probably dating back to the tragedy—and after a brief conference they came to the conclusion that these were most likely the result of brief scavenging attempts after the first spring thaw. Nora knew there would not be many animals at this altitude, and in any case what bones remained would have been covered in dust, dirt, and grass soon enough.

It was around three thirty—with a gorgeous afternoon just beginning to settle toward evening, the sun hanging low over the snowy mountains and bathing them in light—when Clive came over to the square that Nora was carefully photographing.

"Have you got a minute?" he asked. "I'd like to show you something." His voice was calm, but there was a curious expression on his face that she hadn't seen before.

"Sure." She slung the camera around her neck and followed him over to the far end of the dig site, away from the others. Here, in these grids farthest from the main camp, the ground was already under the shadow of the pine trees. A late breeze swept through the meadow, rippling the fresh grass and bringing with it the scent of flowers.

Nora saw that Clive had excavated the square she'd assigned him, E10, down to ten inches and—finding nothing, having secured and documented it in the manner she'd demonstrated—he had moved on to the adjoining square, E9. It was toward this that he pointed.

Nora knelt for a closer look. Clive had carefully removed the carpet of grass in a single section, and excavated down no more than two inches. Something wrinkled and rough was protruding from the soil. At first, Nora thought it might be a saddle or the hide of some animal, but a closer look revealed it was the rotting remains of an old boot. Peering even more closely, she could see toe bones peeking out from within.

"It was so near the surface," he explained, "that I barely did more than remove the grass. A few whisks of the broom, and the earth just fell away."

Nora examined it from various angles. "Might be a burial," she said. "Or it might have just been left where it—where the man—died. The boot leather is the one thing nobody would have eaten: even a starving person knew it was madness to eat the only thing protecting you from the cold and snow."

"Makes sense. But that's not what I brought you here to see." He knelt down beside her. "This is." And, taking up a paintbrush, he turned to a small mound of disturbed dirt at one side of the ancient boot.

Nora watched as the first whisk of the brush exposed a small leather bag, bound with a thong and crumbling into dust. A second gentle whisk revealed where the bag had rotted and split. It revealed the glint of gold.

For a minute, Nora just stared at it. Then she looked at Clive.

"Once I discovered what it was, I covered it back up," he explained. "I wanted you to see it before...before anyone else did."

Nora glanced over her shoulder. Salazar and Jason were on the far side of the old camp, busy with the midden. She looked at Clive. Normally one didn't cover something back up unless it was at the conclusion of the dig, but in this case she nodded her approval.

"What we need to do next is figure out exactly what you've discovered," she said. "And get it out of the ground and under lock and key."

Taking over from Clive, she gently excavated the rest of the square. The earth was just as soft and yielding as Clive had said it was, and within half an hour she'd exposed the lower legs, feet, and crumbling leather boots of what appeared to be two adult men lying side by side, positioned away from the gridded area. Neither the foot bones, the tibias, nor the fibulas showed any sign of dismemberment or cannibalism. In the boots, each man had hidden a pouch of coins. After carefully photographing and recording them in situ, Nora removed the two pouches and placed them on a small conservator's tarp nearby.

"Hey!"

Nora looked over quickly. It was Salazar, waving from the midden heap. "We never ate our lunches. Can we secure things and call it a day?"

She glanced over at Clive. He met her glance, shrugged.

"Bruce, Jason—you finished your quads?"

"Yup!"

"Uploaded all your survey and coordinate data?"

"Sure have."

"Go ahead then, stow your gear and head back. Clive and I will close up the site. You can shut down the network, too—I won't have any more data to add today."

"Okay."

"Tell Maggie to save some dinner for us. We won't be long."

As the two assistants took off their masks, hair nets, and gloves and began to stow their tools, Nora and Clive returned to the moldering leather pouches. Using a thin pair of forceps and a loupe, Nora pried gently at one. It immediately fell apart, revealing five pieces of gold.

With a gloved hand, Clive picked up one of the coins by the edges and turned it around. Even covered with dust and soil, it glinted in the sun.

"It's a ten-dollar gold eagle," he said. He peered closer. "Looks uncirculated, save for a high degree of bag marks. Struck in 1846—from the Philadelphia mint."

"Wolfinger's treasure?" Nora asked.

Taking the forceps from Nora, Clive teased open the remains of both bags. They each held five ten-dollar gold pieces, virtually identical.

"The year is right," he said. "The mint is right. It's just the number that's wrong. There aren't a thousand here—only ten."

"After all this, you're the last one I'd figure for a pessimist."

Clive broke into a smile. "Pessimist? With those coins winking back at me? I don't know about you, but that's what I'd call proof. Now let's find the rest."

"If it's here."

"It will be," said Clive. "Think about it. These two were already suspected of foul play. They were ostracized, not allowed to join the others in their shelter. So they made their own little camp here. And hid their gold somewhere close by. Don't you agree?"

Nora felt a little uncomfortable speculating like this, but she couldn't fault Clive's logic. "I agree."

She picked up the broom and the trowel and went to work on the site, moving quickly but expertly, wasting no time but missing nothing. Within an hour she had both skeletons exposed as far as their rib cages. Not only that, but she had uncovered some exceedingly rotten planks that appeared to be the remains of a small, crude shelter made from wagon pieces.

She sat back on her haunches while Clive used her camera to photograph the exposed portions of the skeletons and the pieces of wood.

"Well?" she asked. "What do you think?"

"You're the archaeologist."

"You're the historian. But okay. Two individuals, both in their thirties, as best I can tell. Their skulls aren't exposed yet, so I can't be sure of the sex, but they appear to be male. No signs of violence so far. No cannibalism, either. Based on the fact that there are two of them placed here together, away from the main group, and judging by the gold on their persons—specifically, 1846 ten-dollar gold eagles hidden in their boots—I would say they are almost certainly Reinhardt and Spitzer."

"All that's missing is the gold. And, like I said, they would've hidden it around here somewhere." Growing more animated, Clive added, "Nora: think what we've accomplished. We've been here less than a week, and look! Not only this—" he gestured at the money pouches— "but the Lost Camp. *The Lost Camp.* And we found it. Or rather, *you* found it."

Nora considered herself an old hand at dirt archaeology, and she'd found several important sites over the years. But this sudden enthusiasm, this praise by an amateur—not an amateur, actually, but a historian who'd made this very discovery his life's work—left her blushing with pleasure.

Without speaking further, they wrapped up the remains of the coin purses and their contents and placed them in an artifact container; secured the grids and exposed skeletons with tarps and fixed them carefully in place; returned to the HQ tent and placed the coins in the strongbox—and then headed down the trail, toward the campsite and dinner.

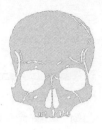

20

May 9

SHORTLY AFTER LUNCH the following day, Nora took a break from working in the dirt. She, Clive, Adelsky, and Salazar had focused on the Spitzer and Reinhardt site all morning. After explaining the discovery to the two assistants, Nora had finished exposing the skeletons, while the others had extended the excavations on either side, stretching out another meter into undisturbed ground. They had taken the entire area down to the 1847 soil horizon and even farther, in case the gold had been buried right at the site. But so far they had found nothing—no gold or any signs of a burial, only ragged scraps of clothing and a few buttons.

After lunch, Clive and the two assistants continued to work in that area. But Nora decided to take a break. Over the course of her career, she had discovered that, from time to time, she had to stop and let an archaeological site speak to her. Just speak. In the midst of digging, sometimes she got so focused on a square meter of dirt that she would start losing the overall story that the site was trying to tell her. That had happened while searching for the gold, and she had to remind herself that it was only a small part of the archaeological treasures the site was yielding.

So now she laid down her trowel and wandered about the site, shutting down the intellectual side of her brain, pushing out thoughts of gold, and "letting the history rise from the earth," as one of her professors had put it. She tried to re-create in her mind the conditions of the site—the drifting snow, the bleak cliffs, the absolute wilderness—and how the people stranded in it were focused on one thing: survival. As she drew in the mountain air and looked around, she got a taste of the strangeness, the isolation, they must have felt. Today, they were a mere fifteen miles from a major interstate highway, yet it still felt like the ends of the earth. In 1847, the travelers would have been farther from civilization than anything conceivable today.

As she wandered around, her footsteps took her to an area down by the creek—the row of parallel grids labeled F that were farthest from the Hackberry trail. Here, in one isolated spot, the magnetometer had registered a small shadow, something unnatural, in or around grid F2. For some reason, this spot spoke to Nora. She wasn't sure why. Maybe she was attracted to it because the place was more pleasant than most in the valley. She had not opened up this grid yet, but she felt it might contain something special, even important. It whispered to her professional instincts of history; of stories long hidden, waiting to be told. And there was something about untouched ground, before the first trowel had bit into the dirt, that seemed almost magical.

Most important, it would take her mind off the search for Wolfinger's gold.

Carefully, she prepared to excavate F2. As she worked, she could hear the low chatter of Adelsky and Salazar floating down from higher ground, where they were finishing up the Spitzer and Reinhardt section—still with no success. Out of the corner of her eye, she could see Clive. He'd wandered away from Adelsky and Salazar and was standing near the far line of trees, hands in his pockets, looking skyward, apparently lost in thought.

As she began work on the grid, carefully sweeping the dirt away, a shadow fell over her. She turned to see Clive, hands still in his pockets.

"Decided to try your luck over here?" he asked.

Nora wiped her forehead with the back of one glove, then nodded.

"Mind if I watch?"

"Not at all."

Clive squatted beside her, careful not to disturb any of the grid lines. He pulled out one of his cigars and lit it up.

"Do you mind?" Nora said, pointing downwind.

"Oh. Sorry." Clive changed position. "I used to be a cigarette fiend, three packs a day. So I switched to cigars—these expensive Dunhills—hoping the cost would keep my habit down."

"That's only the second one I've seen you smoke."

"Yeah. I've cut back over the last couple of years. Now I only smoke to relax, calm my nerves—you know, that kind of thing."

For about five minutes, he watched her work. And then he shook his head. "I've been thinking…" He stopped.

"Thinking what?"

"What a goddamn idiot I've been."

Nora stopped working and sat back on her heels. "Care to tell me why?"

"Those two, Reinhardt and Spitzer, were carrying the gold in their boots. Why?"

"Why do you think?"

"Because that's all the fucking 'treasure' they had."

Clive said this in a low, bitter voice, eyes on the ground. It was the first time Nora had heard him use such profanity. "And how do you figure that?"

"You and I both agree they would have kept the gold close. Well, we just excavated their entire miserable hovel and found nothing."

"Maybe they hid it beneath a nearby tree," Nora said. "Or buried it in the snow."

Clive shook his head. "That's not what my gut tells me."

Nora could hardly believe what she was hearing. "But, Clive, it was you who did the historical research on all this. It was impeccable. You laid it all out, for me and Dr. Fugit, back in her office. Wolfinger withdrew that gold."

Clive puffed on his cigar. "All I found was a withdrawal note. Its details in regards to Wolfinger are, technically, debatable."

"But still, we know there was a robbery and murder."

"Sure, by a couple of jackasses who got a hundred dollars for their trouble. When we first found those coins, I said they looked uncirculated, although with heavier bag marks than usual. But I've thought about that some more. If I'm honest with myself, I have to admit that's not the case. They're scratched, dinged up, far beyond what any bag marks would cause. And do you know why? Because Reinhardt and Spitzer had been walking around with those coins in their boots ever since they killed Wolfinger."

"But—" Nora began, then stopped when she saw the expression on his face.

"They murdered him expecting a fortune—and found only ten gold pieces. Not exactly chump change in 1847, but no treasure, either. It's exactly from such things that legends are born, and this particular legend was just credible enough to gull this particular historian."

"Clive, what makes you think that gold isn't hidden somewhere else—?" Nora began, but Clive cut her off.

"Put yourselves in their shoes for a moment. Think about what you would do."

Nora thought. "I suppose I wouldn't have let it out of my sight."

"Exactly! I made a fatal mistake. I'm a trained historian, and I should have been more careful. I have no excuse."

"What mistake, exactly? Excuse for what?"

"For making an assumption. I assumed Wolfinger made that withdrawal. But Nora, the fact is those bank records were incomplete. Dr. Fugit was right to be skeptical. Sure, Wolfinger made a withdrawal that week—but it was for one hundred dollars. The other nine hundred must have gone out in other withdrawals, lost in the bank's incomplete records. *That's* why Reinhardt and Spitzer divided the gold equally between them— five coins apiece. That's why it was in their boots. And...and that's why I've let you down." As he'd done earlier, he looked up at the sky. "Nora, I'm ashamed. I guaranteed the Institute we'd find that gold—and instead all we have is ten lousy coins."

Nora was silent a moment. Listening to Clive talk, she felt something she hadn't expected: regret. As an archaeologist, she'd always told herself that gold—treasure—didn't matter. After all, *she* wasn't going to get any of it. Here she was, surrounded by the real treasure—an important archaeological discovery—and yet despite her best efforts, she, too, was experiencing more than a pang of disappointment.

She pushed these thoughts away. "Those ten coins are still worth a lot of money," she said.

"Not enough to fund this expedition," Clive said. "And they're not uncirculated. Their historical value might up the price a little, but they're still only worth a thousand dollars each, perhaps a bit more."

"Maybe so. But don't you see? We were never sure we'd find that gold. And the fact is, *it doesn't matter anymore*. We found the Lost Camp. That's what's important. This is going to be such a coup for the Institute that Dr. Fugit will probably be able to raise a lot of money based on the site alone."

"I hope she can," Clive said. "But that doesn't change the fact that I let you down." He dropped his half-finished cigar and ground it out in the grass.

"Better take that away with you."

"Of course. Sorry." Clive wrapped the cigar stub in a tissue. "Here I've interrupted your work, feeling sorry for myself. Go ahead: let's see what's in this grid."

Nora took the whisk and began brushing her way down through the soft soil, removing it with the trowel for later screening. Almost immediately, she felt the whisk encounter an obstruction. She set the whisk aside and resumed work with a paintbrush, brushing in a gentle semicircular motion. A delicate human jawbone appeared—the maxilla.

"Tiny," Clive said.

"It's a child," said Nora. "See the baby teeth? I'd estimate this came from a person six to eight years old." Her voice faltered; in a moment, all thought of the gold was gone.

"There was only one child of that age in the group," Clive murmured, peering closely.

Working slowly, with something close to reverence, Nora continued to brush dirt away from the jaw, freeing it from the earth that had held it prisoner for more than a century and a half.

"Why don't you take pictures while I work, to document this," she murmured.

Clive photographed the jaw from a number of angles. Soon the rest of the skull appeared. It was intact.

Quietly, as if sensing an important discovery, Adelsky and Salazar had left their quads and come to observe.

Working downward, Nora began uncovering cervical verte-brae and a small rib cage. A silver hair clasp appeared, in the shape of a ribbon, with a lock of blond hair wedged in it. Seeing this, she paused. The others were looking on, mesmerized. She could feel the intensity of their gaze as they stared at what were quite clearly the remains of Samantha Carville, the only child in the Lost Camp. The skeleton was lying on its back, skeletal arms folded lovingly across the chest.

Clive broke the silence. "Amazing her hair survived all these years."

"It's the cold," Salazar said. "And the altitude."

Suddenly, Nora realized both her legs had gone to sleep. She stood up with effort, massaging her calves. As she did so, she was startled to notice that someone was standing behind them, at the edge of the clearing.

It was Jack Peel. They had all been so focused on the dis-covery that they hadn't heard his approach. He was wearing a cowboy hat and a long duster, and was staring at them intently.

Nora pulled off her gloves and waved. Adelsky did the same.

For a moment, Peel stood there, half-obscured by shadow. At this distance, his expression was unreadable. Then he raised a hand in acknowledgment, turned, and disappeared into the gloom of the trees, duster billowing behind him as he headed back to camp.

"He's an odd one," said Clive.

Adelsky and Salazar went back to their own tasks and Nora continued working, assisted by Clive, until she had finished the quadrant. At last, she put aside her tools and sighed. A pair of ravens cawed back and forth between two dead trees. A mist began settling down as evening darkened the sky. She gazed upon the delicate skeleton, with its silver clasp and tight braid of golden hair. Only the top part of Samantha was exposed in this quad; the body below the waist ran into the next quad, which Nora had not yet opened. That would be a job for tomorrow.

She reached over, grabbed a tarp, unfurled it, and secured it over the remains of the little girl.

* * *

Dinner around the campfire that evening was a quiet affair. Nora and her crew were bone-tired from the initial work of getting the dig under way. Clive was unusually quiet, and Nora thought he must still be ruminating about the failure to find the gold. Only Maggie seemed to be in her usual high spirits, dishing out extra helpings and needling Adelsky when he couldn't finish his four-alarm chili, the sweat pouring off his brow. The dark came down quickly, and with it, a bitter night chill. Burleson built up the fire, and Maggie, after she'd refreshed everyone's coffee, started in on one of her drawn-out jokes—this particular vulgarism involving a prostitute, a one-eyed parson, and a parrot that spoke French. Nora's mind drifted away, coming back only when a burst of raucous laughter at the punch line interrupted her thoughts. But then she heard Maggie start in on one of her endless speculations about the Donner Party. With a twinge of dismay, Nora realized she was about to tell another ghost story concerning Samantha Carville.

"Maggie," she interjected as mildly as she could, "I don't think this is a good time for a story like that."

Maggie fixed her with a look of mock indignation. "Why not? What else is there to do around a campfire but tell stories?"

"It's just that particular story..." Nora took a deep breath. "We found Samantha Carville's skeleton today."

There was a brief, stunned silence. Maggie was the first to recover. "What about her leg?"

"We've only exposed the top half of her remains," Nora said. She noticed that Peel dug viciously at the coals with a stick, scowling.

Clive came to Nora's assistance. "As for Samantha's leg, Maggie, I like a tall tale as much as anyone, but there's not a shred of historical evidence to support that story. No doubt we'll unearth it tomorrow."

He was stopped by Wiggett, who'd put a warning hand on his shoulder and nodded out into the darkness.

For a moment, there was no sound beyond the crackling fire and the cold wind in the trees. And then Nora heard it: the thud of iron shoes, the snorting of a horse.

Nobody moved.

The slow, thudding steps came closer. And then, abruptly, a figure emerged out of the darkness: a young woman in a heavy jacket and gloves, a palomino horse trailing on a lead behind her.

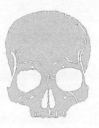

21

THE WOMAN CAME to a stop in the firelight and looked over the group, an uncertain expression on her face. Closer up, she looked even younger than Nora had first thought, with a small upturned nose, pale face, and short brown hair in a choppy but professionally layered pixie cut. She stood just outside the circle, as if respectful of their space. Her body might have been still, but her eyes were busy, taking everything and everyone in.

Burleson rose. "I see you've ridden one of our horses up here," he said.

"I did," the woman said. "I rented it from your ranch. I...I'm sorry to intrude on you like this." She hesitated, then pulled a badge out from under her coat, hanging on a lanyard. "I'm Special Agent Corinne Swanson of the FBI. I'm here as part of an investigation."

Nora stared in disbelief. An FBI agent? This had to be a joke. What kind of investigation would take place out here? Anyway, she didn't look old enough to be an agent—she looked barely out of high school.

Burleson was the first to recover. "Welcome, Agent Swanson." He turned to Wiggett. "Drew, could you please take her horse over to the corral?"

Wiggett got up and took the reins from the woman, leading the horse off into the darkness. Agent Swanson stood there, looking uncertain.

"Well," said Burleson, "won't you sit down?"

"Thanks." She came forward and took a seat in one of the folding chairs around the fire. "We didn't have a way of contacting you in advance. I was hoping to get up here before sunset, but the ride was longer than I imagined. They told me to bring a guide. I should have listened. I got lost once or twice along the way."

She gave them a slight smile and brushed back her short hair. "I imagine you're all wondering what I'm doing here."

"That's an understatement," said Maggie. "Was somebody murdered?" Her tone sounded almost hopeful.

"I'll be glad to explain." The girl—woman—shifted in her chair. Nora wasn't sure what an FBI agent was supposed to look like; she had known only one, and he was obviously in a category all his own, but Agent Swanson was about as far from what she'd imagined as possible.

"I just want to say up front that no one here is suspected of any wrongdoing," she said.

"That's good," said Wiggett, "because I was ready to panic about that damn speeding ticket I tossed two years ago in Utah."

A ripple of forced laughter went around.

"I'm investigating a case involving grave desecration, homicide, and a missing person."

At this the laughter dropped away and a silence fell.

"What does this have to do with us?" Nora asked, speaking up for the first time.

"In the past seven months, three graves have been illegally opened and the remains disturbed. A woman in Arizona has recently gone missing under suspicious circumstances."

"Oh, Lordy," said Maggie, pouring herself another glass of wine.

"It turns out that all the individuals I've just mentioned, including the missing woman, share a commonality."

"Whoa, you said 'graves illegally opened,'" Maggie said. "You mean grave robbing? Did they steal the corpses or something?"

"Well, this information is confidential, but, yes, portions of the remains were removed."

"Holy crap."

"So where do we fit into this?" asked Nora.

"The commonality I referred to. All four individuals were descended from a single person: a man named Parkin."

Nora saw Clive start in surprise. "Albert Parkin?" he asked. "Of the Donner Party?"

"Exactly. And I've been led to understand he's one of the individuals in the camp you're excavating."

"And how did you come by this information, exactly?"

"As a by-product of my investigation into the violated Parkin graves, the family ancestry came to light—including their link to the Donner Party. I learned of your expedition and contacted the president of the Institute, who provided the rest of the details—including a list of the missing persons you hoped to locate."

"But hold on," Nora said. "If Parkin died here, how did he leave any descendants?"

"He abandoned a wife and six children back in Illinois."

"The plot thickens," said Maggie with relish. "But wait—didn't you mention a homicide?"

"A body was found shot to death in one of the disturbed graves. We believe he was hired to uncover the body."

This brought a silence, which the FBI agent eventually broke. "So. Have you identified any remains belonging to Albert Parkin?"

"No," said Nora. "We've only identified three individuals so far: a child, Samantha Carville, and two male adults named Spitzer and Reinhardt. Even those are only provisional IDs, since we've not yet done DNA testing."

"How many individuals have you uncovered?"

"It's hard to say, given the fact that a lot of the bones are broken and commingled. Including the three people I've already mentioned, we've located six partial or complete skulls so far."

"So you may have already uncovered Parkin, but don't yet know it?"

"It's possible."

Clive broke in. "This is very interesting, but I fail to see how what we're doing could be connected to these grave robbings. You've already said that none of us are under suspicion."

At this Swanson shifted, and Nora could see that the veneer of confidence she was trying to project was not very robust. "We're in the information-gathering phase."

"In other words," said Burleson, "it's a fishing expedition."

"It seems quite a coincidence that the very person whose descendants were being dug up illegally was also being dug up at the same time."

"Yes, but dug up *legally*," said Nora. "You've talked to Dr. Fugit. So you obviously know our excavation is fully authorized, with federal and state permits, not to mention being sponsored by one of the leading archaeological institutes in the country."

Swanson responded to this in a level voice. "Tomorrow, I'd like to go to the dig site and examine the human remains. I would also like the opportunity to ask you and your staff a few questions—if you don't mind, of course."

"You're free to ask all the questions you like," said Nora. "But like Clive said, it's hard to imagine what a man's death in 1847 has to do with his descendants getting their graves robbed almost two hundred years later."

"That's exactly what I'm trying to determine."

"This is an active and extremely sensitive archaeological site," Nora said, "and as director of this dig I can't have uncredentialed individuals tramping around, touching things. Shouldn't you have some sort of warrant?"

Swanson said, her voice as flat as a Kansas prairie: "This is federal land. I am a federal agent. I don't need a warrant to search federal property or conduct whatever investigation I see fit. But just to reassure you, I have a master's of science in forensic anthropology from John Jay College of Criminal Justice." She paused. "And from what I know of your CV, posted on the Santa Fe Archaeological Institute website, I am at least as 'credentialed' as you to handle human remains, Dr. Kelly."

Nora stared at the young woman's face in the flickering firelight—determined and yet, at the same time, lacking confidence. For someone so seemingly qualified, she was awfully defensive.

Nora had the sudden insight that this was probably her first case.

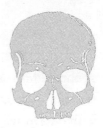

22

May 10

Special Agent Corrie Swanson rose before dawn—as was her habit—and did a hundred sit-ups in her makeshift tent to get the blood flowing before dressing and exiting into the chilly air. Her arrival at breakfast shut everyone up, and she was relieved when they finally set off for the archaeological dig. It lay about half a mile up the trail from the camp. When Corrie arrived, she found the place to be an oppressive-looking valley, shut in by cliffs of dark rock, skirted by broken scree and boulders that had fallen from above. A circle of gloomy peaks, covered in patches and drifts of snow, surrounded them. On the floor of the valley, a number of dead spruce trees were interspersed with patches of sickly grass. There was a small, sad-looking pond at the far side, fringed by rocks. Even though it was midmorning, the sun hadn't yet topped the eastern bluffs and the bowl was still in shadow. The only birds to be seen were a quartet of ravens in a dead tree, cawing back and forth.

She approached the edge of the excavated area, looking out over an expanse of blue tarps pegged to the ground. She thought back to an investigation of human remains she'd stumbled into as a student in Colorado a few years before, and realized she could easily develop a similarly morbid fascination with the Donner ordeal: the twenty-five feet of snow, the starvation so extreme they were forced to eat their own family. Almost unthinkable—but at the same time, a testament to the human will to survive.

The dig and its associated work tent and screening areas were neat and crisp-looking—at least to her inexpert eye. As she took in the site, she couldn't help but wonder if this was a wild goose chase. Morwood certainly felt so. He'd nixed her first two requests, and it was only after continued pestering that he'd finally relented. He'd given her a Friday, plus her own weekend, which with travel time allowed her one full day at the site: today.

But as she continued looking over the meadow, the mystery returned with greater insistence. Why all those Parkins dug up all of a sudden? She had been racking her brains for a hypothesis. Could it be an inheritance issue? No: the descendants of Albert Parkin didn't have significant money, nor was there evidence of family conflict, legal or otherwise. The dead whose graves had been despoiled were all second or third cousins who evidently hadn't even known each other. Could it be related to an obscure medical issue, a rare disease or syndrome that ran in the family line? But there was no evidence for that, either, at least from her search of medical records. Maybe a bizarre form of revenge against the family? Or maybe some obscure religious practice, perhaps with a connection to voodoo?

Every idea she came up with was more outlandish than the one before. The truth was, she had no idea what she should be looking for. But she sure wasn't going to show her uncertainty.

As she surveyed the site, Nora Kelly came over, with the historian, Clive Benton, following.

"So, what do you want to see?" Kelly asked, arms crossed. Her voice carried a note of suspicion.

Corrie tried to muster a firm, confident demeanor. "If you could remove the tarps, I'd like to take a closer look at the remains."

"As you can see, the dig involves several discrete areas. It would be helpful if you could give me some idea of what you're looking for."

Corrie found herself growing defensive at the question. "Dr. Kelly, we are generally not authorized to discuss the details of our cases until we refer them for prosecution."

"If we could narrow down the parameters, it would speed things up. I'd prefer not to uncover the entire site, which would be a waste of your time—and ours."

Corrie nodded to the set of pegged blue tarps at the far end of the site near the tree line. "What's out there?"

"The men I mentioned last night. Spitzer and Reinhardt. They were camped away from the rest."

"And that other, smaller tarp, down by the stream?"

"The remains of Samantha Carville, a young girl who was one of the first to die."

"Only Samantha Carville? Nobody else?"

"Not that we know of. We're still excavating those quads."

Corrie returned her attention to the main part of the dig. "And what about this large area—what does it represent?"

"It's a midden heap, essentially a trash pile. It's where the majority of remains have been discovered so far. We haven't yet uncovered the camp's hearth and shelter, but we think they're over at that gridded area, there."

"Last night you mentioned six skulls. Are the other three in the midden heap?"

"Yes, two males and a female. Along with a great deal of other bones, bits of clothing, boots, and so forth. And remnants of the camp's dogs and oxen, which were of course consumed long before any human beings."

"Could one of those three skulls be Albert Parkin's?"

"It's certainly possible," Dr. Kelly said. "We haven't made any identifications from the midden. Nine people are known to have died up here, so we still have three skulls to find—those of a male and two females. All of the males were adult, so it'll be difficult to identify Parkin without DNA analysis."

Corrie felt a faint sense of satisfaction at the realization that here she had a chance to put this know-it-all in her place. "Really? I don't think Parkin's identification would be difficult—depending on the location of his body."

Nora Kelly uncrossed her arms. "And why is that?"

"He was injured by an arrow during a desert crossing. It broke his collarbone."

"That's correct," the historian, Benton, spoke up. "Indians took potshots at the wagon train at several spots along the route."

"The fracture should still be visible," said Corrie, "healed or not."

Nora said nothing.

"Good. I won't need to look at the outlying sites, just this midden heap. Could you please remove the tarps?"

There was a pause. "As you wish," Kelly said. "We'll take it a few quads at a time—I don't like to leave the bones uncovered and exposed to light for any length of time." She turned to one of her assistants. "Jason, will you and Bruce uncover B3 and B4, please?"

As the two got to work, Nora Kelly pointed to a worktable,

on which sat several boxes. "You'll need to put on nitrile gloves, booties, a mask, and a hair net. And I would ask you please not to touch anything. We're trying to prevent any stray human DNA from contaminating other remains."

"Of course."

The quads were soon exposed and Corrie, now kitted up, brought out a hand magnifier. When she did so, she detected some sniggering from behind and caught a whispered "*Watson, the game is afoot!*"

"These square meters," Nora explained, "expose the center of the midden heap. We think most of the remains are concentrated here."

Swanson gazed over the area. It was a dense aggregate of bones lying willy-nilly, a mixture of partials, with a couple of complete bones, very few articulated, and no complete skeletons. Most lay in what looked to the untrained eye like a broken tangle.

She carefully stepped to the edge of the closest quad and knelt on a board placed there, the smell of fresh earth rising to her nostrils. With the magnifying glass held close to the bones, she could see butchering marks made by iron knives, areas of burning, and rough breaks where the marrow had been scraped out—all classic signs of cannibalism. She took a suite of photographs with her agency-issued camera. The three skulls all showed signs of having been cooked in a fire and broken to extract the brains. Despite their damaged condition, it was obvious they were adults, two men and a woman, as Dr. Kelly had said.

Leaving aside the woman, she focused on the first male skull. It lay in two adjacent pieces with the associated mandible. The cranium showed burn spalling and flaking on the back, where it had been placed in the fire. The other skull lay not far from it and showed a similar pattern of cooking and spalling. The skulls were surrounded by a jumble of other bones and postcranial scrap. Almost all were broken, and some were processed beyond recognition. A few small flags bearing numbers and letters were inserted here and there in the matrix of the midden.

It was a dumping spot for food scraps, where the remains of one stew after another had been discarded over weeks or even months, and many of the bones were covered by others. There was no obvious way to tell which ribs, vertebrae, or collarbones were associated with any particular skull. She did her best to conceal her chagrin; so much for putting Nora Kelly in her place by identifying Parkin's broken collarbone right under her nose.

"As I mentioned last night," Kelly said, "this is an active dig site—with an emphasis on 'active.' As you can see, we still have much to do."

"What about these flags?" Corrie asked, rising and pointing to the small colored markers.

"Those are checksum tags, placed by my team at the start of each new work session. They help in associating the digital information our computer model uses with the physical excavation—matching the data to the dirt, so to speak."

Corrie nodded. This was obviously a professional, well-organized operation. There was nothing she could do for the moment except await further results. And she had to be back in Albuquerque tomorrow.

"I'd really appreciate knowing a little more about your investigation," the archaeologist said. "Whatever you can tell me."

"I really can't go into any more detail than I already have. If you are able to identify Parkin, could you please let me know right away? And of course if you could ensure these remains are properly curated, that would be much appreciated."

When Nora frowned, Corrie realized she had probably come off as condescending, and she added hastily: "Naturally, I don't want to tell you your job. It's just that, since we're not yet sure how Parkin's remains might fit into the investigation, it's vital that they are kept secure."

Kelly nodded. "Anything else?"

"Just keep me in the loop. If Parkin is identified, we might ask for the bones to be turned over to us for analysis. But for now, that's unnecessary."

Nora Kelly asked her two assistants, Salazar and Adelsky, to re-cover the quads.

"I have a few questions for you and Dr. Benton," Corrie said. "If I may?"

"Let's have a seat."

They walked toward the headquarters tent and settled in director's chairs set out under a tarp.

Corrie took out a notebook and pen. "Just to confirm, you've identified the three bodies at the two more distant sites, two adult males and one female child, and in the midden heap you've found three adult skulls, again two male and one female, as yet unidentified."

Dr. Kelly nodded.

"You mentioned nine individuals died in this camp, out of eleven. What happened to the other two?"

"A man named Boardman escaped and managed to get to the Donner's camp, and died there. Another man, Chears, was saved, but he died soon after returning to civilization. Of the nine individuals left, we've found six and identified three."

"Do you expect to find the other three in this midden?"

"We're still excavating the rear section, so it's a little early to say. I wouldn't be surprised if most of the remains are there. We might find one or two additional outliers there, or perhaps at the site of the shelter."

"The shelter?"

"Yes. They built a rude shelter out of wood from the wagons, and inside was a hearth. Our magnetometer survey suggests it's in that area gridded out beyond the midden heap, but we can't be sure until we open it up."

"So Parkin's remains might be there?"

"It's a possibility. There's still an adult male we have not located yet."

Corrie made some notes. "So please tell me: how did this excavation originate?"

"Clive can give you the background."

Benton then proceeded to tell, in exhausting length, the story of how he'd spent years searching for Tamzene Donner's journal; how he'd found it; and how he'd gone to Nora Kelly and the Institute and convinced them to look for the site. Kelly then took over and explained how the excavation had reached this point and what their plans were, going forward. It was all Corrie could do to keep up with the flow of information. Everything seemed aboveboard, with the exception of Benton's theft of the journal—but that was out of her bailiwick and frankly, in his place, she would probably have done the same, at least back in her scofflaw days.

She asked a few more general questions and received equally general answers. She could find nothing the slightest bit suspicious; nothing, at least on the surface, to tie the expedition to her own investigation. She wondered how Morwood would react when she briefed him.

She shut her notebook and looked at her watch. "I've gotten what I need for now. I'd better ride back to town while it's still early. I want to thank you for your cooperation."

She rose and Kelly did likewise. "If you do identify Parkin," Corrie told her, "please remember to let me know. And be careful—there may be no connection, but you never know, and my case does involve a homicide and a probable kidnapping. So be on your guard."

The look of relief on Nora Kelly's face as she shook her hand goodbye was unmistakable.

23

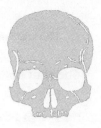

May 11

THE FOLLOWING DAY dawned clear, and the night had been cloudless, allowing Nora and the rest an excellent view of the comet Skip had reminded her of before she set off. Around noon, however, thunderheads began piling up over the surrounding peaks. Nora's first task was to open the quad containing the lower half of Samantha Carville's body. After removing the layer of grassy turf on top and putting it aside, she and Clive began, using paintbrushes and bamboo picks in addition to the ever-present whisks, working with agonizing slowness down through the soil to the level of the bones. As before, the dirt was piled in a tray to be sifted and floated later.

Working even a shallow quad like this was a lesson in patience. Nora was used to it, but Clive was sweating and had a tendency to hurry. While they worked on the Carville quads, Salazar and Adelsky were opening another quad at the edge of the midden heap.

"Easy there, Clive. Those bones aren't going anywhere."

"Sorry," he said. "Curiosity makes me impatient. Does it do that to you?"

"Yes. I had to learn to slow down—just like you need to."

Clive laughed and turned his blue eyes on her. "We seem to have a lot in common, you and me."

Nora said nothing, but Skip's parting words came to her mind unbidden. Opening herself to new people was not being disloyal to Bill. She needed to move past him and get on with her life. She had already dated a couple of losers, but Clive was certainly no loser: smart, a Stanford PhD—but most important for her, someone with real intellectual passions. And he was obviously interested in her.

She found herself coloring at this train of thought and the guilt that it caused in her, and she quickly bent her head to conceal it and continue digging.

"Got something," Clive said.

Nora looked over. It was clearly the leading edge of a small bone.

"I'll take over, if you don't mind." This had become their informal working arrangement, Clive turning over the delicate labor to Nora.

She moved to the spot and began brushing away the dirt, exposing more of the bone, while Clive watched. She could feel his breath on her hair. "Looks like the left patella."

"That's the knee bone, right?"

"Right."

Working down, Nora exposed the bottom of the femur and the top of the tibia, along with a stray button and a scrap of cotton, which she placed in artifact envelopes with tweezers. As she worked down the leg toward the foot, a ragged row of buttons appeared, along with some withered scraps of leather—the girl's tiny button-down boot. Leaving it in situ, Nora worked around it, uncovering the entire left leg. When it was fully exposed, she took a series of photos.

Meanwhile, Clive moved over and began working the opposite side of the quad, loosening the surface with the bamboo pick and gently working the dirt off with the whisk. Nora felt a certain unease as he deepened his half of the quad, exposing more and more of the right leg.

"Oh boy. Here's something else," Clive said, backing away for Nora to look.

It was the right femur. Nora brushed the soil from around what turned out to be a ragged end of bone. Its termination was a splintered mess and there was nothing below. She placed a magnifying stand over it. Deep chop marks from butchering leapt into view.

There was a silence, interrupted by a sound of distant thunder.

"I'll be damned," said Clive. "The legend is true, after all."

Nora sat back and took a deep breath. "The leg's been chopped off with something crude, like a hatchet, right at the knee."

"I can't believe it. The historical record..." Clive's voice trailed off.

There was a silence.

"What do you think?" Nora asked. "Should we tell the team? With Maggie riling people up with her ghost stories, maybe we should keep quiet."

Clive stroked his incipient beard. "They already know we've found the girl's remains. They're going to ask."

"But there's a negative vibe already circulating in the camp," said Nora.

"True. And that damned FBI agent showing up out of nowhere didn't help things."

Nora nodded. "Let's decide later. We should finish excavating the quad on the off chance we can locate Samantha's missing—"

She paused as a shadow fell over the excavation. Jack Peel stood at the edge of the quad, dressed in his long duster, staring down at them, his face creased with mingled sorrow and anger. He slowly raised his arm and pointed at the skeleton with a trembling finger.

"Samantha Carville?"

"Yes," said Nora.

Peel didn't respond. He simply stood there, immobile.

"Is...is there anything in particular you'd like to know?" Nora asked, spooked by the man's intensity.

"I've already heard everything I need to know." And with that, Peel turned and walked fast across the meadow toward the trail, duster flapping behind him.

"If we had any plan to keep this on the down low," said Nora, "it's walking away with that man right now."

"What is it with that guy? He prowls around like an extra from *The Good, the Bad and the Ugly.*"

Nora shrugged. "Let's cover this up. Adelsky is already waving us over for lunch."

Clive looked over. "I swear, for a skinny kid, that guy's got a hell of an appetite. I wouldn't want to be snowbound in a tent with *him.*"

★ ★ ★

After lunch, Clive and Nora resumed work on the quad. "I hope that FBI agent is safely strapped to her desk in Albuquerque by now," Clive said.

Nora worked with her brush. "If she'd identified the Parkin skeleton, she might have shut down the dig—or taken the bones."

"With that jigsaw of a midden heap? Good luck." Clive shook his head. "The look on her face when you had the tarp pulled away was epic."

"Actually, luck is only a part of the equation."

Clive glanced at her. "What do you mean?"

"Meaning parts of the jigsaw puzzle might be easier to put together than you might think."

"How so?"

"You know how we've been plugging all our data into the HQ computer? The Institute purchased the latest, most powerful archaeological software available—I showed you the rudiments on the iPad—and once you get up to speed on its intricacies, it's pretty amazing."

"It must be—you three hunching over your tablets every chance you get."

Nora put down the brush. "I'll show you how it works in a minute."

They walked past the tent to the midden heap, which was still partially covered with tarps. A worktable adjacent to the excavation, in the shade of a tarp, held a variety of equipment as well as a few bones in a tray, removed for specific analysis.

"Help me get this tarp off."

They unpegged a tarp covering the area of the midden heap that Agent Swanson had looked over the day before. Nora donned a fresh pair of gloves and reached into the padded neoprene case where they kept the expedition's twelve-inch iPads.

"As I started to explain the other night, we enter every pertinent detail of the dig into our iPads—survey coordinates, grid points, depth markers, artifact locations, photographs, and so forth. The software crunches all the data, creating an extremely accurate 3-D rendering of every object, placed in a detailed topographic map of the location."

"So you told me."

"But that's only the beginning. We can't access the internet, of course, but using this local VPN, we can communicate with each other and the host laptop via Wi-Fi. Obviously, to conserve power, we use the computer only at specific times, such as when we make our uploads and downloads at the end of each day."

"I was going to ask about that."

"We've got that small generator and solar boosters to charge up all this electronic stuff." With the iPad in hand, she stood at the edge of the midden heap. "As confused as this looks, the AI suite makes sense of it all. The cataloging and mapping software can show us this midden in any number of ways: by depth, by types of artifacts, locations of particular bones, even who exca-vated what and when—all overlaid on X, Y, and Z axes. You can also slice the midden heap any which way to look at a cross-section."

Nora showed Clive a wireframe image of the midden. As he looked on, she swiveled it in various directions. In turn, the screen displayed sections illuminated in different colors.

"Looks like an Atari arcade game," Clive said.

Nora laughed. "It means a lot of work up front, inputting the data, but once that's done we're able to do stuff that would have been impossible even a few years ago." Using the iPad's stylus, she made some markings, tapped a few icons. On the screen, one wireframe section of the midden was suddenly highlighted in green: irregularly shaped, filled with darker green shapes. The rest of the midden receded to gray.

"This is the section Jason worked on two days ago," she said. "The dark areas are individual artifacts. Extensive metadata exists for each one." She tapped one dot at random with her stylus, and immediately the screen zoomed in on it in 3-D, showing what looked like an old wooden button, with a panel of text scrolling up one edge of the display.

"So you actually know who dug up what, and when?"

"Yes. And more than that—the AI is powerful enough to help us reassemble artifacts. At a Paleolithic dig site, it could reverse-engineer a scattering of flint flakes into the original point they were struck from. Here—as an example, I'm going to ask the software to locate all the metatarsal bones and likely fragments it can. Watch."

She tapped with the stylus and the screen changed once more, zooming out to show the surface of the midden, several bones highlighted in green and blue.

Clive whistled. "I'm beginning to see what you meant about the jigsaw puzzle."

"Now," said Nora, "I'm going to ask it to locate all the clavicles we've unearthed."

Nora tapped the screen again. This time, instead of a particular cross-section, a small scattering of bone shapes and fragments were highlighted.

"You'll see there are a total of eleven pieces, none intact. Note how in at least two instances they tend to be clumped together—these three pieces, here, and those four over there. And now, let's look at them in reality."

Walking over to the midden, and using the tablet as a guide, she carefully removed three bone fragments from the matrix with a gloved hand. Then she set them on a black velvet cloth in a specimen tray atop the worktable. Putting the iPad aside, she examined the pieces closely, moving them this way and that with her gloves. After a moment, she managed to fit them together.

"See?" she said.

"That's incredible," said Clive. "You've reassembled somebody's collarbone—just like that!"

"Not 'just like that.'" Nora smiled. "This is the result of meticulous excavation, good data entry and documentation, months of software training, years of classwork—and, of course, good financing." She pointed at the broken collarbone. "No signs of recent fracture here." Picking them up, she returned to the midden, knelt, and carefully replaced them where they had originally been.

"You're just going to put them back?" Clive asked in disbelief. "Now that you've established those pieces form a single bone?"

"Of course. The pieces belong in their original locations—for now. That's the beauty of this method. We are documenting every millimeter of the site so precisely that, if we wanted, we could re-create it in software at any time—long after it's been backfilled and the bones put in their final resting places."

"So... can you identify other clavicle bones?"

"You mean, like Parkin's? Let's see."

She consulted the tablet once again, then—using it as a guide—moved to a different section of the midden and, over the course of several minutes, removed four more fragments of bone: the other cluster identified by the software. She laid them out on the cloth, brushed them off gently with a paintbrush, fitted them together, and then looked at them with a loupe.

"Poor old Parkin," she murmured. "That looks painful."

"You mean—?" Clive began.

He fell silent as Nora handed him the loupe. He leaned in to look at the bones himself.

"My God," he murmured. "Is that what I think it is?"

Nora nodded. "A sharp nick in the bone, no doubt made by an arrowhead, with a partial fracture, almost healed."

Clive straightened. "Incredible. But can we find the rest of him?"

"Let's see." Nora applied herself to the tablet again. After a moment, she showed it to Clive. "I'll ask the computer to assemble—based on bone placement, anatomical analysis, and other relevant factors—the best fit of bones to go with this clavicle."

She consulted the iPad again. Now the display lit up with additional bones and pieces of bone, outlined in green. She turned back to the midden, gently removed three large pieces of a skull, plus a jawbone, and brought them over, placing them on the velvet cloth next to the clavicle. They consisted of the maxilla and lower face, the relatively intact cranium, and most of the occipital bone and mastoid process. Missing was only an orbit. The cranium displayed a distinctive star-shaped imprint on one temple: a sign of being bashed on the head, either how he died or the initial attempt by survivors to get at his brain.

"So this..." Clive paused. "This is—?"

"Allow me to introduce Mr. Albert Parkin."

Clive exhaled. "Wow."

"It'll take a DNA test to be sure, but I think we can find some confirming evidence in these butcher marks." She pointed at the pieces of collarbone. "As that FBI agent examined the midden, I noticed her observing the cut marks. And I knew why. You see, when someone is butchering with a single tool, the tool leaves its own telltale marks. Look." Nora handed

Clive the loupe again. "See how the cut marks look the same, here, and here—and then again here?" She pointed first to two pieces of the collarbone, then the cranium. "It's textbook." She reached for the section of jawbone, held it up beside the skull. "And notice how the condyle matches up with the mandibular process."

"You mean, how well the jaw fits in there? I see."

Nora carefully returned the bones to their respective places in the midden and covered it all with the tarp. When she was done, she turned and gave him a smile. "What were you saying about luck?"

Clive just shook his head in amazement. "But how sure are you?"

"Well, I'm ninety-nine percent sure."

In the silence that followed, Nora could see Clive's brows contract.

"What is it?"

"It's just that... well, what are we going to do now? Swanson asked us to tell her if we identify Parkin. I mean, you could've done this identification yesterday for her—right?"

"There was no way to know unless I actually attempted it. But yes—probably. And then what? Have her take the bones and possibly shut down the site, to boot?"

"But... it's the FBI," said Clive. "You don't want to be accused of withholding evidence."

"Here's how I see it. Is this truly Parkin?"

"Well, you just said—"

"I said I was *ninety-nine percent* sure. To truly identify Parkin, we need DNA confirmation in the lab, after the excavation phase is complete."

"Okay... But—"

"But if I'd given that demonstration to Swanson yesterday, we'd still have no *proof* this is Parkin, and it would have caused our expedition a lot of trouble."

"I understand."

But Nora wasn't finished. "Here's the bottom line. Up until five minutes ago, I had no idea who those bones belonged to. Lacking DNA testing, I still don't."

"I get it."

Nora looked at him, a little surprised by the expression on his face. "Don't tell me you have a problem with this?"

There was another rumble of thunder and a dark cloud blotted out the sun, plunging the valley into shadow. Nora waited as a silence descended. Slowly, the look on Clive's face changed to a smile. "I believe that what I just witnessed was a hypothetical example of a hypothetical identification," he said at last. "Nothing worth reporting until we know for sure."

The sense of guilt Nora had been feeling eased off a little. "Exactly. And we'll keep Agent Swanson in the loop, as promised. As soon as the excavation phase is complete and we have a DNA identification back in the lab, we'll let her know."

The wind picked up, rattling the dead branches of the trees.

"Come on," she said, taking a quick glance at the sky. "Let's get this site secured and head for camp. Looks like it's going to pour any minute."

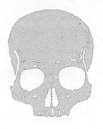

24

THAT NIGHT, THEY all sat around the fire after dinner. Maggie chunked on another log, sending a swirl of sparks upward. There had been a brief, savage thunderstorm, but the sky was now clearing, the stars appearing. The mood in camp was somber and uneasy, but Nora didn't think it had much to do with Agent Swanson's visit. She guessed Peel had said something to his co-workers about Samantha Carville.

Maggie was silent, without her usual chatter and ghost stories—and her guitar remained in its case. Peel had skipped dinner and was nowhere to be seen. That, too, made Nora apprehensive.

As if summoned by her thoughts, Peel abruptly walked in from the darkness, carrying a blunt stick in one hand and his bowie knife in the other. He sat down on a log, staring into the fire. After a moment he started whittling, not making anything but just peeling off strips of wood. The conversation, already sporadic, quickly faltered.

Into the silence, Peel spoke in a low voice. "I've got a question. For the archaeologists."

Here it comes, thought Nora.

"Those human remains up there—what's going to happen to them?"

"Well," said Nora, "once they are fully documented on-site, we'll remove them, do additional study in the lab, and then see them reburied."

"What does that mean, *additional study?*"

"Extract DNA, identify who they are by name, and look for signs of disease, starvation, cannibalism, and a host of other factors. We'll try to identify descendants and work with their wishes for a respectful reburial."

The bowie knife slowly carved off a long strip. "And that little one you've uncovered up there—Samantha—what's going to happen to her?"

"First, we have to make one hundred percent sure it really is her. And then, as I said, she'll be given a proper burial."

Another strip came off. "And why weren't they given a *proper* Christian burial back then? Why were the bones left lying around?"

There was a silence. Nora glanced at Clive.

"I can answer that question," Clive said. "When a member of the relief team reached the Lost Camp in the spring of 1847, the snow was still twenty feet deep. You couldn't bury anyone in those conditions. And there was no way to haul out the remains. It was all the man could do to rescue the one survivor, Chears."

"Why didn't they come back later and bury them?"

"This was exceedingly remote country at that time. One reason might have been superstition—a fear of lingering evil, perhaps, or revulsion at what happened. The rescuers saw scenes of appalling horror at the camps, and the newspapers sensationalized it to the hilt. That deterred others from coming up here after the snows melted."

"And so the bones were left unburied for one hundred and seventy-five years."

"That's unfortunately correct."

Another long strip curled off and landed at Peel's feet. "So this rescuer—what did he find when he got up here?"

"Josiah Best was his name. He never left a written record of what he found. However, he did mention it—briefly—to a couple of people after bringing Chears back to the main camp at Truckee Lake. After that, he apparently never spoke of it again, nor did he make note of the location—which is why the camp was lost these many years."

"What exactly did he see, this Best?"

At this, Burleson broke in. "Jack, are these questions really necessary? It's been a long day."

"We're up here because of the Lost Camp, and I'd like to know what's going on. There's no reason to be hiding anything from us—but when I was up earlier, there they were, hiding the body of Samantha Carville from me."

"Just a minute," Nora said. "Nobody was hiding anything. Covering an excavation is standard procedure."

"There's nothing secret," Clive said. "The problem with Best's account is, as I said, he didn't write it down. All we have are secondhand reports, which were later collected by a newspaper reporter and written up as if in the first person. The oral reports of what Best originally said have been lost, which makes the reporter's article a thirdhand conflation. There's no way to know how accurate it is—or how embellished."

Peel stared at him. "So what did it say?"

"The newspaper account? You want me to read it?"

"Yes," Peel said.

Clive got up and went over to his tent, then returned a moment later with a notebook. He turned on his headlamp, opened the notebook, cleared his throat, and began to read.

The Lost Camp was the most appalling spectacle ever to greet my eyes. A crude shelter had been erected from wagon boards, almost entirely buried in snow, with an entrance like a hole, trampled and stained with human blood. Bones lay scattered around as so much trash. Inside the hut was an iron kettle setting on a dead fire, containing a foot and a head split from top to bottom. The face was unrecognizable. In one corner of the shelter a scalp had been flung, a mass of black hair tied in a bun, which I took to mean the remains of the poor soul in the pot were of a woman. In another corner were two corpses. Mr. Chears was outside, heedless of the elements and singing to himself. He was fashioning something out of pieces of bone, but did not object when I raised him to his feet and tied on snowshoes for the journey out. He never to my knowledge spoke a word of sense while I was there or after. It looked as if the devil himself had unleashed hell upon that bloody ground. I never in my life witnessed such a dreadful thing and I pray never to see the like of it again.

A horrified silence fell on the group. Nora wished Peel had not pushed for this grisly passage to be read, but it seemed Clive had done the best he could under the circumstances.

At last, Peel spoke again, his voice quiet. "Why isn't there a clergyman up here? To oversee the handling of these remains?"

"Once we've confirmed the identities back in the lab," Nora

said, "we'll involve clergy. As I said, the remains will be interred with the appropriate religious rites, according to the wishes of their descendants. Or in the case where there are no descendants, the State of California will make the reburial decisions."

"After 9/11," said Peel, "they had clergy on call for whenever human remains were found. But here, it seems to me you scientists are digging these folks up with no respect or consideration of their immortal souls."

"Jack," said Burleson sharply. "I was very clear with everyone what we were going to be doing up here. It's a little late to be registering objections."

Peel turned to him. "I didn't realize it involved *this*."

"That should have been obvious," said Burleson angrily.

"I'm sympathetic to Jack's sentiments," said Nora, intervening. "And as I said, we plan to involve clergy. But not until we've finished. This area is too difficult, logistically, to bring in anyone. We don't even know the faith of most of these victims—whether Protestant or Catholic, or perhaps Jewish."

"You're messing around with some powerful stuff," said Peel. "And you can sugarcoat it all you want, but it sounds an awful lot like desecration to me. The consumption of human flesh, that talk of hell on earth, the people going mad, the bodies unburied. This is the devil's playground. Ever since I got here, I've had a bad feeling about this godless place. And nothing any of you all have said—or done—has made it go away."

Nora's feeling of apprehension rose. She'd never considered such serious objections might be raised. "I realize the details are disturbing," she said, trying to keep her voice calm. "As archaeologists, we're only trying to understand what happened. We're not desecrating anything."

Jack Peel stood up. "This isn't right."

Clive suddenly spoke again. "As a descendant of one of the Donner Party families," he said, voice rising in anger, "I resent your attitude. *I* want to know the truth, all of it, even the worst. Voltaire once said, 'To the living we owe respect, but to the dead we owe only the truth.' And that's the way we can best serve these people's memories—by learning their stories. I'm not going to let some Bible-thumping wrangler tell me what's right and what isn't."

Peel stared at him for a long moment. Then he slowly holstered his bowie knife, tossed his stick into the fire, and turned and walked off into the night.

Burleson turned to Clive. "I'm sorry. I had no inkling of this. I can't have this kind of disruption on my team. I'll replace Peel."

"Let's not do anything hasty," said Nora. "Let's see how things stand in the morning."

As they broke up to go back to their tents, Nora turned to Clive. "What the hell's gotten into you?" she asked in a low voice. "Riling up Peel the way you did? You think that's going to help?"

"I can't stand these sanctimonious religious types, dictating to scientists what they can and can't do."

"Sanctimonious," said Nora angrily. "That's rich, coming from you—*and* Voltaire. Well, you can pat yourself on the back for standing up for science—and royally screwing up in the process."

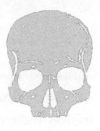

25

May 12

Nora awoke well before dawn to hear Burleson talking in a raised voice to Wiggett. From the tone, she knew immediately something was wrong. She dragged herself from her sleeping bag, dressed, and went outside. The breakfast fire was just lit and Maggie was working on a Dutch oven full of biscuit dough. Clive and her two assistants had yet to emerge from their tents.

"What's going on?" Nora asked.

"Peel's gone," Burleson said. "Packed and left during the night. Seems like he quit."

"I can't say I'm all that surprised," said Nora.

"I'll bring another horse wrangler up from the ranch. No worries about that. It's just a goddamned annoyance. Peel was a fine wrangler—too bad he got so self-righteous and worked up."

The party gradually assembled around the fire, and they ate breakfast as the sun broke over the trees and a cloudless day dawned. *A good day to work*, Nora thought. With the excavation of the midden heap nearing completion, they could move on to opening up the shelter and hearth area of the camp. There would undoubtedly be a concentration of artifacts and bone fragments there, a mother lode of sorts.

She and Clive filled their day packs with lunch, water, and a few tools, then set off with Adelsky and Salazar. The usual ravens followed them as they hiked, cawing their displeasure. When they arrived, the valley was still in shadow, a cold mist rising in tendrils from its grassy floor.

Suddenly Clive's voice broke through the cawing. "What the hell?" he burst out.

They had just rounded a bend, bringing the meadow into sight. Even from this distance, Nora could see that several of the tarps had been pulled aside and were lying loose.

They broke into a jog. The tarps covering the midden were askew, the pegs pulled up. For a moment, Nora thought the previous evening's thunderstorm might have done the damage—but then she noticed fresh hoof marks and boot prints around the muddy site.

"A horse has been up here," she said. "Walking all over the damn place."

"We've been robbed!" Clive cried out as they reached the edge of the midden, now exposed to the elements.

Nora stared in dismay. The midden had been badly disturbed. All three skulls they'd found were missing, as well as several of the larger bones and bone fragments—literally ripped out of the ground. Boot prints could be seen everywhere.

Nora looked around wildly. Down by the stream, the tarp that covered Carville's body was also askew.

"Oh, no." She rushed down with Clive and the others. The little skeleton was gone—every last bone picked cleanly out of the earth.

"Peel," said Clive. "That son of a bitch did this."

"He must have taken them for reburial," Nora said.

She glanced over at the shocked faces of Adelsky and Salazar. This was an almost unthinkable development. A stain on her professionalism, a scandal for the Institute—and, potentially, a flat-out archaeological disaster.

"The strongbox," Clive said. "I wonder if he took that, too." He jogged off to the HQ tent while Nora continued to assess the damage. The area with Reinhardt and Spitzer hadn't been touched, at least, its tarp still pegged down. But quite a few of the more intact bones were missing from the midden, and— almost as bad—the site had been seriously contaminated.

Clive emerged from the tent. "The gold's still there."

Nora turned to her assistants. "Jason, Bruce, please rephotograph the entire site, and document the boot and hoofprints as well—then stabilize and tarp down everything as best you can. Clive and I will go back to camp and report this."

As they walked down the trail, Clive asked: "What next?"

"What next? Next we call the Forest Service and report the theft. And then . . . I'll have to call the Institute."

Clive was silent for a moment before speaking again. "I agree you have to call the Institute. But don't you think it's a little premature to call in the authorities?"

"Why?"

"You spelled it out yesterday. As soon as you report it, that Agent Swanson is going to be back up here, all hot and bothered. And maybe shut us down."

Nora cursed under her breath, recalling that Parkin's skull was among the three taken. "But how can we avoid reporting it?"

"It's likely the value of those stolen bones is under a thousand dollars, which would make stealing them a misdemeanor."

"Less than a thousand dollars?" Nora said. "Those relics are priceless."

"To you and me, yes. Not so much to the local police. Most likely, this would be viewed as a misdemeanor violation of the National Historic Preservation Act of 1966."

"What about the Antiquities Act?"

"Look, Nora, let's not go off half-cocked. Let's see what Burleson says. Maybe Peel hasn't gone far. Maybe he's going to show up in town and turn the bones in to some priest or something."

Nora sighed. "Okay. Good point. Let's see what Burleson has to say before we decide anything."

* * *

Back at camp, Burleson was beside himself with fury when he heard about the desecration and looting. The lanky man stomped around, letting fly a string of curses that shocked even Nora. He turned and collared Wiggett. "Saddle our horses. We're going after Peel. Catch that damn-fool son of a bitch and get your bones back. I mean, it's not like the sheriff would get off his fat ass for something like this."

Nora exchanged a look with Clive.

Burleson took a deep breath, calming down. "What do you think Peel's going to do with those bones? He's not going to sell them, and he's not going to destroy them. I'll call my staff at Red Mountain Ranch. They'll talk to the local clergy, stake out Peel's house, watch the trail exit, maybe the nearby cemeteries—there's only two of those, after all. We'll get your bones back. Give me forty-eight hours and then, if we haven't resolved this, we'll call in the cavalry."

"Thank you," Nora said.

"I apologize again for Peel's behavior. Meanwhile, let's keep the specifics—his looting of the bones, I mean—between us. No point in agitating Maggie and Drew more than they already are."

Nora nodded.

"One thing you can be sure of: Peel is taking tender care of those artifacts."

Nora hoped Burleson was right, and that Peel and his stolen loot would be back in short order. She let him get on the satellite phone and notify his people at the ranch. Then she and Clive watched as the man saddled up and rode off with the assistant wrangler.

"You know," Clive said as the two riders disappeared, "there were a lot of things to worry about with this project, but I never expected something like *this*."

Nora sighed as she reached for the sat phone. "I guess I'd better call the Institute."

Clive groaned. "The optics of this are terrible. First, I promised them twenty million in gold and all we found were ten dinged-up coins." He paused. "And now a good portion of the artifacts have been stolen. I'm sure glad I don't have to make that call."

"Thanks," said Nora sarcastically as she dialed the Institute.

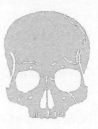

26

An hour later, Nora and Clive hiked back up to the dig site. Nora's conversation with Dr. Fugit had not been pretty. After hearing about the theft, the president had delivered a chilly lecture on security and professionalism. And then she asked about the gold, and Nora had to admit they'd found only ten coins so far and there was a good chance no more existed. Fugit seemed even more upset about this than about the stolen bones and threatened to shut down the excavation entirely. In fact, she was going to call an emergency meeting of the trustees to discuss just that.

A total disaster.

As Nora looked over the site, Adelsky brought over the list of specific damages to the individual quads. Nora felt, if not exactly relief, a little less sick to her stomach. It wasn't quite as bad as it had seemed at first. Peel had tampered with six of the quads—the four that made up the front face of the midden heap and the two containing the skeleton of the Carville girl. He hadn't touched Spitzer and Reinhardt, the rear of the midden, or the test quads they'd done some preliminary work on.

"We noticed something odd," said Adelsky. "The midden heap is all messed up, the bones pulled out higgledy-piggledy, boot prints all over. But the Carville bones were taken out piece by piece, with the utmost care—and with no boot prints in the excavated area."

He took Nora over to the Carville quads. Nora peered in. "It looks as if that skeleton simply got up and walked off on its own."

"Maybe it did," Salazar said with a snort.

Nora grimaced. "Hey, Clive, take a look at this."

Clive came over. He frowned, looking into the shallow hole. "Maybe he was more careful because it was a child—and the skeleton was almost intact."

"Or," said Nora, "perhaps Peel took the Carville bones first and then, while he was collecting bones from the midden heap, he realized it was taking him too long, or he thought he heard someone coming, and began to rush things."

"Maybe," said Clive. "What now?"

"I think we'd better remove any artifacts of value," she said, "and lock them in the strongbox. I don't want the chance of any more thefts."

"Agreed," Clive said.

There weren't many: a gold medallion, a silver cross, some gold and silver rings, and a silver belt buckle. Nora used tweezers to remove each one from its matrix of soil and place it into a labeled artifact bag. Then she carried them into the work tent. She opened the strongbox and took out the plastic container with the ten gold coins, and then—on a whim—unlatched the container's lid. They were all there, gleaming, nestled in the withered and split remains of the leather pouches that had once held them. One at a time, she took out each coin, laid it in a specimen tray, and examined it. All were ten-dollar gold eagles minted in Philadelphia, uncirculated when withdrawn from the bank, but scratched and dented after having been carried inside boots for a couple of months.

"Sad, isn't it," said Clive, peering over her shoulder. "Pretty low grade from a numismatic point of view."

"Yeah. Funny how the rumor grew—that Wolfinger was carrying a fortune. They murdered him over a hundred dollars."

"They were fooled. Just like we were."

A silence fell over the work tent as Nora looked at the coins. All dated 1846. Out of nowhere an idea began to form in her head. A strange idea.

She turned to Clive. "Remind me, please. When you found that Independence bank ledger, you said a withdrawal of a thousand ten-dollar coins had been made. Correct?"

"Not exactly. The ledger indicated the bank had received a thousand coins in anticipation of a withdrawal. But beyond that, the records were damaged. I couldn't determine who withdrew the money, whether it was a single person or many people. I only know Wolfinger made a withdrawal because of that note from the bank."

"Were other people listed? Who'd made withdrawals that week, I mean?"

"It's possible, but as I told you and Dr. Fugit, those ledger pages were spoiled by silverfish. I assumed Wolfinger had withdrawn the entire ten thousand in preparation for his trip west. That was my big mistake."

"Let me put this a different way. When we found only ten coins on Spitzer and Reinhardt, and nothing else in their camp, we decided that's all there was."

"Seemed logical."

"What happens if, instead, we assume Wolfinger did withdraw a thousand coins?"

Clive shrugged, as if to humor her. "So where are they?"

"Hold on and let me finish. If we assume Spitzer and Reinhardt did steal a chest with a thousand coins, what would they do? Hide it, of course. But before they hid it, they'd take some money out and keep it on their persons."

Clive shook his head. "If that was the case, why would they be carrying around any money at all, when they had no place to spend it?"

"Because *they anticipated being rescued*. They would need that money when they got to California, so they could outfit an expedition to come back and retrieve the rest."

Clive looked at her.

"Think about it. If they didn't have some gold on their persons, they'd arrive in civilization destitute." She gestured toward the coins. "These coins aren't evidence that Wolfinger's treasure doesn't exist—but that it *does*."

Clive was silent a long moment, thinking. "You know, that makes a lot of sense. But then why didn't we find the strongbox at their campsite?"

"Because they hid it well. They weren't going to leave it lying around their camp or hidden in the snow nearby. They'd put it in a place where they could come back and get it later without fear of someone else finding it. Especially after the snow melted."

"Nora? Clive?" A voice boomed out. They turned to see Burleson in the doorway to the tent. He was staring at the coins spread out on the tray.

A silence settled.

He stepped inside. "Drew and I tried to catch up to Peel,

but with no luck. It seems that instead of going directly down the trail to town, he took some other route through the mountains." He pushed his hat back on his head. "I've got Wiggett tracking him, and I've got Red Mountain staff on horseback looking to intercept him if he emerges on any of the Forest Service roads around Truckee. One way or another, you'll get your bones back."

His gaze swiveled up slowly toward their faces. "Now. What's with the gold?"

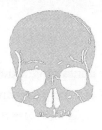

27

W<small>HAT ABOUT IT?</small>" Nora said, after a moment.

"What *about* it? Looks like you all found yourselves some treasure."

"It's not treasure. These are artifacts, just like the bones, and they don't belong to us. We found these coins on two of the victims—they were carrying them in their boots. We also found some gold jewelry and rings. No big deal."

Burleson fixed her with his eye. His face was slightly flushed. "That doesn't quite square with what I heard outside this tent a moment ago. Something about a thousand gold coins in a chest?"

"You were eavesdropping?" Nora asked.

"You were talking loudly enough for me to hear what you were saying." Burleson paused. "Sounds like you've been keeping me in the dark—and I have a feeling it has to do with that gold right there in that tray."

Nora reddened and tried to formulate an answer as she returned the coins to their plastic case. "I'm sorry we had to deceive you. The fact is, we knew from the outset that a chest containing a thousand gold coins might be hidden somewhere around here. But all we've found so far are these ten coins."

"Then why the deception?"

"Not deception," said Clive. "We were simply trying to keep sensitive information confidential."

"So how much is it worth?" Burleson's voice was getting louder. "This chest of gold you didn't tell us about?"

Nora glanced at Clive. The cat was out of the bag. "About twenty million dollars—in numismatic value," she said. "But none of it belongs to us. If the gold *is* found, it gets divided among the feds, the state of California, and the Institute. It's written into our excavation permits—all legal and aboveboard."

"Legal, maybe, but sure as hell not 'aboveboard.' You've kept us in the dark, and I for one don't appreciate it. My people are on edge as it is, what with Peel riding off and all this wild talk of ghosts."

"If they're already on edge," Nora said, "what do you think would happen if word got out that twenty million dollars in gold might be hidden up here?"

"There wouldn't be a problem if you'd been up front from the beginning. You've been feeding us bullshit, Nora. You should have trusted me."

"Hey, just take it easy," said Clive, stepping forward. "Don't talk to her like that."

Burleson whirled on him. "No, *you* take it easy, mister. I've suspected something underhanded was going on here, and so has my team. Now we know what it is."

"Maybe you should have kept better control of your 'team,' then, instead of letting one of them destroy a priceless archaeological site."

Burleson stepped forward, fists clenched. "Why, you little turd."

"I'm not fighting you, old man," Clive said with a sarcastic laugh. He skipped back just as Burleson, now enraged, took a swing at him.

"Going to have to do better than that," Clive said.

"Stop it!" Nora grabbed Burleson's arm. "What do you think you're doing?"

"Teaching this shitbag a lesson."

"You want to get charged with assault? You should know better!"

"Or is it your temper that got you in trouble and forced your abrupt career change?" Clive demanded.

Burleson stood there, breathing hard, a vein throbbing in his forehead. "What the devil are you talking about? How dare you!"

The sound of a galloping horse reached them, approaching quickly. All three froze. The thundering of hooves came right up to the tent, then the animal shivered to a halt with a loud blowing and stomping.

"What the hell?" Burleson swung around and strode out of the tent, Nora and Clive following.

It was Prince, Peel's horse, terrified, eyes rolling. It pranced about in agitation, lathered up, the saddle turned over and hanging down, much battered. The animal was trailing his lead rope, which was frayed and caught up with brush. Burleson approached him, hand out, moving slowly and speaking in a soothing voice.

"Easy now, Prince. Easy. It's all right."

He approached the horse. It danced away a bit, ears flattened.

"Easy, there."

He gently took up the dragging lead rope and followed it up to the horse's head, stroking his neck. The horse began to calm down. Adelsky and Salazar watched from a distance. Working gently, Burleson undid the latigo of the saddle and let the saddle slip to the ground.

"This riderless horse—what does it mean?" Nora asked.

Burleson led the horse away without responding, his face still inflamed from the exchange. He stalked off toward the trees and down the path, leading the horse with one hand and carrying the saddle under his other arm.

There was a long silence. And then Clive said, "Guy's got a frigging temper."

"I suppose. But what did you expect? The fact is, we *have* been deceptive. And you egged him on. What was that business about his career change?"

"I just wonder how come a guy like that, making tons of money as a high-powered divorce lawyer, suddenly gives it all up for some horse ranch?"

"I'm worried about that horse and what it might mean for Peel. I hope he isn't out there lost in the mountains."

"His own damn fault," said Clive.

Nora sighed. What had started out as a textbook-perfect archaeological dig was rapidly turning into a nightmare.

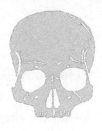

28

That evening around the fire, the riderless horse was the talk of the camp.

Maggie vigorously stirred a pot of beef stew, talking almost nonstop. "I think Peel got thrown and is out there somewhere, hurt, maybe even dying."

"I disagree," said Burleson. "I think Peel got to wherever he was going, slapped Prince on the rump, and sent him back. A horse, as everyone knows, will retrace its route if set loose."

"How do you know that's what he did?"

"Because he's a damn good rider, and it's not likely he'd be thrown."

"What do you mean by 'wherever he was going'? Like *where?*"

This caused a momentary silence.

Burleson finally sighed. "Well, the answer to that opens up a whole can of worms. Doesn't it, Nora?" And he glanced her way.

Nora nodded. She understood the look. Earlier, Burleson had wanted to keep Peel's theft from the rest of the crew—but with his horse returning carrying nothing but an inverted saddle, there was no longer any point in doing so. "When we went up to the site this morning," she said, "we found it had been robbed."

"What?" Maggie said. "*Robbed?*"

"It looks like Peel decided to take some of the bones. We think perhaps to rebury them or, at the very least, prevent them from being studied."

"Which bones?" Maggie asked.

"Several of the more intact bones we've uncovered so far—in particular, the skeleton of Samantha Carville."

"He stole Samantha? *All* of her?"

Nora hesitated. "So it seems. Well…except the missing leg bone."

There was a silence.

"God*damn*," Wiggett muttered.

"Maybe we should open a bottle of wine," said Burleson—in almost the same soothing voice he'd used with the horse— "and all join in a glass."

Hearing this, Nora felt a sudden tickle of alarm—despite, or perhaps because of, Burleson's calm voice.

"That's the best suggestion I've heard all week," said Maggie, covering the simmering stew and sitting herself down in a chair by the fire.

Burleson produced a couple of bottles of wine from his stash, opened them, and filled everyone's tin cups. He settled himself in his own chair and looked around. "First, I want you all to know my men at the ranch have been alerted, and it's only a matter of time until they find Peel. We don't want to involve the police unless we have to—Jack may have some strong religious beliefs, but at heart he's no thief. I'd rather we found him ourselves and talked some sense into him than see him put in jail."

"How do you know it's him who stole the bones?" asked Wiggett. He looked a little put out, having spent a good part of the day looking for Peel without being told the real reason why.

"We found his boot and horse prints all around the site," said Clive.

"Well, I'll be damned," said Maggie. "Still waters run deep, that's what I always say. To think that poor girl, after all she'd been through in her short life, disturbed again..." She took a swig of wine.

Burleson gently interrupted. "And now there's something else I think you deserve to know. Something I myself just learned this afternoon. Nora will explain."

And he gave her another look, different this time. This one had something of a warning in it.

She felt Clive begin to stir beside her, preparing to object, but she put a hand on his arm. At this point, with the expedition in disarray, it all might as well come out. She took a deep sip of wine.

"There's more to the story of the Donner Party than you've heard," she began. "During their journey, rumors started to swirl that one pioneer named Wolfinger was carrying a chest of gold coins. At a certain point he was murdered by two fellow travelers, who stole the chest and told everyone Wolfinger had been killed by Indians. I guess that later, the Donner tragedy itself became so infamous people forgot about the possibility that the gold might still be around somewhere, hidden by the killers before they died of starvation. Historians certainly never focused on it. But four days ago, we found the skeletons of the two murderers up at the site. They had ten gold coins hidden in their boots—confirmation, it would seem, that the story is true.

And if it is true, they may have hidden the bulk of the gold up there somewhere before they died."

"How much?" Maggie asked.

"Ten thousand dollars."

Abruptly, Maggie leapt to her feet. "I *knew* it! That's just what I was telling Drew the other day. I said, 'They're looking for something else besides just a bunch of old bones.' Didn't I say it? And I was right!" She turned from Nora to Clive, her face shining with eagerness. "What's it worth today?"

Clive glanced at Nora. She nodded.

"About twenty million dollars," he said.

No one said anything as this sank in.

"Twenty *million*?" Maggie asked at last.

Clive nodded.

"And you haven't found it yet?"

"No."

"So there's twenty million in gold buried up here somewhere?" Maggie couldn't seem to absorb it.

"It's a possibility."

"Holy smoke!" She whistled. "Who gets it?"

"Every last coin belongs to the government or the Institute," Clive said, articulating each word crisply. "None of us are getting any of it."

"Taking even one coin," Nora added, "amounts to felony theft from the government. It's no different from bank robbery, and it'll get you twenty years in San Quentin."

"Come on!" cried Maggie. "That ain't fair!"

Wiggett stirred. "Surely there's got to be some reward."

"That's the way it is," Nora told him. "No reward. It's the law."

"The hell with the law," said Maggie. "Finders, keepers!"

"What are you suggesting?" Burleson asked her sharply. "Are you going out tomorrow to start searching for the gold? That's probably why we weren't told about this in the first place. Listen up: there's no finder's fee. There's no reward. You are *forbidden* to search for it. This is an archaeological dig, not a damn treasure hunt!"

"Not fair!" said Maggie.

"I can't deny that's how it might sound. But that's how it has to be. And if you don't like it, I'll accept your resignation. Right here and now."

There was a silence. Maggie downed her wine with a gulp, smacked the tin cup down, wiped her mouth. "All right. Don't get your panties in a bunch. I just think it's rotten not to let us at least help. I've always wanted to find a buried treasure."

"I don't like it any more than you do. But this isn't the Wild West. Any gold the archaeological team finds is already spoken for. I want to know you both are clear on that."

Wiggett sighed deeply, then nodded. After a moment, Maggie did the same. It was strange, Nora noticed in a detached kind of way, how news of the gold had led the camp members through a quick succession of emotions: shock, delight, dismay, resentment—ending in grudging acceptance of the legalities involved.

Burleson slapped his knees. "I guess that about covers it. I hope by daybreak we'll have both Peel and the stolen artifacts back, so the archaeologists can restore their site to its proper condition. As for the gold, remember: I won't tolerate anyone on my team going out looking for it. And now, Maggie, if you'd please finish up that beef stew, I'll bet I'm not the only one who's famished."

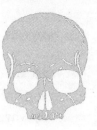

29

May 13

NORA TOOK A seat at the worktable outside the HQ tent as the others gathered for their customary morning meeting. As she glanced around, she noticed a distinct air of expectation. She was still flustered about another call she had placed to Skip earlier on the sat phone. Skip told her Fugit was still furious about the theft. If that wasn't bad enough, Mitty was depressed and spent most of the day at the window, waiting for her to come home.

"Until we get those artifacts back from Peel," she said, shaking away her negative mood, "there's little point restoring the sections he disturbed. And so today we're going to make an organized search for the gold. If it really is here, the sooner we locate it—and get it out of temptation's path—the better."

Salazar and Adelsky both looked so eager that Nora added hastily, "That is, Clive and I are going to begin searching. Jason, Bruce, with the rear of the midden basically finished, you can open up those last four quads you've surveyed. With any luck, they'll encompass the site of the original shelter and cooking fire."

"You know," said Adelsky, "four people will find treasure more quickly than two."

"Maybe," said Nora, "but the dig has to keep going, one way or another. The archaeological value of what you'll be doing—uncovering the heart of the camp—is greater than a chest full of gold."

Salazar rolled his eyes.

"But a lot less fun," said Adelsky.

"I hear you, and I get it. You'll both get a chance to help us secure the gold if we do find it. In fact, the main reason for today's meeting is to see if we can't brainstorm where the gold might have been hidden. I had some ideas I wanted to share with you."

"Sure thing," said Salazar. "I've been speculating about that myself. I figure that a thousand ten-dollar gold eagles, at half an ounce each, weigh about thirty-one pounds. Add to that the weight of the strongbox or chest, and I'll bet the treasure is fifty pounds, at least."

Nora was surprised he'd gone so deeply into the problem already. But then, she'd made the calculation herself. "Right. Good work. And two starving men couldn't have carried a chest that heavy very far in deep snow."

"They probably made an improvised sled out of a few planks and dragged it," said Adelsky.

"That's an interesting idea," Nora said.

"And another thing," Salazar interjected. "The gold couldn't have been buried in the ground—it being frozen and all. They wouldn't have left it in the snow, either, to be exposed by the spring melt."

"Right on both points," said Nora.

Clive laughed. "Looks like you two have thought through this as much as we have, and more."

"I think we can rule out the chest being hidden in a tree, where it might fall or be seen," said Nora. "So we're left with one very obvious hiding area: the cliffs."

"Unfortunately," said Adelsky, "there must be a thousand holes and cracks up there that would fit a chest. And maybe they blocked it with rocks so the hole doesn't even show."

"I think we can safely narrow the number down," said Clive.

"How?"

"By estimating how deep the snow was when the chest was hidden."

"Right." Adelsky leaned forward with excitement. "Right. Because if the snow was twenty feet deep, the chest would be, say, twenty to twenty-five feet up in the cliffs."

"Exactly."

A pause. "So...how can we know how deep the snow was when they hid the chest?" Adelsky asked.

Nora smiled. "Piece of cake."

"Yeah?"

"Take it step by step," she went on. "The party arrived at this valley in the afternoon, during a blizzard. It snowed two feet that night, the first storm of the season. Then it was one snowstorm after another. By February, the snow reached its maximum depth of approximately twenty-six feet. So if we know *when* the chest was hidden, we'll know how high up the cliffs it must be."

"And how can we possibly know that?" Adelsky said.

"As Clive would be the first to say: examine the historical record." And she turned expectantly to the historian.

"Tamzene Donner kept track of snow depths and dates in her journal," Clive said. "And the Lost Camp escapee, Boardman, told her a good deal about what happened here. Now help me reason this out: initially, the two killers must surely have hidden the gold somewhere in their wagon. They were not allowed to join the others in their shelter and were forced to camp some fifty yards away. Around November fifteenth, they broke their wagon up to make a shelter. We know the gold's not in their shelter, so the chest had to have been hidden *before* their wagon was broken up, no doubt shortly before November fifteenth. Agree with me so far?"

Nods all around.

"According to Tamzene's journal, in mid-November the snow was six feet deep. If it was six feet deep at Donner Pass, it would be six feet deep here, too. Given that, the chest should be in the cliffs at a height of six to twelve feet. QED." He looked around with a smile. "Anyone disagree with the logic?"

No one did.

"But," said Salazar, "that still leaves a ton of holes up there in those cliffs. You've got your work cut out for you."

"I can't deny that," said Nora. "Especially since we don't know what the tree cover was like back then—that is, what areas would have given them camouflage from the camp. Because they had to be able to hide the gold unseen by the others."

"What's the plan, then?" Adelsky asked. "Look for a patch of hundred-and-seventy-five-year-old yellow snow as a marker?"

"No. We'll divide the cliff faces into sectors and search each one in turn." She rose. "You two get to work on those final quads, while Clive and I start searching."

Salazar and Adelsky groaned in unison.

"I promise: with this amount of cliff face to cover, I'm pretty sure everyone will have a chance to search."

While Salazar and Adelsky got out their tools and put on

masks and gloves, Nora laid out a diagram of the cliff faces she'd
drawn from camera images in her tent the previous night.

"I already divided the cliff into six sectors," she told Clive.
"Three on each side of the canyon, just as if it were an archaeological dig. We'll start with sector one and proceed from there."

"Looks like you've been busy." Clive leaned over the diagram.
"The far part of sector six is under *that*, you realize." He pointed
toward the far end of the meadow, where the rock walls came
together. Some thousand feet above, a gigantic curl of rotten,
melting snow along the lee side of a ridge—what they'd jokingly
come to refer to as the "death cornice"—still hung menacingly
over the narrow fissure.

"I realize that. Let's hope we find the treasure before we have
to search that area. Anyway, that's nearly a quarter mile off—a
long way for two starving men to lug a strongbox." She folded
the diagram and shoved it into a pocket. "As we proceed, we'll
mark off each searched zone on this master diagram."

Clive nodded. "Good plan. Just keep an eye open—I'll bet
those rocks are prime rattler habitats." He hesitated and lowered his voice. "When we find the treasure, let's sneak it out
and take it to Mexico and live happily forever after on the beach.
What do you think?" He laughed merrily and gave her a fond
nudge.

"We'd both die of boredom," said Nora.

The two started scouting the base of the cliffs in sector one.
A fair number of the holes were reachable by free climbing. But
there were other sections with few hand- and footholds, and
Nora could see that, eventually, climbing with the protection of
ropes would be necessary.

"Ever done any technical climbing?" she asked.

"Nope. But I've always wanted to learn."

"Well, if it comes to that, I'll show you the basics of how to belay first, while I rope up—that'll save time."

Nora and Clive started free-climbing to every crack, hole, and fissure they could reach in the first sector, probing with hiking poles and headlamps. The first half dozen holes Nora shone her light into were empty, with at most a little brush at the entrance that she swept back with her pole. In one, a messy crow's nest could be seen, with half a dozen babies sticking their necks up and peeping loudly, beaks open. The mother crow circled above, screeching furiously. Another fissure revealed a coiled rattlesnake, which buzzed angrily when Nora illuminated it, whipping into striking position. Nora jerked back so fast she almost fell. She scrambled down.

"Jesus," she murmured.

"I just saw one, too," said Clive.

In an hour, they had exhausted all possible hiding places that could be reached with a free climb. Nora and Clive then put on harnesses and she showed him how to belay her. Given the heights they had estimated, the climbs wouldn't present much difficulty.

She tied the rope off, then checked their equipment. "On belay?" she asked Clive.

"Belay on," he said, patting his carabiner and bracing himself.

"Climbing." She began making her way up the vertical slope, fixing a cam at twelve feet. Using that as an anchor, she worked sideways six feet in either direction, peering into holes. A crow shot out of one, scaring the hell out of her, and she felt herself fall about a foot before Clive caught her rope tight with the belay device.

"Sorry," he called up.

"Remember—never take your brake hand off the rope." She

removed the cam, eased herself down, then moved twelve feet farther along the cliff, where she started the process over again.

As the morning wore on, what had begun as an exhilarating treasure hunt started to grow wearisome. The climbing, so close to the ground, was neither fun nor challenging. The holes were mostly empty, except for old crow's nests and the occasional pissed-off rattler to get her heart racing. Clive soon got the hang of belaying and it didn't take long for the novelty to wear off for him, either.

Around noon, they heard a shout from the middle of the meadow. A few minutes later Salazar appeared through the trees, waving. "We found it!"

Nora descended, marking her position, and the two of them followed Salazar back to the dig.

Salazar and Adelsky had opened two of the four quads before hitting pay dirt—wooden planks, nails, spikes, and what was obviously the camp's hearth: a mass of charcoal surrounded by stones.

Nora examined the area. Not all of it was uncovered yet, of course, but there was enough to make out the general outline: extremely rotten planks, along with crude bent nails and hand-forged spikes embedded in the boards or lying on the ground.

She looked closer at the hearth. It was a grim spectacle. Pieces of what was obviously a skull lay in the remains of a pot. Mingled in with the charcoal beneath were more burned bits and gnawed nubbins of bone. About two feet from the hearth, at the edge of the excavated quad, was a ghastly sight: the perfect skeleton of a dismembered hand that, for some reason, had not been eaten. Perhaps it had been stored for later consumption and either forgotten about or, more likely, left because everyone had died.

A silence settled over the group. As Clive photographed everything, Nora turned to her assistants. "Well, this is it. Very clean work. Nicely done, both of you."

"And the gold?" asked Adelsky.

"Nothing so far."

Salazar cleared his throat dramatically. "Any possibility we might help search this afternoon?"

Nora looked at Adelsky and then at Salazar. There was a glow in their eyes that she didn't remember seeing before. Strange how gold brought out that kind of reaction, even in archaeologists who should know better. However, they were both experienced climbers—and she could use a break.

"Tomorrow. Once you complete those other two quads. You can trade off climbing and belaying."

After lunch she and Clive hiked back to the cliffs, and Nora once again harnessed up. "I hope we find it soon," she said. "Because I'm a little worried about gold fever taking hold around here."

"Me, too," said Clive, looking up at the nearest cliff face, its flanks riddled with openings. "But it's like looking for a needle in a haystack—a haystack full of rattlers."

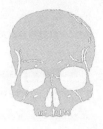

30

WHEN NORA AND the archaeology team returned to camp late that afternoon, with one quad of the shelter thoroughly searched and the other three well along, they found the place strangely deserted. Nora sat down near the fire as the afternoon chill settled, her arm and leg muscles aching, throwing on a few sticks to get the smoldering coals going.

"Where is everybody?" Salazar asked.

"Out hunting for gold," said Adelsky with a laugh, settling in his chair and firing up his vape.

"I hope not," said Nora.

As if on cue, she heard the sound of voices, and then Burleson and Maggie came riding up. They dismounted and Burleson led the horses off while Maggie bustled into the kitchen area and began opening up camp cupboards and pulling out pans, working up supper.

"Where were you?" Adelsky asked Maggie, blowing a stream of smoke. "Looking for something, by chance?"

"Lay off, wise guy. Yeah, we were looking for Peel. We're not allowed to hunt for treasure—remember?"

Adelsky gave a cynical chuckle. "Peel. Sure."

Burleson returned and settled down in his chair. "Took another look downtrail, just in case he'd fallen from the horse and was out cold, lying off among the rocks. But no sign of him." He paused. "Anyone seen Wiggett? He was supposed to stay back here with the horses."

"Probably out looking as well," said Adelsky.

"Three guesses as for what," said Salazar.

"Cut it out, you two," Nora told them.

The golden glow gradually painted the peaks around them as Maggie served up dinner. Afterward, as twilight filled the valley with purple shadows, Nora heard a call, distant but urgent.

A sudden silence fell as they all listened.

Another yell, followed by the sound of hooves beating the ground. A moment later, Wiggett burst out of the forest at a lope, bringing his horse right into camp and reining up without dismounting.

"I found Peel," he gasped. "Up by Black Buttes."

Burleson jumped up. "What? You mean he was headed west? Deeper into the mountains?"

Wiggett nodded. "And that's not all. He's dead."

"*Dead?*" Maggie cried. "Are you sure? What happened?"

"Fell off a cliff. The way he's lying, all twisted up... Yeah, I'm sure."

"Jesus." Burleson glanced skyward. "There's still some light left, and tonight's the full moon. Let's go—take me back up there."

"We'll all go," said Nora.

* * *

Nora and Clive accompanied Burleson and Wiggett as they rode from the corral up past the dig. Wiggett led them away at right angles from the canyon and up a small draw, following the crude trail as it continued into high country. The ride brought them to a landscape of granite domes, ravines, and twisted bristlecone pines. As the trail petered out and the last of the light faded, a great buttery moon rose in the east, casting a pale light over the landscape that was almost as clear as day.

After half an hour of riding, Wiggett halted amid a labyrinth of ridges. The others rode up beside him. They were ranged along a ridgeline that narrowed abruptly as it approached a small peak.

"It's just below that peak," said Wiggett. "The body's down in the ravine to the left. I wouldn't have noticed it myself, except I had to dismount while traversing the ridge because the footing was so tricky. Be careful and stay away from that edge." He paused a moment. "And there's something else you should see. It's what first caught my attention. Looks like Peel was building a cairn—or a grave."

He urged his horse on and they rode single file along the ridge. A sheer chasm plunged downward on their left, a chill wind blowing up from below.

"We should stop here, tie up the horses, and go the last few hundred feet on foot," Burleson said. "I don't like the footing, and I'd rather disturb the area as little as possible."

"Good idea," said Clive.

They dismounted and tied their horses by their lead ropes to some dwarf pines below the ridgeline, out of the wind. Wiggett led the way, snapping on his headlamp, as they walked over the rounded granite rocks. A half-built cairn came into view, stones tumbled about.

Burleson shone his headlamp over it. "Looks fresh, all right. And over there are some pieces of wood, like he was going to make a cross. Guess I was wrong—he wasn't headed into town to find a clergyman, after all; he was going to bury those bones in the wilderness, where nobody would disturb them again." He paused. "Looks as if he was building it when he fell. That's one hell of an edge."

Nora shone her light on the oblong pile of rocks and then toward the cliff edge, about thirty feet away. Only blackness yawned beyond.

"He's down there," said Wiggett, pointing.

Nora and the others approached gingerly. She knelt at the edge and looked down. The valley was flooded in moonlight and she could see, perhaps five hundred feet below, the horribly twisted body of a man. Scattered around him were bits of white. She took out her binoculars and saw immediately that the bits were scattered fragments of bone, spilled from a pair of torn saddlebags that had tumbled down the cliff with him.

Clive knelt next to her. Silently, he took the binoculars from her hands. "Jesus, how awful. And I suppose those are the bones he stole—or what's left of them—lying around him."

For a moment, everyone was silent, wrapped in their own thoughts. Then Burleson abruptly spoke.

"How is it possible," he asked, "that a man as experienced in the wilderness as Peel would fall off a cliff like this?"

"Late at night," Wiggett replied. "The moon had set. He's collecting rocks for his grave. He's agitated, upset, not thinking clearly."

"Maybe even had a drink or two," Clive added.

"Peel didn't drink."

Nora looked down again, fighting off a sense of vertigo

despite her long experience with heights. The cliff edge was, in fact, so sharp it could have been cut with a knife. Anyone might have walked over the edge. Except…

"Wouldn't he have had a headlamp?" she asked.

"You'd think so," said Burleson.

Nora backed away from the edge. Then she rose to her feet. "I think we'd better ride back to camp and notify the police."

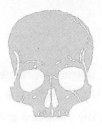

31

May 14

Sᴘᴇᴄɪᴀʟ Aɢᴇɴᴛ Cᴏʀʀɪᴇ Swanson rode at the rear of a string of horses winding their way up the ridgeline. Ahead of her was the wrangler who was acting as guide; the county sheriff, a burly man named Blake Devlin; his deputy; and two Forest Service law enforcement officers—all on horses supplied by the Red Mountain Ranch. The county coroner was up there, too, a funny, small man who didn't seem to have anything much to say and looked silly perched on a very large horse. It was quite a motley crowd, Corrie mused, to be making its way along a series of rocky ridges high in the Sierras. They were at an altitude of over seven thousand feet, in a country of barren granite peaks and knobs, with little twisted pine trees growing here and there. Beyond stood higher mountain peaks heavily patched with snowfields.

Corrie did not like horseback riding. The holster carrying her Glock was digging into her ribs, and the handcuffs tucked into her back—why the hell had she brought those?—were rubbing against her spine. Her bulging saddlebags carried the paraphernalia she had brought for collecting evidence—booties, gloves,

mask, hair net, evidence tubes, digital camera, Ziploc bags, penlight, and tweezers. Normally an FBI response team would handle evidence collection, but in this case Morwood had declined
to provide one, since all initial reports suggested the death was
an accident. And, he pointed out, Corrie was supposed to be a
forensic expert herself. Which she was, in theory—but with no
field experience yet.

When she had arrived that morning at Red Mountain Ranch,
the other four in the law enforcement group—middle-aged men
all—seemed to know one another already and were saddling up.
It was pretty clear from the unenthusiastic way they greeted her
that she was an unwelcome interloper. Corrie was acutely aware
of how young and inexperienced she looked. But she was determined, for that very reason, to be cool and correct in all her
interactions. *Even if it's a straightforward accident*, Morwood had
told her, *it'll offer you some valuable experience.*

As the group rounded a bend in the ridge, she could see
where someone had strung rope across the trail as temporary
crime scene tape. That was good. She wondered who had
done it.

They all halted their horses and Corrie dismounted. She untied the saddlebags and draped them over her shoulder. The
wrangler from Red Mountain who had guided them up came
over and took the reins, leading her horse away with the others.
She looked around. The guys were confabbing in a group.
Abruptly, they all broke into laughter about something.

Stepping over the rope, Corrie made her way to the edge of
the cliff. It was a long, sheer drop. At the bottom, she could
see the body of the victim, saddlebags lying nearby. On the
ridge next to her stood a half-built pile of stones, and not far
away were two freshly carved and peeled sticks. Evidently, the

man had been in the process of making a cross when he fell. The ground was mostly solid granite, with patches of moss and alpine flowers in the cracks—pretty much the worst possible ground to record evidence, and a close examination of the edge of the cliff and the cairn of stones did not reveal a single trace of man or horse.

Taking out her camera, she snapped a number of photographs. Meanwhile, the sheriff and deputy and the two Forest officers came walking up behind, still talking and laughing. They stood around, obviously uninterested but nevertheless, she thought, having a grand time playing cowboy in their hats and boots.

She felt a presence behind her and turned. The archaeologist, Nora Kelly, approached rather tentatively. Behind her was the man Corrie recognized as Benton, the expedition's historian, and two other familiar faces.

"Any idea what happened?" the woman asked.

"I don't think there's much to find up here," said Corrie. "I'd like to get down below to examine the body. Do you know the way?"

"I'll show you. Looks like the coroner is heading down there already."

Corrie followed Nora Kelly along the ridgeline to a steep couloir that led down into the ravine below. They descended carefully to the bottom. A stream flowed through the ravine, with meadows and stands of tall firs on either side. Hiking alongside the stream, they soon came to another piece of rope.

"Who put up this rope?" Corrie asked.

"I told Wiggett to do it, before everyone came up. I didn't want anyone tramping through here and picking up things. Especially the old bones Peel stole."

"Wiggett, the assistant wrangler?"

"Yes."

"Thank you for doing that."

Behind them she could hear the four cops descending the couloir, still talking loudly.

Around a bend in the ravine, a graphic scene of death presented itself. Corrie paused, taking it in and struggling to maintain a professional expression. The coroner was bending over the body, taking its temperature, a process she had studied in depth but never actually seen performed. It was not pretty.

"Who's been up through here before us?" Corrie asked.

"Just Wiggett and the coroner. We told everyone to stay away."

Corrie nodded. She took a few more steps forward. The body lay about twenty feet in front of her, among jagged boulders. It was horribly mangled. She wondered if it really made sense to put on booties, gloves, a face mask, and a hair net to collect evidence, given that the coroner hadn't. In the end she decided she'd better do it by the book, just in case. She pulled the requisite items out of the saddlebags she was carrying and put them on.

"If you wouldn't mind waiting here," she said to Dr. Kelly, "I'd like to take a closer look."

"Of course."

Corrie proceeded to the body. The coroner nodded a greeting. "I'll just be a few more minutes and then it's yours."

"Thanks."

She took another series of pictures of the overall scene, the cliff, and the various bones and other items scattered about from Peel's torn saddlebags. The old bones from the excavation—the ones Peel had apparently made off with and planned to bury—were scattered about in profusion, including a badly shattered skull. The victim's headlamp lay near his body.

She leaned over the headlamp, photographing it.

"Agent Swanson?" the coroner said. "I'm done here."

The coroner backed off to one side and began jotting in a notebook while Corrie approached the corpse and examined it at close range. The damage was massive. The neck was so badly broken it was partially severed from the head. The back of the skull was crushed and a large pool of blood lay beneath it, the extensive exsanguination indicating he had been alive when he fell. Both arms and both legs were fractured in dozens of places, with exposed bone and more bleeding. Abrasions and contusions could be seen everywhere. The victim's shirt and pants were ripped and abraded. One boot was gone, lying a good twenty yards off.

Moving around the body, she continued photographing.

Devlin, his deputy, and the two Forest Service officers came walking up, yakking away, having made no effort to put on protection, not even gloves. "Well, well," said the sheriff. "Have you solved the case yet, Special Agent Swanson?"

Corrie spoke through the face mask. "Just gathering evidence." She bent over the victim's head, taking more pictures of the cuts and contusions.

"Think it's...murder?" Devlin asked. Stifled laughter came from the deputy.

"As I implied, I haven't drawn any conclusions."

"Well, I have."

Corrie did not respond, hoping he wouldn't continue, but he did. "What we have here is what's technically known as a *bad fall*."

Ignoring him, she put her lens in macro mode and shot a series of close-ups of the facial contusions.

The sheriff went on. "The guy was building his little grave up there, hunting around for rocks, and just walked right over the edge."

Corrie continued taking pictures.

"Isn't that how you see it, too, Special Agent Swanson?"

"The question is not whether he fell. The question is how."

"I can tell you that, too," said Devlin, hiking up his utility belt with a jangle of metal. "Two nights ago—the night he died—the moon set at three AM. He's up there, building a grave for these bones with no ambient light; it gets really dark. But he just keeps going, working away, and—off he goes."

Corrie couldn't help but point to the broken headlamp. "He had light. The switch is in the on position."

"Yeah, but he's agitated, he's in a hurry. On that knife edge of a cliff."

Corrie straightened up and looked at Devlin. He was smiling at her indulgently. *Just be cool*, she told herself. "Thank you, Sheriff Devlin, for your opinion." She turned to the other three, who were doing nothing but walking around and gawking. One of them had inadvertently stepped on a bone fragment, and Corrie heard Dr. Kelly call out in protest.

Corrie turned back to Devlin. "I'd like to ask those of you not involved in active evidence collection to please stand behind the rope."

The sheriff stared at her. "We are collecting evidence. I'm looking around with my two little eyes. So are they."

Corrie's heart accelerated, and that old boiling feeling of anger—the feeling she had tried so hard to control in recent years—began to rise up. She took a long breath in, let out a long exhale, then repeated the process, feeling a bit of equilibrium return.

"When I'm done," she said, "you may resume your examination of the scene. But for now, I'd appreciate it if you could step back behind the rope and allow me to complete my work."

A long silence from the sheriff. And then he said: "May I ask, miss, where you acquired the authority to give orders to the elected sheriff of Nevada County, California?"

It was the *miss* that did it. In a cold voice, Corrie said, more loudly than she intended: "This is federal land. On federal land, the FBI has jurisdiction. That includes priority over local law enforcement. You are here as a *courtesy*, Sheriff. I might also point out—" she turned her stare at the two Forest Service officials— "that you two gentlemen are directly under my authority."

The Forest Service officials stared back at her. For a moment she feared they might push back, and she realized she didn't have the slightest idea how to deal with that. But then one of them mumbled, "Yes, ma'am," and the two turned and walked back behind the rope.

Corrie returned her gaze to the sheriff and his deputy. Devlin had gone red. He opened his mouth to say something, thought better of it, and then retreated, scowling, with his deputy.

Breathing a secret sigh of relief, Corrie finished up her series of macro photos. She did a walk-through of the site, transects in four directions as she had been taught—seeing nothing more of interest—then returned behind the rope to where the others were standing around, chatting and glancing in her direction.

"If you gentlemen want to examine the area, it's free," she said.

"We don't need to examine anything," said the sheriff. "It's clear as day what happened."

As Corrie started packing up her gear, Dr. Kelly and the

historian, Benton, approached. Kelly leaned over. "I heard that exchange. Good for you."

Corrie tried to stay neutral, but inside she felt enormously grateful for the comment. She nodded.

"I wanted to ask you," Kelly said. "What's going to happen to the bones Peel stole from the dig?"

Corrie thought for a moment. "They're evidence. And as such, they'd normally be kept in our custody."

"May I offer another suggestion?"

"Go ahead."

"They're human remains—of great value archaeologically. Also, as human remains they must be treated with sensitivity. They've obviously been damaged in the fall, and they should be curated, conserved—and, if possible, reassembled. We won't be able to do that if you lock them up as evidence."

Benton broke in. "As a Donner Party descendant, I agree with Nora. I wouldn't like to see my ancestor's remains locked up indefinitely as evidence."

"If they're needed in the future," Kelly added, "the FBI will always have access."

Corrie thought for a moment. "Are you familiar with the term 'chain of custody'? If the bones are ever to be used as evidence, we have to be able to document who had access to them and when."

"That's not a problem. Since these bones are to be DNA tested, they'll be protected from contamination. Part of the DNA testing protocol is maintaining a strict chain of custody."

Corrie thought about it for a moment. "Very well. As soon as the coroner removes the body, you can collect the bones."

"Thank you."

Corrie finished up her notes while the coroner and the two

Forest Service officers bagged the body, draped it over a horse, and tied it down. They departed, along with the sheriff and his deputy.

Corrie turned to Kelly. "Feel free to collect the bones."

She watched as the team of archaeologists began scouring the area, picking up every last fragment of bone with rubber-tipped tweezers. The bits and pieces went into labeled Ziploc bags that in turn went into hard plastic cases, meticulously documented. Many bones were still in Peel's saddlebags, and those appeared to have survived the fall better than the others. She had to admit that an FBI evidence response team could not have done a better job.

By the time the team had finished, it was late afternoon. They switchbacked up the cliff, the wrangler brought over their horses, and they rode back to camp as the sun cast a golden glow over the surrounding peaks.

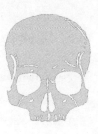

32

May 15

THE NEXT AFTERNOON, in the dig site's HQ tent, Nora stared at a long plastic table on which a black piece of velvet had been laid. Spread out on the velvet were all the bones recovered from the site of Peel's death, carefully cataloged and arranged. She and her assistants had been meticulous in their recovery work, combing over the site where Peel had fallen, and she was confident they had retrieved all the bones he'd stolen. Many of them had been damaged in the fall, but over the course of the morning the team had managed to identify and reassemble each one from their database of photographs. The specialized archaeological software they used to curate the excavation had sped up the task considerably.

"This is disturbing," said Clive, standing next to her. "To say the least."

Nora could only shake her head. "When that FBI agent hears about this..."

"Do you think we missed something at the base of the cliffs?" he asked.

"I'm sure we got every last piece."

"So he buried it somewhere else?"

"Looks that way. But why?"

A voice outside interrupted their conversation. "May I?"

Oh God, Nora thought: here she was, as if on cue. To Nora's annoyance, Agent Swanson had set up her tent right next to the main camp and showed every intention of extending her stay.

"Come in," said Nora.

The FBI agent stepped inside. "Are these the bones found with Peel?"

Nora sighed. Better to just get it over with.

"They are," she said slowly. "And it seems we have a problem."

The agent pulled out her notebook. "Yes?"

"We're missing a skull and, apparently, some vertebrae."

"Whose remains?"

"Parkin's."

At this, she saw a look of surprise in the agent's eyes, quickly turning into a gleam of—what? Eagerness.

"Are you sure it's the Parkin skull? Albert Parkin?"

"Yes."

"And you're certain it wasn't overlooked at the scene of the fall?"

"Yes."

"And nothing else is missing?"

"Not to my knowledge."

The agent took a moment to write in her notebook.

Clive said, "We can only assume Peel buried that skull somewhere else before he fell."

Swanson turned to Nora. "Is that also what you think?"

"I don't know," Nora said. "It seems odd Peel would bury a partial body somewhere else. But the whole thing's odd. If he was so worried about getting them a proper Christian burial, why would he take them up into the mountains instead of bringing them back to hallowed ground?"

Clive shook his head. "He was crazy, that's why. I mean, think about it: Samantha Carville's remains were the most properly buried of any of the corpses we'd found. And he took them anyway."

Nora found Corrie looking at her with a penetrating eye. "When I first visited, you hadn't identified the Parkin remains. We agreed you would notify me if and when you identified Parkin. But now you say you're certain Parkin's skull is missing. So you *did* identify it but failed to tell me?"

The faint tickle of self-reproach Nora had felt when she located Parkin's remains—showing off just a little for Clive's benefit—now came back, big-time. She hoped it didn't show. "We conducted further analyses after you left. Your mentioning the broken clavicle provided additional information. We used our artifact database and topographical software tool set to identify the skull, but it was not a hundred percent certain—not without a DNA analysis. All this only happened a day or two ago."

"So you did find the broken clavicle."

Nora nodded.

"But you say the skull and some vertebrae are missing. So I assume the clavicle is still on-site?"

"That's right."

"May I see it?"

"Of course. It'll take a bit of time. Do you need it immediately—?"

"It can wait a little, thanks. Right now, I have some questions I'd like to ask you and the others."

"You mean, as in an interrogation?"

"No—just gathering information on a voluntary basis. I'd like to use this work tent if I may, since it's private and away from the camp."

"Is this really necessary?" Nora asked.

"Yes. And I'd like to start with you, Dr. Kelly."

Nora heaved a deep sigh. "Me? When?"

"Right now."

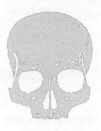

33

CORRIE WATCHED AS Kelly and Benton carefully packed away the bones and locked them in a cabinet. They cleared a small worktable for her to use.

"Thank you, this will do fine," said Corrie as she sat down, laying out her cell phone to record the conversation.

She turned and saw the historian lingering at the flap of the tent. "If Dr. Kelly and I could have some privacy?"

"Of course," he said. "I'll go help Bruce and Jason."

He left and Dr. Kelly took the seat opposite her.

"I'd like to record you, if I may."

The archaeologist shrugged. "Go ahead. And if you don't mind, it's Nora, not Dr. Kelly. We operate on a first-name basis here and you're beginning to sound like one of my students."

"Very well. But for the purposes of the questioning, it'll still be Dr. Kelly." Corrie turned on the cell phone recorder, gave her name and the date, and then slid it toward the archaeologist. "Please state your name."

"Nora Kelly."

Corrie took a deep breath. "Dr. Kelly, you told me earlier that Clive Benton was the originator of this excavation. When exactly did he approach you?"

"Last November."

"Could you go over the circumstances for me?"

Even with the recorder going, she took notes as Nora described how he'd found Tamzene Donner's journal and brought the idea to the Institute.

"And who at the Institute approved it?"

"The president, Dr. Jill Fugit. And the board."

"So the Institute agreed to finance it? On the strength of an old journal? This would seem to be an expensive expedition."

"Yes, the Institute is financing it."

Corrie picked up on the uneasiness in her tone. "Financing it how? Through private donations? Grants?"

The archaeologist hesitated again. "There's something you probably don't know yet. Regarding the financing."

"Go on."

"The Institute hopes to recoup the cost of the expedition by...recovering a hoard of gold believed to have been hidden near the camp."

Corrie could hardly believe what she'd just heard. "You mean, as in buried treasure?"

"Essentially, yes."

"Would you please explain?"

Corrie listened as Nora related the history of Wolfinger's chest of gold, his murder, and the gold coins they had discovered on two sets of remains. "We believe the rest is hidden close by," she said in conclusion.

"Have you been looking for it?"

"Yes. After Peel left. We thought it best to—to get that part of the expedition safely out of the way, if possible."

"But you haven't found it?"

Nora shook her head.

"What's the total estimated value?"

"Twenty million dollars."

It took Corrie a moment to process this. "Twenty *million*? And it goes to the finder?"

"No. It's to be divided, a third to the state of California, a third to the feds, and a third to the Institute. For obvious reasons, we have to keep that aspect of the expedition under wraps. But it's all spelled out in the fine print of the permits."

Corrie scribbled in her notebook, trying not to appear incredulous at this revelation. She considered asking Nora why she hadn't mentioned it before, but realized she'd probably get an evasive answer. The archaeologist had not exactly been cooperative, failing to notify her when she found the Parkin skeleton, and she sure as hell hadn't mentioned anything about any gold on Corrie's brief first visit to the camp. There was something bizarre, if not fishy, going on up here, she now felt sure—and she felt equally sure that, one way or another, it was linked to the missing Parkin remains she was investigating.

"Who else knows about the gold?" she asked.

"Everyone in camp. A few individuals at the Institute. We've obviously been keeping the information restricted. The last thing anybody wants is for this place to be overrun with treasure seekers."

"So Peel knew of the gold?"

"Actually, no. He left before we confided in the full team."

"And Dr. Benton?"

"He was the one who first became aware of its existence."

Corrie paused. This was such an unexpected turn, she was finding it hard to formulate questions.

"Getting back to Peel's death," she said. "What were his relations with the others in camp?"

"He was a bit of a loner. I never got to know him well."

"No conflicts?"

"Not that I knew of. No friends, either."

"Nobody who might have reason to want him dead?"

Nora stared at her. "You don't think Peel was murdered, do you?"

Corrie pondered this. She wasn't sure of the answer herself—but stirring the pot now just might produce results.

"It's possible."

"*Anything's* possible. Why would you think that?"

"My understanding is that Peel was an expert horseman and wilderness guide," said Corrie. "He had a headlamp. Most important, there was a contusion on his head that looked like it might have happened prior to the fall."

"You mean, he was clobbered on the head and then thrown off the cliff?"

"Yes."

"I saw Peel's head. It was a mess, and I noticed several contusions—not just one. How can you be sure they weren't caused by the fall?"

This was, unfortunately, a fair question. Given the environmental conditions and the state of the body, Corrie couldn't answer it—not without a meticulous examination at a forensic lab. So she said nothing.

"But who would have done it? I mean, as far as I know, we're the only people up here."

Corrie let the tension build. Silence, she had been taught in interrogation classes, was one of the most effective tools.

"Are you suggesting," Nora said, her voice rising, "it was one of *us*?"

"We can't rule out unknown persons up in these mountains, but that scenario seems less likely."

Nora stared in disbelief and growing anger. "And this is why you want to question us?"

"Yes."

"I can tell you, none of us are killers. Besides, why would anyone murder Peel?"

"In recent months, three Parkin graves have been robbed and a grave digger murdered. A living Parkin has disappeared, presumably murdered as well. And now another Parkin skull is missing—and the man who stole it is dead under suspicious circumstances." She paused. "Someone seems awfully interested in the Parkin family."

Nora shook her head. "It just seems so crazy. Why?"

"That's what I'm trying to find out."

Corrie could see Nora was shaken up. "Could you please ask Dr. Benton to come in? And after him I'd like to question your archaeological team, and the others tomorrow."

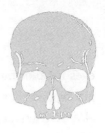

34

AFTER NORA LEFT, Corrie took a moment to jot some questions in her notebook and check the recording she'd just made while waiting for Dr. Benton to arrive. The tent was pleasantly warm, the air fresh. It was nice being in the mountains, even if this was her first real job in the field and she felt stressed out as a result. She took another deep breath and tried to tamp down her nervousness. The practice interrogation sessions at the Academy had been straightforward, leaving her ill-prepared for the sort of investigation she was engaged in now—in which she could see no motive, develop no hypothesis of a crime. All she had were a lot of disconnected facts and coincidences, along with a gut feeling.

One of the things she'd been taught at the Academy was to clarify the facts, work chronologically, and—especially—resist forming ideas. But as Clive Benton entered the tent, Corrie realized she had already formed an idea about him, and it wasn't good. The man was not a slope-shouldered, meek, bespectacled historian; he was tall and fit, not rugged exactly, but with a good-looking, weather-beaten face from which two baby-blue eyes looked out at her own. Maybe it was the good looks that put her off, but more likely it was the fact that he, and no one else, had set in motion the events that led to the discovery of Albert Parkin's skull—now, unfortunately, missing.

"Please have a seat," she said.

He pulled up the folding chair and sat down. His attractive face was marred by a scowl he made no effort to hide.

Corrie turned on the recorder again and went through the preliminaries.

"Dr. Benton," she said, "I'd like to know the source of your interest in the Donner Party history."

He gave a sigh of impatience. "I'm a collateral descendant of the Breen family. They were one of the families that formed the Donner Party. I've been fascinated with the subject from childhood. I majored in history in college and got a PhD from Stanford. My dissertation was on the Donner Party. You know most of this already."

"I know we've discussed some of this before, but I'm going over these points for the record, if you don't mind. How did you get from that interest to this specific excavation?"

He gave a distinct sigh of annoyance. "Historians had known that Tamzene Donner, George Donner's wife, kept a journal. It had never been found. I managed to track it down."

"How?"

"I found it in a deserted house that once belonged to the daughter of Jacob Donner."

"How did you know to look there?"

"An educated guess."

"That's rather vague. You didn't have more specific information?"

"I was pretty sure the daughter had it, and I figured it must still be somewhere among her stuff, given that no one else ever saw it or remarked on it."

"You found it and...what? Bought it from the family?"

A hesitation. "Well, no. The house had been vacant for many years." He sat back rather defiantly. "I entered the house to save it from imminent destruction."

"Let me just clarify this point," Corrie said. "You trespassed and took the journal, even though you had no legal right to it. In other words, you stole it."

The defiant look grew more pronounced. "It was a priceless historical document. It would have been lost forever. The bulldozers were about to tear the place down. So yes, I broke the law. Go ahead and arrest me." He held out his hands in dramatic fashion, as if for handcuffs.

"Dr. Benton, you can put your hands away." *For now*, she almost said.

He withdrew his hands.

"That explains the first step. So how did you go from the journal to this project?"

"When I read the journal, I realized it contained vital information regarding the location of the Lost Camp. Since I'm not an archaeologist, I brought the idea to Nora and the Institute. I suggested they finance it with the gold presumed to be hidden in the area." He spread his hands. "End of story."

Interesting that, unlike Nora Kelly, Benton had not hesitated to bring up the gold. "And you're the one who figured out there was gold hidden up here?"

"Historians have known forever that one of the pioneers, Wolfinger, was carrying gold, but I was the first to determine the amount."

"How?"

"Old bank records."

"I see. And where do you think this gold might be hidden?"

"Somewhere in those cliffs that surround the dig site." He leaned forward. "I might note that, having realized almost a year ago the gold was up here, I could have come up on my own, found it, and bugged out with no one the wiser. But I didn't."

"Why not?"

He laughed. "You certainly are direct. I didn't because I'm an honest man. I care more about history than money. It was important for the gold to be recovered in the right way, through a legitimate dig. Even though it meant I wouldn't get a penny of it."

These points were all hard to refute, Corrie thought as she made notes. She moved on to the next set of questions in her notebook. "Where were you on May second?"

"What happened then?"

"That's the day Rosalie Parkin disappeared. The floor of her bedroom was covered with so much of her blood, it's being treated as a likely homicide."

"And I take it you're looking for an alibi?" He laughed again. "I don't even need to check my calendar. I was driving up here from Santa Fe, along with all of the scientists now here on the dig."

"And on April twenty-second?"

"April twenty-second." He pulled out his phone and did examine his calendar. "I temporarily put aside preparations for this expedition and took a flight from Santa Fe to attend a western history conference. At the University of Oklahoma in Norman, with hundreds of witnesses. Did something sinister happen on that date, as well?"

"That's the night a Parkin corpse was exhumed from the

cemetery in Glorieta Pass. And a body was shot and left on top of the coffin."

"Looks like I'm off the hook, then," he said, wiping his brow in mock relief.

"These are routine questions, Dr. Benton."

"Routine?" He rose and placed his hands on the table, leaning toward her. "Let me just tell you to your face: this whole idea is ridiculous."

Corrie was about to respond, but she remembered what an instructor at the Academy had said: when they're angry, shut up and let them keep talking.

"From what you've told us," he went on, "it seems these Parkin disappearances have been going on for less than a year. My research into the Donner Party and the Lost Camp has been a *twenty*-year project. Not to brag, but my scholarly credentials are impeccable. I've already demonstrated my honesty by not scooping up the gold. You are absolutely barking up the wrong tree, and I doubt if you're doing your career any good in the process."

Corrie waited. He seemed finished.

"Any more questions?" he asked.

"Not for now. I may have more after I interview the others."

"I'll bet they're just lining up." He turned to leave.

Corrie said evenly, "Could you please send in Jason Salazar?"

"Sure, why not?" He exited the tent, shaking his head, and called for Salazar.

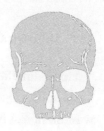

35

After Corrie finished interviewing Salazar and Adelsky—they had little of note to add—she asked Nora to show her Parkin's broken clavicle, then packed up her stuff and hiked the half mile down the trail to the camp. She arrived around three in the afternoon to find the place deserted. She went back to her tent, organized her gear, read through her notes, and made a few more. And then she began writing a preliminary summary for Agent Morwood.

She heard Maggie outside, banging pots and pans as she started to get things ready for dinner. Corrie emerged from the tent and sat down by the fire, next to Burleson, who was reading *The Education of Henry Adams*.

"Mr. Burleson?"

He looked up.

"I'd like to address the group tonight at dinner. If you could please make sure everyone is present, I'd appreciate it."

She found his eyes lingering on her questioningly. "Is it about Peel?"

"That—and other things."

He nodded.

By sunset, everyone had straggled back into camp. Burleson was opening a bottle of wine—apparently, an evening ritual.

"If you'll all gather around the campfire," he said, "Special Agent Swanson wanted an opportunity to speak to the group."

As Maggie stirred a simmering pot of stew, all eyes turned to Corrie. She swallowed and tried to tamp down her nervousness.

"Thank you," she began. "Tomorrow, I'd like the opportunity to question the three of you from Red Mountain Ranch. I've already spoken to the archaeological team."

Wiggett, the assistant wrangler, raised a finger. "The sheriff already spoke to us. He says it was an accident. What's there to talk about?"

Corrie shifted. She could feel the resistance from the group. "I'm not sure I agree with the sheriff."

At this, a collective murmur rose. "Come on," said Wiggett. "You don't actually think Peel was murdered, do you?"

"I'm still gathering information." She hesitated, then decided to go ahead and share her suspicions. "But in my opinion, at least one of the injuries to Peel's head looked as if it predated the fall."

This caused considerable consternation.

"You think one of *us* did it?" Maggie asked.

"I haven't drawn any conclusions." Corrie began to feel annoyed by this questioning.

"But you *think* it," Maggie said. "I can see it in your face!"

Nora broke in. "Hold on. I'm as unhappy about this as anyone, but Agent Swanson is only doing her job."

Thank you, Corrie thought. She was surprised—especially given Nora's own feeling about drawing conclusions, given the state of the corpse.

"Why the hell would anyone kill Peel?" Maggie repeated. "Where's the motive?"

"That's what I'm trying to find out," Corrie said. "The twenty million dollars in gold hidden around here might well be motive enough for a homicide. I noticed nobody was in camp when I returned this afternoon. I wonder what all of you were up to."

"Now just a minute," Burleson said. "If you're suggesting we were out treasure hunting, I've already forbidden that."

"All I'm asking," Corrie said, trying to keep the exasperation out of her voice, "is everyone's cooperation."

There was a restless movement among the group.

"If you really think it's murder," Maggie said, "then you've got to suspect one of us. Right? It's like an old mystery novel, where everyone's trapped on an island or something. Ain't nobody else up here."

"There's no need to speculate," Corrie said. But she could see that what Maggie said was already beginning to take root.

"The honest truth is, we don't know who might be in this neck of the woods," Burleson said. "This is big country—anyone could be wandering around up here. Camping. Eavesdropping. And who knows how far the rumors of gold might have leaked?"

"Are you suggesting one of us has a hidden partner, out there in the mountains?" Salazar asked.

"I'm only saying my team didn't know about the gold until we were already here—and our only connection to the outside world is your satellite phone."

"So by elimination, one of us from the Institute set this up?"

"I'm not saying anybody set anything up," Burleson told Salazar. "Besides, even if Agent Swanson is right, it's not necessarily us, or you—there are people at the Institute who know about the gold."

"Only the president and chairman of the board," said Nora. "And there's no way either one of them would divulge it."

"I'm sorry, but I don't understand why we're even talking about this," Wiggett said. "The idea that one of us was involved in Peel's death is bullshit. The idea that Peel was *murdered* is bullshit."

"Maybe so," said Corrie. "But if we are dealing with a homicide, regardless of whether it's someone in the group or outside, it might be a good idea for you all to stay in pairs when leaving camp from now on—especially after dark."

That, she noted, shut them up.

★ ★ ★

Dinner was a silent affair. Corrie ate fast and then retreated to her tent to work on her notes. Being an FBI agent was hard in ways she hadn't expected. She wasn't quite sure how it happened, but it seemed that, in trying to do her job, she had managed to piss off just about everyone: the archaeologists and the ranch staff, the sheriff and Forest Service guys. What was she doing wrong? Or was this how it always was?

As she lay on top of her sleeping bag long after everyone had gone to bed, wondering if there was a way she could be handling things better, she heard a blood-curdling scream. Leaping up, she grabbed her holster and pulled out the Glock. She raced out of the tent. Headlamps and flashlights were going on all over as everyone piled out to see what had happened.

The cook, Maggie Buck, stood before her tent in her pajamas, hugging herself, sobbing and shaking.

"I saw her! She came into my tent!"

"Who?" Burleson asked.

"Who do you think? It was so awful. She was hobbling, and she smelled like rotten meat and her eyes were all white and she said she was looking for her leg...and then *she started to reach out...!*"

Burleson gave her a gentle shake. "It's okay, Maggie. You've had a nightmare."

Maggie turned her wide eyes toward him. "It was no nightmare! She was right in front of me. And her touch was as cold as clay!"

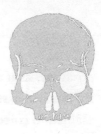

36

May 16

THE NOONDAY SUN cast a welcome heat over the dig site as Nora examined the hearth and shelter area. It had now been fully cleared by Salazar and Adelsky, and the two field assistants stood to one side, proud of their work.

And it was good work. Very good work. The hearth had been meticulously uncovered, a stain of charcoal surrounded by nubbins of bone. It lay inside the shelter built by the stranded travelers, with many of the rotting boards still surviving. She could see its basic shape. The boards had been pried from the wagon and reassembled using nails and spikes to form a sort of lean-to, supplemented by a few slender tree trunks. It gave Nora's heart a twist, looking at these remains of a pathetic shelter where human beings had struggled and died. Incredible to think of so many crammed into this tiny hovel, covered in twenty-five feet of snow.

To one side of the shelter Adelsky and Salazar had uncovered another area of bones, consisting of two almost complete skeletons, apparently among the last to die, in twisted, grotesque positions, as if they had expired in convulsions. It wasn't normally how a starving person died, Nora thought. Rather, it seemed to corroborate the accounts that some members of the Lost Camp had kept on raving to the last.

She did a mental count. Samantha Carville; the two Wolfinger murderers; the three skeletons in the midden heap; the pathetic remains they'd found in the shelter pot; Boardman, who'd managed to escape the camp after his crazed wife tried to attack him; and Chears, the lone person to be rescued. Those, along with these two sets of remains her assistants had just uncovered here, totaled eleven—precisely the number of people believed to have been stranded at the Lost Camp. Nora couldn't resist a feeling of professional satisfaction at this summing up. And they'd managed to achieve it despite Peel's theft. Of course, a portion of the Parkin skeleton remained missing. But they had combed both Peel's route and the location where he died, and Nora was certain they'd recovered every last bone and fragment. The fact was, despite the missing skull, the success of this archaeological project had proven remarkable. There was only one thing still undiscovered.

"So, what more do we need to do?" Clive asked as he looked over her shoulder at the remains of the shelter.

"We're essentially done with the excavation phase. All that's left is to remove the bones and artifacts and seal them up for transportation back to the Institute. Then we can backfill the site." She turned to Salazar and Adelsky. "Fine job, you two."

They smiled, hesitated, and Nora said, "Now I suppose you want to do some gold prospecting?"

"Well," said Adelsky. "You did promise."

Nora had to laugh. "You've earned a break. Okay, we'll wait for tomorrow to get the bones tagged and sealed for shipment."

★ ★ ★

After lunch, Nora unfolded her diagram of the cliffs. She and Clive had managed to get some more searching in here and there since the first serious attempt, and now only two sectors remained.

"You really think it's there?" Adelsky asked, peering upward.

"I'm sure it is," said Clive. "It wasn't on the bodies, and there isn't any other place they could have hidden it, given all the snow."

"What about this area of the diagram, here?" Salazar was pointing to a spot Nora had recently shaded red, at the far end of the last sector.

"That area is threatened by that stubborn cornice up on the ridge. We can't search that sector until the cornice either melts or falls."

"The 'red sector,'" Adelsky said melodramatically, looking at the diagram. "Sounds like a spy novel. What do you want to bet that's where it ends up being hidden?"

They gathered the equipment and packs and hiked up the valley. Nora put on the harness and began climbing to various cracks and holes. Salazar belayed her while Clive and Adelsky searched the lower openings that were reachable by scrambling.

Around four in the afternoon Nora called for a halt. They had now covered all of the areas not threatened by the cornice. At the bottom of the cliff, still roped up, Nora cast her eyes over the remaining holes and cracks in the red sector.

"That's it?" Salazar called over to her.

"That's it."

"Damn," said Adelsky. "As long as we're here, let's finish up."

"Go ahead, knock yourself out," Salazar told him. "I've seen cornices like that fall before. You wouldn't get me to search in there now for fifty million in gold."

Nora's eye traveled upward to the scree slope and avalanche chute leading to the ridge. The chute was swept clear of trees— obviously many avalanches had come down in the past. She raised her binoculars. The cornice was still a good hundred feet deep, and it slumped over the cliff edge as if it would give way at any moment.

"Jason's right," she said, taking off her gear. "It's far too dangerous."

She looked around at the downcast expressions. Even Clive looked a little disappointed. But as the expedition leader, she knew she couldn't take such a crazy risk.

Then an idea hit her. She turned back to Adelsky and Salazar. "You guys swept the entire site with the magnetometer. Right?"

They looked at each other. "Right," they chorused.

"Well, before we pack up for good, let's use it for one more careful sweep around the corpses of Spitzer and Reinhardt."

Clive frowned. "Why? We already excavated out several feet from those bodies."

"I know. But we've checked all the cliffs that we can for now. And who knows—maybe they hid the gold a little farther away from their camp than we've dug."

Salazar shrugged. "I'm game."

The other three walked over to the burial site while Salazar went back to the main tent, retrieved the proton magnetometer, and returned. Nora and the rest stood well back while Salazar set up the sensor and cabling and made the necessary calibrations to the device. Then, with even more than the usual amount of care, he began to traverse the site in an ever-widening spiral.

Nora followed his progress from her iPad. At first, Salazar noted lots of hits on the magnetometer's console, but Nora could see these corresponded to what they'd already found. As he began to circle the bodies at a greater distance, the hits dropped to infrequent, then to none.

The air of expectation that had settled over the group despite this strategy being a long shot disintegrated. Clive glanced at Nora as if to say, *Well, it was a good idea, anyway.*

"Got something," Salazar said.

Immediately, the others snapped to attention.

"What?" Adelsky asked.

"Just a shadow. I'll check the surrounding area." Salazar made another few transits with the magnetometer, farther from the bodies, then returned to the spot where he'd gotten the hit and went over it again, still more carefully. "This is it. Whatever's buried is here."

"Could it be an iron chest?" Clive asked.

Salazar shook his head without looking up from the console. "Not that large and not ferromagnetic. But there's something, and it's subsurface."

He marked the spot, then stepped back and turned off the magnetometer. Adelsky had already run off to fetch a set of tools, which he handed to Nora. She gloved up, knelt, and began exposing the area Salazar had marked.

It took only ten minutes of careful digging. The magnetometer had picked up a small grouping of bones. Nora excavated below and around it, but there was clearly nothing else.

"It looks like a tiny leg," said Salazar. "Oh, God."

Nora already knew exactly what it was—she had recognized

it even as she was uncovering it. "It's Samantha Carville's missing leg." And after a moment she added, "To be precise, what we have here is a tibia and fibula, along with the foot bones, belonging to a small child. If you look closely at the tibia, you'll see knife and teeth marks in addition to the scorching."

"Jesus," murmured Salazar.

"Are you sure it's Carville's?" Clive asked.

"Who else's?"

The question needed no answer, and none was offered.

★ ★ ★

Half an hour later, Clive was following Adelsky and Salazar back down the trail. Nora watched them disappear into the trees at the edge of the meadow, then returned to the work tent to get the tarps out in preparation for pegging down the site. She had mapped and logged the final bones into the database.

As she was working, she saw a figure emerge from the trees. It was that FBI agent, Corrie Swanson. *Damn, will she never leave us alone?*

She stood up and waited for the agent to arrive.

"Am I disturbing you?"

Nora shook her head. "Just about done. What's up?"

Corrie paused. "I had a few more questions."

Nora sighed. "Okay." She noticed the agent didn't have her cell phone out to record. That was a good sign—she hoped. "Shoot."

"It's about Dr. Benton."

"What about him?"

"I've now spoken to everybody, and I'm still a little confused about precisely why he approached you for this project, and not a place like Stanford or the University of California."

"I'm an archaeologist. The Santa Fe Archaeological Institute is world class. End of story."

"It just seems that Stanford or UC would be the first choice, given they're California institutions and Stanford is where he went to school."

Nora tried to suppress an upwelling of irritation. "Why are you so suspicious of Clive?"

"I didn't say I was suspicious—"

"It's obvious. Why?"

"Because everything seems to revolve around him, in one way or another. The journal, the dig, the gold."

Nora stared at her. "What you have are a bunch of vague notions. You're trying to put them in order, but you can't. Because there *is* no order."

"I'm still in the evidence-gathering phase—"

"Look at it from my perspective. You come up here, hurl around a bunch of accusations without really knowing what you're talking about. You say a guy who fell off a cliff might have been pushed—without proof. I *know* Clive. He's a straight shooter. He could've come up here and taken the gold. But he didn't."

"How do you know he didn't?"

"Well, if he'd already collected the gold, what would we be doing here?"

Corrie didn't answer.

"And if he didn't find the gold, why would he pull in the Institute, when that prevents any chance of him profiting from the gold himself? You're fishing—and hindering an excavation that's already had more than its share of problems." She paused, irritation increasing. "Look, everybody else in law enforcement who's seen the site is satisfied. It's pretty clear you're a rookie, and you're eager to see bogeymen where there are none."

Corrie flushed deeply. Nora realized she had hit home with the comment, and immediately regretted it.

After a moment the agent said a terse "Thank you," turned, and left.

★ ★ ★

As Corrie walked into camp, the group sitting around the fire fell silent. She headed for her tent and Burleson rose.

"A Special Agent Morwood called on the sat phone. Wanted you to call back. Phone's in the equipment tent."

Corrie headed to the tent, picked up the box with the sat phone, and carried it to her own tent, where she could speak in privacy.

"How are things going?" Morwood asked when she reached him.

Corrie hesitated. "I'm making progress. Everyone's been interviewed, and I've assembled quite a lot of information."

"Any hard evidence connecting the missing Parkin skull with your case?"

"No hard evidence, but I'm still working on it."

A silence, and then Morwood said, "We've got a lot to talk about, and we can't do it over this phone. I'd like you to come down tomorrow and meet me at the Truckee sheriff's department."

"But I haven't finished my investigation up here—"

"Agent Swanson, I want you to come down. I've already

spoken to the sheriff, and he can make available a conference room where we can speak privately. If you leave in the morning, you should reach Truckee around two o'clock. Can we make it for three?"

"I...Yes, sir."

"Good. Bring your tent and gear."

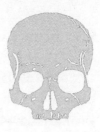

37

May 17

THE NEVADA COUNTY Sheriff's Office in Truckee was an ugly midcentury modern building with a flat roof, surrounded by a parking lot. Low dark clouds accumulated in the afternoon sky as Corrie headed across the asphalt lot to the building. Her butt hurt from the ride down the trail, and her knees were stiff. As she approached, she hung her badge around her neck.

"Special Agent Morwood is waiting for you in the conference room," the receptionist said as she entered the building. "Third door on the right."

Corrie walked quickly with her head down, successfully evading Sheriff Devlin, whose door was open. Morwood rose as she entered, extended his hand.

"This is a nicer town than most to conduct an investigation, don't you think?" he asked, closing the door. "Beautiful mountain scenery and fresh air. Too bad about the altitude, though—for me, anyway." He punctuated this with a cough.

"Thank you for coming out here, sir."

"Let's get down to business."

Corrie took out her notebook and thumbed through the pages that summarized her findings. She quickly described the examination of Peel and the surrounding site; the fact that the Parkin skull was missing; her suspicions about Benton; the supposed existence of the treasure; and her conclusion that Peel had likely been hit over the head before being pushed off the cliff—making it a homicide. In conclusion, she reviewed her interviews with each member of the group.

She lowered the notebook. Morwood had listened intently, and now he eased back in his chair and let out a long exhale. What was that—disapproval? Frustration?

He fished a file out of his briefcase and put it on the table, sliding it toward Corrie. "The autopsy report on Peel."

Corrie took it and opened it, but already Morwood was speaking again. "Conclusion: death by misadventure."

She skimmed the contents before replying. "With respect, sir, I think he's wrong."

"He's not just some amateur county coroner. This guy is highly trained and experienced, with a degree in forensic pathology."

"But my degree is—"

Morwood held up a hand. "Corrie?" he said gently. "If I may?"

Corrie fell silent.

"Let's get back to basics here. Was a crime committed up there at that dig?"

"I think Peel—"

"Forget Peel. It's officially an accident. Outside of that: where's the crime?"

"Before I got here, we had Parkin bodies disappearing all over. Now the Parkin skull found at this site is gone, too. There's twenty million in gold hidden up there. I think the missing

Parkin bones are related to other crimes I'm investigating, and the gold is, at the very least, a complicating factor."

Morwood issued another sigh. "The bottom line is, once again: where's the crime? And the answer is: there is none. You've gathered a lot of scattered evidence and drawn some unfounded suspicions, but that doesn't amount to a coherent theory. Nor does the evidence offer a link to the other Parkin disappearances. The FBI doesn't investigate rumors or conjectured crimes. We operate on facts. We need an actual crime— and there's none here."

"I still think there must be a connection. It can't all be coincidence."

"Corrie, I've been ghosting people now for almost ten years. I've seen this happen many times with young agents freshly minted from Quantico. They're bursting with energy, they want to make their bones, and they see suspicion in every face and conspiracy in every coincidence. I authorized you to come here to look for a Parkin connection. I was skeptical, as you know, but you were persuasive and you were persistent, and in the end that's what ghosting is all about: letting the new agent find things out for herself. And your own briefing just now has convinced me this is a genuine archaeological site, it is being excavated properly, and everyone is doing their job. There may or may not be gold here, but there's no mystery surrounding it. Everything is aboveboard and accounted for."

He paused. Corrie remained silent.

"And in the process, you've made some missteps."

"Like what?" She blurted it out before she could stop herself.

"Well, you should never have spoken of your suspicions about Peel's death. Maybe you hoped to rattle them, shake out a suspect. But you did it before you *knew* it was a homicide. The first rule of an investigation is to keep your suspicions to yourself and only reveal information if there is an extremely pressing need to do so—and if the information is solid. I shouldn't have to remind you of FBI procedure: Say nothing. Do *not* opine. Do *not* speak of your evidence. Do *not* discuss any aspect of the case with civilians."

Corrie felt herself flushing deeply. She knew, of course, Morwood was right. It was one of the things they drilled into you at the Academy.

"The second thing is that you have not worked well with local law enforcement."

"You mean Sheriff Devlin? And those Forest Service guys? They were tramping all over the site like bulls in a china shop. They were disrespectful of my authority and pretty much forced me to pull rank."

"I have no doubt they were difficult. But locals are often difficult when the FBI shows up. They don't like us butting into their territory. You have to learn how to handle that."

So Devlin went whining to the Bureau about our little standoff in the ravine. Figures. "But, sir, I was totally respectful of them."

"You managed to seriously piss off Sheriff Devlin. He's one of these good old boys: a bit sexist, not terribly smart, but in essence a decent guy. You're going to meet a ton of Devlins—*and* Turpenseeds—in your career. You've got to find a better way to get along with them."

"Yes, sir."

"At any rate, I'm shutting down this branch of the investigation. It's a dead end. You're going to shift focus on this case back where it belongs: New Mexico and Arizona."

"Yes, sir," Corrie said again. She felt the heat in her face and hoped to God she wouldn't start to cry.

Morwood reached across the table and gave her a pat on the shoulder. "Corrie, you're going to make a good FBI agent. I know it's a truism, but we were all rookies once."

"Thank you, sir."

"I've booked a room for you at the Truckee Motel tonight. We'll drive back to Albuquerque in the morning."

Corrie looked at him. "Albuquerque?" It was a stupid question; Morwood's announcement was still sinking in. She should have expected it when he told her to bring down her gear.

Morwood nodded. "It's over. With Peel's death being ruled an accident, there's nothing to investigate."

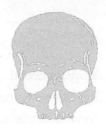

38

Nora sat in her tent, using the last of the evening light to update her journal. It had, in its own way, been a momentous day. They had completed the excavation. And though Parkin's skull was missing, they'd recovered Samantha Carville's leg and could reunify it with the rest of her remains. While they hadn't yet found the gold, they still had time during the wrapping-up period to search. Maybe, she thought, the cornice would give way in the storm forecast for the coming days. If not, they could always come back later, in the summer, after the snowfields disappeared from the high country.

"Champagne!" she heard Clive call from the kitchen area. "Come and get it!"

With a smile, she shut her notebook and exited her tent. Clive was standing by the fire, waving a bottle around. "Time to celebrate!"

"For God's sake, man, don't shake it up!" Burleson said, emerging from his own tent. The atmosphere in camp had improved considerably since the FBI agent had left. Morale was high, and even Maggie, who had been dour of late, was in a buoyant mood—perhaps because Nora had told her of the finding of Samantha Carville's missing leg bone. She hovered over the fire, a pile of raw steaks and roasting ears ready to toss on the grill.

Clive worked off the cork with a pop. As it flew into the air, Wiggett snagged it with a deft one-handed catch.

"The man who makes the catch gets the first glass." Wiggett stuck out his tin cup and Clive poured champagne into it, then went around the circle, opening a second bottle when the first was empty.

He raised his glass. "To the Donner Party—those who died and those who lived."

"Hear, hear."

Everyone drank and now a third bottle went around.

"So what's the takeaway?" Burleson asked. "Give us a rundown on your discoveries."

"In any archaeological excavation," Nora said, "ninety percent of the real discoveries come in the lab. But we've already learned a lot."

"We're all ears."

"It's obvious the Lost Camp was the hardest hit of the three. We found many signs of the struggles they must have endured. They built a shelter, ate their oxen, ate their dogs. But they refrained from eating human flesh for a long time, except for one early moment of weakness when the two murderers, it seems, dug up Samantha Carville's frozen body and began to eat her leg. But finally, in late February, when Albert Parkin died, most of the others finally broke down. That's when the real cannibalism set in. Followed, according to Boardman's account, by madness."

"Why did they go nuts?" Maggie asked.

"Extreme starvation is known to cause neurological problems, including temporary derangement. Even the other two camps, which did not endure quite such extreme hardship, were affected—admittedly, to a lesser degree."

"And how many of the dead have you identified so far?" asked Burleson.

"People's remains were processed, boiled, gnawed on, and reboiled to extract every bit of nourishment—that's how desperate they were, and that's what will take the most lab time. So far, we've identified four individuals to a high degree of confidence: Samantha Carville, Spitzer and Reinhardt, and Albert Parkin."

"And the gold?" Wiggett asked.

"I still believe we'll find it." She turned. "Clive, do you want to add anything?"

The historian took a sip of champagne, composing his thoughts. "I just want to say how grateful I am to everyone. Every single person here, in one way or another, did their part to make this possible. And I'm especially grateful to you, Nora. You know how strongly I felt about this, and you not only helped get the expedition on its feet—you were patient." He paused. "Knowing what happened here matters. This is not just a story of cannibalism and death; I see this as a testimony to courage and survival."

The fire had died into coals and Maggie began loading the steaks and corn on the grill, with an accompanying sizzle of roasting meat. Nora realized the discussion of cannibalism seemed to make that particular sound, and smell, a little repellent to her. But at least the corn looked appetizing.

★ ★ ★

They all went to bed rather jolly from the champagne. Nora drifted off to the scent of the campfire and the trilling of crickets—only to be awoken in the middle of the night by loud voices. She unzipped her tent as flashlight beams swung through the darkness and Maggie stood in the middle of everything, wearing her voluminous pajamas, talking loudly. It seemed she had had another nightmare.

Nora pulled on her jacket and came out. The night air was chilly. Nobody else had heard anything.

"I saw it—off in the trees," Maggie was saying loudly. "A green light. Moving."

"A flashlight?" Burleson asked.

"No. And then I swear I heard a voice. It sounded like someone trying to shout—a gurgling shout."

Burleson put his hand on her shoulder. "Are you sure it wasn't another nightmare?" he asked gently. "They found Samantha's missing leg bone today. Is that on your mind?"

"I swear to God..." She broke down, sobbing loudly, shoulders heaving.

"There, it's okay," said Burleson, putting his arm around her.

"Where's Wiggett?" Clive suddenly asked.

"He's a hard sleeper," Burleson said, and then after a moment: "Let me check."

His flashlight went weaving off into the darkness. A moment later his voice came back: "He's not in his tent."

Burleson returned to the group. "His boots are gone, PJs tossed on the cot. He must have gotten dressed and gone out."

There was a silence. "Maybe it was his voice I heard," Maggie said. "It kind of sounded like it."

Burleson shook his head with annoyance. "He may be looking in on the horses. I'm going to check the corral."

"I'll go with you," said Nora.

But Wiggett was not at the corral. The two returned to find an anxious group waiting for them.

"All right," said Burleson. "I think we'd better have a look around."

"I'll bet he was out there looking for the gold," said Maggie. "You know, he wouldn't stop talking about it when you all were away from camp."

"Let's all get dressed and meet back here in five." Burleson looked around. "Everyone needs to pair up, and then we'll do a quick search. Nobody goes anywhere alone."

Clive turned to Nora. "You and me?"

She nodded.

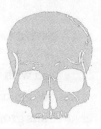

39

May 18

As they assembled in the chilly dark, dressed and ready, some-one chucked some brush on the coals. The fire flared up, paint-ing their faces in flickering yellow light. In the darkness of the trees, an owl gave a series of low hoots, like the tolling of a bell.

"All right," said Burleson. "Everyone got headlamps?"

There was a chorus of assent.

"Nora, Clive, you go up to the dig site. Bruce and Jason, fol-low them up the trail, then cut east and search the area around the tarn. I'm going to scour the immediate vicinity of the camp with Maggie."

He looked around, firelight gleaming in his eyes. "Don't go far. Be careful and stay together. There's always the chance someone else is out there."

He flashed his headlamp on his watch. "It's three twenty. We'll search for an hour. Meet back here at four twenty—sharp."

Nora and Clive set off up the now-familiar trail leading to the dig site, Adelsky and Salazar close behind. Nora took the lead, hiking fast. It was a dark night, with a heavy cloud cover casting an inky blackness over the mountains. It was like swimming through a sea of darkness with only tiny circles of light to guide them. The night was full of sound—the breath of wind in the treetops, the calling of owls, the chirping of crickets, and the occasional eructation of a bullfrog along the stream.

"I feel like we're cursed," said Clive bitterly. "No sooner do we celebrate our success—with champagne, no less—than this happens."

"We don't know if anything has happened," said Nora. "Maybe Wiggett just quit and took off, like Peel."

"Without his horse? No way."

"Maybe it's like Maggie said and he's out there searching for the gold."

"If he is, you can bet Burleson's going to have words with him."

They emerged from the trees into the broad meadow of the Lost Camp. Ahead she could barely make out the rectangle of gray that marked the work tent. The cliffs were like black walls, the sky almost as dark. Adelsky and Salazar headed off in the direction of the tarn. Nora looked around for the gleam of Wiggett's flashlight, in case he was searching the cliffs, but all she could see was blackness.

"Let's check the tent," Clive suggested.

They approached the tent, which loomed out of the darkness in the beams of their headlamps. Untying the flap, Nora entered. All was exactly as they had left it. They next inspected the excavation area, tarped over and pegged down. It, too, looked undisturbed.

Clive glanced around, as if trying to pierce the darkness. "I guess that just leaves the cliffs," he said.

They hiked over and began making their way along the base

of the cliffs, shining their lights up and around the stone flanks. But there was no sign of Wiggett, and the heavy dew that lay on the grass also looked undisturbed. When they had finished examining one side of the cliffs they went across to the other, but again found no sign of the wrangler.

"He wasn't up here," Nora said. "Which sort of eliminates the idea he was searching for the gold."

"Unless," Clive said, "he had his own ideas about where it was hidden."

"Could be." Nora checked her watch. "It's been almost an hour. We'd better head back."

Even as she spoke, she heard a scream coming from down the canyon. It went on and on, echoing grotesquely among the peaks before trailing off.

"Oh Christ," said Clive.

They started for the trail at a jog and the forest quickly closed in on them. Their headlamps stabbed into the darkness, tree trunks illuminated one by one as they passed like columns in an endless cathedral. As they approached the camp, Nora could make out, alongside the stream, a cluster of lights and uneasy voices ringing across the night. Another piercing scream erupted, the voice now distinguishable as Maggie's.

They turned off the trail and jogged toward the lights. They found the rest of the group gathered at the base of the cliffs near the camp. Maggie was breathing loudly between sobs, leaning on Burleson.

"In there," said Burleson, shining his headlamp at a broad crack at the base of the cliffs. Nora went over and made out a hiking boot, grotesquely wedged into the crack. Peering deeper, she could see a body, soaking wet.

Wiggett.

"What the *hell*?" said Clive, peering in beside her. "Who found him?"

Maggie hiccupped. "Samantha showed us."

"Come now," said Burleson sharply.

"I saw the light. The greenish light, it led us over here. You saw it, too!"

"It was just the reflection from our headlamps on something," Burleson said impatiently. "For God's sake, let's get him out of there."

Nora, Clive, and the rest started pulling out loose rocks that had been piled into the crack in a feeble attempt to hide the body. Wiggett had been shoved in upright, arms dangling. Nora seized an arm—it was cold and damp—and pulled, while Clive and Burleson grabbed a leg and the other arm. After a struggle, they managed to slide his body out of the crevice and lower it onto the grass. His eyes were staring and his mouth open, a dribble of water draining out from his lips.

Burleson felt his neck. "No pulse."

They all stood around the body, shocked and staring.

"But how..." Maggie stuttered, "how did he get in there, all wet like that?"

Nora recovered her wits. "Excuse me, everyone, but I think we should leave everything just as we found it, go back to camp, and—" she swallowed— "phone this in."

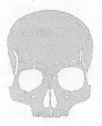

40

Corrie Swanson sat bolt upright in bed as her cell phone blasted out the theme to *The Man from U.N.C.L.E.* She fumbled the phone off her bedside table.

"Yes?"

"It's Nora Kelly. I'm calling because..."

Her voice on the satellite phone seemed very far away.

"What's happened?"

"There's... a murder."

Her voice kept cutting in and out.

"Who? How?"

"Wiggett. They found him... crack of rock near..."

The sleep cleared swiftly from Corrie's brain. "I'm not getting all of what you're saying. But I'm getting enough. Don't touch anything and keep everyone back. What's this about a crack?"

"His body was jammed... hidden with rocks..."

"Any idea who did it?"

"No idea... Someone shadowing us... God knows..."

"Listen, get everyone into camp and keep them together.

Nobody should go anywhere alone. Even for visits to the bathroom."

"Okay."

Corrie looked at her watch. Almost 5 AM. Sunrise was still an hour away. Maybe the sheriff or local Forest Service would have access to a helicopter. "We'll be up there as soon as we can."

"Thank you."

"In the meantime, tell everyone not to discuss anything or do anything. That's going to be hard, I know, but I need everyone's observations to be fresh and uncontaminated. Nobody is to go back to bed."

The only response was a crackle of static.

Corrie hung up and dialed Morwood's room.

★ ★ ★

The sheriff department's helicopter was in Sacramento undergoing maintenance, and the two FBI choppers in the area were both occupied in a drug interdiction effort with the DEA. And so Corrie found herself once again on the back of a horse, riding into the mountains with the usual suspects—Sheriff Devlin, his deputy, and the two Forest Service LEOs. Morwood could not accompany them due to his lung condition, but he had made it clear to her she was in charge, and that she was responsible for evidence collection and keeping the bulls out of the china shop. And then he reminded her that she'd better get along with Devlin and the others.

She wondered how the hell she was supposed to balance all those things.

And just before she left, Morwood had concluded with an unwelcome observation. "Agent Swanson, this presumed murder in no way proves any connection with the Parkin case. So don't let your speculations run amok. Just gather evidence, keep your thoughts to yourself... and do your best not to alienate the locals."

Great.

On top of everything, a storm was approaching. It was something the local papers called a "pineapple express": a river of moist air that flowed in from the Pacific and drove across the Sierras, unloading on the high country. It was the same kind of weather system that had trapped the Donner Party— only this time it was coming down as rain and sleet instead of snow.

Corrie made sure to ride in front, right behind the wrangler, while the good old boys rode at the end of the train, their loud talk and laughter drifting forward. Once again, they seemed to be having a grand time. At first it irritated her afresh. But then she thought: Why shouldn't they enjoy themselves? There was nothing in the book that said law enforcement officers had to be grim and silent, and she imagined that being a sheriff in Truckee wasn't the most exciting job in the world.

The county coroner, Dr. Anand, wasn't part of the jolly little band, preferring to keep to himself. He was a small, aloof, studious-looking man with round glasses and a shiny bald head. She wasn't sure he was all that good, given what she believed to be his error in classifying the Peel death as an accident. But she hoped for the best.

They arrived in camp around 1 PM. Everyone was standing around waiting for them, looking agitated. Corrie dismounted as Nora approached.

"Show me the body," Corrie said as she untied the saddlebags containing her forensic evidence collection gear. "I want to secure the site immediately." *Before the others get here*, she thought to herself. "The rest of you, please stay here."

She sensed that Nora understood the situation. "Just up the creek a bit and through the forest."

Corrie draped the bags over her shoulder and followed Nora upstream through a stand of fir trees, then cutting off-trail toward a line of cliffs. Wiggett's body lay on its back in the grass next to a large cleft in the cliff face that rose before them.

"He was in there?" Corrie asked, pointing at the cleft.

"Yes. Wedged in vertically, soaking wet. Those rocks on the ground, there, had been stacked inside the crack to hide the body."

"Who found him?"

"Maggie and Burleson. Maggie, ah, claimed she saw a light or something that guided her over."

"Light? As in a flashlight?"

"No. She said it was the spirit of Samantha Carville."

Corrie gave a snort of derision and then instantly regretted the display of disrespect. "Did Burleson see it, too?"

"He says he did see a light, but thought it was a reflection from their own headlamps."

Corrie looked around. A reflection off what? There was nothing. Perhaps there was someone shadowing the group after all.

"What was the temperature of the body when you found it?"

"Cold."

Pulling a roll of tape from her pack, Corrie tied it to a nearby tree and walked it around the area, unrolling it to enclose the crime scene. When she arrived back at the initial tree, she tied it off. As she was pulling booties, mask, and a hair net from her pack, Sheriff Devlin arrived, with the others in tow.

"Sheriff," Corrie said, trying to sound welcoming. "Thanks for assembling your men so quickly. I was hoping...perhaps you and the rest could help me while I go over the crime scene."

"Well, sure." Devlin hiked up his duty belt with a grunt, eyes fixed on the body. "You see the marks on his neck?"

Corrie had seen the marks right away, but she said: "Oh. I'd missed those. Thanks for pointing them out—significant, wouldn't you agree?"

The sheriff nodded, pleased.

"If you and the others could control the perimeter," Corrie said, "keeping people out while I work—that would be greatly appreciated."

"Sure thing."

Corrie ducked under the tape and slowly approached the body, looking around carefully. A heavy dew lay on the grass, but unfortunately it had already been trampled by many feet during the discovery of the body. She snapped pictures of the ground and surroundings, finally focusing on the corpse.

Judging from an area of flattened grass beyond the trampled area, one thing was clear: Wiggett had been killed elsewhere and hauled over to the crack. The problem was, the grass disappeared into the woods—and drag marks didn't show well under the trees.

As she bent over the corpse, she could see unmistakable abrasions and bruising on the neck typical of strangulation. Dragging a body any distance and wedging it into a vertical crack was no mean feat. That meant the killer was almost certainly a man, which would eliminate Maggie and Nora, at any rate. Or would it? The cook, at least, looked pretty damned tough, even if she was a bit overweight. The weight might even be a plus when strangling someone.

Corrie took another series of photos, then started to examine the body. Kneeling, she placed her hand on the victim's sternum and pressed down hard; fluid dribbled out of the mouth. Wiggett's lungs were full of water—that meant the actual cause of death was drowning, perhaps after being rendered unconscious by strangulation.

So where had he drowned? The stream was only a few feet deep. That gloomy little lake uptrail, the tarn, was a more likely place. She took a series of photographs of the drag marks and used her compass to note the bearing; she'd check that out later. For now, it seemed obvious they were dealing with a disorganized, spur-of-the-moment homicide.

She examined the victim's hands but found no traces of biologics under the fingernails. Still, the killer might be scratched or otherwise injured from the struggle. She made a note to scrutinize—subtly—everyone in camp.

She glanced back and saw the four law enforcement officers and the coroner standing behind the tape, waiting for her to finish. They didn't look happy, but at least they were cooperating.

After taking a few more photos and picking up what little evidence she could find at the site—a few bits of hair, a piece of trash, some damp pine needles—she went back to the group.

"Thank you all for waiting so patiently," she said.

There was some nodding and shuffling.

"Dr. Anand? The body is ready for you."

"Thank you, Agent Swanson," said Anand, ducking under the tape with his equipment.

She turned to Sheriff Devlin. "When the doctor is done, I'd appreciate it if you and the others could apply your evidence-gathering expertise to the site as well—to see if there's anything

I've missed." She said this with an effort at a self-deprecating smile.

And as Devlin gave a curt, manly nod in response, Corrie realized something: amid all the sudden scurry, the activity and crime scene analysis, she'd forgotten she was a rookie—and that she had just completed the initial investigation of her first undeniable homicide.

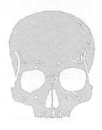

41

AGENT SWANSON WALKED back to the main camp and retrieved the sat phone. She carried it into her hastily reassembled tent and called Morwood, down in Truckee.

"It's Corinne Swanson, sir."

"What's the news?"

"Definitely a homicide. Strangulation and drowning."

"Any thoughts on who?"

"Almost certainly a man. It's possible the killer is someone on the expedition. But a light was seen near the place where the body was hidden, so it's also possible someone from outside could be involved."

"Any forensic evidence?"

"I gathered what I could. Nothing dispositive."

"Any idea where the drowning took place?"

"Not yet. In the stream, perhaps, if he was already unconscious. There's also a pond up beyond camp which seems the more likely place, but I haven't examined it yet for signs of a struggle."

"And your next action step?" In the weekly meetings, Morwood was always talking about "action steps."

"I think we should shut down the camp. Send everyone back to Truckee while we conduct a thorough search."

A long pause, and then Morwood answered. "That's drastic."

"I know. But if it's someone in camp, there might be evidence in their tent. Wet clothes, perhaps, or blood."

Another long pause. "Okay," Morwood said. "I respect your call."

"Thank you, sir."

"As you're always reminding me, you've been trained in forensic evidence collection, so here's your chance to max out that skill set. It's our case, for better or worse, until we can pull in the Sacramento Field Office."

"You're bringing in Sacramento?"

"Not just bringing them in. Turning this case over to them."

Corrie felt surprised and stung. "But why?"

"There's no connection to the Parkin case. I'd bet ten to one this is about the gold. The Parkin case is *our* case; let Sacramento take this. So keep that in mind, do everything by the book, and make sure all your evidence is solid. In other words, no speculation; just the facts, ma'am."

"Yes, sir."

"Have at it."

She racked the phone, then shut and latched the box, leaving it in her tent in case she needed to call Morwood again. She felt crushed that he was turning the case over to Sacramento. Despite everything, she felt there must be some connection between the missing Parkin bones and the homicide.

But this disappointment faded temporarily as she considered what would be a daunting task: evacuating the camp. It was going to be a tough sell, and she sensed Nora Kelly was not going to agree without a fight.

She emerged from her tent in time to see the sheriff and his buddies returning from the crime scene. She caught his eye and motioned him and the others over.

"Any luck?"

The sheriff held up a collection sack. "We found some stuff, but nothing suggestive. Maybe in the lab?"

"Thanks." Corrie took the sack and set it among her other evidence. She took a deep breath. "I've just spoken to my supervising agent. I'm going to order that the camp be shut down for evidence collection purposes."

Devlin stared at her. "They're going to have a fit," he said.

"Can't be helped."

The sheriff looked at his deputy, then they both exchanged glances with the Forest Service LEOs. "Your call," the sheriff finally said.

"Your call." Translation: "Covering my own ass." But Corrie only smiled and nodded, then walked into the camp, the sheriff and his gang following. Nora Kelly was waiting for her, and the other expedition members quickly crowded around.

"So what did you find?" Nora asked.

"I'm sorry, but for now I have to keep the details confidential."

"Who do you think—?"

"Nora, can we speak privately?" Corrie broke in. Then she turned. "You, too, please, Mr. Burleson."

She led them away from the group.

"What's up?" Nora asked.

"I'm afraid we have to ask that the camp be evacuated."

"Evacuated? What do you mean?"

"I mean everything has to be closed down—the dig site,

the camp—leaving all in place. You and your crew will need to go down to Truckee until we can complete the evidence collection."

"Are you crazy?" Nora said. "We can't just leave! I've got an open dig site up there, with exposed human remains!"

"I'm afraid it's necessary."

"Bullshit." She turned and called out. "Sheriff?"

Son of a bitch, thought Corrie. This woman was a real pain in the ass.

"Yes?" Devlin and his deputy, who had been hovering in the background, came over.

"Agent Swanson is saying we have to shut down everything. I'm trying to explain to her that's impossible. Not just impossible, but it threatens the integrity of the dig. It puts the human remains up here at risk of damage, vandalism, even theft. I can't allow that. You're the county law enforcement officer, and I protest this."

Devlin shuffled a bit and didn't answer at once. He slipped a pack of cigarettes from his vest pocket, shucked one up, and stuck it in his mouth, taking his time lighting it. He exhaled a stream of smoke.

"Well, ma'am, shutting down a crime scene is standard operating procedure."

Corrie realized she'd been holding her breath. She released it.

"But this isn't the crime scene!" Nora said. "We found Wiggett's body at least a couple hundred yards upstream. Look, at least keep the dig site open so we can protect it. Nothing happened up there."

"We don't know that." Corrie shook her head. "And last I saw, the dig site was already tarped and secured. Law enforcement will be very careful not to disturb anything."

Nora fumed for a moment in silence. "When do you expect us to leave?"

"Now."

"Like, *right* now?"

"That's correct. And without anyone being allowed to return to their tents, take their possessions, or disturb anything."

"That's insane. I've got my notes, wallet, credit cards, phone, everything in the tent!"

"Take absolute necessities only. We'll make sure the rest is safe."

"Don't you need some kind of warrant?"

"Nora, as I've already explained, since we're on federal land, no search warrant is required. I've also taken a closer look at your permit, and I noticed it allows for federal law enforcement entry without notice—pretty standard language, actually, for any activity in the National Forest."

Nora stood there, arms akimbo, a dark expression on her face. "Who made this decision? You? What does your boss say about this?"

"Special Agent Morwood agrees with me." She glanced over at the sheriff. "What's more to the point, *I'm* in charge and that's the end of this discussion." Corrie realized with relief that, this time, she was managing not to raise her voice. She turned to Burleson. "Please get the horses saddled and ready to take everyone down. I want them on their horses and gone, leaving everything untouched. And I'll need your personnel—in addition to Nora's—to remain in Truckee, available for questioning."

"Are you shitting me?" Nora asked. "For how long?"

"As long as necessary."

Nora turned to Devlin. "And you. Sheriff. You're good with this?"

Devlin cleared his throat, took a moment to take another drag on his cigarette, puckered his lips, and spit out a piece of tobacco. "Well, maybe we could put a time frame on things. How about that, Agent Swanson?" He looked at her sideways.

Corrie suppressed an upwelling of irritation. She didn't like Devlin interfering, but the suggestion wasn't out of line.

"Seventy-two hours," Corrie said.

"Twenty-four," said Nora.

Corrie had just about had it with this woman. "Forty-eight. And you don't come back up here until you've cleared it with me—face-to-face."

A long silence.

"All right," Nora said at last.

Burleson spoke. "I'm guessing you think one of us killed Wiggett?"

"I can't speak to that. Now, are we clear?"

"As a bell," said Burleson with a wry smile. "We're going to have to hurry if we want to get back to the ranch before dark. You ready, Nora?"

Nora swore briefly and colorfully, her face white with anger, then turned and stormed off.

"What about that pineapple express headed our way?" Burleson asked Corrie.

She hesitated. Son of a bitch: in the course of everything, she'd forgotten about the approaching weather. "We'll do the best we can. But I need forty-eight hours up here, storm or no storm."

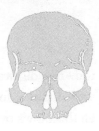

42

May 19

At nine o'clock the next evening, Nora sat alone at the bar in the faux-quaint saloon of the Truckee Inn: old movie posters and roadside attraction signs hung on the wall, along with random gold-mining tools—picks, shovels, pans, sluice boxes, hand drills. She was nursing a beer and a sense of grievance. She'd spent a long, boring day stuck in this crappy town. Wiggett's death had horrified her, and she couldn't get the image of the wrangler's white, staring face out of her mind. Her brother, who'd started hearing rumors about the dig site, had called her full of concern, and it had taken her half an hour to persuade him not to drop everything and drive up immediately.

She felt a presence behind her and Clive swung onto the next barstool.

"Hendrick's straight up, with a twist," he told the bartender, then turned to Nora. "How are you doing?"

"Extremely shitty."

"I know. Just when we thought we were finished. But I've been doing my best to look on the bright side—and you should, too. The dig was an unqualified success. We found the site we were looking for, and an incredibly rich one at that. And when all this blows over, we still might find the gold."

"It would have been an archaeologist's dream," said Nora. "If it weren't for the murders."

"Plural. So you think Peel was murdered, too?"

"I don't think an experienced guy like Peel would just walk off a cliff with his headlamp on."

"I heard the coroner is going to take another look at his body."

"Good. If he hadn't screwed up the autopsy, Wiggett might still be alive."

Nora finished her beer and ordered another as Clive's martini arrived.

"That FBI agent seems to think it was one of us," Nora went on.

"Can't blame her, I guess." Clive shrugged. "But who?"

"That's just it. Me? Maggie? You? Burleson? Adelsky or Salazar? The idea that any one of us six is a killer is totally absurd." She hesitated a moment before continuing. "I didn't want to say anything earlier, but now I've begun to wonder if some person or persons *were* in the forest. Watching us."

"Now you sound like Maggie."

Nora made a moue.

"But why?"

"It all comes down to the gold. Maybe Wiggett or Peel found it and got killed as a result. Maybe they found it together, and had some kind of secret pact. Or maybe word of the gold somehow leaked—and somebody's trying to scare us off so they can hunt for it unencumbered."

"Maybe, maybe, maybe." Clive sipped his drink. "Burleson

says we're slated for the third degree tomorrow. When Agent Swanson gets back."

"Oh, God."

Clive finished the martini and tapped the glass, signaling for another.

"Those look strong," said Nora.

"They're just what the doctor ordered." He waited, watching the bartender fill a cocktail shaker. "There's something I've been meaning to mention to you. About Burleson."

"What?"

"Well, I did a little checking up on him. It wasn't easy to dig up, but I'm a historian and I'm good at finding obscure stuff on the web. You know he used to be a big-shot divorce lawyer in California, right?"

"Yes."

"He says he switched careers because he got tired of the rat race. But the real truth is he got into trouble. He was representing this young woman who married a rich asshole, it seems, with a prenup. He hired a shady detective, who illegally broke into the guy's mansion, got caught, and ratted him out. Burleson lied to the cops. And when they tried to arrest him he got all pissed off and took a swing at one of them. They charged him with perjury, assault, B-and-E, attorney misconduct, obstruction of justice. He barely escaped jail time. It looked like he was going to get disbarred, so he resigned his license to practice law and came out here."

"Wow. He mentioned to me something about getting an unfriendly push out of the profession but nothing like this."

"I mean, Nora, if you look at all the problems we've had, every single one originated with Burleson's crew—not us."

"You think he's got a hidden agenda?"

"I don't know. He's got a temper, he drinks a lot, and now we know he's dishonest, hires crooks, and is a liar. And there's twenty million in gold buried out there. Motive enough for all kinds of evil deeds."

Nora thought about this. Even though Burleson seemed like a straight shooter, Clive had a point—a good point. "We'd better keep an eye on him," she said.

"Dr. Kelly? Dr. Benton?" came a crisp voice from behind them. They turned to see Dr. Jill Fugit, President of the Institute, approaching them from across the saloon.

"I've been looking for you two," she said, a displeased look on her face. She glanced around. "Let's talk in private. My room."

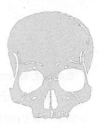

43

Fugit had taken the best lodging at the inn, a large room under the eaves with a kitchenette and a sitting area with a gas fireplace. A row of dormer windows looked out over the forest, rising steeply into the mountains. As they entered, Fugit waved them into wing chairs on either side of the fireplace while she took the sofa.

"You can guess why I'm here," she said. "I'm very concerned about what's going on. I'm especially worried for the safety of our people." She paused. "And I'd also like to know how a simple, uncomplicated archaeological expedition spiraled into murder and scandal."

She sat back in the sofa, arms crossed, her gaze on Nora.

Nora felt a flaring of anger at her attitude. After dealing with that arrogant FBI agent, the last thing she needed was Fugit's interference. But getting into a fight with her boss was a bad idea, so Nora swallowed and tried to modulate her voice. "Let me start by saying the excavation has been an unqualified success. We've mapped the entire camp and uncovered a trove of information and artifacts that will be studied for years to come."

"Except, of course, for the stolen bones."

"Dr. Fugit, the bones had to be kept in situ, and there was no way to protect them or lock them up until they could be removed for curation at the close of the dig. Nobody had any idea Peel would steal them. And in any case, all the bones we'd found have been recovered, except for one cranium and a few vertebrae."

"What about the death of this man Wiggett?"

"The FBI are investigating. They won't give us any information."

"I intend to speak to this FBI agent as soon as she comes back down from the site. I talked with her once before, and she sounded out of her depth, hurling accusations left and right."

God help her, Nora thought, not without satisfaction.

Fugit turned to Clive. "And your views on the situation?"

"I agree with Nora. It's been a successful expedition. I don't see how these problems could have been anticipated or avoided. Certainly none of them are Nora's fault. To be blunt, all the difficulties seem to lie with the wranglers hired by the Institute—not us."

"Speaking of the Institute, do you have any idea how much this project has cost us to date? Just shy of half a million dollars. You need to get back up there, finish the dig, and if possible find that gold."

"Agent Swanson said we could return in forty-eight hours."

"Maybe, but that doesn't account for the big storm that's rolling in. If it's as bad as they're predicting, it could be days before you can get back up there."

"We'll deal with that once Nora gets the green light from Agent Swanson," Clive told her. "I'm certain the gold is up there. We've narrowed the search to a single area."

"I certainly hope that's the case. Now, I understand the FBI are going to be conducting detailed interviews. Keep in mind the Institute needs to be cast in a favorable light." She leaned forward. "As you said, these troubles originated with the Red Mountain Ranch and their wranglers. Nothing to do with us. Right?"

"Right," said Clive.

"Thank you. Now I'd like a few private words with Nora, if you don't mind."

Clive rose and left the room. Fugit turned to Nora, her look softening. "I'm sorry to seem so critical. I know this has been difficult. And I suspect my arrival was not exactly a pleasant surprise."

Nora hadn't anticipated this change of tone.

She went on. "I was truly concerned when I heard there had been an accidental death, and then a murder. I didn't want to mention it in front of Dr. Benton, but I hope you understand that I couldn't stay away."

"I'm glad you're here," Nora lied.

"Now we need to talk about the press. So far, nothing's come out. But it will. You'll have to be prepared."

"How?"

"You're going to be asked questions—pointed ones. My advice is to say as little as possible without seeming evasive. Anticipate the questions and write out your bullet points ahead of time. The dig was a great success; you accomplished everything you came here to do; the historic importance of the discovery is peerless. Yes, there were some unfortunate events, but only involving the wranglers hired to support the expedition—nothing to do with the Institute."

Nora nodded. It was, after all, true, and not just spin the president of a prestigious organization would be expected to employ.

"Do you agree with Dr. Benton? That you'll find the gold, I mean?"

"As a matter of fact, I do."

Fugit seemed to relax a little, and then she actually smiled. "I didn't want to embarrass you in front of him, but I want you to know: I think you're doing an exceptional job under difficult circumstances." She leaned over. "You're a first-rate archaeologist, Nora. The best at the Institute. And I'm going to make sure that FBI agent doesn't impede the completion of your work. I know people in Washington. I can pull strings and, with any luck, rein in that overeager rookie."

"Thank you," Nora said sincerely. "I'd appreciate that very much."

"When the FBI releases the site, make it a priority to get the bones prepped for transport and the dig secured—just in case they try to bother you again. And find that gold. The Institute can hardly afford to go half a million dollars in the red."

"We'll do our best."

Fugit laid a hand on her shoulder. "We're going to get through this. Whatever you need, just let me know."

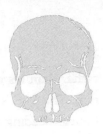

44

May 20

CORRIE RODE DOWN the canyon from the camp, unaccompanied. She had managed to squeeze in her forty-eight allotted hours, and then some, before the storm was to arrive, and for that she was grateful. On the other hand, a meticulous search of the camp had yielded no smoking gun. In fact, she had to admit they hadn't found any incriminating evidence at all. If the killer was a member of the team, he had been a lot more careful than Corrie initially assumed.

They had made one significant discovery: the glacial tarn in the little cirque up behind the camp was the actual site of the homicide. The killer had tried to cover it up, smoothing the ground along the shore and replacing overturned stones, but a careful inspection revealed it to be the place of a struggle. Beyond it they had found imperfectly concealed drag marks heading toward the spot where the body was found.

But this only raised more questions. What was Wiggett doing up at the lake in the middle of the night? Was he meeting someone? Had he been lured there? He'd left his tent with obvious deliberation, dressing warmly and putting on his hiking boots

rather than his cowboy boots. So he was expecting rough terrain. The M.E.'s report would hopefully verify the sequence of
injuries leading to his death—but she wasn't sure that would
help her reconstruct the crime.

If someone in camp had killed Wiggett, he or she had left
no obvious evidence. Corrie was starting to favor the idea that
someone on the outside, lurking near the camp, had been shadowing the group and committed the murders. She'd sent Devlin
and his group to search the surrounding forest for signs of
recent disturbance, but they had turned up nothing.

They'd all left at noon, but Corrie had stubbornly stayed
behind, unwilling to leave the area, thinking there must be
something—*something*—they had missed that would point to a
killer. How many times had she made one "final" pass through
camp? But now the window of opportunity had closed and she
had to hustle back down the trail. Even hurrying, she would
probably not arrive before dark, and already the wind was rising.
The storm was predicted to move in around dawn. Waiting for
her at the head of the trail would be Morwood and, perhaps, the
new special agent from the Sacramento office who was going to
take over the investigation.

And that would be it.

As she rode, she found herself filled with frustration: at the
lack of evidence; at her inability to develop a theory of the
crime; at her failure to find a connection to the Parkin case.
She couldn't help but go over the mistakes she'd made: talking
too much, telling people she thought Peel might have been murdered, alienating Devlin, and letting Nora Kelly push her into
limiting the camp closure to forty-eight hours.

But maybe the case was as simple as Morwood believed—this
was a sordid murder involving the twenty million in gold and

nothing more. He had decades of experience under his belt, and she had just a few months. One thing they'd hammered into her in the Academy was that the right solution to a crime was usually the one most obvious. *Avoid the temptation to look for devious motives and unlikely conspiracies*, one instructor had said. *Life is not an Agatha Christie novel. Criminals are stupid and most crimes are banal and obvious.*

Suddenly she looked up, realizing she was in unfamiliar territory. A giant spruce, split in half by lightning, stood in front of her—she'd never seen that before. She cursed out loud. Wallowing in self-pity, she had ridden off the route.

She took out her cell phone and checked her location on the GPS app. Even though there was no cell reception, the phone's independent GPS was working and she had previously downloaded the requisite maps of the area. It showed that instead of riding down Hackberry Creek from the Poker Creek junction, she had missed the turn and instead ridden half a mile up an unnamed side canyon on the far side of the creek.

Four o'clock. Dark clouds covered the sky and the air smelled of gathering electricity. "Let's go, Sierra," she said, awkwardly turning her horse around. "Come on, boy. Faster!"

The sluggish horse, unmoved by her entreaties, slowly turned and plodded back down the canyon.

"Hurry up, for Chrissakes!" She shook the reins, but the horse ignored her.

She would never get used to riding. Her whole body seemed to ache. As she rode alongside the creek, she passed through a clearing and noticed the remains of a fire ring. She drew a sudden breath. Maybe this was the camp of the person or persons shadowing the group.

"Whoa, Sierra! *Whoa*, goddamn it!"

The horse reluctantly came to a halt. Corrie dismounted and tied his halter rope to a tree. She approached cautiously, trying not to disturb anything. But on getting closer, she was disappointed to see the fire ring was old. Autumn leaves and pine needles had collected in the fire pit, which meant the rude camp had to date back to before the previous fall. Nobody had been here since.

Still, it was an odd place to camp, off any trail, next to a stream too tiny for fishing, in a dark and depressing canyon. She picked up a stick and stirred the old ashes, uncovering a few pieces of trash, singed here and there but still relatively intact. Feeling a little silly, she slipped them into an evidence bag. That was something else the Quantico instructor had said: *If in doubt, take it out.*

She untied the horse and remounted, urging him along. The rising wind was tossing the treetops, making a hissing noise. She had three hours to ride a dozen miles before the sun set, on a rugged trail. Son of a bitch, she was really cutting it close.

She gave Sierra a vigorous kick and finally got him into a slow trot. She hated trotting—it bounced her all over the place— but she'd rather have a sore ass than get lost at night in the mountains on the leading edge of a storm.

★ ★ ★

She arrived at Red Mountain Ranch as the last light was disappearing in the west. Sure enough, Morwood was waiting as she rode in.

"Jesus, Swanson, I was getting worried!" he said as she got off the horse and handed the reins to a wrangler, then hobbled over. She could barely walk.

"You okay?" Morwood asked.

"No worries, just crippled for life from riding that glue plug," Corrie said.

"You shouldn't have ridden down alone."

"I wanted to go over the site one last time."

"And?"

She shook her head.

They walked toward the parking lot. "I wanted to tell you that Special Agent Nick Chen has been assigned the case," Morwood told her. "He'll be arriving from Sacramento tomorrow morning. He's got a spotless record and—just as important—a rep for being a nice guy. I think you'll enjoy working with him on the transition."

"Okay."

Morwood smiled like a matchmaker. "I'm heading out tonight on a late flight for Albuquerque. Corrie, you'll stay here long enough to bring Agent Chen up to speed. I've booked you at the Truckee Inn for the next several days. Transfer all your notes, evidence, and so forth to him. I'm afraid you'll have to wait out the storm that's coming, but after it passes I'd like you to take him up to the camp, show him around, and introduce him to the group. And then rejoin me in Albuquerque."

"Okay."

"Any questions?"

"No, sir," she said.

They got into Morwood's car and he drove down the highway toward the Truckee Inn. As she got out, he offered her his hand. "If I weren't headed to the airport, I'd buy you a big steak. Good job, Agent Swanson—and if you need anything, don't hesitate to call."

* * *

As Corrie passed through the lobby, heading for the check-in desk, a tall, well-dressed blond woman came striding up, glasses dangling from her neck on a thin gold chain.

"Special Agent Swanson?" she asked.

"Yes."

"I'm Dr. Fugit, president of the Santa Fe Archaeological Institute. We spoke on the phone, as you'll recall." She shook Corrie's hand and then slid her glasses on, examining Corrie as if she were an archaeological specimen. "Do you have a minute?"

"Ah..." She remembered Morwood's warning about getting along with everyone. "Yes, I do. How can I help?"

Fugit led them over to a private area at one side of the lobby. They sat down on an orange sofa and Fugit leaned toward Corrie, her voice suddenly ice cold. "It seems you think my team is harboring a murderer. Is that right?"

Corrie took a moment to ponder the best reply. *Stay neutral, don't take offense.* "Nobody's been accused of anything," she said, "and nobody's making allegations. We're conducting a routine homicide investigation."

"Routine? You shut down an entire archaeological site!"

"We're done with our evidence gathering. As soon as I see Nora I'll be releasing the site to her and the team."

"Not much good now, is it, with the storm bearing down on us?"

Her tone had become bitingly sarcastic, and Corrie didn't respond. As if dealing with Nora weren't enough, her boss was a straight-up bitch.

"Do you have any suspects? A motive? *Anything?*"

"I'm sorry, we can't share specifics." She shifted on the couch.

"What I can tell you is that the investigation is being transferred to the Sacramento Field Office."

"And what am I supposed to infer from that?"

"That a Special Agent Chen will be taking over, and I'll be heading back to New Mexico. You can address your concerns to him." *And he can tell you exactly where to stick your archaeological dig.* Corrie smiled.

Fugit took off the glasses and let them drop. "It appears to me the handling of this investigation to date has been incompetent and inconsiderate. I'll be filing a complaint."

"That's your privilege, of course," said Corrie. "But I think you'll find everything's been done by the book."

"We'll see."

"Let me just assure you the FBI fully expects to solve this case and apprehend the perpetrator." Corrie struggled to keep her voice neutral as she fed the president this platitude.

Fugit stood up. "I sincerely hope you do." She paused. "And about the gold up there. I assume you know about that?"

"I was briefed."

"So how does it fit in? Is the murder connected in some way?"

"Again, Dr. Fugit, I can't go into that."

"What *can* you go into?"

"As I've repeatedly explained—nothing."

Fugit frowned. Then, without another word, she turned and left, not offering her hand, the heels of her black slingbacks echoing on the wooden floor.

Corrie took in a shuddering breath. She had to work on not letting bullies like Fugit get under her skin. She'd been bullied as a teenager and was hypersensitive to it. This was a weakness, and if she was ever to make a good FBI agent, she'd better learn to deal with it.

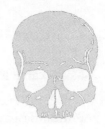

45

May 21

Burleson was adamant: no horses, no wranglers, nothing.

"We can't go up there," he said, still groggy from sleep after being roused by Nora showing up on his doorstep at seven in the morning. "Not in this weather. And we sure as hell can't be responsible for your well-being."

He'd been saying the same thing for the past ten minutes, and no amount of begging, threatening, or wheedling could shift him. "But I'm not asking you to go—" Nora began again.

"End of discussion. Sorry, Nora—you're just going to have to wait it out."

* * *

Back in town and on her way to the inn for a badly needed cup of coffee, Nora came around a corner and nearly ran into Agent Swanson, headed in the other direction.

Nora frowned and looked away, hoping to dash by. But no such luck.

"Nora," Corrie said. "Do you have a moment?"

Nora was in no mood to talk to this woman. "What now?"

"There's one other thing I meant to tell you. The Wiggett homicide is being turned over to the Sacramento Field Office. Special Agent Chen is arriving today to take over."

Nora gave a brusque nod, then started for the entrance to the inn. Maybe this Chen would be easier to work with.

Corrie turned to follow her. "As soon as the transition is complete, I'll be headed back to Albuquerque."

"I wish you the best." *And good riddance.*

"Unfortunately, with the storm it may be a few days before I can show Agent Chen the campsite and dig."

"*Unfortunately*, you were supposed to hand off the site to me after forty-eight hours. That meant yesterday at two PM. Instead, you didn't live up to our agreement. You got back after dark—and now we can't get to the dig, either."

She walked into the inn, Corrie Swanson still following. "I was late. Sorry. But the fact is, you couldn't have gone up yesterday afternoon anyway—not with the approaching storm."

Nora didn't answer. She knew this was true, given her reception from Burleson just now. But she was in no mood to admit it to this interfering FBI agent.

"I've got one last question," Corrie went on. "It's just a loose end, but I'm not sure how to write it up in my report. Do you know of anyone who might have been camping near the dig last summer or fall?"

"Nope, sorry." Nora glanced around the lobby, looking for the urns. Damn, she needed that coffee.

"I ask because yesterday I found a fire ring dating back to last year or earlier, up a side canyon."

"I didn't even learn of the site's existence until December, as you know. It must be just some random camper."

Corrie frowned. "Okay."

Nora located the coffee urn and began heading for it, but then something made her hesitate. She recalled her growing feeling that someone had been watching their camp. "Are you sure the fire ring wasn't more recent?"

"A bunch of pine needles and aspen leaves were lying over the dead coals, along with a stray patch of snow, so I assumed it had to be abandoned before the leaves fell in the fall."

Nora waited.

"Funny place to camp," Corrie went on. "No fishing, no scenery, just a dead-end canyon and a big split tree."

Nora hesitated. *A split tree.* Why did that ring a bell? "Maybe it was a hunter's camp?"

"Hunting season starts in late November, *after* the leaves have fallen."

This sounded a little strange. "Did you find anything else up there?"

"I scoured the site, but it was pretty clean. Just some trash. A gum wrapper, cigar butt, stray piece of cellophane—that's it."

Nora paused. "Cigar butt? Did it still have its label?"

"I didn't notice. I'd have to check."

"You saved it?"

"Of course."

Nora quickly dismissed this as a meaningless coincidence—which, if mentioned to this FBI agent, would only create more unnecessary suspicion. Still, she hesitated, uneasiness tugging at her. "Where was this canyon, exactly?"

Corrie paused to recollect. "If you go down Poker Canyon, cross, um, Hackberry Creek, and go up the canyon on the opposite side—that's the one. No name on the map."

Nora took a deep breath. Now she remembered where the

memory of the split tree had come from. When they were first riding up Hackberry Creek, before they found the Lost Camp, Clive had mentioned something about a giant tree split in two by lightning. But in what context?

"Where's the cigar butt?" Nora asked.

"In my room."

"Can we go take a look?"

Corrie's gaze turned speculative. "Why?"

"Let's just check it," said Nora. "I'll tell you why later."

"All right."

Nora followed Corrie over to the stairs and up to her room. The agent walked over to an evidence case placed on a luggage rack, opened it, and took out a sealed plastic envelope with a few items inside, including the butt end of a fat cigar. She handed the envelope to Nora.

Nora turned it over, feeling an odd tightness in her chest. "Dunhill," she murmured. She handed it back to Corrie.

"Is that significant?" Corrie asked.

Nora hesitated. Should she tell her? It was only going to lead to more trouble. But she heard herself saying: "Clive occasionally smokes Dunhills."

"Is that so?"

"Yes. He said it calms him when he's feeling frustrated. And..." Now she feared she was really taking a step she'd regret. "You mentioned a tree split by lightning."

"Yes. It was right next to the fire ring, one half leaning out like it was about to fall. I'd never camp there for fear of getting clobbered while I slept."

"When we were looking for the camp, riding up Hackberry Creek for the first time... Clive said something about a split tree."

"In what context?"

"I can't fully recall. I think he was joking about the danger of being struck by lightning up in those mountains. He mentioned a spruce he'd seen that was split top to bottom. Very dramatic, he said. Is the tree...visible from the trail?"

"No."

Nora went silent, thinking.

Corrie asked, "Is Dunhill a common brand of cigar?"

"No idea." This was precisely what she'd been afraid of, setting off more speculation. "Look, anybody could have left that cigar. It wasn't Clive. Why would he be camping up there last year? He told me he'd never been in this area before."

Corrie took a moment to answer. "Looking for the gold."

"Come on. *Really?* Then why bring this project to the Institute? Why didn't he just take the gold himself?"

"Maybe he tried but couldn't find it. So he enlisted your expertise in locating the camp."

"That makes no sense. Once we found the gold, how was he supposed to get his hands on it? Steal it from the Institute?"

Corrie said slowly, "Perhaps he's already found the gold. And that's why *you* haven't found it yet."

Nora laughed mirthlessly. "You're hanging this entire theory on an old stogie."

"And a split tree."

"There must be dozens of those in the forest."

After a moment, Corrie took the evidence bag from Nora. "There's going to be DNA on this. Maybe even a fingerprint. Let's show it to him and ask if he was camping up there last year."

"He'll say no."

"Of course he'll say no. But we'll get a chance to gauge his reaction to our question."

"*Your* question. I'm not going to ask him that to his face. He's a partner in this expedition—and a friend."

"Fair enough." And Corrie led the way to the door.

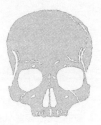

46

BUT WHEN THEY knocked, Clive didn't answer.

Standing just outside his door, they spoke in low tones. "Think he's still asleep?" Corrie asked.

"He always seemed to be an early riser."

"Well, he wasn't downstairs at breakfast. And there's not a whole lot of other places to go in town this early in the morning, with a storm bearing down on us." Corrie knocked again, harder this time. As she did so, the door came ajar.

"That's funny," Corrie said, inspecting the knob. "Looks like the lock is stuck. If the shower in my room is any indication, the hardware in this fleabag is in as bad shape as the plumbing."

Nora stuck her head past the open door. "Clive?" She could see the room was a whirlwind of disorder—suitcases open, drawers ajar, personal items scattered around. About the only thing that wasn't a mess was the bed—it was still made.

"Doesn't look like Clive went to bed last night," she said. "But whenever he left, he left in a hurry."

"That probably explains the door," Corrie replied. "He

locked it, but didn't check to make sure he'd pulled it tight. Hey, wait—!"

As she was speaking, Nora stepped into the room.

"You can't go in there," Corrie said. "Not without a warrant."

"What warrant? I'm the expedition leader. A friend. Clive left something in his room that belongs to me. I came to get it and found his door open."

"What thing of yours would that be?" Corrie asked.

"I'm not sure. But I'll know it when I see it."

"I'll wait here, if you don't mind."

Nora gazed around at the disorder, trying to make sense of things, her friendship with and respect for Clive at odds with the inexplicable mess surrounding her. It didn't look like he'd taken any clothes. Even his camera was still sitting on a nightstand. She approached the desk, which was covered with historical documents. Riffling through them, she found photocopies of old letters; contemporary newspaper reports; yellowed reproductions of microfilm pages; even penny dreadfuls purporting to tell the gruesome and unadulterated story of the Donner tragedy. There were dozens of items; Clive was nothing if not thorough in his research.

"Do you see a coat?" Corrie said, looking in through the door.

"No. He must have gone out."

Nora continued sorting through the documents on the desk. She picked up a stapled photocopy of what she quickly recognized as Tamzene Donner's journal. Clive, of course, had left the original back in Santa Fe for safekeeping. As she turned the well-thumbed pages, a single sheet fell out.

Curious, she picked it up. This was something new—new and strange. It was another photocopy, written in an uneven spidery script, with names and dates and biblical quotations and even grim little drawings that served as punctuation: tombstones and weeping angels and sheets of fire that, apparently, depicted the apocalypse. Here and there, she could see newer markings: a few highlighted lines and brief notes scribbled in the margin— in Clive's handwriting.

This looked like an important historical document. But she had never seen it. If Clive had found it stuck into Tamzene's original diary, he'd never mentioned it to her.

"He must have gone out," Corrie said. "Let's go."

"Just a minute." Nora carried the photocopy to the door and showed it to Corrie.

"What's that?" Corrie asked. "Looks like the doodlings of a madman."

"Maybe that's what it is." Nora folded the sheet and stuffed it in her pocket. "All right. Lead the way."

* * *

At the front desk, the receptionist said Clive had left that morning before dawn, with a day pack. He had not said where he was going.

They looked at each other. Corrie pulled out her cell phone and dialed Clive's number. It went straight to voice mail. She dialed again, this time the Red Mountain Ranch.

She spoke for a few minutes, then hung up.

"The folks at Red Mountain Ranch found one of their horses missing this morning," Corrie told Nora. "Burleson thought it might have been you."

"It wasn't me."

"Of course not," Corrie said, arching her eyebrows.

"Come on. Clive, a horse thief? Why would he take a horse—and in this weather?"

Corrie didn't reply.

"You keep jumping to conclusions," Nora said, her tone dubious. "Clive's no criminal."

"Everyone's a potential criminal," Corrie replied. "All it takes is the right incentive."

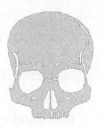

47

Burleson came out on the porch to meet them, coffee cup in hand, face red. "We've never had a security problem here before," he said, fuming. "But someone came and helped themselves to a horse, a saddle, and tack."

"When?" Corrie asked.

"After the morning feeding. One of my hands turned the horses out in the corrals, as usual, for exercise. That was at six—around the time the rain started, maybe an hour before Nora here arrived and woke me up. At eight, I noticed someone had latched the back gate wrong; went out—and saw Blaze was missing. Not only that, they took my .30-06 Springfield down from over the damn fireplace in the lodge. Brazen bastards."

Corrie looked at Nora, then back to Burleson. "Blaze was the horse Dr. Benton rode, correct?"

"That's right. You think it's Clive?"

"I do," Corrie said.

"But why? I'd have *loaned* him Blaze once the weather cleared. Why would he steal a damn horse he could have for free?"

"Because he didn't want anyone to know what he was doing," said Corrie. "And the gun? What about ammo?"

"I don't keep loose ammo around, and the gun was un-loaded." Burleson was shaking his head in disbelief. "You really think Clive stole my horse? To do what—ride up to the dig?"

Corrie nodded. "I need to go up there, too. I hope you can spare another horse."

"I already told Nora here that I can't let my horses out in this—"

"One's out already. I'll bring him back. Don't force me to requisition Sierra."

Burleson cursed under his breath. "Well, if you're going to put it like that, I've got an excellent wrangler that—"

"No wrangler," said Corrie. She couldn't involve any citizens in this.

"You can't go up there alone. You're no horsewoman, and you've only got a handgun. I'll go with you."

"No."

"*I'm* going with her," Nora said.

Corrie turned to Nora. "Excuse us for a moment," she told Burleson.

She took Nora off to the far end of the porch and lowered her voice. "You can't come with me. This is a law enforcement matter."

"And it's my dig site. It's crazy for you to ride up there alone. It's already raining, and look at the damn sky. If you won't take me, at least get the sheriff and some others."

"No time. I've got to get up there now."

"Why? What's the hurry?"

"I'm sure you can guess. I think Clive has gone up there to retrieve the gold he already found."

Nora's dubious expression returned. "You really think so?"

"I do. It's the only theory that fits the facts. He couldn't find it on his own, so he enlisted you to locate the Lost Camp. As soon as the camp was established, he began a determined search for the gold—and found it. And now, with the camp shut down, he has a chance to recover it." She took a deep breath. "If I catch him with the gold, it's an open-and-shut case. Otherwise, I've got no case at all—just supposition."

"What about that new FBI agent you mentioned? Wait and go up with him."

"Clive started up the trail maybe two hours ago. By the time Agent Chen arrives, it could be too late."

"All the more reason you need me. You can't go alone."

"Forget it. You're a civilian."

"I'm also an expert horsewoman, and you can't ride worth shit."

"You're wasting my time with this arguing," said Corrie hotly. She turned back to Burleson. "Get Sierra ready, I'm leaving now."

"And get Stormy for me, too," Nora said.

Burleson stood motionless a moment, staring at them. Then he told Corrie firmly: "I'm saddling two horses, one for you and one for Nora. And I'm issuing rain gear. That's my decision, or neither of you go—law or no law."

* * *

As they started up the trail, the gray skies grew darker, bringing with them a feeling of dusk despite the early hour. So far the rain was relatively light, though it was terribly cold. Thank God Burleson had given them rain jackets and pants. Corrie trotted on her horse behind Nora, gripping the saddle horn with one hand, feeling like she was being jackhammered.

Corrie had her Glock and an extra magazine. But Clive was armed with a .30-06. She wondered if he'd managed to get ammo; realized she needed to assume he had. If they were going to confront him, her handgun—accurate out to about fifty feet—was no match for that rifle.

Of course, all this depended on whether her theory about Clive and the gold was right. She wondered once again if she was jumping to conclusions. But the historian's abrupt departure, the condition of his room, and most especially the stealing of the horse all struck her as additional reasons for suspicion.

What would Morwood say about all this? She hadn't been able to raise him by phone. And Chen...maybe she should have waited for him. She should not have taken Nora. She should have rousted the sheriff and his deputy.

But who knew when Chen would arrive in this weather, and coaxing the sheriff out from his comfortable hole would have taken at least an hour. Besides, she wasn't sure they'd be an effective backup. But Nora? She had to admit, Nora was resourceful, smart, and tough.

After a while the trail turned slick and muddy, and she could clearly make out the hoofprints of Clive's horse. They had been moving fast, and despite his head start weren't all that far behind him—at least, judging from the freshness of the prints. When they turned off the established trail, along Hackberry Creek, she could see where Blaze had left prints in the damp grass and pine needles.

"Nora? Hold up for a moment."

Nora reined in her horse and swung it around.

"That .30-06 is a hunting rifle with a range of a thousand

yards. If Benton really is the killer, it'd be suicide to just ride in on him."

"I was thinking the same thing. But I can't believe he's a thief *and* a murderer. How sure are you—exactly? We don't want any mistakes that might end in tragedy."

This was true, and Corrie answered carefully: "I'm not sure. But Benton is up to something, and we need to find out what it is. And he did steal a gun, which suggests he's ready to use it."

"Then what we should do," said Nora, "is find a way to observe him from afar—before we determine how to respond."

"Makes sense. Any ideas?"

"Yes." Nora plucked the portable GPS from her pocket, gave it a moment to acquire satellites, then consulted its small screen. "We can ride up Sugarpine Creek to where it tops out, then climb the ridge between it and Poker Canyon. From the top, we should be able to see down into the valley."

"Is it rideable?"

"We can probably get at least halfway up the ridge, but the last part we'll have to hike."

Corrie nodded. "Let's go."

They rode up Hackberry Creek to Sugarpine, then turned their horses up the canyon. Nora led the way, occasionally crossing the burbling stream. The rain continued to mist down and the sky darkened to the color of iron. The wind picked up further, the treetops bending before it and exuding the sharp smell of pine resin.

The creek eventually led them into a cirque carpeted by meadows that rose to a series of bare granitic ridges. Here they were close to timberline, and the few surrounding trees were dwarfish and twisted from the harsh wind and weather.

They tied up their horses and started hiking up the grassy

slope. It grew steeper, finally turning into a scramble among lichen-splotched boulders. Near the top, they crouched to work their way up to the ridgeline and peered over.

Bingo, thought Corrie. It was a perfect lookout.

About a quarter mile below, she could see the large meadow where the dig site was. The HQ tent appeared as a crisp white rectangle next to the excavated area, which was covered with the bright blue tarps. The trail the expedition had made over weeks of work could be seen winding down through the meadow and into the trees, where it emerged at the campsite half a mile down the canyon. Everything appeared undisturbed, exactly as she had left it the day before, except a whole lot wetter.

She took out her binoculars and glassed the area. There was no sign of Clive, either in the camp or at the dig site. Had he already collected the gold and split?

But then she saw something—a horse. It was Blaze, and he was tied to a tree about a quarter mile above the dig site. Scanning the area, she noticed movement—then spied Clive at the base of the cliffs. He was hard at work, but at what she couldn't immediately make out. She watched him collect a rock, then another, then carry them to the base of the cliff. There, he fitted each of the rocks into a small cavity at ground level, blocking its entrance.

"I see him." She handed the binoculars to Nora, who took them and peered through.

"He's concealing something."

"That's what I thought," said Corrie excitedly. "He's hiding the gold. Or rather, moving the gold that was already hidden to a more secure location. My forty-eight-hour search must have spooked him."

"That area he's in is the red zone," Nora said. "The portion of cliffs we haven't dared search because of that huge rotten cornice above it."

Corrie raised her eyes to the row of peaks far above. The cornice was still there, among snowfields, hanging menacingly. "Makes sense. He knows that's precisely the place you won't look. Let me see those binocs again."

Nora handed them to her. Corrie watched the historian move the rocks, cleverly obscuring the cavity. Then she took a few photos of the scene with her agency camera. "I bet he plans to come back and get it later, once the cornice has fallen. He'll make some excuse for borrowing the horse and rifle. Then he'll return once everything has died down—probably in the summer."

Corrie continued observing as Clive finished placing rocks into the hole at the base of the cliffs, arranging them to look natural. Then he gathered pine needles and leaves and sprinkled them around the area.

"Okay, Agent Swanson—what's the plan?" Nora asked.

"We can't face off against a man with a rifle. But we don't have to: we know where the gold is now. When Clive leaves we can retrieve it. What we've just seen is testifiable in court. There's no need for a confrontation."

"That means going in the avalanche zone."

"The overhanging snow has been like that for weeks," Corrie said. "It didn't deter Clive. And it won't fall in the few minutes it takes us to pull out those rocks and retrieve the gold."

"Clive will get away."

"One of the first things you learn at the Academy: evidence is key. Get the evidence and you've got the perp. The evidence we need of wrongdoing is right there behind those rocks."

She observed Clive again with the glasses. He was now

brushing away the marks he'd left in the grass with a branch. Walking backward, he collected Blaze, untying him and leading him away. Once at a safe distance, he mounted and rode down the canyon. She followed him with the binoculars as he carefully went past the dig site and then down the trail. Another moment and he had disappeared past the camp and into the forest.

They waited fifteen minutes to make sure he was gone before rising and making their way down into the canyon. It was a steep descent, made worse by the slippery pine needles and mud. A rumble of thunder echoed off the peaks and a rising wind pressed down the grass. The rain was increasing.

Once they reached the meadow, it took them only a few minutes to cross to the spot where he'd hidden the gold.

"Let me take some pictures first," Corrie said, camera in hand.

She took a quick series from a couple of angles, then put the camera away. "Okay. Let's get these rocks out."

This was it—the moment that would prove her suspicions had been right all along. Heart pounding, careful not to smile out of sheer relief and pride, Corrie knelt beside Nora and began to uncover the cavity.

Suddenly, she heard the sound of a distant gunshot.

"Get down!" she said, instinctively grabbing Nora and pulling her to the ground.

They flattened themselves in the grass as a series of shots, evenly spaced, rang out, echoing off the canyon walls. It was impossible to pinpoint their source, but the shots sounded far away—and, oddly, they didn't seem to be directed at them.

There was a pause. Then another series of five shots sounded: regular, unhurried, like target practice.

"He's not shooting at us," Corrie said. "Those shots are too far away. Besides, he couldn't possibly see us from down the canyon."

"So what the hell *is* he shooting at?" Nora asked.

As Nora spoke, Corrie heard a strange sound like thunder erupt from above, followed by a low vibration and a rising wind. And that was when she realized exactly what Clive had been shooting at.

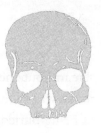

48

THE MASSIVE CORNICE of snow slid off the top of the cliffs and descended toward them with terrible speed. Nora leapt up to run at the same moment as Corrie, but it was too late: the avalanche hit her from behind, wet and cold and terrifyingly heavy, knocking her down and tumbling her over and over. Abruptly, she was caught up in a horrifying elemental fury the likes of which she'd never known: churned about, beaten, help-less, unable to breathe. She vaguely remembered hearing some-where that if caught in an avalanche, you should try to swim—breaststroke your way upward. But which direction was up? The sudden fury had left her dazed, disoriented, and half-crushed. She flailed about in a panic, thinking she could just as easily be digging herself deeper into her own frozen grave.

Abruptly the violent motion stopped. Her entire body lay frozen in place, immobilized. Her ears were plugged with snow, and sound was reduced to a cocoon-like whisper. For a moment Nora lay where she was, stunned. Then she opened her eyes—and saw only a dim gray blur. She tried to breathe in, got a mouthful of slush, and coughed it out immediately. She tried to scream, but she had no breath to spare, and a muffled, distant moan was all that resulted. Panic flooded through her; the panic of being buried alive. She could feel her heart pounding faster and faster.

Frantically, she tried moving her limbs—and realized that, incredibly, one arm was unencumbered. It had to be above the level of the snow—and that, at last, gave her a sense of which way was up. She sank her free hand into the icy mush, scooping away the slush, even as she felt the lack of air taking hold. She scooped again, then again and again. Just when she thought she'd black out, her lungs afire, her desperate fingers cleared the snow and ice from her mouth and she took a vast, gasping breath.

She paused to rest, gulping in the delicious air, breathing strength back into her body as the stars cleared from her eyes and the pain in her chest subsided. After a minute or two she began wriggling her limbs, slowly, carefully, checking to see if anything was broken. She felt like a mass of bruises, but otherwise seemed to be intact. Now she began digging again, clearing the area around her face, twisting this way and that to loosen the heavy white tomb that encased her. The snow was wet and dense and it was remarkably difficult work, but within five minutes she had managed to free her upper body, then heave herself up and crawl out of the snowy grave onto the irregular surface.

"Corrie!" she cried, looking around. "Corrie!"

The avalanche had spread out across at least a third of the width of the valley, snow boulders mingled with twigs and branches and bits of debris. She could see no sign of the FBI agent.

"Corrie!" she called again, coughing and staggering to her feet.

She frantically began wading through the slush, postholing

with each step, calling out Corrie's name and looking for a sign—something, anything, a hand, foot, bit of clothing—that might indicate where she was buried. But there was nothing save a vast and lumpy snowfield: deep at the base of the cliffs, spreading and thinning out as it moved toward the center of the valley.

She needed a probe. She looked around frantically, pulled a stick from the debris, then began tromping back and forth, plunging the stick into the snow.

"Corrie! *Corrie!*"

The stick kept getting stuck in the heavy, ice-packed snow, and soon it broke. She threw it away with a curse and cast about for another one.

"A brave show," came a voice.

Nora whirled. It was Clive—rifle leveled at her.

"*You* did this!" she said. "You brought down that cornice intentionally!"

Clive nodded. "I knew you were following me, so I set a trap. Too bad it didn't get you both. Now, get down off that snow pile."

"But Corrie! She's—"

"Dead, of course. It's been, what, ten minutes? She suffocated five, maybe six minutes ago."

"You bastard."

Clive raised the gun and fired over her head. "Shut up or I'll kill you here and now." He lowered the muzzle and pointed it at her again.

Nora fell silent.

"Now get the fuck down here and do as I say."

Nora wallowed through the snow and reached solid ground. It was horrible, thinking of how Corrie must have suffered. She hadn't escaped that horrible, crushing, suffocating whiteness.

Nora's mind reeled, barely able to process the shock and tragedy of the last few minutes.

But Corrie had been right. She'd been right from the start. It was Clive. And he was carrying a blue artifact box, lashed to his day pack.

"So it was just the gold, after all," she said bitterly.

At this, Clive started to laugh. "Ah, the *gold!*" He nodded toward the box. "You know what? I couldn't give a shit about the gold. In fact, when everyone learned about it, my job got ten times harder: Maggie with her bionic ears, people hunting around at night. People like Wiggett. I can't believe how fast you found his body: maybe some goddamned ghost was helping you after all. Anyway, in the end the gold did prove useful. It got you up here. Right? You bought into the same story as your dead friend."

He jerked the muzzle of the gun. "Enough chit-chat. Start walking."

"Where?"

"The dig site."

He was going to kill her; she knew that. Why hadn't he already? She'd been supposed to die in the avalanche, like Corrie. Shooting her might raise too many questions and leave evidence: he would probably do it some other way, make it look like an accident. She tried to push away the feelings of fear and horror and figure out how to get away from him. Her mind came up blank.

Just then, she saw movement. Seconds later, a horse and rider appeared at the edge of the meadow, coming toward them through the trees, still in shadow. Nora's heart leapt. Was it Burleson? Of course. He'd come to make sure they were all right—exactly the kind of thing he'd do.

"Look out!" she screamed. "He's got a gun!"

Clive shook his head. "You poor, dumb bitch," he said, seemingly unconcerned about the figure, still in shadow, who was approaching. He waited, gun trained on Nora.

The wind had picked up and the trees were now thrashing about, the rain coming down hard. Nora shivered uncontrollably, and she began to feel light-headed and unaccountably warm. Hypothermia. Maybe his plan was that simple: let her die of cold and exposure.

The figure on horseback emerged into the open and Nora saw, with perfect astonishment, that it was Dr. Fugit.

"What's she doing here?" Fugit asked Clive as she rode up, nodding at Nora.

"Dr. Fugit!" Nora called, uncomprehending. "What's going on?"

Clive gestured at her with the gun. "Shut the fuck up."

Fugit halted her horse and gave Nora a cold smile. "You're a fine archaeologist, Nora. But when it comes to understanding the way the world works, you're exactly what Clive just said: a dumb bitch. I'm sorry for you." She removed a six-gun from a holster under her arm and pointed it at Nora. Absently, as if in a dream, Nora noticed she was wearing nitrile gloves.

"You were supposed to take care of this," Dr. Fugit told Clive.

"She got lucky. Dug herself out. The FBI agent is dead, though."

"Well, stop gloating and give me the box. Put your gun down: I can cover Nora. Just *be careful*."

Clive put down the rifle, shucked off the pack, and untied the artifact box. He gingerly handed it up to Fugit. Still sitting on her horse, she tucked the six-gun under her arm and opened the box, glanced inside for a moment, then sealed it back up.

She slipped it into one of her saddlebags, buckled it shut, and pointed the gun once again at Nora.

"You going to, ah, *do* her?" Clive asked. "I was going to put her in the tarn, make it look like an accident. Like I did with Wiggett."

"Some accident. You screwed that up rather nicely. I'll deal with her—don't you worry."

"They said you were going to arrange the wire transfer. Has it been done?"

"Don't worry, Dr. Benton. You'll be paid. In fact, I can take care of that right now."

The gun in her hand turned from Nora to Clive. A shot rang out and Clive's head suddenly snapped back. The rest of his body stood motionless for a moment, then toppled backward as well, hitting the ground with a soft thud. He lay unmoving in the falling rain, except for one finger that twitched a few times before going still.

"Stupid bastard," Fugit muttered to herself. The gun swung back toward Nora. More briskly now, Fugit raised it, aimed, and fired.

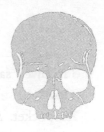

49

THE TWO SHOTS were not quite simultaneous. The first came unexpectedly from behind, knocking Fugit off balance just enough to make her own shot go wide, the gun flying out of her hand. Another shot punched her over the saddle horn. The horse, terrified, reared up and bucked, throwing Fugit's body up and to one side, and it somersaulted through the air before slamming to the ground. Despite all that, the Institute president was still alive: she screamed shrilly, grasping and tearing at her clothes in the most horrible way, as if trying to find a wound.

Nora whirled to one side and saw Corrie—bleeding, sodden, the snowy Glock in her hand—stumbling toward the edge of the avalanche debris. She fell to her knees, still holding the Glock. She struggled to stand again.

Nora rushed over, catching her before she collapsed and easing her to the ground.

"Help me," came a feeble voice. Fugit.

Ignoring her, Nora leaned over Corrie. "You're hurt," she said.

"I'm alive," said Corrie.

"How—?"

"Air pocket. And just enough room to work my way out. Thanks to you."

"I thought you were dead."

"If you hadn't grabbed my hand and heaved me up, I *would* be dead."

Nora stared at her. "I didn't grab your hand."

"Of course you did. I was blacking out when I felt your hand grasp mine..." Corrie's eyes fluttered as she began to drift in and out of consciousness.

Nora said nothing. Obviously Corrie's oxygen-starved brain had been hallucinating.

"Please help me," came the pathetic voice of Fugit.

Nora went over. The president lay on her back, blood staining her shoulder. Nora quickly unbuttoned the woman's shirt and pulled it aside, revealing an ugly exit wound on her anterior shoulder. Shivering, she tore off a piece from her own shirt and balled it up, handing it to Fugit. "Press down with this."

Fugit took it. "I'm cold," she said.

Nora's teeth were chattering. "We're all cold. You just keep pressing."

She went back to Corrie, knelt, and took her hand. The agent's eyes fluttered back open. "Nora?"

"Yes?"

"Go...see what's in that blue box."

Nora turned. Fugit's horse was standing fifty feet away, sides heaving, still frightened. The box bulged inside the left saddle-bag, one corner peeking out.

"That can wait. We need to get you out of this rain."

Corrie pressed Nora's hand. *"Please go see what's in the box."*

Nora realized she wasn't going to leave the subject alone. She stood up and approached the horse, holding her hands out and speaking soothing words. The horse took a few nervous steps back before Nora could grab the lead rope and stroke his neck reassuringly.

She untied the saddlebags, slipped them off, and draped them over her shoulder. Then she tied up the horse and returned to Corrie, who was now sitting up.

Corrie nodded for her to open it.

Nora slipped the blue box out of the saddlebag, unlatched it, and handed it to Corrie. She removed the lid. A wan smile spread across the agent's features as she stared inside. "I *knew* it."

"What?"

"Parkin's skull."

She handed the box to Nora, who looked inside. "What the hell? How is this supposed to be worth more than gold?"

"That," said Corrie, "is the twenty-million-dollar question."

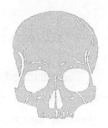

50

Nᴏʀᴀ ʜᴇʟᴅ Cᴏʀʀɪᴇ tight in the driving rain, trying to think through their situation.

"I'm so cold," Corrie said, her entire body shivering.

"We've got to get out of this weather. Can you stand up?"

Gripping Corrie under her arms, Nora tried to help her to her feet. Corrie cried out and staggered, sinking back to her knees, cradling her left arm. "I think it's broken," she gasped.

"Hold it still with your good arm," Nora said. "It's only a hundred yards to the tent."

She helped Corrie up, bracing her by the shoulders, trying to avoid the broken arm. Corrie managed to remain standing, and one painful step at a time, they reached the tent and got inside. Unfortunately, there were no blankets or sleeping bags—just tarps. Nora laid Corrie down and covered her with several. Then she rummaged in the equipment box and pulled out a camp stove, along with packets of tea, sugar, and cocoa.

"Better get Fugit in here," said Corrie.

"Screw Fugit," Nora said as she set out the stove, fired it up, and poured water into a pot. The wind was now shaking the tent, the rain pounding down, making an almost deafening noise.

Corrie shook her head. "No. Key witness. Can't let her die."

"I'm going to make cocoa first, because we're both suffering from hypothermia." Nora dumped cocoa into the water and stirred, dissolving it. When it began to simmer, she poured out two mugs and put one in Corrie's pale hand.

"Thanks."

Nora helped Corrie raise the mug to her lips and take a sip, then another. In between, Nora drank hers, feeling the warmth slide down her throat. The effect was dramatic as strength and mental acuity immediately flowed back into her body.

Nora got out the medical kit and sorted through it for ibuprofen, giving two pills to Corrie and taking the same dose herself. Corrie had finished her cocoa and Nora poured out two more mugs.

"Let me see your arm," she asked Corrie.

Corrie eased her left arm out from under the tarp, wincing. With great care, Nora took a pair of scissors from the medical kit and cut open the sleeve to expose the skin. Corrie's forearm was oddly crooked and already sported a massive purplish welt—a bad break, but at least it wasn't a compound fracture.

"That must hurt," said Nora.

"You have no idea," Corrie said. Her voice was stronger now. "Look, if you don't help Fugit, she's going to die."

Nora nodded. "I'll go get her."

She wrapped rain gear tightly around herself, even though she was already soaked through, then opened the flap. Wind and rain gusted in, lashing her skin. Hunching into the tempest headfirst, she went to where Fugit lay prone. The president's eyes were slits, and rain-diluted blood was pooled on the ground beneath her. She looked dead.

Nora knelt, put her finger to the woman's neck. Still a pulse.

"I'm going to move you into the tent."

Fugit gave a moan.

God, how was she going to do this? The woman's shoulder was shot to pieces. It looked terrible.

While she pondered the problem, Fugit moaned and turned her head toward Nora. She wasn't sure how conscious the woman was—if at all.

"I'm going to have to drag you," Nora said. "By your feet."

Nora grabbed Fugit's boots, braced herself, and started pulling. The grass was wet, which made sliding the body easier. She pulled, rested, pulled again, moving a few feet each time. Fugit made no sound. It seemed she had definitely lapsed into unconsciousness.

With a final struggle, Nora got the woman into the tent and onto a tarp. Now she could examine the wound more closely, cutting away Fugit's rain jacket, coat, shirt, and bra strap to expose the area. One bullet had only grazed her, but the other had gone in through the back of the shoulder and come out the front, expanding as it exited. The wound was ugly, but it was just oozing now, no longer bleeding heavily, and it appeared to have been well rinsed by the rain.

Nora carried the medical kit over, smeared some antibiotic ointment on a pad, pressed it gently against the wound, then bandaged it in place. When she was done, she covered Fugit with plastic tarps. Then she returned to Corrie.

"How are you doing?" she asked.

Corrie tried to smile. "Better." She looked over at Fugit. "We need to get a medevac up here. Where's the sat phone?"

"Down in the camp."

Corrie hesitated. "I hate to ask…"

"I'll go make the call. You just watch Fugit in case she revives."

Corrie eased her good arm out from under the tarp and Nora saw she had her Glock in it. "Sorry I can't go with you. I just don't want her to die."

"I don't, either. She has a lot to answer for." Nora stood up. "I'll be back."

After getting the number from Corrie, she went out again into the driving rain and staggered over to Fugit's horse. It looked miserable, soaked and steaming. Nora swung into the saddle and set off, a fresh blast of rain hitting her face.

Under the downpour, the empty camp looked bedraggled. She tied up the horse and went into the equipment tent, found the phone, and dialed the number Corrie had given her.

An Agent Morwood answered immediately. "Swanson?"

"Nora Kelly. It's an emergency. I'm up at the campsite with Agent Swanson—"

"The campsite? In that storm?"

"It's a long story. Corrie's injured. She's got a broken arm. There's been a shooting. Clive Benton is dead, Dr. Fugit is shot and badly wounded. We're going to need a medevac up here."

"What the devil happened? Can I speak to her?"

"She's uptrail. Too much to explain. Just get a medevac to the dig site."

"Right, I'm on it. Stay by the phone." He hung up.

Nora shut the phone, took a pack from storage, put the phone in it, tied on two sleeping bags, and went back out into the storm.

She arrived at the dig site ten minutes later, shivering afresh. She tied the horse outside the tent and carried in the sleeping bags. One she unzipped and laid over Fugit as a makeshift blanket. She took the other one to Corrie.

"Can you get out of your wet clothes and in here?" Nora asked. "You'll be a lot warmer."

"I think so."

Nora helped her remove her sopping clothes and slide naked into the sleeping bag. She was shocked by how many bruises covered Corrie's body. It must be the avalanche; Nora probably looked the same herself.

"What did Morwood say?" Corrie asked, clutching the bag to her chin.

"He's getting a medevac."

She nodded, still shivering.

At that moment the phone rang. Nora answered it, putting it on speaker.

"Agent Swanson?" came the voice. "Are you there?"

"I'm here."

"Tell me how you're hurt."

"A broken arm, some bruises. I'll be fine. But Fugit's going to die if she isn't medevac'd out of here soon."

"I've been working on it. It's hell to put a bird in the air in this storm. But they've got two heavy-duty search and rescue choppers flying up from Sacramento: a primary and a backup. We're looking at ninety minutes. Can you hold out?"

"Nora and I can. Not sure about Fugit. And, sir—Fugit should be put under arrest."

"What did she do?"

"Murder, attempted murder."

"Jesus. I'll send in a marshal with the chopper."

"Thank you."

A pause. "Corrie," said Morwood. "What in God's name is this all about?"

Corrie seemed to hesitate. "It's about Parkin, sir. Parkin's skull. Beyond that, I've no idea."

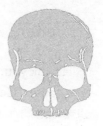

51

After the call, Nora prepared hot tea and dumped in extra Cremora and sugar.

"More ibuprofen," said Corrie.

"I already gave you—"

"Just hand it over."

Nora fished one more tablet out of the bottle. Corrie swallowed it with a gulp of tea. The storm shook the tent, the rain sweeping across in gusts.

Fugit groaned. She seemed to be regaining consciousness. Nora checked her bandages and saw that blood was soaking through. Rather than remove them, she added another layer and applied pressure.

After a long silence, Corrie spoke again. "Why would Parkin's skull be more valuable than a boatload of gold?"

"We can worry about that later."

Corrie winced. "I want to worry about it now."

"Why?"

"It matters to me. I feel like…" Corrie hesitated. "Like I've got all the information I need and *should* be able to put it together. I don't want to face Morwood and have to tell him, *Sorry, five people are dead and I don't have a clue why."*

Nora didn't respond at first. The whole business was stranger than she'd ever imagined. A skull, apparently worth millions—how could that possibly be? "Maybe there's some crazy collector out there, willing to pay a fortune for a historic skull. Look what some people pay for a baseball card."

Corrie shook her head. "This skull isn't old enough to be rare. We're not talking about Taung-1 or Cheddar Man."

"True," Nora said. "Then perhaps someone wants the skull for DNA identification to prove a family inheritance."

Corrie again shook her head. "I'm guessing this is about more than money."

That seemed true enough, Nora thought.

"It seems somebody, or some organization, has been scouring the world for Parkin family remains, digging up graves, and even kidnapping, perhaps murdering, a living Parkin. Clive killed two people for that skull. Fugit killed one and was ready to kill again." Corrie closed her eyes, then after a moment opened them again. "After crossing everything else off the list, all I can think of is that it's some sort of genetic thing Parkin and his descendants have. Something desirable."

"Like what?"

"I don't know. But if you forget any truly freaky theories, like a nut with a penchant for Parkin skulls, what else is left?"

"Nothing," Nora admitted. "But with genetics, you're casting a net that's almost ridiculously broad. A genetic mutation that could, theoretically, confer a resistance to cancer? Or promote longer life? I mean, of course, something like that would be worth millions—even billions." She looked at the blue plastic box, sitting to one side, that contained the skull. "Did you see a connection such as those among the Parkin descendants you investigated? Remarkable intellect, long life, resistance to disease?"

"No. But I never got that specific." Corrie looked up at Nora. "What about Albert Parkin himself? Anything odd about his life?"

"We don't know much. He abandoned his wife and kids in Missouri to go to California. As you know, he was struck by an arrow in an Indian attack in Utah, which cracked his collarbone and helped us identify him. He died of starvation in late February of 1847, and he was the first person cannibalized. Except, of course, for Samantha Carville, whose leg was partially eaten."

Corrie winced. "So that's all we know about Parkin?"

"I'm afraid so."

"And he was cannibalized how, exactly?"

"His skull was roasted upside down in the fire and the cooked brains scooped out, the rest of him presumably chopped up, butchered, and cooked."

The wind buffeted the tent.

"And the rest in the Lost Camp? What happened to them?"

"They continued to starve, went mad, died, and were eaten. Like Parkin—he just happened to be first. Except for two people: one made his way to the Donner's camp on Alder Creek, and another was found by a rescuer, but died later raving mad."

"They all went crazy?"

"It's not unusual: extreme starvation usually triggers a mental breakdown before the end."

"In what ways did they go nuts?"

"The man who escaped the Lost Camp, Boardman, said his wife had tried to kill and eat him. He said they were fighting with each other, hallucinating, that sort of thing."

"What happened to Boardman?" Corrie asked.

"He died of starvation in the Donner camp."

"Did Boardman eat Parkin?"

Nora thought. "He claimed to Tamzene Donner that he didn't 'indulge' in cannibalism. He was a preacher and said it was a mortal sin. Or so she said in her diary."

"So we have essentially a secondhand account of what Boardman told Tamzene, who then wrote it down."

"Right. Although Mrs. Horne's journal mentioned Boardman's surprise arrival in camp, we know the specifics— secondhand—only from Tamzene." Then Nora hesitated. "*Except...*"

Quickly, she dug into her rain gear and pulled out the sheet of paper that had dropped from the journal she'd found in Clive's hotel room. She unfolded it and looked over the old, uneven handwriting, the quotes from the Bible, the strange drawings here and there among the words. It seemed to be primarily a list of names and dates, with additional information mostly in Latin:

MORS COMMENTARIUS

In this dismal place where, after the blizzard of 23rd Oct. 1846, abandoned by man & forgotten by God:

Widow Morehouse agt 50 years; died of Cupid's disease 20th Dec. 46.

Sam. Carvil agt 6 years; died 25th Dec 46. "Neither can they die any more: for they are equal unto the angels; and are the children of God."

Spitzer et Reinhartt non potuerunt incipere
Aug. Spitzer, died 21 Jan 47 unrepentant; Joseph Reinhartt agt 35 confess't his sin of murder before expiring
28 Jan 47. Both taken by starvation. "At the hand of
every man's brother will I require the life of a man."

‡ *Nobis maledictum:* ‡

Albert Parkin, agt 38 years; died 20 Feb 47.

Coeperunt malis festum
"And I will destroy your high places, and cut down your images,
and cast your carcases upon the carcases of your idols, and my
soul
shall abhor you."

† Jul. Carvil †, anthropgs., agt 27 years; died 23 Feb ex
insania

† Leander Widnall †, anthropgs., agt 17 years; died 24
Feb ex insania

† Mrs. Jul. Carvil † anthropgs., agt 30 years; died 24
Feb ex insania

"Depart from evil, and do good; and dwell for evermore."
25 Feb 1847
As witnessed by Asher Boardman
husband of † Edith Boardman †
Lamented and lamentable
Et anthropgs.

"Is that the document you picked up in Clive's room?" Corrie asked.

"Yes. The one that slipped out of Tamzene's journal."

"What is it?"

"It's a list of names, sort of a death almanac of the Lost Camp. Given all the biblical quotations and Latin, it might have been compiled by Boardman himself."

"You know Latin?"

"If you'd taken as many grad-level zoological courses as I did, you'd know it, too." She read the document over and over. It was like a puzzle written in shorthand.

"Keep going," Corrie said.

"It says that the widow Morehouse was the first to die, of 'Cupid's Disease'—a euphemism for venereal illness—followed shortly by Samantha Carville. Then it mentions the two killers, Spitzer and Reinhardt. There's an aside about them: *non potuerunt incipere*. That translates roughly to 'could only begin.'" She put down the note. "Could only begin what?"

"Eating Samantha Carville," Corrie said. "Remember where you found the missing leg bone?"

"My God, you're right." Nora began examining the document again. "Then, in January of 1847, the killers died. Boardman writes that Spitzer was unrepentant to the last, but Reinhardt confessed to murder. That must mean Wolfinger."

"Go on," Corrie said.

But Nora paused a moment. "After that, the tone of the document seems to change. Boardman prefaces the rest with *nobis maledictum*, 'our curse.' He makes a big deal about Parkin's death in late February, following it with a dire biblical quotation and something in Latin like, 'the beginning of the terrible feast.'"

"So the cannibalism started in earnest once Parkin died."

"And the deaths also started mounting more quickly," Nora said. "Julius Carville. Leander Widnall. Carville's wife, Julius Carville, and Widnall are all described as dying insane. There are little daggers surrounding the names of all three, also, and some Latin abbreviation—*anthropgs*. I've no clue what it means." She looked up. "The last date recorded is February 25. Boardman concludes with the mention of his wife. She has daggers around her name, too, and that same strange abbreviation—*anthropgs*."

"Didn't you say Boardman ran away from the camp because his wife had gone nuts? She was trying to kill and eat him?"

"That's what Tamzene recounted in her diary."

There was a pause, during which the only sound was the shrieking of the wind and the pelting of the rain against the tent.

"So Boardman wrote up this death almanac after he reached the other camp," Corrie said.

"It's the only possibility." Nora's eye fell to the brief, cryptic notes Clive had made in the document's margin. One said *daggers!* with a circle around it.

"Odd," she murmured.

"What?"

"The names notated with little daggers—Clive seems to have thought them important."

Corrie stirred in her sleeping bag. "Why?"

"All three—Carville and his wife, Widnall—bear the notation '*anthropgs*.' And Boardman also labeled them as *ex insania*—insane. His wife's name is just surrounded by those daggers."

"Well, unlike the others, he didn't actually see her die. He was too busy running away from her at the time. It's a safe bet his wife also went crazy. I think that's what those daggers by the names stand for—the people he knew went insane." Corrie sat up, winced, then lay back.

"He was a carrier," she murmured. "A Typhoid Mary. Maybe that's what this unknown group digging up all the Parkin bodies was after. It wasn't something nature had gifted Parkin with. They wanted his skull to get the microbes from a *disease*."

Nora shook her head. "Microbes don't get inherited down the generations. You don't pass along an infectious disease—not genetically. And genetic diseases aren't infectious: you can't get them from eating someone."

Corrie closed her eyes. "Damn, I hope they bring some morphine."

Nora checked her watch. "Any minute now."

Corrie remained a long time with her eyes closed. "Boardman didn't go mad. Samantha Carville didn't go mad. The two killers who started in on her leg didn't go mad. Parkin didn't go mad—just the people who ate his body. If it wasn't a disease, what else could it have been?"

It was a drowsy question, more rhetorical than anything else. But it rang a bell in the back of Nora's mind. *Going mad from eating flesh*. She'd studied a case like that in college, a famous case.

The story of the Fore tribe in New Guinea.

"Oh, my God," she said.

Corrie opened her eyes at this sudden change of tone. "What?"

"There's a case every student of anthropology learns about. There was this tribe in New Guinea, the Fore. Around a hundred years ago, many of them started going mad and dying. It wasn't until the 1960s that doctors figured out what was causing the epidemic—ritual cannibalism. When a person died, they were eaten by the family as an expression of love. Doctors discovered the deadly agent wasn't any ordinary disease. It was a *prion* disease."

"Prion?"

"Like mad cow, or Creutzfeldt-Jakob disease in humans. Prions are not a microbe, like a virus or parasite. They're not even alive; they're a protein particle with a very strange property. When you eat them, the prions spread through your body, and when they come in contact with other proteins, those proteins are changed—into something deadly. Prions especially attack the proteins of the brain... and drive people mad."

"But how did something like this start in the first place?"

"Around the year 1900, a single Fore individual suffered a random mutation and his body began to produce prions. He became the first carrier. When he died and was eaten, the disease started spreading. And spreading."

Corrie groaned. "So you think Albert Parkin was like that tribesman? A mutant carrier?"

"Maybe. CJD is a horrible disease—there's no vaccine, no cure, and the protein particles can't be killed by sterilization or disinfectant. It's inevitably fatal." Nora frowned. "But prion disease takes up to fifty years to kill—and the people in the Lost Camp died within a week of eating Parkin."

"So Parkin carried an incredibly fast-acting form of the disease."

"It's possible," said Nora.

Corrie sat up again, ignoring the pain. "Nora, think about it. Here's a disease that kills in days, has no vaccine and no cure, and is a hundred percent fatal. Sterilization can't kill it. What does that describe to you?"

"Something terrible. Demonic."

"More than that. *It describes the ultimate weapon.*"

"Holy shit."

"Holy shit is right. A biological weapon that makes anthrax, Ebola, or smallpox look like a head cold. No wonder it's worth more than gold, worth killing for—worth any effort. Think about what would happen if you weaponized that prion protein and dispersed it over a city with a crop duster. Or put it in a bomb. Or dumped it in a water supply—"

Suddenly Nora heard a grotesque sound, a gurgling hiccup from Fugit, lying prone across the tent from them. The sound resolved itself into low, ugly laughter. Fugit's eyes were open and she was staring at Corrie, a trickle of blood dribbling from her mouth.

"So," Corrie said to her. "You've been listening."

Fugit stared back at them.

"Are we right?"

Fugit's bloody mouth opened again. But whether she planned to explain or just emit another gibber of laughter, Nora never found out, because the howl of the storm—quite suddenly—was drowned out by the beating of an approaching helicopter.

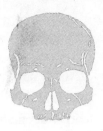

52

May 27

CORRIE SWANSON PULLED her well-traveled 2002 Camry over to the curb of 7227 North Ninety-Eighth Way and killed the engine. It was a cloudless day, and hot as hell—it took only a minute before the car started heating up like an oven cranked to high. But as long as she was going to be based in Albuquerque, she supposed she'd better get used to it.

She looked up at the façade of the condo before her. Other than the 3-series BMW parked at the end of its walkway, it looked the same as the last time she'd seen it, less than a month before. So what, exactly, felt different?

Me, she thought. It was Corrie herself who was different now.

The Garmin GPS on her windshield—her car was way too old to have such niceties built in—was still on, sucking juice from her battery. As she unplugged it from the cigarette lighter, she noticed on the map that she was no more than a mile from Troon North, the famous golf course. She'd played Troon at least fifty times and remembered the course well, especially the par-five number three, with its brutal dogleg and cactus-fringed rough. Of course, that had been on a PC golf sim during her time at Phillips Exeter. She'd always wanted to learn the real game, with its beautiful vistas and sense of freedom. Maybe she'd find the time for that here.

She realized such reminiscences were just delaying the inevitable.

After she had been discharged from the hospital, Morwood had given her a mandatory vacation that she sure as hell didn't need. Nora and her team had also been caught in a kind of limbo—between the red tape caused by three murders and the scandal at the Institute following the sudden loss of Fugit. They were waiting to be allowed to go back up to the site to finish removing the artifacts and restoring it to its previous natural state. But none of that enforced delay really explained this day trip Corrie had decided to make. Why exactly had she taken the time to drive all the way here? Was it because she felt somehow it was her duty as an FBI agent to tie off all the dangling threads? Or was it something else?

Enough psychoanalyzing already. Just get out, go up the steps, and ring the goddamn bell.

Her stalling became moot when the door opened and a figure emerged, holding a huge bundle of loose clothes, and headed for the BMW. Right away she recognized him, and before he could look over and see her just sitting there, she opened the door, got out—awkwardly, as usual, given the sling on her arm—and approached. He looked the same—beat-up jeans, faded T-shirt— but there were no new tattoos, and a quick glance reassured her there were no fresh cuts on his arms.

He frowned as she came closer. She wasn't dressed for work, and it was obvious that it took him a minute to recognize her.

She used that moment to inspect his features more closely: no bruises or marks, hair combed, even freshly shaved. Well, relatively.

A knot of concern that had been tightening in her chest as she made the drive to Scottsdale now began to relax.

"You're that FBI person," he said. "Agent..."

She could tell the name was never going to come. "Swanson. But just call me Corrie."

He nodded, then opened the door of the BMW and threw in the clothes. Corrie noticed that his stereo and record collection were already on the backseat, arranged with significantly more care than this fresh load of stuff.

"No real reason for my visit," she went on before he could say anything. "Just thought I'd stop by, see if you have any outstanding questions, you know—just part of the job."

It wasn't, but he didn't have to know.

"No questions. I've already heard more than I want to know."

Rosalie Parkin's body had been found, without its head, five days before, dumped in a storm drain on the outskirts of Gary, Indiana. Her kid brother had been cleared of any possible suspicion, and so had that married dick of a lawyer, Damon, who had been using Rosalie as his side piece. But Corrie wanted to check on the kid anyway. If all this had happened to her, she sure as hell would have wanted someone to do that. Of course, with her, no one ever did. Not until...

A shirt fell out onto the curb. The youth picked it up, threw it back into the car, closed the door. Then he turned to her.

"Got a minute?" she asked.

He thought a moment, shrugged. "Sure."

They sat on the front steps. It seemed easiest: least formal, least threatening.

"Is that your sister's car?"

He nodded.

"Looks like you're headed somewhere."

"Tucson."

"Yeah? What's there?"

"Got a couple friends with a place."

This was a fair enough answer. But Corrie remained silent, giving him time to say more.

"They're into vinyl, like me," he added at last. "One of them works at the Southwestern Museum of Rock. Got me a job there as a researcher."

Corrie looked at him. "No shit. That's great."

He shrugged again. "Part-time at first. We'll see." He nodded at the sling. "What happened to you?"

"Cut myself shaving." Corrie turned her gaze away and they both looked past the BMW, toward the lawns—some with manicured grass, others with colored lava rock—that lay across the street.

"Ernest, I just wanted to tell you I'm sorry about your sister," she said in a lower voice. "Really sorry. And I know it doesn't mean much coming from me, but I'm told she didn't suffer."

"That cop, Porter, told me the same thing," he said, still gazing straight ahead. There was a beat. "But thanks."

Corrie took a breath. "Think you're going to be okay?" Shit, she was winging this, big-time. Maybe it had been a bad idea, coming here. But it had seemed the right thing to do.

"I guess," Ernest answered after a while. "Yeah, I think so." Another pause. "You know, it sounds messed up, but—somehow, her death, the shock of it, was like a wake-up call. I was spiraling deeper and deeper into self-pity. Now..." He let the thought drift off. "It hurts like a motherfucker. All the time. But at least I have that pain to keep me going. Before, I didn't even have that."

Corrie nodded. It sounded like he'd been jump-started into the cycle of grief. Hopefully, he'd work through it in a healthy way.

There were no leads on his sister's killers, and she wasn't going to waste his time in speculation. In fact, she realized she'd done what her gut had told her to—show her face, make sure he was okay—and that she should leave.

"I brought you something," she said.

"Hope it isn't a subpoena."

Corrie grinned as she dug into her pocket and pulled out a flash drive. "When I was in high school, a lot of kids made mixtapes. Not in the way it's meant now, but, you know: compilations of favorite songs, to give to friends or make for yourself to fit a certain mood." She handed him the USB stick. "I made one for you. Back in the day, we had to burn CDs. This is much more convenient."

Ernest turned it over in his hand. "You made this for me?"

"Sure. Remember how I started to basically lecture you about 'The Ocean' in your room that night? Well, consider this the rest of that lecture. My hard rock golden oldies: Zep, Guns N' Roses, Aerosmith, AC/DC. Enjoy. And when you graduate from that, let me know and maybe I'll send you one covering my other weakness: dark ambient."

For a moment, the youth didn't say anything. Then he dropped the USB stick into his shirt pocket. "You clear the copyrights on all these songs, Agent Swanson?"

"It's your word against mine." Then she stood up with a grunt, rearranged the sling into a more comfortable position, and returned to her Camry. She started it up, spun the wheel one-handed, and did a one-eighty.

"Hey, Corrie!" she heard Ernest call. She glanced out the window.

He patted his shirt pocket. "Thanks."

Corrie smiled, gave him a thumbs-up. Then she gunned the Camry's wimpy motor, pointed the car toward Albuquerque, and took off.

EPILOGUE

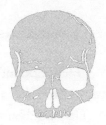

One week later

In the HQ tent, Nora Kelly stepped back and examined the skeleton she had carefully reassembled. The bones and fragments were arranged on black velvet in a tray, every bone in place. After a maddening temporary shutdown of the site while the dust settled, everything was now back on track. All the other bones from the excavation of the Lost Camp had been packed away and were headed to the lab in Santa Fe, except for this: the skeleton of Samantha Carville.

For the first time in 175 years, Samantha Carville was whole again, the butchered, scorched, and gnawed bone of her leg restored to the rest of the body.

One task remained before Nora could pack up the work tent and the last of the equipment and leave the valley of the Lost Camp to the deer and the crows and the snow and rain. Using long rubber tweezers, she began transferring the bones of Samantha Carville from the tray to a small coffin she had constructed. It was made of rough, unfinished pine, with no adornment and no lining, as required by the religion of

Samantha's family—of which, as far as she could learn, no descendants remained.

"Knock, knock?"

Nora turned to see Agent Swanson poking her head in the tent flap.

"Hi, Corrie, come in. You're just in time for the interment."

Corrie entered, her arm still in a sling. "I want to introduce you to someone very special to me."

Nora looked up as Corrie pulled aside the tent flap to allow the entrance of a man. He slipped in: tall, pale, dressed in black, two eyes that glittered like diamonds set into his chiseled features. For a moment Nora thought she must be hallucinating: the man was the spitting image of Special Agent Pendergast.

It *was* Special Agent Pendergast.

"Greetings, my dear Nora," Pendergast said, stepping over and extending his hand.

Nora took his hand in hers. "Agent Pendergast. What... what the heck are you doing here?"

"Wait," said Corrie, looking from one to the other in astonishment. "You two *know* each other?"

Pendergast turned with a mischievous smile. "Nora and I worked on several intriguing cases back in New York."

"*What?*" Corrie cried. "But you never said a word. I've been sending you updates on this case for weeks!"

"I ask your forgiveness. When I heard you two were working together by sheer happenstance, I admit that I withheld the fact I knew both of you. I simply cannot resist a bit of drama." He spread his hands.

Nora gathered her wits. "Sorry about my shock. It's nice to see you again. But how do you know Corrie?"

"I am pleased to serve as a sort of Dutch uncle to her, in her previous life and now in the FBI. She helped me on an unusual case in Kansas some years ago, and we worked together on another little difficulty in Colorado. I encouraged her to go into law enforcement. What a charming coincidence that her first case would involve you."

Nora laughed, shaking her head. "You're full of crazy surprises. I'll never forget the first time you visited my museum office. Almost gave me a heart attack, sneaking up like that."

"I take exception to that characterization," said Pendergast. "I never 'sneak.' I *glide*." He moved toward the coffin and peered inside. "Who is the dear departed?"

"These are the restored remains of Samantha Carville, a six-year-old girl who died in the camp." Nora took a deep breath. "I've decided to bury her here. Properly."

"Really?" Corrie asked. "You're not going to send her remains to the lab?"

"No. She's already been positively identified, so no DNA test is necessary. It seemed the right thing to do—lay her spirit to rest, I mean."

"Right here?"

"Yes. Right here—right now."

"What about a clergyman?" Corrie asked.

"Samantha and her parents were Quakers. Quakers don't bury their dead with ceremony, music, clergy, or even a grave marker. Just a plain coffin, put in the ground in the presence of friends." She continued to transfer the bones and fragments, one by one, into the coffin. "What news on the case?"

Corrie hesitated. "I'm sorry, it's confidential."

"Naturally." Nora raised her eyebrows quizzically.

Corrie grinned. "Okay, but this is for you only. Fugit flipped, trying to save her ass, and laid it all out for us. It was pretty much as we figured—an effort to weaponize the prion protein by some shadowy international organization."

"Who?"

"The ever-present, ever-elusive 'shadowy international organization,'" Pendergast said, arching his eyebrows. Whether he was serious or not, Nora couldn't tell.

"The FBI doesn't know—and may never know. The organization covered its tracks with incredible care and layers of intermediaries. Their reach and sophistication suggests a government is behind it, engaged in a search for potential weapons of mass destruction. It seems their research focused on the Donner Party cannibalism, and the interesting fact that everyone in the Lost Camp who ate Parkin went mad—with all the classic symptoms of prion disease. They concluded Parkin was probably an exceedingly rare genetic carrier of a fast-acting form of CJD. And that's what started this whole thing."

"So they needed to get his skull?"

Corrie nodded. "They had to sequence Parkin's genome to find out exactly how the prion protein was made before they could start to weaponize it. In addition, they needed a sample of the prion protein itself—which is only found in brain tissue—for synthesis. So they undertook a two-pronged attack: They set out to find the Lost Camp and retrieve Parkin's skull. And they started digging up or even killing Parkin descendants to see if they carried the genetic code. The latter didn't work. But the former did."

"And where did Clive come in?"

"They hired him because of his expertise in Donner history. The fact he was a descendant of the Donner Party was icing on the cake. We can't be sure, but it appears they put him on the trail of Tamzene's journal and dangled in front of him the possibility of a grand discovery that would both bring him renown and clear up the lingering mark on the Breen family name. They topped it off by offering Clive a massive sum of money, which they probably never intended to pay—easier to kill him instead. By the time Clive realized who he was working for, it was too late and backing out would have meant certain death. After finding Tamzene's journal last fall, Clive tried to locate the camp on his own and failed—hence the campsite I found. He realized he needed expert archaeological help—and he turned to you."

"And Fugit? How did she get drawn in?"

"She was insurance. They brought her on board when they grew worried Clive might have second thoughts. He'd been reluctant and hard to seduce. But Fugit, it turns out, was eager for the money and morally flexible. She was subverted last winter, while the expedition was being put together. Finding Parkin's remains in the Lost Camp was the group's last chance to get the necessary prion samples and DNA—and so they weren't taking any chances."

"And the gold?" Nora asked.

"It had nothing to do with the case. A distraction. Except that Wiggett was secretly looking for it when he happened on Clive at the tarn, where he'd hidden Parkin's skull by sinking it into the pond in that waterproof box. That's why Clive killed him, of course. After reclaiming the skull from Peel. Clive discovered Peel stealing the bones and took advantage of the opportunity to follow him, kill him, and throw most of the bones over the cliff while keeping the skull. In this way he hoped to confuse the issue and maybe even cover up the fact that the skull was missing. Clever man. But you put all those bones back together."

Nora shook her head. "All those deaths, for such an awful purpose. And we didn't even find the gold."

"I'll bet it's long gone," said Corrie.

"The investigation," said Pendergast, "has moved up to the highest levels at the Department of Homeland Security. I doubt even I will hear of the final disposition. Parkin's remains are now being guarded under exceptional secrecy. And, more to the point, Corrie's career at the FBI has gotten off to a promising start."

"That's something, anyway." Nora put the last bone in the coffin. "Help me with that lid."

Together, they fit the lid on, and Nora screwed it down through predrilled holes. "Let's go."

Corrie and Nora raised the coffin to their shoulders—it was quite light—and together they brought it out of the tent and into the brilliant sunlight, Pendergast following. Nora led the way up the valley a few hundred yards to where she'd dug a grave. It was a dramatic if not exactly cheerful spot, with dark cliffs all around, framed by the skeletons of dead trees.

Using a pair of ropes, they lowered the coffin into the ground.

"Now we each say a few words," said Nora. "That's the Quaker way."

A silence, and then Corrie said: "I don't know who led Maggie and the rest of us to Wiggett's body, or who it was that pulled me out of the snow. But if that was you, Samantha, thank you. May you rest in peace, little one."

Nora said: "Your life was short and your death tragic. But I find inspiration in your courage and spirit—both during life and after. The least I could do was make you whole again. May you rejoin your family in a better place."

Both women looked at Pendergast. He raised his head and

cleared his throat. *"Samantha Carvilleae ossua heic. Fortuna spondet multa multis, praestat nemini, vive in dies et horas, nam proprium est nihil."*

Corrie looked at Pendergast. "What exactly does that mean?"

"'Here lie the bones of Samantha Carville. Fortune makes promises to many, keeps them to none. Live for each day, live for the hours, since nothing is forever yours.'"

"That's rather dark," said Corrie.

"It's a favorite quote of my ward, Constance. Besides, the graveside is no place for pleasantries."

All three took turns shoveling, dirt hitting the coffin lid with a hollow sound. When they were finished, Nora packed down the area and restored the clumps of grass she had removed earlier.

"You'd never know it was there," Corrie said.

"I've recorded its GPS location in case we ever need to find it again."

As they began walking away from the gravesite, Pendergast murmured: "Tell me more about this missing gold, if you please."

Nora gave him a quick summary of Wolfinger, his withdrawal of gold from the bank, his murder, the death of the two killers at the Lost Camp, and the gold pieces she and Clive had found in their boots.

Pendergast listened intently. "A curious story. And where exactly have you searched?"

"We scoured the lower sections of the cliffs, from the base to about twelve feet up."

"And why did you choose that area?"

"We figured that the two men must have hidden the gold before the wagon was broken apart for a shelter. We know the snow was six feet deep at the time of the breakup, in mid-November. So we figured it had to be in the cliffs somewhere between six and twelve feet up. Six feet would have been ground level, relative to the snowpack. Twelve feet was in case they put it as high as they could reach. The cliffs are the only place to hide something, since the ground was frozen."

Pendergast nodded. "All perfectly logical."

"We searched every damn hole on both sides of the valley. Below the six-foot level, too, in case they buried it in some crevice beneath the snow line. Yesterday I even searched the area underneath the cornice that fell on us and broke Corrie's arm. Nothing."

Another slow nod from Pendergast. "And you have a record of snow depths and dates?"

"Yes. Tamzene Donner kept a chart in her journal."

"When did the two robbers die?"

"Spitzer died on January twenty-first, and Reinhardt on January twenty-eighth."

"And what was the snow depth on January first?"

"I'd have to check the journal. It's in the tent."

They reached the work tent and Nora took out the photocopied journal. She turned to the page where Tamzene had recorded snow depths.

"On January first, it was eighteen feet."

"And on January fifteenth?"

"Um, let's see. Twenty-one feet."

"And January twenty-eighth?"

"Still twenty-one feet."

"And the maximum depth?"

"It reached twenty-six feet by early March before it started to go down."

"Most intriguing."

"I'm not sure of the relevance of the later snowpack. They had to have buried it back in November, when the snow was a lot shallower."

But Pendergast simply wandered back outside and stared up at the cliffs, his silvery eyes glittering in the sunlight. "Investigating every hole and crack up there would be an exercise in futility."

"You're not kidding," said Nora.

"You mentioned earlier that the camp was marked by the profile of an old woman in the cliffs, since fallen. Where was that?"

Nora pointed. "See that area of lighter rock along the upper bluff? That's where we believe the old woman was."

Pendergast squinted up at the bluff. "Would you, perchance, have a pair of binoculars?"

"Right here." Nora pulled a pair from her day pack. Pendergast took them and examined the cliff face for some time. He handed them to Nora.

"Do you see those holes below the patch of lighter rock?"

Nora raised the binoculars. "I see."

"Count five holes down."

"Done," Nora said, peering up.

"The treasure is in that hole."

Nora lowered the binoculars. "But that's over twenty feet high!"

"Indeed."

"Why would it be way up there?"

Corrie snorted. "He's pulling our legs. We're going to climb up there and find nothing, and he'll be laughing his ass off."

Pendergast turned to her. "Agent Swanson. I do not engage

in low pranks and ignoble humor. I assure you, the gold is there. Or, just perhaps, in one of the holes directly above or below."

"And what makes you so sure?"

"I'll explain once the treasure is safely in our possession."

Nora looked at Corrie. "The climbing gear is still in the tent. You want to belay while I go up?"

"Why the hell not?"

Nora unpacked the gear and they brought it to the base of the cliffs. Nora climbed into the harness, buckled on the carabiner, and tied a figure eight knot. Corrie put on her own harness and braced in a belaying position.

Nora began to climb. It was not difficult, the pockmarked basalt offering numerous hand- and footholds. In no time she reached the hole in question. She anchored a piton and threaded the rope while Corrie took in the slack. She peered inside.

"Oh, my God!" About three feet in, she could make out the dull outline of an iron strongbox. "It's here!"

"Excellent," the dulcet voice drifted up from below. "Most excellent."

Nora reached behind and pulled a small cargo net out of her pack, slipped it around the chest, and dragged it to the edge of the hole. She rigged up a pulley, fixed it to the piton, threaded a second rope through it, and dropped the end of the rope to the ground.

"That's for lowering the box. Someone grab the end and hold tight, because this sucker must weigh at least fifty pounds."

Pendergast took up the end of the rope. Nora tightened the slack and eased out the chest, letting it swing free. She steadied it with her hand.

"Ready to lower."

Pendergast played out the rope and the chest slowly descended. When it reached the ground, Nora climbed back down, removing the pitons as she went.

The box sat in the grass, rusty but intact, with a brass padlock. "Should we break the lock?" Corrie asked.

Pendergast knelt. A pale hand slipped into his suit jacket and brought out a small, strange-looking tool. He fiddled with the lock and it clinked open.

Nora felt her heart quicken.

Pendergast opened the lid. Inside were various leather-wrapped packets; where the leather had rotted and shrunk, it revealed gleaming stacks of gold coins.

The Wolfinger treasure.

Nora stared. "I can't believe it. There's a thousand holes up there. We've been looking for weeks. And in ten minutes you point to *one* hole—and bingo. How?"

Closing the lid, Pendergast reattached the lock and rose. "It's all about snow depths. You were undoubtedly correct in assuming that Spitzer and Reinhardt originally hid the chest in that six-to-twelve-foot range. But the snow kept falling and growing deeper. They still hoped to be rescued and wanted to keep close track of the gold's precise location. So as the snow deepened and threatened to bury the gold and make it inaccessible, they moved it up. And up. They kept doing so until they became too weak to move it any further. Given that they died at the end of January, I estimated that point came early in the month, when the snow was eighteen to twenty-one feet deep. So I examined the cliff face for a hole at about that height."

"Clever. But there are still countless holes at that level all over in these cliffs. How did you know exactly where to look?"

"I asked myself what landmark the two would have chosen—

and the face of the old woman you mentioned sprang to mind. Based on what I can see at present, it must have been the only distinctive landmark. And that cliff is like Swiss cheese: if the treasure had been hidden in any other hole, it would have been very difficult to find again. Knowing that, I looked to the holes directly beneath where the old woman's face had been situated before it fell. I saw likely holes at around eighteen, twenty, and twenty-two feet. I guessed the one in the middle. Correctly, as game theory could have predicted."

"Jesus," said Corrie. She turned to Nora. "Why didn't you think of that?"

"Because she didn't follow the logic to its bitter end," said Pendergast. "A common human failing, even among quite intelligent people."

He hefted the strongbox. "My goodness, what a lot of gold! And now, I think we are well and truly finished here. I suggest you arrange to get this out at the earliest possibility—perhaps by helicopter, then armored car to a suitable safe deposit vault at the Golden Pacific Bank in Sacramento."

"Sounds like a good idea," said Nora.

"I congratulate you both on solving this case. I understand Agent Morwood is to receive a commendation for his excellent work." He paused with a cynical smile.

"And not Corrie?" Nora asked.

Corrie smiled ruefully. "Aloysius tells me I'm learning the ways of the Bureau."

"Indeed. Your turn will come."

"Can't come soon enough."

Pendergast looked from one to the other. "The forensic anthropologist and the archaeologist—one wonders if you two might have reason to partner on a future case?"

"Professionally?" Corrie scoffed, with an amused sideways glance at Nora. "Seems unlikely. Nora can be a real pain in the ass."

"And you're a short-tempered punk." Nora turned to Pendergast. "*I'm* a pain in the ass? That goes double for her. We'd be at each other's throats."

"And that," Pendergast replied placidly, "is precisely why such a partnership just might work."

About the Authors

The thrillers of **DOUGLAS PRESTON** and **LINCOLN CHILD** "stand head and shoulders above their rivals" (*Publishers Weekly*). Preston and Child's *Relic* and *The Cabinet of Curiosities* were chosen by readers in a National Public Radio poll as being among the one hundred greatest thrillers ever written, and *Relic* was made into a number one box office hit movie. They are coauthors of the famed Pendergast series, and their recent novels include *Verses for the Dead, City of Endless Night, The Obsidian Chamber*, and *Blue Labyrinth*. In addition to his novels and nonfiction works (such as *The Lost City of the Monkey God*), Preston writes about archaeology for *The New Yorker* and *National Geographic* magazines. Lincoln Child is a Florida resident and former book editor who has published seven novels of his own, including such bestsellers as *Full Wolf Moon* and *Deep Storm*.

Readers can sign up for The Pendergast File, a "strangely entertaining" newsletter from the authors, at their website, PrestonChild.com. The authors welcome visitors to their Facebook page, where they post regularly.

A Note to the Reader

Old Bones is a work of fiction. As such, it mingles the history of the Donner Party with imaginary events, locations, artifacts, and individuals. For example, Samantha Carville, Albert Parkin, and certain other characters who feature in the novel never existed. As far as anyone knows, there is no Lost Camp. However, many of the historical details in the novel are accurate. Those interested in learning more about the fate of the Donner Party are encouraged to read one of the many excellent nonfiction books available on the subject.